Jor
for
Th
Th
ma
bes
wo
and
An
and

Jes
pla
wo
(fo
liv

'Tl
log
in

'Tl
is e

'So

'W
sto

JONATHAN & JESSE
KELLERMAN
CRIME
SCENE

HEADLINE

First published in the United States by Ballantine Books,
an imprint of Random House, a division of Random House LLC,
a Penguin Random House Company, New York.

First published in Great Britain in 2017 by
HEADLINE PUBLISHING GROUP

First published in paperback in Great Britain in 2018 by
HEADLINE PUBLISHING GROUP

1

Cataloguing in Publication Data is available from the British Library

ISBN 978 1 4722 3849 8 (B format)
ISBN 978 1 4722 5414 6 (A format)

Typeset in Fournier MT by Jouve (UK), Milton Keynes
Printed and bound in Great Britain by Clays Ltd, St Ives plc

Headline's policy is to use papers that are natural, renewable and recyclable
products and made from wood grown in sustainable forests. The logging
and manufacturing processes are expected to conform to the environmental
regulations of the country of origin.

HEADLINE PUBLISHING GROUP
An Hachette UK Company
Carmelite House
50 Victoria Embankment
London EC4Y 0DZ

www.headline.co.uk
www.hachette.co.uk

1

DON'T MAKE assumptions.

Every now and then, I remind myself of that.

Every now and then, the universe does the reminding for me.

When I meet new people, they're usually dead.

A young white male lies on his back in the parking lot of a Berkeley frat house. According to the license in his wallet, his name is Seth Lindley Powell. He is four months past his eighteenth birthday. The license gives a San Jose address. It's a fair bet his parents are at that address, right now, asleep. Nobody has notified them yet. I haven't had a chance.

Seth Powell has clean gray eyes and soft brown hair. His palms are open to the three a.m. sky. He wears a misshapen brown polo shirt over khakis. One shoelace drifts loose. Except for a few shallow abrasions on his left cheek, his face is smooth and content, with a bluish tinge. His skull, rib cage, neck, arms, and legs are intact. There's little visible blood.

Down at the end of the driveway, beyond the yellow tape, a throng of students snap photos of Seth. And selfies. Some of them hug and weep, others just look on, curious.

Crushed red Solo cups pile high on the sidewalks. A banner strung from the eaves declares the theme: SATURDAY NIGHT FEVER. Boys slur their statements to uniformed officers. Girls in platforms fidget with the buttons of loud polyester shirts fished from the five-buck bins on Telegraph Avenue. Nobody knows what happened but everyone has a story. From a third-floor window come the lazy flickers of a disco ball nobody has thought to still.

Standing over Seth Powell's body, I make an assumption: I wonder how I'm going to explain to his parents that their son has died of alcohol poisoning during his first week of school.

I'm wrong.

The following afternoon, a technician comes into the squad room, calls me away from my computer and down to the morgue so I can see firsthand a body cavity sloshing with busted organs; lower vertebrae punched out of alignment; a pelvis smashed to gravel, consistent with a four-story fall, the small of the back taking the full brunt of impact.

There's a reason we do autopsies.

Toxicology confirms what Seth's friends insisted on, what I hesitated to believe: he wasn't a drinker. He was That Guy, caught up in righteous notions of purity. He wrote songs, they said. He took arty black-and-white photos with a camera that used actual film. Rush Week depressed him. Someone heard he went up to the roof to look at the stars.

How depressed?

At some point you need to make a decision. Boxes need checking. It says a lot about our desire for simplicity that there are an infinite number of ways to die but only five manners of death.

Homicide.

Suicide.

Natural.

Accidental.

Undetermined.

My job begins with the dead but continues with the living. The living have telephones with redial. They have regret and insomnia and chest pain and bouts of uncontrollable weeping. They ask: *Why*.

Ninety-nine times out of a hundred, *why* isn't a real question. It's an expression of loss. Even if I had the answer, I'm not sure anyone could stomach it.

I do the next best thing. The old switcheroo.

They ask for *why*. I give them *how*.

Knowing that it's impossible to live without assumptions, I try to choose mine carefully. I think about the loose shoelace. I rule Seth Powell's death an accident.

Five years on, I still think about him whenever I get a callout to Berkeley.

I don't get called out to Berkeley often. Alameda County covers eight hundred square miles, of which Berkeley is a speck, and, compared with its neighbors, basically untouched by serious crime, unless you object to homeless people or fussy vegan reinventions of diner classics, which I don't. Who doesn't enjoy a good tofu Reuben?

Five years after Seth Powell's death, near to the day, at eleven fifty-two a.m. on a Saturday in September, Zaragoza was hanging over my cubicle wall, probing the flesh behind the lower left corner of his jaw in search of the latest development that would widow his wife and orphan his kids.

He said, 'Yo, Clay, touch this.'

I did not look up from my work. 'Touch what.'

'My neck.'

'I'm not touching your neck.'

'You can feel it if you push hard.'

'I believe you.'

'Come on, dude. I need a second opinion.'

'My opinion is that last week you asked me to touch your stomach.'

'I checked WebMD,' he said. 'It's cancer of the pharynx. Maybe salivary glands, but that's kind of rare.'

'You're kind of rare,' I said. My desk phone was ringing.

I pressed the speakerphone. 'Coroner's Bureau. Deputy Edison.'

'Hey there, this is Officer Schickman in Berkeley.' Friendly voice. 'How are you?'

I said, 'What's up, man?'

'I'm out on a DBF here. More than likely it's natural but he's at the bottom of the stairs so I figure you might want to have a look.'

'Sure thing,' I said. 'Hang on a sec, I'm all outta my little forms.'

Zaragoza absently handed me a blank worksheet, continued prodding his neck. 'I should get an MRI,' he said.

On the speaker, Schickman said, 'Sorry?'

'Never mind,' I said, picking up the receiver. 'My buddy here's got cancer.'

'Shit,' Schickman said. 'Sorry to hear it.'

'It's all right, he gets it every week. Go ahead. Decedent's last name?'

'Rennert.'

'Spell it?'

He did. 'First name Walter. Spelled like you think.'

I asked questions, he answered, I wrote. Walter Rennert was a seventy-five-year-old divorced white male residing at 2640 Bonaventure Avenue. At approximately nine forty a.m., his daughter had arrived at the house for their weekly brunch date. She let herself in with her key and found her father lying in the foyer, unresponsive. She called 911 and attempted, unsuccessfully, to resuscitate him. Berkeley Fire had pronounced him dead at ten seventeen.

'She's next of kin?'

'Believe so. Tatiana Rennert-Delavigne.' He spelled it without being asked.

'Is there a primary doctor?'

'Uh . . . Clark. Gerald Clark. I haven't been able to reach him. Office is closed till Monday.'

'Any medical conditions you know about?'

'Hypertension, per the daughter. He took meds.'

'And you said he's at the bottom of the stairs?'

'Nearish. I mean, he's lying there.'

'Meaning . . .'

'Meaning, that's his location. It doesn't look to me like he slipped.'

'Uh-huh,' I said. 'Well, we'll have a look.'

'Okay. Listen, I'm not sure I should be mentioning this at all, but his daughter's pretty insistent he was murdered.'

'She said that?'

'What she told dispatch. 'You have to come, my father's been murdered.' Something like that. She told patrol the same thing when they got here. They called me.'

So far I liked Schickman. All indications were that he had his shit together. I attributed the hesitation in his voice to uncertainty over how to interact with the daughter, rather than any concern that she might be correct.

'You know how it is,' he said. 'People get upset, say things.'

'Sure. Can I get your badge number real quick?'

'Schickman. S-C-H-I-C-K-M-A-N. Sixty-two.'

Berkeley. While I get that it's not for everybody, you have to admit there's a certain boutique charm in a PD small enough to have two-digit badge numbers.

I gave him my data and said we'd be there soon.

'Cheers.'

I rang off, got up, stretched. On the other side of the cubicle wall, Zaragoza had opened up Google Images and was scrolling through a ghastly catalog of tumors.

'You coming?' I asked.

He shuddered and closed the browser.

2

I THINK about the dead, wherever I go. It's inevitable. In eight hundred square miles, there's pretty much no place untainted in my memory by death.

A bend in the freeway and I reflexively slow to avoid the invisible lump of a woman who leapt from the overpass, causing the nine-car pileup and five-hour traffic jam that would become her legacy.

The motel in Union City where a tax lawyer's celebration of his impending divorce ended in a speedball overdose.

Certain blocks in Oakland: take your pick.

It's not that I'm haunted. More like I never quite manage to feel alone.

The work clings to us in different ways. That's how it is for me. Zaragoza, he gets hantavirus, or flesh-eating bacteria, or whatever.

'Lymphoma,' he said, thumbing his phone. 'Fuck, I didn't even consider that.'

'I still get your Xbox, right?'

'Yeah, fine.'

'Lymphoma it is, then.'

Propped on the dash, my own phone instructed me to exit the 13 and continue onto Tunnel Road, skirting blind driveways drowned in redwood shadow. A hard yellow at the entrance to the Claremont Hotel had me stomping the brake, causing the gurneys in back to rattle around unhappily.

Pairs of wide-set brick columns marked the southern edge of the neighborhood, stern iron gates left open in a gesture of generosity. The homes beyond were tall and bright and stately, weathered brick and wood shingling, thoughtful drought-tolerant landscaping. A sign encouraged me to drive like my grandkids lived there. I saw a Volvo with a roof-mount bike rack, bumper sagging under several elections' worth of stickers. I saw a Tesla and a seven-seater SUV shouldering together in the same driveway, a winking attempt to acknowledge and then ignore the distinction between living well and living good.

'You know it around here?' Zaragoza asked.

He meant from my student days. I shook my head. Back then I hardly left the safety of the gym, let alone ventured off campus. I'd never come in a professional capacity, either.

Bonaventure Avenue meandered east for three hundred yards, narrowing to a single lane that terminated in a cul-de-sac plugged up by residents' vehicles, two Berkeley PD cruisers, and a full hook-and-ladder. Backing the truck out was going to be a pain in the ass.

Three houses clumped on the south side of the street, along the gentler downhill slope. To the north, a towering Spanish was set high atop a knob of bedrock, accessible via a long, steep driveway lined with crushed stone. At the crest I could make out the boxy silhouette of an ambulance, flashers on.

I eased the van up the driveway, which widened to a fissured asphalt parking area forty feet square and hemmed in by conifers. Aside from the ambulance, there was a third cruiser and a silver Prius, leaving me inches to slot the van parallel to the entrance portico. The secluded neighborhood and the layout of the property meant we had the scene pretty much to ourselves. Good: no one enjoys crowd control.

We got out of the van. Zaragoza began taking flicks of the exterior.

In the far corner of the parking area stood a stick-straight, slender woman in her twenties, the sole civilian among a dozen emergency responders. She wore black yoga pants and a lightweight gray sweatshirt, one shoulder fallen to reveal a teal tank top beneath. Down her neck lay a bundle of lacquered black hair; her throat was concave, her posture so impressive that she appeared to dwarf the female patrol officer standing with her, though they were about the same height. A patchwork handbag slouched against her calf. She had a hand up against the sharp, slanting light, obscuring her eyes, so that I saw only cheeks, smooth and contoured nicely and slightly smoky. Beveled lips pursed and relaxed, as if sampling the flavor of the air.

She turned and stared at me.

Maybe because I'd been staring at her.

Or I didn't matter at all, and she was looking past me, at the van – the gold lettering, the finality. Ambulance arrives: you hope. Cops arrive: you keep hoping. When the coroner shows up, you lose all rational room for denial. Though that doesn't stop some folks.

No. Not the van. Definitely looking at me.

A wiry redheaded guy in a black BPD polo shirt cut between us.

'Nate Schickman,' he said. 'Thanks for coming.'

I said, 'Thanks for leaving the driveway open.'

We didn't shake. Too casual, with kin looking on. There's no class, no textbook, on how to act in the presence of the bereaved. You learn the same way you learn anything worthwhile: by observing, employing common sense, and screwing up.

You don't crack jokes, obviously, but neither do you go overboard with grim sympathy. That's false and it reeks. You don't say *I'm sorry for your loss* or *I'm sorry to inform you* or any version of *I'm sorry*. It's not your place to be sorry. To claim sorrow on someone else's behalf is presumptuous and, occasionally, dangerous. I've had to notify families whose sons have been killed by the police. Do I tell them I'm sorry? They don't care that I'm not the cop who pulled the trigger or that I belong to an entirely different department; that I'm the one charged with caring for their child's physical remains. When it's your kid, a uniform is a uniform, a badge is a badge.

Remember where we are, too. Nobody in the Bay Area likes cops.

'That's the daughter,' I said.

Schickman nodded.

'How's she holding up?'

'See for yourself.'

Tatiana Rennert-Delavigne didn't appear hysterical. She had stopped watching me and turned away, wrapping her free arm around herself like a sash, self-soothing. She was nodding or shaking her head in response to questions posed by the patrol officer. That she was not crying or screaming did not, to my mind, make her any more or less credible. Nor did it make her suspicious. Grief finds a broad spectrum of expression.

I told Schickman I'd be back in a second and headed over to join the conversation.

The patrol officer angled out to admit me. Her name tag said HOCKING.

'Pardon me,' I said. 'Ms Rennert-Delavigne?'

She nodded.

'I'm Deputy Edison from the county Coroner's Bureau. My partner over there is Deputy Zaragoza. I'm sure you have a lot of questions. Before we get started, I wanted to let you know exactly what our role is and what we're going to be doing here.'

She said, 'Okay.'

'It's our responsibility to secure your father's body. We'll go inside the house and assess the situation. If there's need for an autopsy, we'll transport him so that can get done as quickly as possible. I'll let you know if that's going to happen so it's not a surprise to you.'

'Thank you,' she said.

'Meanwhile, do you have anyone you can call, who can come be with you?' I noticed, in the moment before she cast them down, that her eyes were green. 'Sometimes it can help not to be alone.'

I was waiting for her to say *my husband* or *my boyfriend* or *my sister*.

She said nothing.

'Maybe a friend,' I said, 'or a clergyperson.'

She said, 'How do you decide if an autopsy is necessary?'

11

'If we have any reason at all to believe that your father's death wasn't from natural causes – an accident, for example – then we'll do one.'

'What are the reasons you'd believe that?'

'We examine the physical environment and the body,' I said. 'The slightest question, we'll err on the side of caution and bring him in.'

'Do you do the autopsy?'

'No ma'am. The pathologist, a medical doctor. I work for the Sheriff.'

'Mm,' she said. I couldn't tell if she was relieved or disappointed.

Windless sun beat down. Small animals chittered in the cedar branches.

'He didn't slip,' she said. 'He was pushed.'

She shifted, just perceptibly, to address Hocking. 'That's what I'm trying to tell you.'

Credit Officer Hocking for a good poker face.

'I'm definitely going to want to talk to you about that,' I said. 'Right now, I'm going to ask if we can pause for a bit, and me and my partner can go inside and conduct our assessment?'

I was careful not to use the word *investigation*. More accurate, in a way, but I didn't want to suggest that I'd opened the door to the possibility of a homicide. I hadn't opened any doors, period.

Tatiana Rennert-Delavigne hugged herself tighter and kept silent.

I said, 'I promise that we will treat your father with the utmost respect.'

'I'll wait here,' she said.

3

Approaching the house, I noticed deferred maintenance. Rain gutters sagged. Cracks in the façade had begun to gape. The portico floor was missing bricks. The front door was solid oak, though, coffered and free of damage, flanked by two unplanted planters smeared with lichen. All the windows I could see were unbroken.

I signed in, tucked my Posse Box under my arm, pulled on gloves.

Inside, Zaragoza was busy with the camera. A couple of Berkeley cops hung around in the doorway, spectating.

The foyer was a double-high oval, open at the long ends to a dining room and a den. Expansive but spare: the furniture consisted of a single high-backed chair and a console table with a tray, over which an oxidized mirror hung askew. At the back, a staircase curved up toward a spidery iron chandelier.

No rug to cushion the impact of flesh on tile.

No sign of disturbance, just the body, facedown.

I could imagine Tatiana's shock.

I smelled coffee.

Walter Rennert was dressed in a navy-blue bathrobe, fraying

at the hem. His feet were bare. Medium height. High side of average, weight-wise. His left arm was curled beneath his torso. His right elbow crooked skyward, as though he'd tried to slow his descent. I'd seen plenty of other bodies similarly positioned, which made it hard not to jump to an immediate conclusion.

Ten feet separated him from the bottom step. That's a long way for a grown man to travel. I doubted he'd been pushed from the top of the stairs. It would take a violent and powerful heave, close to ground level.

Or else he tripped on the last few steps, went sprawling, cracked his head.

Or else he'd been moved.

Or someone from our side had moved him.

I turned to the uniforms in the doorway. 'Anyone move him?'

One of them fetched Schickman.

'Not us,' he said.

'Fire?'

'Not as far as I know. He was cold to the touch when they got here, so I think they pretty much let him be. I can ask.'

'Thanks. Do me a favor and ask the decedent's daughter also.'

He nodded and went off.

The source of the coffee smell was a brown puddle to my left. The cup it had come from lay on its side, lid popped off. A crumpled bakery bag coughed out its contents. Bran muffin. Scone. Two croissants.

Weekly brunch.

I pictured Tatiana getting out of her Prius, purse slaloming

14

down her shoulder, coffee in one hand, pastry bag in the other, trying to manipulate a house key with two fingers.

I pictured her walking in.

Seeing him.

Dropping the food.

I didn't see her screaming or freaking out. More like she'd dropped the food because it was the fastest way to get to her purse and her phone.

Assumptions.

I began my circuit at the console table. In the tray were a set of keys and a black leather wallet. The keys included one for an Audi and another for a Honda. I hadn't seen either car. No big mystery: the garage wasn't attached to the house, but down at street level, chopped into the bedrock, a common setup for East Bay hilltop homes.

Rennert's wallet contained an unremarkable assortment of credit cards and forty-six dollars in cash. He belonged to two libraries, Cal and Berkeley Public. Health insurance. Social Security. AAA. Fuzz-edged loyalty card for Peet's.

I checked the California driver's license against the man on the ground. Even with next of kin present, I like to find at least one form of photo ID. Stuff like that seems redundant until it's not.

I knelt down for a better look.

The dead man had a dense gray beard and a scraggly gray-white hairline that had fought to hold its ground. His eyelids were locked tight in an expression of agony, his mouth half open. He looked as though he had just received terrible news, unbelievable news.

He was indeed identical with Walter Jerome Rennert.

In the license photo he wore a dazed smile.

I replaced it in the wallet.

Zaragoza took a few last flicks of the body and turned his attention to the staircase, ascending one step at a time, pausing between shots to wiggle the treads. The walls were white-washed plaster. Blood would stand out. The stairs themselves were uncarpeted – a point in favor of a slip. Rushing down, say, to answer the door.

I stepped to the far side of the body. Rennert's right hand was tucked against his flank, gripping an object, the fingers fixed like pipe straps. I waved to Zaragoza, double-checking that he'd gotten shots in situ. He gave me a thumbs-up and I coaxed the object out: an etched-glass tumbler. Its robust, opaque base tapered to wafer thinness along the walls. The faintest coin of yellow liquid pooled at the bottom. Aside from a minuscule chip in the rim, it was intact, which argued strongly against a fall of any significant distance, whether that fall had come about as the result of carelessness, intoxication, bad luck, or malice.

On the other hand, a person hit with, say, an acute myocardial infarction might have time to realize what was happening. He might struggle to stay upright, succumbing in stages, brought first to his knees, then to palms and knees, elbows and knees, before finally giving out. Clutching the tumbler all the while. Wanting to avoid dropping it or collapsing on top of it. Refusing to accept that this was the end. Thinking a very pragmatic, very defiant, very human thought: *No reason to ruin a perfectly good piece of crystal.*

I bagged and tagged the tumbler.

Schickman reappeared in the doorway. 'She says she tried to turn him over to do CPR but couldn't.'

'Couldn't turn him, or couldn't do CPR?'

'You want me check with her again?'

I shook my head. 'I'll handle it. Thanks.'

The body most often speaks for itself.

I set the tumbler aside and knelt at the top of Rennert's head, pressing my fingers into his skull and neck; moving down the spine and the back of the rib cage; digging through the robe's deep pile, through layers of skin and fat and flesh gone rigid; verifying the integrity of the bones beneath.

No indication of fracture or dislocation.

There's a reason we do autopsies, though: some bodies keep secrets.

Having reached the top of the staircase, Zaragoza came down wordlessly to assist me.

He took hold of Rennert's hips. I took hold under the arms. We did a silent three-count and rolled the body over.

The parts of Rennert's face that had been in contact with the ground were blanched paper white, in contrast to the pronounced lividity in his nose and chin. I didn't observe any marks consistent with blunt impact. His robe pouched open, revealing tufts of gray hair, breast and belly blotched purple and white. No lacerations, abrasions, or gross trauma.

It was getting harder and harder not to make assumptions.

Pincered in Rennert's left hand was an item that, for me, is almost always the single best piece of evidence: a cellphone. People keep their whole lives on their phones. You'd be amazed at how many of them will google *signs of a heart attack* instead of calling 911.

Rennert's was a scratched black iPhone, three or four versions old.

Zaragoza photographed the front side of the body.

When he finished, I examined Rennert's cheekbones, forehead, jaw, sternum, and rib cage. I freed the phone and gave it to Zaragoza to catalog, concluding with a check of the extremities before heading outside to confer with Schickman.

'We'll hang on to his cell for now,' I said. 'If you need something let me know.'

'Right on.'

'We're just gonna have a quick look around the house.'

Schickman nodded. He look relaxed. He was making assumptions, too.

It's the mark of a good secondary when you don't have to waste time negotiating the division of labor. Zaragoza might be a neurotic hypochondriac, but he's a professional: he'd taken it upon himself to cover the ground floor, leaving me the upstairs. I followed on his sweep of the staircase with one of my own, failing to find any evidence pointing to a fall or a fight.

Mostly I wanted to track down the hypertension medication. Say Rennert had missed a bunch of pills. That could point toward a natural death: a stroke, for example. Taking too many pills could lead to light-headedness, which in turn could lead to fainting.

A person's home is also a useful indicator of whether he's taking care of himself, sleeping well, getting proper nutrition, and so on.

In this instance, I got mixed signals. Each of the five bedrooms was tidy and tastefully decorated but gave off a stale, unused odor.

In the master I paused to take in a panoramic view of the Bay.

The medicine cabinet in the master bath was empty. Dust dulled the tub.

Rennert was divorced. Maybe he slept somewhere else because the suite conjured too many unpleasant memories. Or it felt overlarge for a single man, living alone.

Nothing hinted at the existence of a girlfriend. No women's clothes in the closet, no stray pots of makeup. Here and there amid the art hung family photos, various combinations of the same three faces, at various stages of childhood and adolescence: Tatiana and two boys roughly ten years older. Products of a previous marriage, perhaps. I saw them apple-cheeked in ski suits against a backdrop of regal pines; holding hands as they jumped into a swimming pool; riding horses in tall dry grass. They looked happy. If they were in fact stepsiblings, they appeared to have blended well enough.

Then again, you don't whip out the camera when the kids are fighting.

Figuring Rennert for one of those people who keep their medicines by the kitchen sink, I started down the hall, pausing by a narrow door.

I had overlooked it, thinking – assuming – it was a linen closet.

I opened it and instead peered up a cramped second staircase.

As I mounted the steps, a phantom ache stirred in my knee, and I stopped for a moment, gripping the banister, breathing through my teeth.

I climbed on.

The staircase opened to an attic, plywood floors and naked rafters and bulging insulation. Stifling and dark, it ran the length of the second story, lacking interior walls but sectioned by Oriental rugs and file cabinets, lamps and books and odd bits of junk. A comfortable disorder that conveyed movement and intention, unlike the space below.

A monumental kneehole desk, ornately carved and piled high with books and magazines, anchored one zone. There was no desk chair, but rather a pair of chairs set up to face each other. The first was a lounger that looked like it had been slept in a lot: nubby upholstery, blanket limp over the arm, grimy buckwheat neck pillow. The second chair was a wooden rocker with smooth, carved spindles, a rich red cherry stain. The two pieces made for strange companions – one elegant and cool, the other greasy and creased. They seemed to huddle in conversation; they looked like a dude on a bender and his successful younger brother, there to stage an intervention. Yet again.

Along the far wall I spied the components of a basic bathroom: plastic-basin shower, sink, toilet, exposed plumbing.

I'd found where Rennert did his living.

No fridge. Maybe he still went downstairs to eat.

I picked my way through the gloom toward the sink.

No pill bottles.

I got down to check the floor.

I inched back the shower curtain.

The makeshift sleeping area felt like the next most logical place to look.

I made my way there, high-stepping over milk crates filled

with LPs, sliding aside the rocking chair to stand before the desk.

I wondered how they'd gotten the massive thing up those stairs. A crane? The largest window, overlooking the Bay, didn't look big enough to admit it. Maybe it had been taken apart plank by plank and reassembled onsite, imprisoned, never to leave.

As a symbol, it felt kind of over the top.

One glance at the mess of papers smothering the desktop was enough to generate a strong hypothesis about Walter Rennert's profession. Books: *The Teenage Brain* and *Taming the Human Animal* and *Issues in Contemporary Research Design*. Academic journals: *Assessment. Adolescence and Childhood Quarterly. Personality and Social Psychology Bulletin*.

It fit. We weren't far from campus. Although I'd majored in psych, and I didn't recognize his name.

Hospital or private practice?

Maybe he used the attic as his office, put his patients in the lounger and took notes in the rocker. To me it didn't feel like a relaxing place to unburden oneself. Too claustrophobic. But to each his own.

I started opening the column of desk drawers on the right.

Pens, pencils, checkbooks, bills, bank statements, invoices, Post-its, confetti, crap.

Middle right, more of the same.

Bottom right, a .38 Smith & Wesson revolver.

As a rule, we stick to a single camera per scene. It gets too confusing otherwise, having to coordinate different devices. Zaragoza had the Nikon with him downstairs. For the moment

I used my own phone to shoot a few flicks, not so much for the official record as to remind myself.

The mere presence of a weapon did not raise red flags. People own guns. Even people in Berkeley. More to the point, Rennert hadn't been shot.

I checked the cylinder.

Five-round capacity.

Four cartridges, full metal jacket.

The central drawer contained more paper and unopened mail.

The drawers on the left were false, a single door that swung out to reveal a deep cabinet, stuffed with a splendid array of fine scotch whiskys: Walter Rennert's liquid pantry.

At least I think the whiskies were fine. I don't know booze. They had fancy labels with pictures of game animals and dramatic Highland names.

At any rate, they had all been well enjoyed.

Three tumblers, identical to the one I'd found in Rennert's hand, sat in a rack on the inside of the cabinet door. Tucked into the tumblers were three plastic amber pill bottles.

The first two contained a diuretic and a beta-blocker – as expected, with Rennert being treated for hypertension. I noted the dates, the dosages, the prescribing doctor (Gerald Clark, MD). A count of the pills corresponded to the days remaining before refill.

The third prescription had been issued by a different doctor, Louis Vannen, and filled five days earlier at a different pharmacy.

We don't receive any formal medical or pharmacological training, but along the way you pick up the basics. Rennert's third prescription was for Risperdal, which is the brand name for risperidone, which is a widely used antipsychotic.

The bottle contained the complete thirty days' worth of pills. Two refills remained. Large black letters warned the user not to consume alcohol while taking this medication.

I opened up my phone to google *risperdal alcohol interaction*. No bars.

I put the bottles back in the glasses and went downstairs to find Zaragoza.

4

He was coming to find me.

'Fridge is basically bare,' he said. He'd been down to the basement, as well, finding a cityscape of moldy cardboard boxes and multi-tier wine racks, the bottles squeaky clean, indicating a healthy (or unhealthy) rate of turnover.

I described the attic and the desk, showing him the pictures on my phone. He headed upstairs to take some better shots with the Nikon and to bag the pill bottles.

I met Schickman at the door.

'We're going to bring him in,' I said. 'I'll talk to the decedent's daughter and give her a heads-up.'

'Yeah, man. Take your time. You need anything from us?'

Weird as it is to imagine a person researching his heart-attack-in-progress, I find it just as weird that others will literally yell, 'I'm having a heart attack.' But they do, sometimes loud enough for neighbors to hear. Not to mention that a two-hundred-pound man yelping as he spills down a flight of stairs can produce a pretty significant racket.

The distance between Rennert's house and the adjacent properties might dampen any noise. But no charge for asking.

I said as much to Schickman. 'Be good to know if anyone heard anything, so if you're offering, a canvass would be cool.'

Schickman rubbed his sunburnt neck. 'Teach me to offer.'

Tatiana hadn't budged from her corner of the parking area, and neither had Patrol Officer Hocking, though their relationship appeared to have outlived its usefulness. The officer had her hands jammed awkwardly in her pockets, and Tatiana was ignoring her, jabbing at her phone with stiff quick thumbs. She noticed me coming and shoved it in her purse, straightening up and shaking away a streamer of hair.

I said, 'We're almost done inside, and I wanted to let you know that we'll be bringing your father out soon.'

'That's it?' she said.

'Beg pardon?'

'You were in there for like half an hour.'

It had actually been an hour-plus. More than enough time to spend at a scene whose signs point toward a natural death. A smaller house? A guy who kept his medicine in the medicine cabinet? I really would've been done in thirty minutes.

I've learned to think before I speak, and that's what I did, looking at the lovely, angry face in front of me.

I said, 'What we do here is just a first step. In your father's case, an autopsy will give us much more specific information. The police have to wait for us to finish before they go inside and start their work. We want to expedite that.'

She exhaled, a little sheepishly. 'All right. Thank you.'

'Of course,' I said. 'Have you had a chance to call someone?'

'My mom. I don't know when she'll get here. She's coming from the city.'

'Right.' I turned to Hocking. 'I think they could use a hand with the canvass.'

Hocking gave a tight, grateful nod and left us.

Tatiana watched her go. 'She doesn't believe me.'

She tilted her head at me. 'You don't either, do you.'

'I'm not sure what you mean,' I said.

'That he was pushed.'

I took out my notebook. 'Let's talk about that.'

It was their ritual, brunch, every Saturday for the last couple of years. She couldn't remember how it had gotten started. Go to the French bakery on Domingo, get herself a cup of coffee, pastries for them to share. Did I know the bakery? They made the most authentic croissants; they'd won multiple East Bay best-of awards. She thought they imported their butter. She only went there once a week, otherwise she'd gain fifty pounds.

Normally, she stayed with her father for two to three hours, leaving in the early afternoon. She taught the one thirty p.m. class at a yoga studio on Shattuck. Sometimes she returned later in the day, bringing dinner for him, depending.

She didn't say what that depended on. As she continued to talk, I filled in reasons.

He drank too much. He didn't feed himself.

He was lonely.

They both were.

She loved him.

I asked when she had last seen her father alive.

'In person, not since Tuesday. Yesterday I called to ask if he wanted me to pick up anything in particular for today.'

'What time was that?'

'Ten, ten thirty a.m.'

'How did he sound?'

'Fine,' she said. 'Normal.'

'Did he complain of any pain or discomfort, anything like that?'

A burr of suspicion appeared in her voice: 'No.'

'I have to ask,' I said. 'It's important to be able to rule things out. How long has he taken medication for hypertension?'

'I don't know. Fifteen years? But I told the police, it wasn't a serious problem. He had it under control.'

'Aside from that, how was his health?'

'He's seventy-five,' she said. 'Normal things. Backaches. I mean, he was fine. Better than that. He played tennis several times a week.'

'Any other medications or conditions that you're aware of?'

'No.'

'For his mood, or anything like that?'

'No.'

'Any mental health issues?'

Her face tightened. 'Like what.'

'Depression, or –'

'If you're asking me, did he hurt himself, that's ridiculous.'

'I don't mean to suggest that,' I said. 'It's just a routine –'

'I know. Okay. No, no issues. And no, he didn't take anything else.'

I believed that she believed it.

27

I could have challenged her; shown her the bottle of Risperdal; asked her about Louis Vannen. But to what end? I play two roles, and I'm constantly balancing my need for information against my duty to console.

I said, 'Officer Schickman told me you tried to do CPR.'

'I started to.' A beat. 'Then I saw his face, and . . .'

She fell silent.

'It's important for me to know how much he was moved,' I said.

She nodded listlessly. 'Not much. I . . .' Her lips began to tremble and she flattened them against her teeth. 'He's heavy. For me.'

She was reliving it: wrestling with her father's body, the sheer physical frustration, a horrifying and unasked-for intimacy.

I said, 'Let's talk about what you said, about him being pushed. What makes you think that?'

'Because it's happened before,' she said.

I looked up from writing. 'What has.'

'This.'

'Okay,' I said.

'See? You don't believe me.'

'Can we back up, please? Something happened to your father –'

'Not him,' she said. 'His student.'

'Student . . . ?'

'Grad student. Here. At Cal.'

'Name?' I asked.

'Nicholas Linstad. He and my dad ran a study together. One

of their subjects ended up going out and murdering a girl. At the trial my father testified against him. They both did.'

'When was this?'

'Early nineties. I was six, I think. Ninety-one or ninety-two.'

'All right. Your father and his student testify against an individual. What's his name?'

'They never released it. He was a minor. Disturbed. The whole thing was awful.'

'I'm sure.'

'You don't understand,' she said. 'My father – it ruined him. Then they go and let this homicidal maniac out of prison. He's walking the streets, my father helped convict him. You'd think somebody would *warn* us. It's completely irresponsible. A month later, Nicholas falls down a flight of stairs and dies.'

'He fell?'

'He was pushed,' she said.

'Was anyone charged?' I asked.

'They said it was an accident. But I mean, come on. It's not, like, a *puzzle*.'

I nodded. 'What about Mr Linstad's death, when did that occur?'

'About ten, twelve years ago. I don't remember the exact date. I wasn't living in Berkeley then. I do know that my father was completely freaked out.'

I thought about the gun in Rennert's desk. 'You shared this with the police.'

'What do *you* think? Apparently it's all a big coincidence.'

'Did they say that?'

'They didn't need to,' she said. 'I could tell from the way they were looking at me.' Her bag buzzed. 'The same way you are now.'

She bent, snatched up the phone, swore quietly.

'There's traffic on the bridge,' she said, texting. 'She's stuck.'

What did I believe, at that point? What did I assume?

It wasn't the first time I'd been asked by a relative to accept the most sinister interpretation of a scene. Grief makes conspiracy theorists of us all. But in my experience, when death haunts a family, there's usually a banal explanation.

Bad genetics. Bad environment. Alcohol. Drugs.

I once met a woman who'd lost three sons, each of them shot. It fell to me to notify her that her fourth son had been stabbed and had died in the ambulance on the way to the hospital. In her face I saw sorrow. Weariness. Resignation. No real surprise, though.

A clatter: Zaragoza at the back of the van, readying the gurney.

Tatiana finished her text and dropped the phone in her bag.

I said, 'I understand your frustration. Right now the goal is to gather as much information as possible. That includes everything you're telling me.'

'Fine,' she said. 'So what next?'

'The autopsy's the first priority. It'll give us a clearer picture of what happened.'

'How long does that take?'

'Middle of next week at the outside. Once that's done, we can issue a death certificate and release your father's body. If you tell the funeral home he's with us, they'll take care of the rest.' I paused. 'Did you have a specific funeral home in mind?'

30

It was this question, the bleak practicality it demanded, that overwhelmed her at last. She pressed at her temples, shut her eyes against tears.

She said, 'I don't even know where to look.'

'Of course,' I said. 'It's not something people think about.'

I gave her a moment to just be.

She wiped her face on her sleeves. 'Who do I call?'

'I'm not allowed to make recommendations,' I said. 'But in my experience most of the ones around here are very good.'

'What about the bad ones?' A short laugh. 'Can you tell me those?'

I smiled. 'Unfortunately not.'

'Whatever. I'll figure it out.' She wiped her face again, regarded me soberly. 'I'm sorry if I lost my temper.'

'Not at all.'

'He's dead, and I feel like nobody's . . . No excuses. I'm sorry.'

'You have nothing to be sorry for.'

She gazed up at the house. 'It's so fucked up. I don't know if he has a will. I can't reach my brothers. Nobody's picking up at the studio, they're expecting me in twenty minutes.' She breathed out sharply. 'It's a mess, is what it is.'

'Did your father have an attorney?'

'My mom might know. If she ever gets here.'

'We can notify your brothers, if it'd help.'

'No, thanks, I'll do it.'

'Before I forget,' I said. 'I have some of your father's possessions, his wallet and his phone. They might yield additional information, so we're going to take them with us. Do you happen to know the passcode for the phone?'

She looked lost.

'Don't worry if not,' I said. 'Usually it's a birthday, or –'

'You can't just, like, crack it?'

'Knowing the code would be a lot faster.'

'God. Okay, try these.'

I scribbled as she rattled off numbers.

'If none of those work, let me know,' she said.

'Will do. Thanks. Anything else you want to tell me? Other questions?'

'I'm sure I'll think of something.'

I gave her my card. 'That's my direct line. Think of me as a resource. Here if you need me, not if you don't. This can be a confusing process, and one of our goals is to make it easier for you.'

'Thank you,' she said.

'Of course.' My turn to look at the house. 'Some people find it tough when we bring the body out. You might want to hang out elsewhere temporarily.'

She didn't reply. She was studying my card.

I said, 'Even if you just want to go down to the street for fifteen or twenty minutes. Or you could drive over to your work.'

She put the card in her pocket. 'I'll stay.'

5

ZARAGOZA HAD left the gurney collapsed by the front door, laying out sheets in the foyer next to the body. He glanced up, spiking an eyebrow as I entered carrying brown paper bags and zip-ties.

We bag hands for trace evidence but only in suspicious cases. I said, 'Can't hurt.'

He shrugged agreeably and we moved the body to the center of the sheets, knotting handles in the fabric. We'll use whatever happens to be in the van, but at that particular moment I felt grateful that it was sheets and not a body bag; sheets move more naturally and are less likely to wrench you in the wrong direction. Ever since the second flight of stairs I'd had a low-level hum in my knee – what I call leg nausea.

Whoever said there's no point worrying about what you can't control clearly had a poor memory, a poor imagination, or both. I take precautions. I ice. I stretch. I get to the gym whenever possible. Still, I worry. I have a decent imagination and an excellent memory.

As I squatted down, braced, put my weight on my heels, I wondered, as I always do: is today the day my own body fails me?

'One,' Zaragoza said, 'two, three, *up*.'

He rose.

I rose.

The body rose.

No disaster today.

We crossed the foyer, moving slowly to minimize the swinging. As we stepped outside and eased the body down onto the gurney, wrapped it in blankets, and buckled it in, I was aware of Tatiana watching us from a distance, those sharp green eyes.

I went over to Schickman and told him we were releasing the scene to him.

'We'll let you know what canvass turns up,' he said.

'Just to put it on your radar, the daughter said her father had a colleague who died under similar circumstances.'

Schickman nodded. 'She told me, too. I tried to ask her about it but she got kind of pissed off. Told me I wasn't listening. Why. You think it means anything?'

I make judgments based on observable facts. Only rarely does a person's history play a role in deciding the manner of death, the main exception being suicide.

Walter Rennert's positioning, clutched chest, facial expression, skin tone, and medical history told the likely story. I thought about my decision to bag the hands – bothered, now, that I'd let her persuade me to second-guess myself.

'Let's wait for autopsy,' I said. 'I'm off Monday, Tuesday, back Wednesday.'

'Sounds good.' Schickman glanced over my shoulder. 'Is she okay there by herself?'

'Mom's en route,' I said. 'Let me check her ETA.'

Tatiana informed me her mother had cleared the snarl and was a few minutes out.

I said, 'I'll hang out until she arrives.'

'You don't have to do that,' she said.

'It's not a problem.'

She stared at the police officers going in and out of the house. She said, 'What are your other goals?'

'Pardon?'

'You said making things go easier for me is one of your goals.' She faced me. 'What are the others?'

'Taking custody of your father's body. Although that's a duty rather than a goal.'

'What else?'

'Securing property, when there's no next of kin present.'

'Do you keep a list of these on a poster in your office?'

I smiled. 'Right above the coffee station.'

The sound of a car turned us both around. A black Mercedes sedan reached the top of the driveway and jerked to a stop, unable to proceed any farther.

Honk honk honk honk honk.

'That would be my mother,' Tatiana said.

I told her we'd be in touch.

By the time we arrived back at the morgue, got Rennert weighed and intaked and handed off to a tech, it was three thirty, the end of shift visible on the horizon. The mood in the office managed to be both subdued and hyper: what you get from long hours in a close, low-lit gray space, everyone steadily sucking down carbohydrates. I stripped off my vest, flexed my knee, settled in front of my computer to begin the paperwork.

Sergeant Vitti shambled over, waggling his phone. 'What's up, boys? How was Berkeley? You finish your rosters yet?'

Without taking my eyes off the screen, I gave him a thumbs-up.

Vitti opened up the app he used to manage our office fantasy football league. His lips moved as he appraised my starters, running a hand back and forth over his shaven scalp. 'Some questionable choices here, Deputy Edison. Kirk Cousins over Cam?'

'It's his year.'

'It's your funeral. Zaragoza?'

'I respectfully decline to participate.'

'Come on. Again with this?'

'Sir, may I point out that last year's winner —'

'Jolly Jesus Christ, Zaragoza.'

'— did not receive the agreed-upon monetary prize. Therefore I decline to participate. Fool me once, sir.'

Vitti appealed to the room. 'Somebody please resolve this for us. Sully.'

One of the techs arched away from her screen. 'What's that.'

'Tell Zaragoza there was no prize for winning the league.'

'It was twenty dollars a person,' Zaragoza said.

Sully rubbed her nose and resumed typing. 'It was a gentleman's agreement.'

'There you go,' Vitti said, retreating toward his office. 'Thank you.'

'Are you kidding me,' Zaragoza said. 'You're kidding me. It

is impossible to have a gentleman's agreement with y'all, cause y'all aren't gentlemen –'

'Oof. *Burn*' – this from a tech named Daniella Botero.

'– which y'all are proving right now with this bullshit,' Zaragoza said. 'Moffett. Back me up, bro.'

From behind a cubicle wall came a lazy baritone. 'It cost a hundred dollars.'

'Don't. Do not. Don't.'

'It cost five hundred dollars,' Moffett said. He stood up. He was tall like Vitti and fleshy like Vitti and had an identically shaved head, down to the V crease where his hairline used to be. Peel ten years off the sergeant and get Deputy Coroner Moffett; likewise, fast-forward Moffett and behold our unit's next leader. He was grinning, chewing on a bear claw big as an actual bear's claw, icing flecking his shirt, quivering at the corners of his mouth.

'It cost ten thousand dollars,' he said.

Behind me, the technicians were laughing.

'It cost ah crap,' Moffett said. Zaragoza had grabbed his pastry and body-slammed it into the trash. 'The heck, dude.'

'You don't need it,' Zaragoza said.

'You can't decide that for me. That's like communism.'

'Have some fruit. Seriously, screw all y'all.'

The subject of the conversation turned to Moffett's weight. My phone rang.

'Coroner's Bureau,' I said. 'Deputy Edison.'

'Aaaahhh, yes sir, okay, so this is Samuel Afton again.'

Samuel Afton had two noteworthy traits. The first was a drawn-out way of speaking that stretched every statement into a question and every question into an existential mystery. Even mildly novel information caused him to drawl 'Oh my goooodness.'

The second trait that distinguished Samuel Afton was a bottomless hatred for his mother. It was impressive. That he expressed his loathing in the same dreamy voice only made it that much more poisonous.

Samuel Afton's parents had split up when he was a baby, his mother remarrying a guy named Jose Manuel Provencio. That marriage lasted longer, but it, too, ended in divorce. Instead of continuing to live with his biological mother, however, Samuel Afton had chosen to stay with his adoptive father.

Now Afton was in his mid-thirties, and Jose Manuel Provencio had died without sufficient funds to pay for burial. Samuel Afton did not have sufficient funds, either. The only person in the immediate picture who had the money was Samuel Afton's biological mother, Provencio's ex-wife. She had in fact offered to pay, which I thought was pretty nice of her, all things considered.

Samuel Afton would not permit her to pay. No sir. No how.

For two months, the body of Jose Manuel Provencio had lain in the cold chamber of a Fremont mortuary, occupying valuable real estate. The funeral director was going bananas, begging me to cremate Provencio as a county indigent. I'd already put that suggestion to Samuel Afton, who had declined. He'd promised to find a relative of Provencio's to cover burial costs.

We'd been having this conversation for weeks.

'Hi, Mr Afton. What's up.'

'Yes, I have been trying to reach you but I have not been able to do that.'

'Sorry. I've been out of the office. What can I do for you? Did you get a chance to speak to Mr Provencio's nephew?'

'Ahhh, okay. So I left another message, but honestly, he hasn't called me back. He's in Virginia, you see. I don't know what it is over there, do you know the time difference?'

'Three hours.'

'Oh my goodness. What is that, is that around seven in the evening?'

'Something like that.'

'Ah-haaah, so yeah, that is why I have been unable to reach him, probably because probably he's engaged in some activity at the moment.'

I opened up Google. 'Right.'

'Probably he went to get something to eat.'

'Right.' I typed *risperdal alcohol interaction* into the search bar.

'So,' Samuel Afton said, 'what I would like to determine is your time line, because you see that would be helpful for me to know that right there –'

Combining Risperdal with alcohol could trigger a host of unpleasant outcomes: seizures, dizziness, fainting, coma, arrhythmia.

'– about when you need an answer, what's the longest you can wait.'

I rubbed my eyes. 'There's no set time, legally.'

'Ah-hah.'

'But,' I said, 'it's a matter of us needing to act. He's been at the mortuary since July.'

'Ah-hah, yes. I understand.'

'So if the blood family is not going to pay for the burial –'

'Yes, I don't know that, though, you see, cause to tell you the truth his nephew hasn't called me back.'

'Right, but if you can't get ahold of him, or some other relative . . . And you still don't want your mom paying for it, even if she's willing to do that?'

'No sir, I do not want that.'

'I get that you and she have had your differences.'

'Oh my goodness, yes sir. That bitch –'

'I get that, but –'

'That bitch took all my money,' he said. 'That's my own mother right there, you understand.'

'I do. My question is what we do about your stepfather, because he's lying there, and at some point I have to go ahead and classify him as county indigent, and you told me you don't want that, either. So it's fine if you want to keep trying his blood, I can say okay, let's do that a little while longer. But at some point. Out of respect for him.'

'Yes sir, I understand. I appreciate your assistance.'

'Have a good day, Mr Afton.'

'You too, Deputy.'

I rang off. I felt tired.

With the browser still open, I searched for the doctor who'd written Rennert's prescription for Risperdal.

I expected a psychiatrist. Maybe an internist.

I did not expect that Louis Vannen, MD, would run a urology practice in Danville.

The internet yielded plenty of off-label uses for risperidone – depression, OCD, PTSD – but none that targeted areas below the neck, let alone the belt.

I craned around to address my deskmate. 'Hey, Shoops.'

Our fourth DC, Lisa Shupfer, hunkered down opposite me, hiding in her screen, pointedly ignoring the debate raging over low-fat versus low-carb. 'Mm.'

'You ever heard of a urologist prescribing Risperdal?'

'Urologist?'

'Yeah. Some condition I've never heard of.'

Shupfer shook her head. 'Ask Dr Bronson, he'll know.'

'He left for the day,' Daniella Botero said. 'It's his son's birthday.'

Moffett said, 'Know what?'

'My decedent was taking Risperdal,' I said.

'He kept it with his liquor,' Zaragoza said.

'He needs psych meds,' I said, 'why isn't he going to a psychiatrist?'

'Maybe he was ashamed,' Shupfer said.

A fair point.

'Maybe his penis was delusional,' Moffett said.

'Find one that isn't,' Daniella Botero said.

6

I spent most of Sunday at my desk. Samuel Afton called three times with updates. He'd given up on his stepfather's nephew but had obtained the name of a cousin in El Paso.

I said that sounded promising.

I attacked my backlog, did crappy EDRS cases, and filled out as much of the Rennert case narrative as I could, leaving voicemails for Drs. Gerald Clark and Louis Vannen.

The following Wednesday I came to work to learn that Walter Rennert's autopsy had been completed on Monday afternoon. I'd guessed AMI, and while I was off about the precise cause of death, my hunch that we were looking at a cardiac event proved correct. If anything, the pathologist's finding was more conclusive: rupture of the aorta, brought about by acute aortic dissection.

The largest blood vessel in Rennert's body had basically exploded. No going back from that.

I wondered how Tatiana would react to the news.

Not well, I suspected. There's often an inverse relationship between intelligence and adaptability. Smarter people – and Tatiana seemed smart enough – tend to dig in harder, largely because they can. They have the resources to draw on. They comb the internet for talking points. They can produce a million arguments for why I am wrong, why I must be wrong. They can sound awfully convincing. The more supple the brain, the more easily it's enslaved by that furious bloody little dictator, the heart.

I remember a mother and father in Piedmont whose teenage daughter died shooting a hot dose. By all appearances, they were upstanding folks: educated, professional, and — as far as they were concerned — involved in their children's lives. In short: totally unequipped to cope with the gash in their reality.

For months they kept calling the office, pleading with and eventually screaming at me to manner it a homicide. They did the same to the cops, demanding the arrest of the unknown dealer. Over and over I had to explain to them that, in the eyes of the law, the death was an accident. I felt like some cruelly defective vending machine, spitting out their dollar again and again. And I'll admit that I came to resent them a bit for forcing my hand, for making me reopen their wound.

In the eyes of the law, Walter Rennert had died naturally. I needed the final autopsy protocol to close out the case, but based on the finding and my own notes, I had more than enough to manner it and issue a death certificate.

I found it disturbing, then, to realize that a corner of my mind had begun exploring other avenues, ones more pleasing to Tatiana.

That I could entertain such thoughts underscores the inherent murkiness of the process. Where's the starting point? How do you decide? These questions apply at every juncture, but they feel especially relevant when you're talking about death, the end result of all prior causes.

A hot dose kills you. So does the decision to try heroin. Same for the history that leads to that decision. Family. Friends. Experience. Coincidence. I can understand how bringing a child into the world might make you feel responsible for everything that follows. I can understand why you'd prefer to blame the dealer.

Five manners of death, and that's by design. Restricting ourselves to a few choices, we prevent philosophical thumb twiddling. The mercy of a death certificate lies in its limitations. It omits reference to your choices, big or small. It puts a cap on the past. It says *This is what you need to know about what happened*.

With few exceptions, its judgment stands forever. It's important to get it right, both for the dead but more so for the living.

Say I were somehow able to nudge Walter Rennert's manner from natural to accidental. Would that satisfy Tatiana? I doubted it. The story she was writing was about a homicide. It was fiction. I opened up my case narrative and began to type.

An hour into my work, I got a call from Gerald Clark, MD.

Clark had been Rennert's primary physician for three decades, and his demeanor reflected the length and nature of their relationship. He confirmed Rennert's history of hypertension, sounding saddened but unsurprised by the autopsy finding.

'The drinking was the main issue,' he said. 'Everything else flowed from that, so to speak. It gives you an idea of how much he drank, that he could play tennis all the livelong day and still be overweight.'

'His daughter made it sound like he was more of a casual player.'

'You've obviously never seen him on the court,' he said. 'He belonged to the Berkeley Tennis Club. I happened to be there once, meeting a friend. We sit down at the bar, and out the window, lo and behold, there's Walter, running around like a madman, rivers of sweat, red in the face. I mean bright red. He looked like a goddamn gummy bear. It was all I could do not to go toss a bucket of water on him. The next time he came into my office, I said, "Walter, you're not more careful, you're going to kill yourself." '

'What did he say to that?'

'He just laughed and told me to mind my own business.' Clark laughed himself, at the memory. 'He didn't look like he was having much fun out there. Frankly, he looked miserable. I told him that, too. "Why don't you take up something more relaxing? Swim." He could be very stubborn.'

'Was he depressed?'

'I never treated him for depression.'

'That doesn't mean he wasn't.'

Clark sighed. 'Did I think he was a happy person? No. He'd been through one hell of an ordeal.'

'By "ordeal" you mean . . .'

'With the university.'

'His daughter mentioned a test subject of his who killed a girl,' I said. 'I'm a little hazy on the details.'

'There's not much else to know. It was a fiasco, and not only because of what happened to the victim. The fallout was awful. Her family sued the school, who forced Walter out. Of course, he blamed himself.'

It ruined him.

Perhaps feeling he'd overstepped, Clark said, 'I'm not telling you anything that isn't public knowledge. It was all over the news. You can imagine the effect it had on him. I wanted to write him a prescription for Prozac. He wouldn't take it. I said, "Find someone to talk to, at least." He wouldn't hear of it. "I know psychologists, I *am* a psychologist, I don't want to talk to a psychologist." Stubborn. But, look, Deputy, I've known Walter a long time. Even before any of that happened, he wasn't exactly an optimist.'

'Did he ever end up getting help?'

'He never would've admitted it to me.'

'This might sound a little out of left field here, but did you ever refer Dr Rennert to a urologist?'

'Really, now, I'm sure that's got nothing to do with anything whatsoever.'

I told him about the prescription from Louis Vannen.

'I don't know the name,' Clark said. 'He gave Walter Risperdal?'

'Seems that way.'

'Huh.' I heard the phone shift; a mouse click; his breathing slow as he read. 'There's nothing in his chart about it.'

'Would there be?'

'We keep track of current medications. Unless he failed to mention it to the nurse.'

'Can you think of a reason why he'd need it?'

'Well, some of these atypicals work for depression or bipolar. He wasn't bipolar.' More clicking. 'Dammit.'

'What's the matter?'

'I had him on Lasix and Lopressor for his blood pressure. They both interact with Risperdal.'

'How serious of an interaction?'

'Moderate,' he said, the unease in his voice steepening. 'Some cardiac effects.'

Presumably the pathologist had taken note of these interactions and written them off as immaterial to cause of death. I said, 'Thanks for your help, Doctor.'

He hung up. The poor guy now had to wonder if he'd helped kill his patient.

He hadn't. I felt reasonably confident of that. And nothing he'd told me had altered my opinion on Walter Rennert's manner of death. To the contrary. I had a seventy-five-year-old man who had endured major life stress, drank to excess, and cherished a hard-charging brand of tennis. The real wonder was that he hadn't dropped dead sooner.

I thought about how best to present these facts in a way that would make sense to Tatiana. I quickly gave up. I'd just have to wait for her to call me up and scream.

It might have ended there.

It should have. I'd called both doctors prior to learning the cause of death. Now that I knew it, I had no reason to chase them down. Had Clark not bothered to return my message, we likely never would have spoken. It might have ended there.

It didn't.

Because I took an active step, small but crucial. At that very moment, it felt harmless. Meaningless.

I called the office of Louis Vannen, MD.

Looking back, I'm not sure why I did this. I could claim I was trying to marshal extra evidence for when Tatiana did start yelling at me. But I knew well enough that piling on facts rarely changes anyone's mind.

Nor did I call out of morbid curiosity. At that point in my career, I didn't have much of it left.

I explained to Vannen's receptionist who I was and what I was after. Citing confidentiality, she could not confirm whether Walter Rennert had been a patient. She would convey my message to Doctor. Doctor would call me back as soon as he had a chance.

7

ON FRIDAY, a hearse from Mountain View Cemetery arrived to take away the body of Walter J. Rennert.

I felt relieved. The family had chosen a nice place; hopefully that meant they'd resolved to move forward and not raise a stink. I chided myself for assuming the worst of Tatiana, for regarding her not as a person, but as a variable in my caseload.

I thought about her eyes.

Wished her well and made my own resolution to forget about her.

Thursday next, I received a notification request from Del Norte County. A man up in Crescent City had shot himself in the chest, leaving behind an adult daughter in our neck of the woods. We make visits on behalf of other counties, just as they do for us; it's more humane than cold-calling the next of kin, especially with suicides or when they're estranged. Both were true here. I copied down the daughter's address, and Shupfer and I climbed into the Explorer and headed east for Pleasanton.

While I get along with all of my colleagues, there are moments when I'm grateful for one more than the others. On that day, I felt no great need to talk. The morning rush had died off, leaving us to ride most of the way in silence – a situation really only possible with Shoops. Outside, tract homes bobbed on wave after wave of dry yellow grass. My legs kept cramping up, forcing me to shift around, angling for room. She, on the other hand, had racked her seat all the way forward to reach the pedals, the steering wheel lodged in her belly.

Here's Shoops: soft and square and rounded off, as tall as five-two gets, with hair that starts each day slapped down to her scalp but finishes in a frizzy brown halo. She could be the star of a *Sesame Street* sketch teaching kids about disappointment.

Say you were an inmate at the jail, back when she was a guard. You might fool yourself into believing, as a certain idiot in a certain legendary story once did, that you could call her an obscene name. Or that you could suggest an obscene activity she enjoyed in her off hours. You might get cocky enough to grab a part of her body.

Those are mistakes you'd only make once.

Technically, Shoops has been around longer than the rest of our team. She joined the Bureau during the changeover, when the county stopped hiring civilian coroners and replaced them with peace officers. An extended family leave reset her status, so I have seniority on her. When December rolls around and we have to bid for shifts, she's low lady on the totem pole. Better believe I don't gloat. Nobody does.

The GPS guided us off the freeway, through a welter of extended-stay hotels and chain stores, along the divided main drag. Thirty minutes inland hardly seemed enough for the terrain to have morphed so dramatically. Topography flatter;

vegetation bleached. The architecture belonged to everywhere and nowhere. That's not a knock on Pleasanton, which is as its name implies. More a statement about where we'd left from.

Shupfer said, 'I still get nervous.'

I glanced at her.

'Before a notification,' she said.

'Really?'

She nodded curtly. 'Every time.'

'I do, too.'

Another nod from her, different: approval.

Trapped in a seam of ranch homes, sandwiched between an elementary school and a middle school, Homer Court was the last and smallest spur off crooked Chapman Way, lawns left to wither and two-car garages. Unfolding myself from the Explorer, I felt the sun twist in close, a microscope focusing down on us.

My gaze lingered on the portable basketball hoop perched at the curb – sandbags crushing the base, backboard craning into the street.

'I know, right?' Shupfer said. 'Put it in the driveway, for God's sake.'

She meant for safety. Thinking about her own kids, dribbling in circles on the asphalt, hollering 'car' and scurrying out of the way.

I nodded, although that wasn't what I'd been thinking, at all.

I was marveling at how far away the rim looked.

There are several reasons to feel nervous before a notification. People do shoot the messenger, and not just figuratively. A day like that one, brutally hot, tempts you to leave your vest behind. I never do. Better sweaty and alive.

That's rare, of course. Best-case scenario, I'm about to ruin someone's day, week, year, life. If that notion doesn't make you squirm, you lack the requisite sense of empathy and you shouldn't be doing this job.

A nasty paradox. Only a true psychopath could do notifications and not suffer any consequences. But who wants a psychopath informing them that their father is dead?

Part of me always hopes the person won't be home. In the middle of the day, in the middle of suburbs populated by dual-income families . . .

Maybe we'd get lucky. The driveway was empty.

We knocked.

Silence.

Shupfer tried again, louder.

We went to the side of the house. I leaned over the gate, called toward the backyard.

No answer.

A neighbor confirmed that Melissa Girard lived next door. He ogled the Explorer and put on a concerned face and wanted to know why we were there.

'It's a courtesy call,' Shupfer said. 'Nothing to worry about.'

We returned to Melissa Girard's house. Shupfer took out her card, wrote a brief note on the back, and made to tuck it into the doorframe.

Behind us, a blue RAV4 pulled up.

Shupfer returned the card to her pocket.

The driver got out. She was gaunt and fair-skinned, peering

at us through raccoon eyes as we came up the front walk toward her. I noticed a rear-facing car seat in back.

Shupfer said, 'Mrs Girard.'

The woman nodded.

'I'm Deputy Shupfer from the Alameda County Coroner's Bureau.' Talking clearly, not rushing, not dragging. Bearing truth, which is a kind of gift. 'I'm afraid I have some bad news. Your father passed away.'

For a moment, Melissa Girard did not react. Then she opened the back door and reached for the car seat.

She unlatched it and hauled it out, her spine bent at a painful angle. Supermarket bags filled the footwells. No way was she going to be able to manage. I jogged over to help.

'Thank you,' she said.

The neighbor was watching us from his front window. Shupfer shot him a look and he vanished.

We went into the house, into the kitchen.

Melissa Girard said, 'On the counter is fine, thanks.'

I made space for the bags amid a litter of unwashed baby bottles.

'Is there someone you can call to be with you?' Shupfer asked.

'Why would I do that?'

'It can help not to be alone,' I said.

Melissa Girard gestured to the car seat. 'I'm not.' She started to laugh. 'I never am.'

Still laughing, she began unpacking the groceries.

The baby was a boy, about three months old, asleep with his head slumped on his chest. His shirt said I ♥ MY BIG BROTHER.

Behind the fridge door, Melissa Girard said, 'Was there something else you needed?'

Shupfer nodded me from the room. I went outside to wait.

Sitting in the Explorer, I found myself thinking about Tatiana Rennert-Delavigne. She was my most recent point of reference, and I couldn't help but feel the contrast between her response to her father's death and that of Melissa Girard.

I wondered if she was okay.

I couldn't come up with an excuse to call her. Remembering that Dr Louis Vannen had never called me back, I did the next best thing. The old switcheroo.

'Doctor's office.'

I repeated my spiel. As before, the receptionist would not tell me whether Walter Rennert had been a patient of the practice. She would deliver the message to Doctor, et cetera.

'Right,' I said. 'I called last week. Is Dr Vannen around now?'

'He left for lunch a few minutes ago.'

'Can you look on his calendar and see when he'll be free?'

'He's booked solid. All I can do is tell him.'

'Thanks, then. Have a good day.'

'You too.'

Shupfer emerged. I leaned across to open the driver's-side door for her.

'Everything all right?' I asked.

She shook her head, put the key in the ignition.

'Should we wait for someone to show up?' I asked.

Shupfer glanced at the house and thought it over. 'I'm going to say no.'

I said, 'You mind if we take a little detour?'

Twenty minutes later we rolled up to the medical building where Louis Vannen practiced. Shupfer cruised the lot along a row of reserved parking spaces. Three belonged to Contra Costa Urological Associates, the middle slot unoccupied.

She found a nearby spot and parked nose-out.

Shortly before one, a silver BMW coupe arrived to claim the reserved space. The brake lights shut off, and I stepped from the Explorer.

'Dr Vannen?' I asked.

He paused, halfway out of his car. He was mid-sixties, sinewy and tan, sleeves rolled up on woolly forearms. He looked at me, at the Explorer, at Shoops, back at me. He stood up, erect and pigeon-chested. 'Can I help you?'

'Hope so,' I said, coming forward. 'I've been trying to get in touch with you for the last week. I called your office a couple of times and they said they'd give you the message, but I was in the neighborhood, so I thought I'd drop by.'

He made a forbearing sound, half chuckle, half cough: *This guy.* 'It's not the best time. I have patients waiting.'

'It's about a patient, actually. Walter Rennert?'

A beat. Vannen bent into the BMW to retrieve his phone from the cup holder. When he came back out his expression had cleared.

'Sorry,' he said, closing the car door. 'I don't have a patient by that name.'

'You prescribed him some medication,' I said. 'Risperdal.'

He shook his head. 'I don't think so.'

'Your name's on the bottle.'

'Then there's been a mistake. Check with the pharmacy.'

'Will do. Sorry for the interruption.'

'Not at all. But I really do have to go.'

'Sure. Thanks.'

He strode off toward the building.

'Dr Vannen?'

He turned around, annoyed.

'You forgot to lock your car.'

He stared at me, fished out his keys, jabbed the button. The BMW bleeped.

I got in beside Shoops. 'That was weird, no?'

She started the Explorer. 'Mm.'

'What's "mm."'

'What nothing,' she said, shifting into gear. 'Mm. That's all.'

'Drive, please.'

'Mm.'

8

PEOPLE KEEP their whole lives on their phones.

Having a person in your contact list doesn't prove that you have a real relationship with them. My own list includes names – Ike the Plumber, Plaid Glasses Girl – that I can no longer match to a face.

At some point, though, I had reason to care.

As soon as Shupfer and I got back to the office, I went down to Evidence to retrieve Walter Rennert's iPhone.

At my desk, I dug through my notes for Tatiana's suggested passcodes. She'd written down four strings of four numbers. Kids' birthdays plus Rennert's own.

I held up the phone. 'Anyone know how many tries I get before it locks me out?'

'Five,' Moffett said.

Sully corrected him: 'It's ten.'

Another tech, Carmen Woolsey, suggested I take it upstairs to the crime lab.

'I don't want to sift through a data dump,' I said, googling *iphone wrong passcode*. Sully was right: after ten incorrect codes, the phone would not only lock but erase itself.

None of Tatiana's codes worked.

If I still wanted an excuse to call her, I had it.

'Hello?'

'Hi, Ms Rennert-Delavigne. Deputy Edison from the Coroner's Bureau.'

She said, 'Oh.'

You could drive yourself nuts, trying to figure out the meaning of that 'oh'.

Oh it's you. Oh great. Oh shit.

I said, 'I've got your father's phone here and unfortunately none of the codes you suggested seem to be correct.'

'. . . uh,' she said, 'ah, hang . . . hang on.'

I heard a chair scrape.

'Is this a bad time?' I asked.

'No. No, it's fine, I . . .' She cleared her throat. 'It's fine. I meant to call you.'

I tightened up. Let the yelling commence. 'Okay.'

'I wanted to thank you for your help,' she said. 'With the . . . the funeral home.'

'You're welcome,' I said. 'I don't remember being too helpful on that count.'

'Well – no. You were helpful in general, I guess. So thanks.'

'Of course.' Possibly she hadn't seen the death certificate and was still clinging to the idea of a homicide investigation. Or else I was right: she'd come to her senses, let it go.

'The phone,' she said. 'That means you're still working on the case.'

Shit.

'The autopsy was completed last week,' I said. 'There are a few loose ends.'

'Like what?'

Aiming for maximum vagueness, I said, 'It's a process.'

'But you did do the autopsy.'

'The procedure itself was completed. The full protocol's not finished. I'm ready for those codes if you have them.'

'I – right. I gave you birthdays, I think. What do you have?'

I read back the list.

She gave me another set of four numbers. 'That's their anniversary.'

For a broken marriage? 'What about your father's own parents' birthdays?'

'I can't remember them off the top of my head. I can find out and call you back.'

'Or email me. My info is on the card I gave you.'

'When do you think I can have it back? The phone. I'd like to get the photos off it.'

'We like to hang on to it until the case is officially closed out.'

'Do you have a sense of when that'll be?'

For a clear-cut natural death? A month. Two at most.

'Tell you what,' I said. 'If I can find a way into the phone, I'll download the photos and get them to you. Does that work?'

'That's perfect. Thank you so much.'

'Of course,' I said.

'It's not an emergency,' she said. 'I want to have them, is all.'

'I understand,' I said.

Silence.

She said, 'I'll get you those other birthdays.'

The anniversary code failed, as did the two additional codes she sent me the next day. With three attempts left, I'd had my fill of living dangerously. I went upstairs to Forensics.

The IT guy took one glance. 'You're lucky it's a 4S. The newer ones are a pain in the ass. What do you need?'

'Everything. Calls, texts, browser history, pictures, video.'

I returned to the office following my days off to find an email waiting for me.

'It's not super organized,' the IT guy said, handing me the phone and a thumb drive. 'But it's all there.'

It was indeed. Rennert had opted for the sixty-four-gigabyte model, the most memory available at that time. Half of what you could get now, but still plenty of room for crap to accumulate over five-some-odd years, any shreds of useful information squirreled away in folders and subfolders and sub-subfolders, minus the typical user-friendly interface. It was like getting vomited on by the Matrix.

With enough hunting, I found the contact list.

'Shoops,' I said. 'Come look at this.'

She rolled her chair over. I'd highlighted a folder labeled LOUIS VANNEN, opened a text file containing Vannen's email address, along with numbers for home and mobile.

'So,' she said, 'he lied.'

'Yeah.'

'So?' she said.

'So he *lied*.'

She glanced at me sidelong. 'You said this case was a done deal.'

'It is.'

'Then why do you care?'

'Because it's weird,' I said.

'Lots of things are weird. Zaragoza is weird.'

'Heard that.'

'Life is weird,' Shupfer said. 'Death is weird.'

Moffett said, 'Deep thoughts, by Shoops.'

'Why would Vannen lie to me?' I said.

Shupfer shrugged. 'Maybe he's scared cause he wrote the scrip for recreational use.'

'People take Risperdal for fun?'

'People take anything for fun,' Moffett said.

'True dat,' Daniella Botero said. 'I had a friend in high school who used to get high on nutmeg.'

'I didn't know you could do that,' Moffett said.

'Totally. You have to eat, like, a pound, though.'

I said to Shupfer, 'You're getting someone to write you bogus scrips, you're not gonna ask for Oxycontin?'

She shrugged again. 'Rennert was a shrink, he knew his own personal chemistry.'

'*Nutmeg,*' Moffett said.

'I don't like it,' I said.

Shupfer smiled, all lips, no eyes. 'So don't like it, princess.'

She rolled back to her desk.

I returned to my data dump. Rennert didn't have a lot of photos, which felt consistent with the guy I was getting to know: solitary. I burned what there was to a fresh thumb drive, put it in an envelope addressed to Tatiana, and tossed it in my to-do tray.

Someone came around, taking orders for a coffee run.

'Pumpkin spice latte,' Moffett said. 'Hella nutmeg.'

At five thirty I got my stuff together. Instead of dropping the envelope in the outgoing mail bin, I kept walking, toward the door, down the stairs, across the lobby linoleum, ripe with disinfectant. I waved to Astrid behind the reception booth glass and pushed out into the mild evening.

Tucked in a peaceful nook, below a regional park, our headquarters is a smooth new concrete stack surrounded by California live oaks and a deep gully frothing with ivy, like a disused moat. I crossed the gangway to the parking lot, the handrail slick against my palm. Autumn in the pipeline.

I stared down the prospect of the next few hours. Hit the gym. Stop at Chipotle. Go home and watch History Channel on demand. The big question was who I'd be spending my evening with. Would it be Jesus? Or Hitler?

Throwing my bag in the backseat of my car, I drove to Berkeley.

9

Tatiana Rennert-Delavigne lived on Grant Street, near the Gourmet Ghetto, fifteen minutes across town from her father's place. Her digs were more modest: the top floor of an orange, seventies-era duplex, a bit of an eyesore on an otherwise quaint block. The silver Prius shared the driveway with a two-tone Subaru wagon.

Drop off the thumb drive.

Leave without ringing the doorbell.

Go home and watch my stories.

I unbuckled my seatbelt and stripped off my uniform shirt. From my gym bag I took a can of Febreze, hoping to cover the skin of stench picked up on a ninety-second visit to the cold storage locker.

Decomp. *The smell of wrong*, Zaragoza calls it – a persistent sensory stain, chewing up your sinuses, shellacking the inside of your face, hounding you for hours. One good whiff will destroy your operating illusions about the world.

I doused myself with freshener.

The car filled with fumes.

I rolled the window down, choking and waving.

Once the air cleared, I smelled fractionally better.

Didn't matter. I wasn't going to see her, I was a delivery boy. I doused myself a second time.

I took an old Cal sweatshirt from the gym bag and pulled it over my T-shirt.

The man in the mirror: disheveled, bleary, and moderately foul.

What a stud.

The exterior stairs to Tatiana's apartment were made of concrete, silent as I climbed to the second-floor landing. A small hinge-top mailbox hung from the siding. The lid squeaked as I raised it and dropped the envelope inside.

I started back down to the street.

Behind me, above me, a door opened.

'Hello?'

I turned.

She stood barefoot on the landing, wearing leggings and a purple scoop-neck shirt, hair up in a bun.

'Hi,' I said. 'Didn't mean to disturb you. I brought those pictures you asked for.'

She blinked at me. 'You didn't have to do that.'

'It's no problem,' I said. 'I was nearby.'

Of course I was. I'd taken a five-mile detour to get there.

'Anyway,' I said, pointing to the mailbox, 'all yours.'

She fished out the envelope, peered inside. 'I guess they worked.'

'Sorry?'

'The codes I gave you,' she said. 'Which one was it?'

'None, actually,' I said. 'We have our ways.'

I'd meant it as a joke but she nodded distractedly, still gazing at the drive. 'Kind of amazing it all fits on there.'

I didn't have the heart to tell her that her father hadn't been much of a photographer. The folder contained around a hundred pictures, many of which were duplicates. Still, there were a handful of shots she'd want, the two of them together.

'It means a lot to have these.' She clasped the envelope to her chest. 'Any scrap.'

I nodded.

She said, 'I feel like I should offer you coffee. Is that what I'm supposed to do?'

'You don't have to do anything.'

'Please. You took the time. I don't have any coffee. I have tea. Do you want tea?'

All around us, the sky was embers.

I said, 'I wouldn't turn down a glass of water.'

She stepped back to admit me.

Over the years, I've had the misfortune to tour some of California's most breathtakingly slovenly homes. Compared with, say, a crack house, Tatiana's apartment felt positively airy, even with large portions of it swallowed by banker's boxes and sliding piles of paper. Shrink-wrapped five-packs of unbuilt boxes leaned against the wall, waiting to be born, eager to get fed.

She led me along a path cleared through the living room, toward the kitchenette.

'Sorry about the mess,' she said. 'I'm kind of in the weeds here.'

She took down a glass from the cabinet, a filter pitcher from the fridge. 'Please, sit.'

I couldn't. Boxes occupied the kitchen chairs; a paper mosaic on the table. Bank statements and insurance statements and bills, some of them years old, addressed to Walter Rennert or a trust bearing his name.

Tatiana finished pouring and turned to see me still standing. Hurriedly she set the glass aside, stacking documents up and dumping them in an open box.

'I'm the executor,' she said. She slapped the box top on. 'Surprise!'

She cleared off chairs and handed me the glass, and we sat.

'You didn't know?' I asked.

'He didn't bother to tell me.' A thin bitter edge, swiftly trimmed away: 'I'm the logical choice. Stephen's in Boulder, Charlie's in New York. They have their own lives.'

The implication being that she did not?

I took a drink. I'd made the glass my clock. Once the water ran out, I would, too.

'Dad had enough sense to divide the assets three ways,' she said. 'At least we don't have to fight about that.'

As siblings, they'd looked happy enough in their childhood photos. But now money was involved. I gave a noncommittal nod.

She sighed and hooked one leg under herself, spine straight as a candle, chest out, as though presenting herself for military inspection. Freckles strewn across her collarbones; bottom lip swollen in a sweet pout; wide-eyed at the avalanche lying before her.

'You probably can't tell,' she said, 'but I'm a minimalist by nature.'

I could buy that. Edit out the inherited clutter and you saw little in the way of ornamentation. Black-and-white posters hastily slapped up with tape; a ukulele on the futon. A stack of cookbooks and some dried-out flowers standing in a repurposed milk bottle. It looked more like the dwelling of a recent college grad, giving the impression that she'd just moved in. Or that she was on her way out soon. Or that she couldn't decide.

She said, 'The lawyer – he did have one, by the way – he's helping, but it's still a ton of work, mostly cause my dad was so disorganized. I have to get everything appraised. The art . . . I've been going through his credit card statements. He's signed up for all this stuff, bogus subscription services or "fraud alerts" or whatever. The kind of sneaky shit a normal person notices and cancels. He had three dozen bank accounts, and each of them is shooting out checks on a monthly basis to God knows where. Plus he keeps his records in his basement, which fills up when it rains, so everything from about' – chopping her shin – 'here down has water damage. I can't be there for more than five minutes, it sets my allergies on fire, so I've started schlepping it here. Four trips and I'm still not done.'

I thought she might have another, unstated motive: she couldn't bear to be alone in a big, hollow house, listening to her father's ghost repeatedly crash down the stairs.

'Whatever.' She shook off her irritation, smiled. 'So you said you live nearby?'

'Lake Merritt,' I said.

'Oh.' The smile took on a gloss of confusion. 'That's cool.'

I'd be confused if I were her, too. I was nowhere near home. Nevertheless I was glad to have found a neutral topic. 'It helps if you like geese.'

'Do you?'

'They're okay to look at,' I said. 'Up close? They're kind of assholes.'

She snorted. 'I know people like that. For some reason they all seem to come to my yoga class.'

I asked where she taught.

'It's a side thing. Mainly I dance. What about you?'

I said, 'Uh. Well –'

She slapped a hand over her mouth. 'Oh my God. I can't believe I just asked you that.' She started to laugh.

'Reflex,' I said.

'Exactly.'

'To be fair,' I said, indicating the Cal sweatshirt, 'I'm in disguise.'

She grinned. She had beautiful teeth, and I've seen my fair share of teeth.

'Yes,' she said. '*Exactly*. Thank you. It's *your* fault.'

I laughed, too, over my discomfort. That she'd asked the question, even inadvertently, called attention to the irregularity of my presence. It was the sort of question you asked a blind date.

I drained the water and stood to place the glass in the sink.

'Let me, please,' she said, taking it from me. 'Can I get you anything else?'

'No, thanks.'

'Thank you for the photos.'

'My pleasure. Good luck,' I said, or meant to say. I didn't get it out before she spoke again:

'You know, I recognized you.'

I said nothing.

'At the house? I thought – when you introduced yourself, I mean, you're like' – she waggled her hand above her head, meaning *tall*. 'I wasn't sure until you gave me your card.'

'You went to Cal,' I said.

'Oh-seven.'

'I was oh-six.'

'I know,' she said. 'I looked you up, just to make sure I wasn't imagining things. It was reassuring, in a way. *Oh my God, I know him*. Even though I don't, really. That's strange, right, for me to think that?'

I shrugged. 'Not that strange. It happens. People feel a connection.'

'You're used to being recognized.'

'We're not talking about I'm famous.'

'Kind of, you were.'

I brought my thumb and forefinger close together. 'That much.'

Narrowed them further, so they were almost touching. 'For that long.'

'I never went to any games,' she said. 'Is that terrible?'

'It is,' I said. 'I'll still help you, though.'

She laughed. ''Cause that's the kind of guy you are.'

I smiled, shrugged again.

'It was a thing that year,' she said, 'the basketball team.'

It was. I was.

'I'm sure that's why I didn't go,' she said. 'On principle. I was artsy. I'm sorry.'

I waved her apology away.

'Do you miss it?' she asked.

'Not really.'

'Not even a little?'

'I don't mean that it was easy to stop,' I said. 'It's not like I had a choice.'

'And now?' she said. 'Why this?'

'My job, you mean.'

She nodded.

'Why do you do what you do?' I asked.

'Because my mother put me in ballet slippers before I could walk.'

So far she hadn't given any indication she could smell me, either the decomp or the Febreze. But I realized with a start that *I* could smell *her*. Scent has a role in my work; it's another tool in the kit, and my nose has grown both highly attuned and not easily bothered. Every body, living or dead, has its own unique perfume. Tatiana's was dark and rich and alive as she leaned toward me.

'It doesn't get boring,' she said, 'dealing with people like me all day?'

'No.'

'You sound very convincing.'

'It's the truth,' I said. 'When I talk to someone who's grieving, they don't care how many other people I've talked to, that day or any other day. They shouldn't have to. For them, it's the first time. They deserve the same attention and respect as everyone else.'

Tatiana rolled the empty water glass back and forth between

her palms, like she was forming a clay snake. She said, 'I know you don't believe me about my dad.'

I started to object and she cut me off: 'It's fine. I wouldn't believe me, either. But if what you just told me is true, look through my eyes for a minute.'

I wondered if everything to that point – asking me in, every word, every coy shape – was a run-up to this moment, when she could lobby me. But that threw far too much responsibility on her. She'd never asked me to come by to begin with. That was my idea.

I said, 'Do you feel that people aren't listening to you?'

'I feel that the cops don't want to get into it, because that forces them to consider they might've screwed up.'

'Screwed up how?'

'When Nicholas died,' she said. 'They ignored that, also, and now they have to justify their decision. But I remember how upset my dad was.'

'I can imagine,' I said.

She frowned. 'I can't tell if you're being sarcastic or not.'

'I'm not. It must have been terrifying for him.'

She allowed a nod.

'It must have affected you, too,' I said. 'Not just that. All of it.'

'My parents did their best to shield me from what was going on. I was genuinely shocked when they told me they were getting divorced. I mean, I wasn't blind. They'd been unhappy for years. And neither of them were experts at staying married. But for some reason I assumed they'd keep toughing it out. For *me*.' She scoffed at her own naïveté.

I asked how many times they had each been married before.

'Dad, just the once. Her? Boy. She's what you'd call a runner. He was number five.'

'Well,' I said, 'it's not the smallest number I've ever heard.'

'But not the biggest, either,' she said hopefully.

'I had a guy once who was married nine times. Twice to the same woman.'

'People are insane,' she said. 'She told me once that I was her Hail Mary. As in, her last chance to have a kid? Obviously she couldn't get pregnant while she was dancing. It's a refrain of hers. "I've seen it happen to too many girls, your body is never the same again . . ." What's that mean, you "had a guy."'

I hesitated. 'In the course of my duties.'

'Oh,' she said. 'Right. I should've realized.'

'All my stories end the same way.'

'I'm almost afraid to ask what he died of.'

'Motorcycle accident.'

'I thought maybe his last wife killed him.' Her collar had begun to sag. She plucked at it, then reached behind to regather stray hairs at the base of her neck, shirt tautening over her breasts. It was warm in the kitchen. She didn't have air-conditioning. Few East Bay homes do. You don't need it till you need it. Diamonds glistened in the cup of her throat.

I said, 'You mentioned the other day that you left Berkeley for a period.'

'I moved to New York.'

'To dance?'

She nodded. 'I came back three years ago.'

'For your father.'

That I had discerned this appeared first to disarm her, then to please her.

'He never asked me to,' she said. 'He tried to convince me not to, in fact. Somebody had to take care of him, though.'

'I'm sure he appreciated it.'

'Whether he did or he didn't, he needed it, and nobody else was stepping up. Not working was terrible for him. It's not like he couldn't have hung out a shingle or whatever. Independent research. He told me he'd lost his professional credibility. I was like, "You are completely missing the point." I wanted him to keep busy.'

'Besides tennis,' I said.

'Besides tennis. That's all he did. That and wander around the house.'

Idly she tapped the rim of the water glass. 'I don't expect to snap my fingers and voilà. But it's frustrating to have the cops refuse to even ask questions. I mean, what harm is there? Other than for some guy's ego.'

'You want my honest opinion?'

'I do,' she said.

'A lot of harm, potentially. I've seen people sacrifice their entire lives to questions.'

She said nothing.

'I'm not saying you're wrong to ask.'

'But get it together and' – twirling air – '*move on*.'

I said, 'I can't pretend to know what's right for you.'

She bit her lip. 'All I'm asking is for you to please keep an open mind.'

A lying doctor; the echo of a fall; a murderer walking the streets.

It only felt like half a lie for me to say, 'I will.'

She put the water glass in the sink and crouched to open the cabinet beneath. She pulled out a ceramic ashtray and a cigar box, both of which she set on the counter. Inside the box was a Baggie of marijuana, a packet of papers, and several pre-rolled joints.

She lit one off the range burner, took a deep drag.

Offered it to me still smoldering.

I said, 'No, thanks.'

A cloud rolled in her open mouth, licking at her tongue before she banished it in a long white wire. 'I have a medical card.'

'I didn't ask,' I said.

'I get migraines.'

I gave her a little salute. 'Have a good night, Ms Rennert-Delavigne.'

She returned the gesture.

10

I SPEND my days off engaged in single-guy activities. It can be a challenge, because I work weekends. But this is the land of the irregular and irregularly employed; build a billion-dollar company in your underwear and you win. Weekday diversions abound, and I can usually find something to do. Browse the farmers' market outside Children's Hospital and flirt with the mushroom girl. Drag a buddy to Lincoln Square Park to play pickup, or Mosswood, if I'm feeling solid and don't mind waiting for a game.

My one semi-regular obligation comes whenever Zaragoza's wife takes pity on me and invites me for dinner.

Things get dire enough, there's always Tinder.

That week, I stayed inside with my laptop and read.

Newspaper accounts of Walter Rennert's downfall were sketchy. The events in question had taken place pre-internet-boom, and archives of the locals, including *The Oakland Tribune* and *The Daily Cal*, only covered the early 2000s and on. The *San Francisco Chronicle* archive went back further, but evidently they had deemed the story East Bay News, unworthy of too much attention.

I did manage to learn the date of the original murder – Halloween night, 1993 – as well as the victim's name and age.

Donna Zhao, twenty-three years old, a Berkeley undergrad, had been found stabbed to death in her apartment, half a mile south of campus.

Tatiana had gotten the year wrong but not by much. She'd been a child; her knowledge of the case had been acquired after the fact.

One thing she'd gotten right: the offender's name was never released. Like many juvenile hearings, his was closed to the public, and I found no information about its disposition. The bulk of the coverage focused not on the murder but on the resulting civil suit, brought by Donna Zhao's parents, charging negligence on the part of the University of California, the Board of Regents, the Berkeley Department of Psychology, and Dr Walter Rennert.

Tatiana said the offender had been enrolled in one of her father's research studies. What she'd left out, deliberately or not, was the nature of that research.

Rennert, it emerged, had built a career examining the effects of media violence on the developing brain. The theory appeared to be that exposing kids to graphic imagery harmed them in all sorts of ways: lessening their empathy, hindering their academic performance, and – his central theme – priming them to commit real-world violence. Perusing his abstracts on PubMed, I gathered he did stuff like show teenagers clips from slasher films while measuring their heart rates.

That sounded on par. During my senior year, when I suddenly had a bunch of free time, I'd volunteered for a handful of psych studies. I recalled a corkboard in the lobby of Tolman Hall, tabbed flyers promising free cookies in exchange for collaboratively building a tower of wooden blocks; five bucks to put on goofy stereoscopic glasses and follow the bouncing ball.

To earn course credit, rather than cash, you'd have to expend a little more effort. Code video, log data, help conduct the study itself. That was what Donna Zhao had been doing when she was murdered: working in Rennert's lab, assisting with the experiment that would draw her killer into the building.

The Zhaos, Chinese nationals, had hired a San Francisco firm to represent them. The claim was that Rennert, his lab, and the institutions they belonged to had failed to properly evaluate the boy's potential for real violence. By exposing him to violent stimuli, they had triggered an outburst that found the closest available target: Donna Zhao.

A settlement was reached in 1997.

Its terms were undisclosed.

Days later, Walter Rennert resigned his professorship.

There was no mention of him testifying.

The name Nicholas Linstad did not appear anywhere.

Turning my attention to Linstad, I found nothing, not even an obit or death notice.

That was as much as I could learn from the comfort of home. I shut my computer and went out for a run.

When it comes to the gentrification of Oakland, Lake Merritt is old news. Nestled in the northern half of the city, bounded by water and freeways, it lies apart from the truly mean streets, steadily absorbing the drip of wealth that filters down through the stony bedrock of Elmwood, Piedmont, Montclair. I've lived here long enough to witness the change, liquor stores evolving into purveyors of small-batch bitters.

Rough edges remain. Hand-grind spices and pour-over coffee and letterpress all you want. That dude by the off-ramp, with the cardboard sign and the starving Chihuahua in a backpack? He's still on meth.

That day I took my usual route along the lake: down Bellevue, past the bonsai garden, and out toward the boating center, where a group of young, fit white people in ludicrously matching outfits dragged their scull toward water rich with chop. The setting sun did a good job of wiping the world clean. Geese, out in full force, honked obnoxious taunts. For decades they'd used the park as a migratory way station. They'd drop in for a few weeks, like ill-mannered relatives, before taking off for points south. In recent years, it had occurred to them that they liked it here just fine. Maybe they could take the pulse of the real estate market. Installing themselves on a permanent basis, they've gobbled up territory, dropping their waste indiscriminately, so that now the lawns consist of more slime than grass. Even for a neighborhood latecomer like me, it's hard not to view them as a metaphor.

The breeze brought a tinkle of bells from Children's Fairyland.

I jogged along, keeping an open mind.

When, precisely, had Donna Zhao's killer been released from prison?

Where was he now?

Distracted, I strayed to the edge of the path. From my right came a rusty shriek and a blitz of dirty brown.

'*Dammit.*'

I sidestepped the charging goose, leaving it snapping at the air.

Reaching Broadway, I hopped from foot to foot, waiting for the light to change.

I had other questions, too: about the accidental death of Nicholas Linstad, and the lawsuit, and Walter Rennert's experiment gone wrong. About Tatiana.

The WALK sign lit up. I put my head down and barreled into the wind to make it feel like I was going fast. With any luck I could catch the mushroom girl before she left.

On Thursday morning, Sergeant Vitti lumbered into the squad room. 'Ladies and gentlemen, we have a winner.'

I minimized a window and swiveled around to accept his congratulations.

'Two weeks running,' Vitti said, pumping my arm. 'Get this man a frickin cookie.'

'All gone,' Carmen Woolsey said.

'Get this man a cruller.'

Sully tossed a mini-packet of M&M's on my desk.

'Good enough,' Vitti said. He thrust an imaginary microphone in my face. 'Coach. Hey, Coach. *Coach.* What's the secret to your success?'

I said, 'At the present time I can't reveal that information.'

Vitti chortled. 'Lookit Bill Belichick here.'

A hail of boos.

'Don't hate on excellence,' Vitti said. He grinned, grabbed my shoulders, and massaged them aggressively. He was a shoulder-kneader, the sergeant. 'I'm coming for you this week. You know that, right? How's that make you feel, Coach?'

'At the present time I can't reveal that information.'

Vitti squeezed my chin, patted my cheek, and lumbered away, announcing as he went that rosters had to be in no later than five tomorrow, for five thirty kickoff.

Shupfer cast her eyes heavenward: *Have mercy.*

I watched Vitti disappear into his office, then reopened CME.

According to our system, Nicholas Linstad was a divorced white male, age forty-two.

His next of kin was his father, Herman Linstad, residing in Gottenborg, Sweden.

He had died on December 2, 2005, of an acute cerebral hemorrhage resulting from blunt trauma to the head.

The manner of death was accidental.

The coroner's investigator was M. Ming.

I knew Ming in passing. One of the last civilian CIs, he'd retired long ago but was known to drop by the office every now and again. He and Shupfer were close. The *M* stood for Marlborough.

I emailed document storage.

Twenty-four hours later, a box arrived containing Linstad's file, along with several dozen others. His was comparatively thick, containing the full autopsy protocol, a handful of photos, and portions of the Berkeley police report.

Paging through, I noted a number of superficial similarities to the Rennert case.

Linstad lived north of campus, on the upper floor of a duplex, the bottom half of which served as his office. An exterior stair-case offered direct access to the living quarters. It was at the foot of these stairs that the body had been found, by the mail carrier, circa nine thirty a.m. In his narrative, Ming recorded intermittent rain on the preceding day, increasing throughout the night. Linstad's hair and clothing were soaked. The wooden banister on the second-floor landing was rickety, and the door to the upstairs unit was slightly ajar. The interior showed some disorder but no definitive sign of a struggle. There were few furnishings and almost no clutter, which made it hard to tell. A single wineglass on the coffee table; another in the sink; a half-empty wine bottle sat on the counter, a second empty in the trash.

If you wanted to see similarities, you had to see differences, too.

Whereas Rennert's body showed no cuts or abrasions, Lin-stad's bore the hallmarks of a fall. Attempting to arrest his descent, he'd made a desperate grab at the duplex's wooden sid-ing, leaving deep gouges in the shingles, collecting splinters under his fingernails; tearing the right middle fingernail half-way off. Bruises ran down his spine; a long thin bruise marred his right flank, the likely result of slamming against the edge of a stair tread. Scrapes covered his knuckles, and there was blood on and around the bottommost steps, in enough quantity that it hadn't washed away overnight. The pathologist concluded that the major trauma came from Linstad's head hitting the pave-ment, rather than from an object. Toxicology gave a blood alcohol level of .11.

The parallels I did see were better explained as coincidental. Linstad and Rennert both drank. So what? Booze is a versatile killer – death's utility player. Some people drink enough to weaken their aortas. Others drink and fall down the stairs.

Look for connections and you can find them anywhere.

Linstad lived in a duplex. Aha! So did *Tatiana*.

See? Hot garbage.

A statement taken by Berkeley PD heightened my interest somewhat. A rear neighbor claimed he'd heard the sound of an argument, followed by a loud bang – possibly a gunshot – around midnight.

Canvass failed to corroborate him, however, and when pressed, the guy admitted he couldn't be sure the noise hadn't been a thunderclap or that it hadn't come from a television. There was, it appeared, no follow-up.

Nobody – not us, not police – mentioned the offender from the Donna Zhao murder. Either they hadn't known about him or they regarded his involvement as so unlikely as to not merit a phone call.

Yet despite all this, Coroner's Investigator Ming, in his initial finding, had mannered the death undetermined.

I could sense his discomfort radiating off the page. Undetermineds don't sit well with anyone, especially next of kin. We make every effort to avoid them, convening monthly to hash them out in a group session, along with Vitti and our lieutenant. Most of the time we can arrive at a determination, just as Ming and Co. eventually had.

The death of Nicholas Linstad became an accident.

What had made Ming doubt?

I asked Shupfer if she had his phone number handy.

'I got an old case of his,' I said.

She gave me her stare-down, then scribbled on a Post-it. 'Here you go, princess.'

Before I could dial, my desk phone rang.

'Coroner's Bureau, Deputy Edison.'

'Ahhh, yes, hello there.'

'How's it going, Mr Afton.'

'It's going all right, thank you, yeah. Listen, I wanted to tell you that I am ready to go ahead with the arrangements for the burial that we discussed earlier.'

'County indigent,' I said.

'Hahhhuhh . . . ? No sir, I did not mean that, I don't mean that.'

'You found a relative?'

'Yes sir. Well no, not that, but I spoke to the man at the place where they got him at, and originally they said it was going to cost eleven hundred dollars but the man said he can do it for five.'

The mortuary getting rid of the body, even at a loss. Chalk one up for pigheadedness. Though by Afton's own account, five hundred was still more than he could afford.

He beat me to it: 'As a matter of fact and to tell you the truth I do not have that amount in my possession currently, but I am expecting to have it sometime next week.'

'Right.'

'So what I would like from you, sir, is to inform you of that fact, so that we can keep the situation in a holding pattern, okay, a little while longer until this other situation comes through and I can get me paid.'

'Next week?'

'Yes sir.'

'Okay. You're sure about this?'

'Ahhha, yes, yes I am.'

'All right.'

'All right all right. So I'll talk to you next week, then.'

'No need. You can just handle it with the folks at the mortuary.'

'Yes sir. I will do that. You take care now.'

'You, too, Mr Afton.'

I replaced the phone. Studied the Post-it with Ming's number, unsure whether to call.

Moffett decided for me. 'Yo, Coach. Ten fifty-five Alameda, we're up.'

I stuck the Post-it to the bottom of my screen and reached for my vest.

11

Two weeks later, I hadn't heard from Afton or the mortuary, which I took as a good sign. I also hadn't heard from Tatiana, which I chose to regard as not a sign of anything. I still had the Post-it stuck to my screen, but it had drifted to the margins of my awareness.

On a slow Saturday morning, I opened my queue to begin closing out cases.

Click a name, confirm everything's square, send it sailing into history.

I came to RENNERT, WALTER J.

The autopsy protocol had come in the previous day.

I didn't need to read it. I knew what it said. Everything was square.

I moved my cursor to SUBMIT.

The Post-it seemed to light up.

I pulled it loose. Stared at it. Called Ming.

Got voicemail.

I hung up without leaving a message and put the Post-it in the trash.

The cursor sat, ready and willing to flush Rennert Walter J.

and Rennert-Delavigne Tatiana Middle-initial-something from my system.

I couldn't tell her the story she wanted to hear, but I might yet convince her I'd kept an open mind.

I clicked the supplementary tab and opened Rennert's cellphone data dump.

In the week leading up to Walter Rennert's aortic dissection, he'd used his browser sparingly. He read CNN and BBC. He searched Southwest flights from Oakland to Reno. He shopped for a new showerhead, probably to replace the leaky one in his attic quarters. He visited the homepage for the California Psychological Association, following many of the links. He'd abandoned his position but not his passion.

His email was mostly spam. One came from a Charles Rennert – Tatiana's brother Charlie. The REPLY-TO field indicated that he worked for an NGO. He wrote testily that he was still waiting to hear back about using the Tahoe house. He needed an answer from his father by the end of the week, so he could tell Jenna whether to enroll the kids in winter camp or not. So far as I could tell, Rennert had never gotten the chance to write back.

The calendar had him playing tennis on Monday, Wednesday, and – significantly – Friday at noon. The pathologist had placed Rennert's time of death between eight o'clock that night and two o'clock Saturday morning. I could call the tennis club, find out who he played with. Maybe that final game had been extra hardcore. Although if Gerald Clark was to be believed, Rennert played only one way.

For most of that week, he'd made or received fewer than a dozen phone calls. A dry cleaner; Citibank customer service; the pharmacy where he got his Risperdal. A handful of calls to his daughter. True to her word, she had phoned him on Friday at ten twenty-one a.m., a call lasting about four minutes.

Anything special for brunch, Dad?

Then the pattern changed.

Around three thirty p.m., Rennert began dialing an East Bay number. The calls were short, and there were a lot of them – eighteen, in fact, lasting thirty or forty seconds apiece, as though he couldn't get through but refused to give up. They started out at fifteen-minute intervals, but by five o'clock he was retrying every few minutes.

Whoever he'd been calling was quite likely the last person to speak to him. Assuming they had spoken.

I reverse-searched the number. It belonged to the Claremont Hotel, adjacent to the club where Rennert played tennis and a five-minute walk from his house.

If he needed to reach someone that badly, why hadn't he just gone over in person?

Maybe he had.

I called the front desk, identified myself, asked about the extension, and learned it belonged to room four fifteen. I asked who'd occupied it last September 8 and was told that information was private.

'Who'm I speaking to?'

'My name is Emilio.'

'Listen, Emilio, do me a favor and put your manager on?'

Dead air, then he came back. 'I asked her, sir. She's very clear that we can't disclose that. Was there anything else I could help you with?'

I quashed the urge to point out that he had not helped me overly much. I said, 'All right, Emilio. I'll be seeing you later.'

'Yes sir.' Then: 'Sorry, what?'

I hung up.

I went to the Claremont that evening after work. Parking on the street to avoid a sixteen-dollar valet charge, I hiked up Tunnel Road on foot, passing Rennert's tennis club to reach the minty glow of a marquee welcoming guests of the Lamorinda Women's Book Society Autumn Cotillion.

The creamy tiers of the hotel rose tilting from the hillside, out of scale and lost in time, like some elderly politician who will not die. I'd been inside, years ago, for a Cal donor event, where I was trotted out and made to pose for photos with the boosters. Hometown hero, full-court general, savior. Folks had faith in me, back then. Maybe they thought they'd be getting a collector's item, something with eBay value or at least worthy of a place on the den wall, next to their old-timey yellow-and-blue pennants.

The lobby had since been spruced up with jewel tones and aluminum tubing. In the main ballroom, the dance was in full swing. Teenage girls in ball gowns and boys in slouchy suits spilled into the lobby, gabbing and taking pictures.

At the reception desk, I badged, asked for Emilio.

In short order I was sitting in a back office across the desk from Emilio's boss, Cassandra Spitz.

'You understand I can't just tell you that,' she said.

'I wouldn't ask unless it was important,' I said.

'I'm sure you wouldn't. But you don't stay in business for a hundred years by giving out the names of your guests.'

'Nice job with the remodel, by the way.'

She grinned. She appeared to be enjoying the diversion from her usual workweek drudgery. 'Thank you, Deputy. I *can* tell you that we had a variety of events taking place that weekend. You could try asking me about those in broad terms.'

'I'm asking.'

She typed, read from her screen. 'Let's see . . . There was the Ellis-MacDonald wedding in the Empire Ballroom, on Saturday. Cocktails for the Berkeley Public Library Foundation, Sunday evening in the Sonoma.'

'What about earlier in the week?'

'Wednesday through Saturday, we hosted the annual meeting of the California Psychological Association.'

I said, 'The guest in room four fifteen was here for that.'

'I couldn't say.'

I showed her a photo of Rennert. 'What about him?'

Her smile vanished.

'Was he part of the conference?' I asked.

'No.'

'He was here, though.'

She stared warily at the photo. 'This gentleman – I'm sorry, I don't know his name.'

'Walter Rennert.'

'Mr Rennert came to the hotel and requested to speak to one of the guests.'

'The individual in room four fifteen. Doctor . . .'

She smiled. *Nice try.*

I smiled. 'When was this?'

'Friday evening. Around six thirty.'

That fit with the phone log. He'd run out of patience. 'Can I see the CCTV?'

'We only keep the last ten days.'

'Okay. Rennert shows up and asks to speak to an individual, who may or may not be the individual from room four fifteen, who may or may not have been here for the conference. Did he say what he wanted to see this person about?'

'Not that I'm aware of. Our staff offered to deliver a message to the guest. Mr Rennert got extremely agitated and began demanding to know the guest's room number. I came out to try and resolve the situation. I could tell he was intoxicated.'

That fit, too. 'Were you aware that he'd been trying to call the guest?'

'Not right then. Later one of the desk clerks told me she'd patched him through earlier in the day.'

'Eighteen times,' I said.

Her eyes saucered. 'Oh.'

I said, 'Were you able to resolve it?'

'Not in the least. He walked away from me. I thought he'd gone, so I went back to my office. But apparently he started poking his head into the conference rooms, one by one, until he found who he was looking for.'

'And then?'

'There was an incident,' she said.

'What kind of incident?'

'Yelling, mostly.'

'Did it get physical?'

She shook her head. 'Security asked him to leave and he did.'

'What were they yelling about?'

'Not they,' she said. 'Him. It was completely one-sided.'

'Sounds like a night to remember.'

She shrugged that off. 'A hundred years, Deputy. It wouldn't make the list.'

She typed something, then got up, adjusting the angle of her screen. 'Sorry to do this, but I have to go check on the kitchen. Unless you have more questions.'

'Thanks very much for your time.'

'You're welcome. Can you find your way out?'

'I think I can manage.'

She left me alone.

You don't stay in business for a hundred years by having a shitty relationship with local law enforcement. Cassandra Spitz had moved her screen just enough for me to see a page from the hotel's electronic registry.

The booking ran from Wednesday, September 6, through Saturday, September 9, for a total of three nights. The guest had been given room four fifteen – nonsmoking, junior suite, king bed, single occupancy – at the conference rate.

I wrote down the name. While that probably would have sufficed for me to track him down, conveniently enough, the registry entry listed a cellphone number, so I wrote that down, too. The number had a 310 area code: Los Angeles.

Rennert with a jones for a fellow shrink.

To learn why, I'd have to call up this Alex Delaware dude.

12

D<small>R</small> A<small>LEX</small> Delaware didn't have a personal website, but he'd merited joint full clinical professorships at USC's Department of Psychology and med school. I found his faculty page. He specialized in children: anxiety, pain control, trauma, custody; he'd published extensively on the effects of chronic and terminal disease. He belonged to a handful of professional societies, consulted to Western Pediatric Medical Center, had won a graduate teaching award.

More interesting, he served as a police consultant.

At the CPA annual meeting, he'd delivered a lecture titled 'Pediatric Forensic Evaluation: Separating Fact from Fiction'.

I called his office, expecting a receptionist or voicemail.

He picked up with a simple 'Hello.'

I introduced myself.

'Alameda,' he said. Mellow voice, young-sounding for a guy with all that paper.

'I have some questions for you about Walter Rennert.'

Hoping for a reaction, getting none, I went on: 'I understand you had a run-in with him recently.'

He said, 'Would you mind giving me your badge number, please?'

I didn't have a whole lot of standing. I complied.

'I'm going to have a friend of mine call your office.' His voice had taken on some steel. Still mellow, still even, but assertive without being abrasive. Someone who could hold his ground with a ranting drunk.

I said, 'When do you think you'll be getting back to me, Doctor?'

'After my friend clears you.'

Too mellow? Maybe he'd follow through. Maybe he wouldn't. I said, 'Sure, thanks.'

A short while later Vitti came out to see me. 'I just got pinged by some lieutenant at LAPD wanting to know if you're legit.'

'For a case,' I said.

'Yeah, huh.' He scratched his pate. 'Anyhow, I told him you're a bastard.'

'Thanks, Sarge.'

'My pleasure.'

I phoned Delaware. 'Are we okay to talk?'

'If you can make it quick. I have a patient in a few minutes.'

'How did you know Dr Rennert?'

'I didn't,' he said. 'Not personally.'

'It sounds like he knew you.'

'He knew who I was, but that's as far as it went,' Delaware said. 'I haven't had any contact with him in twenty years. More.'

'You did see him this last September eighth, though.'

'I was giving a lecture and he interrupted me. It wasn't a conversation.'

As Cassandra Spitz had said. 'What happened twenty years ago?'

'I served as an expert witness at a trial involving him.'

'The Donna Zhao case.'

A beat. 'Yes. That's become relevant again?'

'There were two trials, criminal and civil. Which were you a part of?'

'Civil.'

'Did you testify for the defense or the plaintiffs?'

'The plaintiffs hired me,' he said. 'The testimony I gave was impartial.'

'Of course,' I said. 'Can I ask what your testimony concerned?'

Delaware said, 'Much as I'd like to get into this right now, we're going to have to stop. My patient's here.'

'I can try you back in an hour.'

'No can do, Deputy. I'm swamped.'

'Tonight, then.'

'I have dinner plans,' he said.

I said, 'Dr Delaware, are you aware that Walter Rennert is dead?'

Another beat, longer.

'I see,' he said. 'Not a natural death?'

'That's what we're trying to determine.'

'I'm sorry to hear it,' he said. 'When did it happen?'

'Shortly after you two had your reunion.'

Now he had me answering questions. This guy was subtle.

I said, 'I'm trying to get a sense of Dr Rennert's last few hours, and it's looking like you were the last person to see or speak to him. I could really use your help in understanding what transpired that night.'

'Let me . . . I'm free to talk tomorrow between three and three thirty.'

'That works.'

'Or – you know what,' he said. 'As it so happens, I'm headed north again in a few days. We could meet in person, if you prefer.'

Face-to-face almost always beats phone – body language, facial expressions, so forth. I've also found that, once people sit down with you, a kind of social glue sets in, and they open up more readily.

Or: Dr A. Delaware, master forensic psychologist, wanting to check out *my* nonverbals, use his shrinky Jedi mind tricks to control the situation.

Or this was just a stall, giving himself time to come up with an unimpeachable story.

Other than a weird feeling, though, I had no cause to suspect him of wrongdoing.

Keep it cordial. 'That'd be great, thanks.'

This time, he was booked in the city, at a hotel on Nob Hill. We arranged to meet in the bar.

Before we got off, he said, 'I really am sorry to hear about Walter. We had our differences, but I always got the sense that he was basically a decent guy.'

Those differences were what I wanted to know about.

I said, 'See you Thursday.'

* * *

95

Traffic into San Francisco was compliant, and I arrived at Delaware's hotel with a few minutes to spare, staking out a lobby sofa that afforded a view of both the bar and the elevator. A jazz quartet played some song that was no doubt famous long ago. No clue. I'm tone deaf. I'm not even sure it was jazz.

I'd done a bit more digging on Delaware, found an undated hospital faculty headshot. Had to be an old photo. I saw a young man with pale, searching eyes, a square jaw, and a wide, straight mouth, all that symmetry topped by a loose mop of curly dark hair.

No reason to update it? A little Southern California vanity?

When he finally stepped from the elevator, I almost didn't recognize him, because I was expecting someone who did *not* resemble the guy in the picture, which he did.

Aside from some gray flecks, a slight deepening of lines, he was the same person, middle height and solidly built, wearing a black turtleneck over black slacks. He must have a great plastic surgeon.

I watched him head for the bar. He placed his order, turned and leaned back, elbows up. Before leaving the office, I'd changed into street clothes, and as he scanned the lobby, his gaze passed over me without pausing.

His drink arrived. Drinks, plural.

Needing to steady his nerves?

He put down cash and took both glasses, walking slowly to avoid spilling.

Coming straight toward me.

At that pace it took him a good thirty seconds to reach me, allowing me ample opportunity to wonder how he'd spotted me.

He set the drinks on the end table and eased into an armchair.

'I'm that obvious,' I said.

He shrugged. 'I know a lot of cops.'

He slid me one of the glasses, tall and clear, a lime wedge spiked on the rim. 'Fizzy water okay?'

'Great. Thanks.'

He'd kept for himself a squat tumbler, a glistening sphere of ice lolling in amber liquid. He sipped. 'I assume you're working and don't want anything harder. If you do, though, caveat emptor.' Jostling the ice ball, he smiled. 'Eighteen bucks for Chivas?'

'How much for fizzy water?'

'Don't ask.' He took a second sip, observing me through pale eyes, blue fading into gray, steady and devoid of anxiety. 'What can I do for you, Deputy?'

Blameless. Or a psychopath.

'Let's start with the night of the conference,' I said. 'In your words.'

'I was scheduled to speak for an hour. Midway through, a man slips in at the back. I noticed he looked a bit fidgety, but no cause for alarm. People change their minds all the time, switch seminars. I kept going. He stands there a few minutes, then comes running up the aisle.'

'At you?'

'Scratch that,' Delaware said. '*Run*'s not the right word. He could hardly stand. He tripped over a chair leg and went down on the carpet.'

The memory seemed to sadden him. 'People tried to help

him up, but he shook them off and planted himself in front of the lectern. "Delaware . . . " ' Wagging a finger. ' "Delaware, I *forgive* you." That's when I realized who he was. I'm amazed I did, given how long it's been.'

'Why would you need his forgiveness?'

'I don't,' he said. 'That's what I told him. "Please, let's not do this right here. There's no need." In his mind, though? I don't suppose he had any love lost for me. I heard he ended up losing his job.'

'He did.'

'Terrible situation. For so many people.' He sipped. 'Put it in context, Deputy: I testify all the time. I've made people angry. It's an occupational hazard.'

'So why was Rennert focused on you?'

'*Was* he focused on me?' Delaware asked. 'Or just drunk and deteriorated and seizing the opportunity because I happened to be in town?'

That stopped me short. 'I don't know.'

'It was a long trial,' he said. 'Lots of moving parts, teams of witnesses on both sides. Including, I presume, other psychologists. Have you talked to them?'

I said I hadn't.

'A child custody case, fine,' he said. 'People resolve not to mess their kids up, but often they do, and it gets ugly. Personal. But with Rennert, nothing I did or said should've inspired any special resentment. I'm not one of those guys who gets inventive on the stand. I tell lawyers that at the outset. More often than not, they hire someone else.'

'But not on this one.'

'They wanted a qualified opinion on a single, narrow issue. I gave mine. I doubt I made or broke anything. And it's not as though Rennert tried to contact me before. So I find it hard to believe he's had it out for me all these years.'

He smiled. 'On the other hand, I could be in denial.'

His take on Rennert's state of mind made sense to me. The iPhone calendar had Rennert playing tennis the morning of the lecture. I pictured him leaving his club, noticing the hotel marquee. I imagined the mix of delight and dread. A psych conference, going on right now, right in his front yard.

He'd be curious, naturally. Enough to look up who was talking and what about. He had indeed viewed the conference webpage on his phone.

Browsing the speakers' list.

Seeing Delaware's name.

Feeling the pinch of a dormant grievance.

Witness for the plaintiff.

Calling the Claremont, getting no answer.

Putting back a few drinks.

Discovering, suddenly, the courage to go on over there and give his old adversary a piece of his mind.

I said, 'What was the single narrow issue?'

'I was asked to evaluate the boy who had committed the murder and determine whether he was psychologically stable enough to participate in a study with the potential to induce a high level of stress.'

'And you said he wasn't.'

'Psychology's a limited science,' he said. 'No one honest can pontificate about the past or the future. I said that, if it were my study, I would have excluded him. That's all.'

'Even so, that implicates Rennert.'

'If the jury took it that way, that's up to them. I can't control how things get spun. Let me be very clear: I never said that a video game could make anyone kill anyone. I never said it, because I don't believe it. I always thought the whole media-violence link is a bunch of horseshit. For one thing, it's simplistic. It minimizes the role of personal responsibility. In my experience, it's the individual that matters most of all. Not to mention that a lot of the studies that claim to prove a connection are poorly designed and haphazardly controlled. Back in the nineties, though, it was a sexy topic. The government liked it, you could get big grant money.'

'You don't think there's any way the experiment could have set the kid off.'

'I can't answer that, Deputy.'

'Can't or won't.'

'Either,' Delaware said. 'I don't know what set him off. People are complicated. A doesn't necessarily cause B. I tried to clarify that but got cut short by plaintiffs' attorneys.'

'At that point you were no longer helping their case.'

'Like I said, I'm impartial,' he said. 'I thought defense might raise it on cross-examination but they didn't.'

'Never ask a question you don't already know the answer to,' I said.

Delaware nodded. 'They wanted me off the stand as quickly as possible. They still had to present their side, and if a jury hears the words *study* and *murder* in the same sentence two hundred times, even if that sentence is "The study did *not* cause the murder," they start to associate those ideas, whether they realize it or not.'

He paused. 'You see the irony, of course. Here's Rennert, year after year, paper after paper, doing his damnedest to show a causal relationship between violent media and actual violence. Then one of these kids actually does what he's predicting, plays a game and goes out and kills someone, and his lawyers have to turn around and argue, no, it doesn't *actually* work that way. Everything our client has written, his entire life's work, all the articles, books, and speeches? Just kidding, guys.' He shook his head. 'I wasn't around to watch him take the stand, but I bet the Zhaos' lawyers had a field day.'

He swirled the ice in his glass. 'Look. I didn't agree with Rennert's methodology. I thought it was sloppy, not to mention based on a silly premise. And what happened to that poor girl was horrific. But that doesn't put the knife in Rennert's hands.'

'If he believed in his own theories, he had to feel responsible.'

Delaware nodded. 'I'm sure he did. From the little I knew him, I thought his intentions were good. When he turned up at the hotel, he looked possessed. He said he forgave me but I got the sense he could've been talking to himself. I felt sorry for him. Still do.'

The idea of Rennert needing a sedative no longer seemed quite so far-fetched. Equally conceivable was that he'd hide that need from his daughter. 'Did you have a personal relationship, outside of this case?'

'You asked me that over the phone,' he said. 'No.'

'What about the boy?' I asked.

'What about him?'

'You evaluated him,' I said. 'You spent time with him.'

'Under the terms of the settlement, there's very little I can tell you. Plus he's a minor. Or was, at the time.'

'What was wrong with him?'

He smiled faintly. Not going to answer that. 'I'll say this: the longer I practice, the less I know. It would be convenient if everyone fit into a diagnosis. Or if a diagnosis was all you needed.'

Thinking of his recent lecture – 'Pediatric Forensic Evaluation' – I asked if he'd chosen the subject with the Zhao case in mind.

'No,' he said. 'It is a coincidence, now that you point it out. But, no, it's a standard talk I give. Comparatively technical, dissecting profiling and other alleged magic bullets.'

Another smile. 'It's one of my favorite topics, because people really *are* complicated.'

'You can see how it might get Rennert riled up.'

'I can. Though I've been to Berkeley before to lecture, and he's never crashed those.'

'He might've, if he'd known about them,' I said. 'What brings you here this time around? Another conference?'

'My girlfriend's teaching a workshop. I'm tagging along.'

'Is she a psychologist, too?'

'She makes musical instruments.'

'Was she with you that weekend?'

'I was solo.'

'Right,' I said. 'You didn't finish saying what happened after Rennert barged in.'

'He shouted until security carted him off.'

'And then?'

'I finished my talk, ate as little rubber chicken as possible, went to bed.'

'By yourself,' I said.

He put his glass down. 'Yes, Deputy. Nobody can corroborate that.'

'You didn't speak to Rennert at any point later that night, phone or in person?'

'No. Whatever he was so worked up about, it was his issue and his alone.'

'You didn't go to his house.'

'Absolutely not,' Delaware said. He seemed more amused than annoyed. 'I have no idea where he lives.'

Easy enough to learn. But no reason to claim he – or anyone – could cause Rennert's aorta to shred, even if he'd sneaked up behind and yelled 'Boo'. Medically, the stress of their confrontation might've been a contributing factor. From my perspective, though, that didn't amount to anything more than a tragic end to a tragic story.

Not an accident. Certainly not a homicide.

'How did he die?' Delaware asked.

I smiled. Not going to answer that.

He laughed. 'All right. I get it.'

He checked his watch, then glanced over at the bar.

A woman – petite, extravagantly curvy, with a full head of auburn hair – waved. Like Delaware, she was dressed in black. Tight black.

He raised a hand to her and stood. 'Got to go, Deputy Edison. Good luck finding whatever it is you're looking for.'

13

TATIANA CALLED the next day asking for an update.

Bad timing. I'd spoken to Delaware in the hope of finding information I could use to cushion her landing.

I had nothing for her.

RENNERT WALTER J.

SUBMIT

One click and it'd all be over.

I minimized the window, thinking: *Coward.*

'I'm finished with your father's property,' I said. 'If you want it back.'

'His property,' she said.

'The phone and whatnot.'

Instantly I regretted it. I could tell that she could tell that I was putting her off.

'Fine,' she said, as if I were a phone voice and we'd never met. 'When do I get it?'

The stock reply: *You're free to pick the items up from our facility, between eight thirty and five, Monday through Friday.*

I said, 'I can bring it by tonight. Six thirty work?'

'I'd planned to head over to his house to pick up the last of the boxes. I'm not sure how long I'll be.'

'I can meet you there,' I said.

'Would you, please? That'd be easier.'

Her tone had softened nicely.

I couldn't bring myself to ask what the hell I was doing. I knew what I was doing. I knew that if Tatiana had the face of a toad, the conversation would've already ended.

Never would've begun.

But Tatiana did not have the face of a toad.

'Of course,' I said. 'See you then.'

I put down the receiver.

Shupfer had leaned around her monitor to stare at me.

'What's up?' I said.

She shook her head, went back to her work.

'Shoops,' I said. 'What you looking at me like that for?'

'I'm not looking at you.'

'You were.'

She met my eye. 'We're not a delivery service.'

'Beg pardon?' I said.

She resumed typing.

An open plan office makes it hard not to form opinions. I do it. But you don't expect to hear them spoken aloud. Keep to yourself and go about your business. It's phony, sure, but only as phony as civilization in general.

That Shupfer was right only pissed me off all the more.

'That's a great tip, thanks,' I said. 'Lemme write that down.'

She ignored me.

I shoved back from my desk and went to the coffee station.

Moffett came up beside me, poured his own cup, spoke low: 'Don't get on her, man.'

'She's the one getting on me,' I said, wringing a sugar packet.

'She's having a bad time. You can't take it personal.'

'What bad time?'

'Danny.'

The anger went out of me, displaced by guilt. 'Shit. Is he okay?'

'I dunno,' he said. 'I think they had to take him to the ER last night.'

'Shit. I didn't know.'

'I don't think I'm supposed to know, either. I heard her ask Vitti for tomorrow off. She and Scott need to take him to some specialist.'

I glanced across the squad room. Shupfer had her head down. 'I feel like a dick.'

'Don't sweat it,' he said. 'I'm giving you the FYI.'

He poked around inside the communal pastry box, pressing down to collect cake crumbs on the pads of his fingers. 'What's the deal, though. You're making deliveries?'

I stared at him.

'Chill, homey,' he said. He licked a sugary thumb. 'I'm just asking.'

He grinned, slapped me on the butt, and sauntered back to his desk.

The ground-floor lights were on as I pulled up the driveway to Rennert's house. Tatiana had left her Prius at an uncomfortable angle. It was her house now – one-third hers – and she could park any damn place she wanted to.

Walking to the door, I was struck by how much cooler and calmer the spot felt in comparison with the last time I'd been there. The seasons, turned over. The frenzy, long gone, leaving behind a stillness both easeful and lonesome, dry trees shuffling in the wind.

Before knocking, I smoothed down my uniform. It didn't smell too bad. I could've changed, but it had seemed prudent not to. Keep me in line. Give me a façade of validity.

Distantly: 'It's open.'

I found her at the head of the dining-room table, clutching handfuls of paper, staring defeatedly into yet another box. An empty juice glass sat on the sideboard alongside an open bottle of white wine.

She didn't look up. 'I'm trying to figure out how much of this I can toss.'

The table was vast, long enough to seat sixteen comfortably, though I doubted it had seen any recent action. Cobwebs entangled the carved chair-backs and laced the sconces. On one wall, a roiling seascape stretched nearly to the rafters.

'It's like he didn't know you're allowed to throw things out,' she said. 'Look at this.'

I stood beside her and she showed me a creased instruction manual for a robotic vacuum. The tendons in her forearms stood out like train tracks. 'I don't even think he owns one of these.'

She tossed the manual to the floor, facing me at last. 'What've we got.'

I gave her the phone, still in its evidence bag.

'I can open it?' she asked.

'It's yours,' I said.

She didn't open it. She stood there, feeling the screen through the plastic, and I reached in my backpack for a second evidence bag, containing the pill bottles from the attic.

'I don't need those,' she said.

'Right, but they were his, so I'm required to return them to you.'

I wondered if she'd notice the Risperdal. But she tossed the bag on the table with a clatter. 'Anything else?'

The third and final bag contained the crystal whisky glass her father had been holding when he died.

'I don't want it,' she said.

I hesitated.

'I mean it. I don't care what you're required to do. Get it the fuck away from me. Those, too.'

I tucked both the pills and the tumbler in my backpack.

She stepped abruptly to the sideboard and lifted the wine bottle. 'Do you want?'

'No, thanks. I should hit the road.'

Perhaps I'd made her self-conscious; she stopped at a quarter glass. She took a quick sip and set it aside, sanding her palms. 'Before you go, do me a favor, while you're here? In the basement. I could use a pair of hands.'

I followed her through the kitchen and into a service porch, down plank stairs lit by a bare forty-watt bulb.

'Watch your head,' she said.

I ducked a jutting two-by-four, stepping down into a long, fusty space that stank of rotting wood. Along one wall ran the wine racks Zaragoza had mentioned. The floor was raw concrete, showing concentric traces left by water pooling and evaporating, time and again. Tatiana continued to the far end of the room, where sat a pair of gigantic gravity furnaces, arms flying off every which way. Lodged between them, like an outmatched referee, was an X-braced steel shelving unit, walling off a group of three boxes pushed into the basement's rear corner.

'That's all that's left,' she said.

'More instruction manuals.'

She smiled tiredly. 'Yeah. And this guy's completely stuck.' To prove her point she grabbed one of the shelving unit's uprights, yanking it back and forth to no effect.

I gave it a tug: wedged in there pretty good. 'We can try brute force, but I wouldn't recommend it. You'll scrape the ducts up, and you don't want to do that.'

'Why?'

'They're covered in asbestos.'

She recoiled.

'It's fine,' I said. 'It's harmless as is. You just don't want particles getting into the air. Did he kept tools somewhere? We could take it apart. That'd be the easiest way.'

'I think there's some upstairs.'

'WD-40 would be great, too, if you have it.'

She disappeared, bringing back a screwdriver, a pair of pliers, and a blue-and-yellow spray can. 'Ask and ye shall receive.'

Disassembling the shelves made for an acrobatic enterprise, me wrangling my long body into position to access the rusted rear bolts, while Tatiana hung on with the pliers for dear life. One particular bracket would not move for love or money.

'Forget it,' I said. 'We'll leave it and do that one instead.'

She rested on her haunches, shook out her wrists. 'I need a break.'

I backed out on my hands and knees and sat cross-legged on the concrete.

'I can't wait for this to be over,' she said. She was staring through the bars of the shelving unit at the trapped boxes. 'But it's sad, too. You know?'

I thought of her apartment, stripped down to its essentials, the lack of attachments, a reminder to herself that her return to California was supposed to be temporary.

I said, 'You think you'll move back?'

She looked at me quizzically.

'To New York,' I said.

'Why would I do that?'

'To dance.'

She shook her head. 'I've missed my window.'

'Come on.'

'That's how it is. You get a few good years and then it's over.'

'I hear that.'

'Mm.' A smile. 'Look at us. Washed up at thirty.'

I smiled, too.

She said, 'People ask me what I do and I tell them I dance. That's what I told you. But I don't, not often enough to call myself a dancer. I *teach* dance. I *teach* yoga. So that makes me a teacher.'

'Why does it have to be one or the other?'

'You can call yourself anything you want,' she said. 'That doesn't make it true.'

'Sure it does,' I said. 'This is America.'

She snorted.

We fell silent, our breath returning in short, flat echoes that shrank the space surrounding us. Then one of the furnaces roared to life.

'Holy shit that's loud,' she said, palming her chest.

I reached for the screwdriver. 'Ready?'

We got back to work.

Eventually we loosened the unit enough to toddle it out. I carried the three boxes upstairs. They were badly wrinkled and stank of colonizing fungus. Tatiana told me to leave them in the service porch, out of reach of her sinuses.

My shirt was dark with sweat, my knee dangerously tight. Sipping on tap water, I followed her to the dining room so she could pour herself another half glass of wine. She was patched under the arms, too, both of us smeared with grime and rust. I needed to sit, to take some weight off my leg, but I didn't want to soil the nice leather chairs, so I leaned on the table to relieve the strain.

'Thank you,' she said.

'Of course.'

'You've been really kind throughout. Beyond the call.'

'No big deal,' I said.

'But it is,' she said. Her voice was raw. 'It's a big thing. A great big thing.'

I made a gesture of demurral.

That seemed to anger her. She turned away and gulped her wine and grabbed for the bottle. Then she reconsidered and set it down with a clunk and took two hungry strides toward me, her body sliding against mine as she lifted her face and rose up on her toes.

It wasn't going to happen. Not without my help. At six-three, I had a good eight inches on her. I was going to have to become an active and equal participant.

I did. I bent down, and we met where we could.

The kiss didn't last long. I drew back with salt on my tongue.

She remained pressed against me, her back in a tight, gorgeous arch; peering up at me with those green eyes, her rib cage biting into my stomach, her slight frame bearing down on me with a paralyzing heaviness. She was waiting for me to move, to move back toward her, and when I didn't, she began searching my face. I could see her taking me apart in her mind, realization dawning, followed by discontent.

She broke away from me and went for her wine.

I said, 'I don't want to do the wrong thing here.'

'What's the wrong thing?'

'I'm not sure,' I said.

She said, 'Let me know when you figure it out.'

She drained her wine and set the glass down hard on the sideboard. She still had her back to me. She put her hands on her hips, kicked at the nearest box, one of many. 'Help me, please.'

14

WE MANAGED to fit eight of the eleven remaining boxes into the Prius, leaving the three rotted ones behind.

'Are you okay to drive?' I asked.

She ignored me and got into her car.

Sitting in my own car, engine off, I watched her brake lights fade.

The case was closed, or would be soon, with one click of a mouse. On paper, Tatiana and I would revert to being strangers. That could create opportunities. Or destroy them.

We're not a delivery service.

I started the car, swung a three-point-turn, and eased toward the driveway, cresting the top and immediately jamming on the brake.

Down at the bottom, a man stood on the sidewalk.

He was gazing up at Rennert's house. I couldn't see his face. The angle was wrong; he was wearing a hoodie, pulled up, and my headlights blew out details, leaving me with no more than a general sense of size and shape.

He was goddamn enormous.

That was as much as I could process before he spooked and ran, disappearing behind a hedge.

I lifted my foot off the brake, rolling to street level.

The cul-de-sac was deserted.

I edged forward to peer along Bonaventure Avenue.

No sign of him.

I was off duty, unarmed, fatigued.

I had my couch, my TV, my ice pack.

Why run?

Peeping Tom?

Burglar, casing?

Someone who pushed people down stairs?

I deal in facts. I try to be pragmatic. But so much comes down to instinct, a tickle in the brain stem that says *This feels wrong*.

Where the hell had he gone?

The street was the only way out for a vehicle. Then I noticed the sign for a footpath, poking out at the opposite end of the cul-de-sac.

BONAVENTURE WALK.

I left my car at the curb.

The path snaked between two of the south-side properties, twisting and dropping. I couldn't see more than five feet ahead. To my left grew towering bamboo hedges; from behind them came the loud burble of a fountain or pond, the owner's attempt to block out the sound of pedestrian traffic. It also meant that I couldn't hear what lay around the bend.

No one would hear me coming, either.

I picked up the pace, boots slapping concrete, knee beginning to complain.

A steep run of crumbling cement stairs fed me into a second cul-de-sac. Less ornate homes, brown shingles and station wagons, funky statuary and overgrown planter boxes.

I spotted him: a block and a half off, headed toward College Avenue at a rapid clip.

I followed.

He glanced back.

Stiffened.

Broke into a sprint.

Definitely wrong.

I went after him.

Within ten feet I could feel the mistake in my knee.

'Sheriff,' I yelled. 'Stop.'

He hooked left down Cherry Street, his receding bulk shored up against banks of moonlight and the icy spillover from living room TVs. For a man his size, he could move. Or maybe it felt that way to me because I was limping like a junker.

I yelled again for him to stop.

He raced ahead.

It'd been a long time since I'd detained anyone, let alone made an arrest. But I'm still a peace officer; I was in uniform, and his failure to heed me amounted to probable cause. Forget whatever hunch had triggered my suspicion. He could be carrying drugs or a weapon. He might have warrants out.

At Russell he went right, westward again, ducking out of sight.

I came stumbling around the bend.

College Avenue was bustling and fragrant, bookstores and

cafés doing a brisk nighttime trade. Hipster dads bounced toddlers awake way past their bedtimes. Undergrads in North Face walked with their arms linked. Bursts of laughter and breath-steam.

Given his height, given mine, I should have been making easy eye contact with him.

He was nowhere.

I hitched along, peering into shop windows. People gave me a wide berth. I was sweaty and red and filthy.

He wasn't in the Italian grocery. He wasn't sampling Tibetan cloth.

I crossed over Ashby and doubled back, passing the movie theater, the gelato shop. Weather be damned, there was a line out the door, patrons corralled by a black velvet rope. Everyone was having fun, except me.

He could have gotten into a car.

Taken a side street.

Hopped a fence.

Air whipped my face as a bus barreled past.

I craned to see if he was on it. Too late; it farted exhaust and plunged into darkness.

I stood with a hand on the back of my head, panting.

He was gone.

I trudged back to my car. My knee felt thick as a barrel, and I considered calling in sick. Physically, I doubted I could do more than shuffle paper. But Shupfer had already left the team shorthanded. She had a sick kid, pretty much the definition of a legitimate excuse.

What was mine? I'd hurt myself in pursuit of a suspect?

Suspect in what? A guy in a hoodie fleeing the scene of a death that had gone down two months ago? What was I doing there in the first place?

Explain yourself, Edison. Make it make sense.

I couldn't.

In agony, I crawled behind the wheel, popped the glove box, shook out four generic ibuprofen from a jumbo bottle, dry-swallowed.

For the next two hours I sat in the cul-de-sac, waiting for him to show himself.

Shortly after midnight I drove home. I wrapped my knee in ice, stuffed a pillow beneath it, and stretched out on my bed.

At four thirty a.m., I woke to the beeping of my alarm. I rolled over. The ice had melted into a sloshing bag. Gingerly I removed it and tested my range of motion. The joint felt stiff, but the pain, at least, had receded to a dull threat.

I hobbled to the shower, letting the hot water loosen me up, praying for a slow day. The hulking silhouette of the man flashed through my mind, sending my heart rate leaping. To calm myself, I turned instead to thinking about Tatiana.

Her dancer's posture. Her collarbones. Her body as I imagined it, all parts seamlessly knitted together.

I dried off, dressed, went to work.

15

Officer Nate Schickman said, 'How old a file are we talking about?'

I hesitated longer than I should have. He said, 'Please tell me this doesn't have to do with Rennert.'

I got where he was coming from. He was a homicide cop. Starting two months behind was his personal nightmare.

'My understanding was you guys had that sewn up. You're changing your mind?'

'Nope. Natural.'

'Uh-huh,' he said. 'So, what. Something else?'

I shifted the phone to my other ear, hunching to gather as much privacy as possible. I didn't have to worry about Shupfer listening in; she had indeed taken the day off. But I was conscious of Moffett, standing five feet away, fake-stabbing Daniella Botero in the neck as he reenacted a scene from *The Walking Dead;* conscious of Zaragoza, behind the partition, humming 'The Final Countdown' to himself. Of Carmen Woolsey giggling at a cat video.

I said, 'I'm sure it's nothing. Rennert was involved, but as a witness. I'm just tying up loose ends. You know the deal. One tiny screwup, all kinds of shit hits all kinds of fans.'

That relaxed him somewhat. Nothing unites the brotherhood of the badge like hatred of red tape. 'Gotcha. What's the name?'

'Donna Zhao. October ninety-three.'

'You want I should send it your way?'

I imagined the file showing up at my office for everyone to see. 'I'll come get it from you, save you the hassle. Tuesday good?'

'Fine by me,' he said. 'I'll be waiting.'

The four spots outside the Berkeley Public Safety Building were occupied. I trawled downtown awhile before finding a space on Allston, opposite the shuttered central post office with its grand and sooty colonnade. An encampment had sprung up on the steps, a mix of homeless people and protestors incensed over a variety of social ills, including homelessness. A man offered me a choice of pamphlets: STRIKE DEBT, SAVE OUR POST OFFICE, SAY NO TO GREEDY DEVELOPERS. I smiled my refusal; ten feet on, I heard him oinking.

It was lunchtime. Outside the high school, I paddled upstream against the exodus of kids bound for eateries along Shattuck Avenue. They spread out on the grass, clotting the sidewalks over several square blocks, eating or yakking or texting or all three simultaneously.

While I waited for the light to cross MLK, skaters ground the rail at the base of Peace Wall Park, the noise raising the hair on my arms.

The lobby of the Safety Building was spruce and silent. Reception paged Nate Schickman, but it was Patrol Officer Hocking who came to escort me back to investigations.

'You,' she said, not unpleasantly.

'Me,' I said.

Schickman wasn't at his desk, either. Someone said he was out back. I couldn't blame him for needing to escape: the room he shared with five other cops was landlocked, windowless, a cave with fluorescent bulbs and whiteboards badly in need of a shave.

'Out back' meant the vehicle lot. Hocking walked me there, about-faced, and returned inside, unimpressed by the unfolding spectacle: Schickman, in gray sweats, grunting as he flipped a giant truck tire end-over-end, while another guy kept time on his phone and exhorted him to fucking hurry the fuck up. Just watching it re-tore my ACL.

'Ten,' the timekeeper yelled.

Schickman collapsed to his knees and rolled messily onto his back, forearm draped across his eyes, belly pumping in and out. 'Fuck that,' he wheezed to no one in particular.

The timekeeper looked at me. 'Help you?'

'I'll wait till he's alive,' I said.

Schickman sat up, groaning. 'Shit. I forgot you were coming.'

He stretched out a hand, and his partner yanked him to his feet.

'Back in a minute,' Schickman said. 'Stay warm.'

The other guy began jumping imaginary rope.

Schickman went slowly up the stairs, pounding his quads as he climbed. He asked if I was into CrossFit.

'I'm more into not being paralyzed,' I said.

He laughed. 'Me, I'm nothing. My buddy there squats five fifty.'

'Well that seems unnecessary.'

'Till you're crushed by a tractor.' He glanced at me. 'Ever had anybody crushed by a tractor?'

'No, but I'm still young.'

'Ha.'

He climbed faster. My knee was feeling better and I kept up with him. Fate had done me a solid: no bodies for me at work, and I'd been religious with the ice and ibuprofen. Shupfer had returned on Saturday without explanation, nodding a truce as she sat down. When I asked how Danny was, she'd shrugged. 'Shit never ends.' Adding: 'He's home.' Adding: 'Thanks.' As close to optimism as she got.

Life had regained its normal rhythm, except for the nagging possibility of a prowler stalking Rennert's house and/or his daughter.

I'd said nothing to Tatiana. I didn't want to scare her before I knew there was something to be scared of.

Schickman, bless him, didn't ask any more questions. Maybe he was a good guy, maybe he didn't care. He brought me to a storage closet adjacent to the investigations room, reaching for the top shelf to take down a cardboard box hand-lettered in black marker.

12-19139 vi: Zhao 31 oct 93
homicide do not destroy

He hauled the box over to the deserted conference room.

'Need anything,' he said, dropping it with a thump, 'you know where to find me.'

'The hospital.'

He strained comically. ''Murica, baby.' Turning serious. 'And it goes without saying, there's something I need to know . . .'

'You got it. Thanks.'

Alone, I spread the contents of the box out on the table. The centerpiece of the Donna Zhao file was a vinyl five-inch binder, its contents tabbed in rainbow colors: yellow for the report, orange for written statements and warrants, so forth, ending with blue jail call transcripts and green A/V files. The scheme suggested an investigation starting off at a boil and cooling as it went.

As a kid I had a habit of reading a book's last page first. I'm not sure where I picked it up. I think I tended to feel a story much too hard, the characters' struggles becoming mine to an uncomfortable degree. Skipping ahead was my solution, a way to establish a critical space between them and me – enough to allow room for pleasure.

Once my brother saw me starting to do this with a book he'd recently finished. I can't recall which. We're fourteen months apart; our tastes often overlapped. Probably it was an athlete biography. We ate those up. *Legends of Sports: Michael Jordan* or whatever.

What I won't forget is Luke's reaction: he went berserk, ripping the book out of my hands and winging it over the rear fence into our neighbor's yard; getting up in my face and screaming about cheating. I was confused. Cheating who? The author? Michael Jordan? Who cared? That's my brother, though: righteous, sensitive, unfit to live in an unjust world. The way he saw it, he'd worked for that ending. I hadn't.

What became of him, I suppose, was nauseatingly poetic, if not inevitable.

What became of us both.

After he'd stormed off, I went around the block and rang the bell to Mrs Gilford's house. She admitted me, watching with a perplexed smile as I went to her backyard and fished a flimsy paperback from the rosemary bush.

I was thinking about Luke distantly as I flipped ahead in search of an arrest report. I didn't consider it cheating to start with information that bore on Tatiana's safety.

Several hundred pages in, I found him.

His name was Triplett, Julian E.

On April 23, 1994, he was arrested and booked on one count of PC 187(a), murder.

At the time he resided at 955 Delaware St #5, Berkeley, CA 94710.

He was a black male, with brown hair and brown eyes, born on July 9, 1978.

The next line made my blood lock up.

At fifteen years old, Julian Triplett stood six-four and weighed two hundred forty-seven pounds.

The man I'd chased was easily that size. Bigger, maybe. Twenty-plus years had elapsed – plenty of time for a growing boy, even a huge one, to grow more.

The arresting officer and lead investigator was named Ken Bascombe.

I paged back to his supplemental and began to read.

At four thirty-one on the morning of November 1, 1993, Bascombe was called to an apartment building on the 2500 block of Benvenue Avenue, just south of People's Park. Upon arrival he found the street roped off at either end in anticipation of a mass of onlookers. Consulting with officers on the scene, he learned that the victim was Donna Zhao, a twenty-three-year-old Asian female, dead of apparent multiple stab wounds to the face, neck, and torso. She shared a third-floor two-bedroom unit with a pair of roommates, Li Hsieh and Wendy Tang. All three were undergraduates, enrolled at UC Berkeley.

It was the roommates who'd found her.

According to Wendy Tang's statement, around nine thirty the previous evening, she and Li Hsieh had left the apartment together to go trick-or-treating. They'd tried to persuade Donna to accompany them, but she had declined, stating she was too tired and had too much work. Wendy Tang and Li Hsieh went out, spending the night hopping from one party to the next before coming home at approximately four in the morning.

Both women admitted to being intoxicated. For this reason, they did not at first realize that a crime had taken place, despite the disorder evident upon entering the apartment. Furniture was overturned, a lamp snapped in half. A trail of blood on the carpet led toward the adjacent kitchen, accessible through a pair of saloon doors, also bloodstained. Wendy Tang said, 'We thought it was a joke.'

Entering the kitchen, they found Donna Zhao's body heaped on the linoleum in a large pool of blood. Drawers had been pulled out. The toaster was in the sink. There were bloody handprints on the refrigerator door, as well as numerous streaks and smears, indicative of the victim fighting back. Spatter on the walls reached a height of eight feet, a few drops grazing the ceiling.

'Grossed out' but still unsure they weren't being pranked, Wendy Tang called Donna's name. Receiving no response, Tang shook her, then ran to dial 911 from the phone in her bedroom.

The first police arrived at 4:11 a.m., EMTs shortly thereafter. At 4:24 a.m., Donna Zhao was pronounced dead.

According to Wendy Tang, nothing of value appeared to be missing from the apartment. She said that Donna did not have a boyfriend, or very many friends at all, speculating that Donna was self-conscious about being several years older than her classmates. Her Chinese given name was Dongmei. Studious and shy, she spoke a halting but grammatical English. Like Li Hsieh, she was a Beijing native; the two of them communicated with each other primarily in Mandarin. Tang, American born, had opted to room with them in order to improve her own Mandarin. She could not think of anyone who would want to harm Donna.

Canvass failed to produce a credible witness to a person or persons entering or exiting the building. BPD did receive an overwhelming number of tips about strange characters running around, covered in blood or wielding weapons. It was Halloween.

The early stages of the investigation had focused on People's Park and its residents, a rotating cast of the mentally ill, the homeless, dealers, drifters, and social dissidents. In general, the cops took a hands-off approach, a policy born of the sixties. Then as now, you could stroll by and observe a multitude of freak flags flying.

That ethos swiftly went up in flames. A young woman, a student, alone in her apartment, doing her homework – butchered – the outcry was immediate and wild. A quirk of human nature is that we're seldom afraid of the things that really might kill us. With the exception of Zaragoza, not too many folks have nightmares about cancer, heart disease, or diabetes. Stranger murders, rare as they are, are the epitome of randomness, and they stoke a disproportionate amount of terror. And terror's first cousin: media coverage.

A sweep turned up a bloody steak knife, wrapped in an X X L hoodie, gray fabric dyed brown and red with blood. Both items had been stuffed into a plastic bag and dumped in a trash can on the corner of Dwight and Telegraph, blocks from the crime scene.

Photographed against a white surface, laid beside a ruler, the knife was a malignant thing, with a stocky black handle and a wide, serrated blade four and a half inches long.

Over the next forty-eight hours, the cops rolled the park up, hauling people in on charges rarely if ever filed in Berkeley — disorderly conduct, public nudity. The strategy was: net as many warm bodies as possible and hope that one of them turns out to be the bad guy. Naturally, the crackdown sparked a protest, which turned into a minor riot, leading to further arrests and head-cracking and outrage. Your basic P R toilet spiral.

Not until several weeks had passed did a plausible suspect emerge, and it wasn't the product of any extraordinary detective work. A man walked into the police station and said he needed to speak to someone right away.

At approximately eleven thirty on the night of the murder, the man told police, he had been walking home from his lab when he noticed an individual loitering outside Donna Zhao's building. He was able to offer a detailed physical description of the individual, including his clothing: basketball shorts, conspicuous in the chill, and a gray hooded sweatshirt that closely resembled the one recovered from the can.

Information about the sweatshirt had not yet been released to the public.

After some hesitation, the man went a step further, stating he could positively identify the individual. However, he declined to provide the individual's name.

The informant, Nicholas Linstad, explained that he was a fifth-year graduate student in the Cal Department of Psychology. At present he was conducting a study in which the individual, a Berkeley High School freshman, was enrolled.

Linstad stated that, upon recognizing the individual, he had grown concerned, wondering why a boy of that age would be on the street at that late hour, on a restless and hectic night. He called out, crossing the street and hoping to engage him in conversation. But before Linstad had reached him, the boy hurried away. Linstad stated that he had not attempted to pursue the conversation. He had to get home to his wife.

16

I SAT back, letting my eyes unfocus.

Nicholas Linstad had pointed the finger at Julian Triplett.

Hard to imagine a better motive for revenge.

Wondering why Linstad had waited over a month to come forward, I flipped through the transcript of his interview with Detective Bascombe.

LINSTAD: You see, it's not simple. He's a boy.

BASCOMBE: I hear that.

LINSTAD: He is a child. This is what you need to realize. He's not . . .

BASCOMBE: I get it. I— it's natural, you feel for him.

LINSTAD: Yes, of course, but also I thought perhaps I was mistaken, perhaps the police will find the real person. If I speak to you, I put him in a terrible position, and in the meantime the real person is walking around, free. You see?

BASCOMBE: I do. I do. Can I clarify something for a second? You thought you were mistaken? You mean you aren't sure it was him you saw?

LINSTAD: No, no. This I felt, I feel quite certain about, it was definitely him.

BASCOMBE: You saw his face.

LINSTAD: I said his name and he turned to my direction.

BASCOMBE: Okay.

LINSTAD: But that is all I saw. I didn't see him go in, I didn't see him come out. It's a boy's life we are talking about, the life of a child.

BASCOMBE: There's also the life of the victim.

LINSTAD: Yes . . . It's all that I saw.

BASCOMBE: You said he was pushing buttons on the gate keypad . . . Nicholas?

LINSTAD: I suppose it's possible.

BASCOMBE: It sounded before like you were pretty sure.

LINSTAD: It could be, it was dark.

BASCOMBE: Are you saying you're not sure anymore?

LINSTAD: I . . . [inaudible]

BASCOMBE: Listen, I appreciate what you're experiencing. I need to know what you saw, exactly like you saw it. It wasn't too dark for you to see his face . . . ? Nicholas.

LINSTAD: Yes, okay.

BASCOMBE: Yes he was messing with it . . . ? I know you're nodding but for the record, can you verbally acknowledge what you're . . .

LINSTAD: I saw that he was pressing buttons.

BASCOMBE: Did it look like he was trying to break in?

LINSTAD: [inaudible] intentions. I thought perhaps he lived there.

BASCOMBE: He looked suspicious.

LINSTAD: I don't know that.

BASCOMBE: That was the word you used. When we first sat down you told me you noticed him because he was acting suspicious.

LINSTAD: Perhaps I should have said he looked anxious.

BASCOMBE: How?

LINSTAD: I don't know. It is an intuition that I had. I work with teenagers, I'm attuned to the way they behave.

BASCOMBE: You didn't alert the authorities.

LINSTAD: No, of course not.

BASCOMBE: Why not?

LINSTAD: Because I didn't know what he's doing, he wasn't doing anything wrong. He's standing there. I called his name and he saw me and left. Why do I call the police? What can I tell them? There's a person? He's not there anymore. It's not my business.

BASCOMBE: All right ... Do you need a minute? Do you want some more water?

LINSTAD: No, thank you.

BASCOMBE: I'll get you some more.

LINSTAD: Fine, yes.

(14:29:36)

BASCOMBE: Can we continue? You said the victim was working on the same study and that this boy Triplett was part of it. Sorry, can you, verbally ... ?

LINSTAD: Yes.

BASCOMBE: Did the two of them have contact with each other?

LINSTAD: She assisted with data collection. She was present at certain times and not at others. The subjects came in for several hours to perform the task and [inaudible] she was there when he was. But I don't know if they met, I can't say that.

BASCOMBE: Were they friends?

LINSTAD: How can I know? I don't think so.

BASCOMBE: Okay, but, what I'm asking is, was there some kind of prior relationship between them that might lead him to want to hurt her?

LINSTAD: I don't, I really don't know.

BASCOMBE: The boy, you knew him a little bit?

LINSTAD: Not very much.

BASCOMBE: Enough to be worried when you saw him.

LINSTAD: I wasn't worried, I was [inaudible].

BASCOMBE: What's the difference?

LINSTAD: In the, the, in a broad sense, I was concerned. This boy, I saw him in the laboratory. You must try to imagine how it is to see him in a setting that is totally different. It was very late, I was tired. I apologize, I find it difficult to explain.

BASCOMBE: It's all right, do what you can.

LINSTAD: That's all I can think of, I don't know how else to say it.

BASCOMBE: In terms of personality, how would you describe him?

LINSTAD: Well, it is really difficult to say.

BASCOMBE: Still, you interacted with him.

LINSTAD: Very briefly.

BASCOMBE: Did he ever do or say anything inappropriate, or threatening?

LINSTAD: I'm not sure what you mean.

BASCOMBE: In your judgment.

LINSTAD: This is not something I feel comfortable speaking about.

BASCOMBE: What makes you uncomfortable?

LINSTAD: He has a right . . . I must respect his privacy.

BASCOMBE: Be that as it may, you're aware, you have to be aware of what he did.

LINSTAD: I don't . . . It's not my intention to lead him to a, a [inaudible].

BASCOMBE: Nicholas. Listen. This was a terrible thing. Just god-awful.

LINSTAD: Please.

BASCOMBE: It was really ugly, what he did to her. I can show you the pictures.

LINSTAD: No. No. No.

BASCOMBE: I've been a cop a long time, okay? Nothing like this.

LINSTAD: I don't want to discuss it anymore. I saw him there, that's all.

BASCOMBE: I'm saying, if you can help us . . . What is it? What's the matter?

LINSTAD: Please, can we stop?

(14:51:09)

BASCOMBE: How are you feeling? Are you feeling better?

LINSTAD: Yes, better. Thank you.

BASCOMBE: You're ready to go on?

LINSTAD: I must tell you I don't think I should say any more before I've had a chance to consult with someone.

BASCOMBE: Okay, that's not a problem, but first let's talk about your study.

LINSTAD: One moment, because it's not my study.

BASCOMBE: I thought it was yours.

LINSTAD: I have an advisor, it's his lab.

BASCOMBE: What's his name? I'd like to talk to him.

LINSTAD: Is that necessary?

BASCOMBE: Well, yeah, I think it is, because we're talking about a kid who was in his study and a victim who was in his study. You can tell me his name. I'm not going to have a hard time finding that out. I can call your department . . .

LINSTAD: Professor Walter Rennert.

BASCOMBE: Okay.

LINSTAD: He doesn't know I'm here. I didn't tell him I was coming.

BASCOMBE: Why don't you give him a call him right now? You can call him from another room and talk to him. Tell him we'd like to speak to him.

A knock yanked me back to the present. Nate Schickman poked his head in. He'd changed into work clothes. 'Doing all right here?'

There was a clock above the door. I hadn't left my chair in three hours.

'Fine,' I said, moving the binder off my lap. 'There's a lot to sort through.'

'You finding what you need?'

'Getting there.'

He came and stood by the table, regarding the file with a bemused expression. Aside from the main binder, it contained a host of stuff I hadn't touched. An entire second binder of crime scene photos. Other agency reports. A box of mini-cassettes; those would be interesting to hear. Seeing Linstad's words transcribed to paper made it hard to know if his waffling was the result of nerves, guilt, or genuine uncertainty as to what he'd witnessed.

Schickman said, 'When I got it for you I took a peek. Crazy shit. I was kind of surprised I'd never heard about it.'

'Before your time.'

'Yeah, but. This place has a long memory.'

'The primary, Ken Bascombe. Is he still around?'

Schickman shook his head. 'Don't know him.'

'Can you think of someone who might be able to reach him?'

Schickman looked at me. 'Be straight. What's the deal here? Either you closed your case, or you didn't.'

'It's done,' I said. 'I'll send you the death certificate if you want.'

'Then what's up?'

I said, 'Rennert's daughter is convinced it's murder because of this other case. My reaction was the same as yours: How come I never heard of it? So I wanted a look, that's all.'

He smiled, too polite to call bullshit on me. 'Curiosity knows no bounds, huh?'

'It's my day off to spend.'

He squinted at the open binder. 'Who's the primary, again?'

'Bascombe.'

'I'll see what I can dig up,' he said.

I returned to the file.

By the time the cops got around to interviewing Walter

Rennert, they'd managed to unearth Julian Triplett's name. It wasn't difficult: they crossed the street to Berkeley High and asked around. In a freshman class of eight hundred, there was a single boy who matched the physical description provided by Nicholas Linstad, in all its freakish proportions.

For his part, Rennert began by denying that he was aware of any contact between Triplett and Donna Zhao. Eventually, though, he allowed that he wasn't around the psych building every minute of every day, overseeing every aspect of his lab.

He refused to describe the nature of the study Triplett had been enrolled in, blustering about academic freedom. Bascombe switched tacks, attempting to coax Rennert into talking about Triplett's personality. Again, Rennert refused. When the detective pressed harder, Rennert asked for a lawyer.

That was the extent of it. Perhaps he could already sense the coming shitstorm.

Ultimately, as the evidence piled up, whatever Linstad or Rennert or anyone else thought about Julian Triplett's capacity for violence ceased to matter.

Triplett's first interview with police took place in late January 1994. In the transcript, he came across as detached, often giving bizarre answers. He became fixated on the tape recorder, asking Bascombe who was listening to them and at one point attempting to shut it off. Unable to account for his whereabouts and actions on the night of the murder, he kept contradicting himself.

He was home.

No, he was walking home.

No, he was playing video games.

Six more interviews would follow, and Bascombe would note that Julian Triplett wore the same outfit to each: navy-blue or black mesh basketball shorts and a gray hoodie.

Bascombe asked Triplett for permission to take his fingerprints.

Triplett consented.

The crime lab matched a partial on the knife handle to Julian Triplett's right thumb.

Confronted with this, Triplett imploded. He confessed to killing Donna Zhao.

BASCOMBE: Where'd you stab her?

TRIPLETT: Here.

BASCOMBE: He's pointing to his chest. Where else?

TRIPLETT: Here.

BASCOMBE: In the abdomen. After you stabbed her. What happened then, Julian?

TRIPLETT: She like disappeared.

BASCOMBE: She disappeared.

TRIPLETT: Okay.

BASCOMBE: It's a question. I'm asking you.

TRIPLETT: Okay.

BASCOMBE: Julian. Julian. Come on, now. Tell me the truth. What are you talking about, she disappeared. Where'd she go?

TRIPLETT: Like in the air.

BASCOMBE: In the air.

TRIPLETT: Can I have a Coke?

BASCOMBE: You can when you stop playing with me. I'm gonna ask you again. What happened after you stabbed her? What'd you do with the knife? You throw it away?

TRIPLETT: Yeah.

BASCOMBE: Where.

TRIPLETT: I want to go home.

As before, lacking voice cues, I couldn't tell what was going on in Triplett's head from reading the transcript. Denial, fear, remorse, confusion? His youth complicated matters.

With the day winding down, I gave up on reading for content and began to flip pages quickly, using my phone to photograph them for later review.

I phone-shot the crime scene photos. Street; building exterior; stairs; front door. Familiar angles, but fewer than you'd find in one of my case files. This was the period before digital cameras, when every frame cost money.

Front hallway.

Living room, in chaos.

Kitchen.

A human being, torn apart.

At five fifty-six, I packed up the file and took it back to Schickman's office. Two other cops sat working their computers.

'Cool,' Schickman said. 'You can just leave it here.'

I set the box down on his desk. 'Thanks a lot.'

'Yeah, no worries,' he said.

I asked if he'd had a chance to look up Bascombe.

'Shit, no. I'm getting crushed here. Tomorrow, scout's honor.'

One of the other detectives called, 'What kinda fuckin scout are you?'

I said, 'Tomorrow's great, thanks.'

We shook hands and I left.

Dusk had flooded the square, skateboarders and students cleared out, leaving men in rags, in sleeping bags, belly-up on benches. They stumbled in and out of streetlight, kicked bottles, sermonized, confronted invisible enemies. They, too, were invisible, pressed down to ground level, stepped over.

Across the purpled lawns, lights burned inside the high school. Extracurricular activities. Math or debate or jazz or fencing.

Julian Triplett had never made it to the end of sophomore year.

Less than half a mile away, due east, lay the Cal campus, steeped in history and flush with resources, a haven for young minds full of hope and folly. They came from around the world to drink at the fountain.

Donna Zhao hadn't graduated, either.

I thought of the two of them colliding like streaking comets. Meeting in a savage heat that left no trace.

17

Julian Triplett wasn't in the system.

I found a last known address for him – his mother's house, on Delaware Street – but it was a decade old, and nobody picked up when I called. Other than a younger sister named Kara Drummond, who lived in Richmond, he had no other kin or associates. He had no adult criminal record. No credit history, no Facebook page, no Twitter, no Instagram, no gallery of faces on Google Images.

The lack of an internet presence is unusual but not unheard of. The denizens of People's Park tend not to be plugged into the social network. Maybe Triplett was living on the street. Or he'd served his sentence and decided to get far away, start over. Part of my job is finding people, some of whom prefer not to be found.

The phone interrupted me.

'Yes, hi, this is Michael Cucinelli from Cucinelli Brothers Mortuary in Fremont.'

'Hi, Mr Cucinelli. What can I do for you?'

'Yeah, so I'm following up with you directly, cause we have the body of a Mr Jose Provencio here, and I gotta be honest with you, this is getting to be a bit much.'

'Wait a sec,' I said.

'Well, yeah, but no, cause I've been waiting five months, so I'm not really inclined to do a heck of a lot more waiting.'

'Hang on. Hang on,' I said, mousing rapidly. 'You said Jose Provencio?'

'Yes.'

'Jose *Manuel* Provencio?'

'. . . yes.'

'He's still there?'

'I'm looking right at him.'

'You're kidding me.'

'Do I sound like I'm kidding?'

'You're telling me he never took care of it.'

'Who didn't.'

'Samuel Afton. Mr Provencio's stepson. He assured me he would handle it. He said he worked out a deal with you guys.'

'Look, I don't know anything about that. I know that my idiot nephew is telling me this guy's been here since the summer. I respect what you do but I'm at my limit.'

'You and me both,' I said. 'Give me five minutes, okay? I'll call you back.'

Samuel Afton's phone went straight to voicemail. I left a message asking him to get in touch immediately, then phoned Cucinelli.

'Here's the deal,' I said. 'If I don't hear from him by the end of the day it's going to county indigent.'

He grumbled but agreed. 'As long as we finish with it today.'

'Five o'clock. You have my word.'

I put down the phone.

'Yo,' Zaragoza said, hanging over the partition. 'We're up.'

I reached for my vest.

He laughed. 'No, dude. Lunch run.'

In the car, he said, 'You okay?'

'Me? Fine. Why.'

'You look kinda tired.'

I'd been up late several nights in a row with the Zhao file. Even after forcing myself to roll over and turn off the bedside lamp, I'd lie on my back, listening to cars bottoming out in the potholes along Grand Avenue, wondering whether to call Tatiana and what to say.

The question wasn't if Julian Triplett was dangerous. I'd seen the carnage. I'd read the autopsy protocol. Donna Zhao had been stabbed twenty-nine times.

The question, rather, was, if the huge guy I'd seen outside Rennert's house was in fact Julian Triplett, or whether he was some other huge guy, and I was caught up in an equally huge mindfuck of a coincidence, victim of my own imagination.

Say it was him. What did I hope to accomplish by warning Tatiana? What did I expect her to do? Run out and get a gun? Like a dancer, Berkeley born and bred, would arm herself. Even if she did, she was more likely to end up shooting herself by accident.

By making her aware of a threat, I was in a sense creating that threat, which in my mind created a responsibility for me – to ensure that no harm came to her. Was I going to sit outside her house, a one-man neighborhood watch? For how long?

I was also concerned about feeding her suspicions. There was no evidence her father's death was anything but natural, and I had no proof of Triplett's ill intent. I had no proof he knew she existed. He hadn't come to *her* address.

I considered other explanations for his presence outside the house. The best I could come up with was that he'd read the obituary and dropped by to gloat.

'Insomnia,' I said to Zaragoza.

'You try melatonin? I have some in my desk.'

'No, thanks.'

'I meant to ask you. Sunday. Priscilla's making ...' He paused, scratching his chin.

'Food?' I suggested.

'Let's hope.'

'Yeah, man. Thanks.'

'Thank her. Her idea.'

That raised my antennae. 'No unmarried cousins, please.'

'*One* time,' he said.

'Once was enough.'

'Telling you, dude, you fucked up. Iris is a quality chick.'

'I don't doubt it.'

Leaving In-N-Out Burger with my arms full of greasy bags, I felt my pocket buzz and hurried to dump the food in the backseat of the Explorer. Too late: I'd missed the call. I was expecting a voicemail from Samuel Afton.

Tatiana. No message.

I squirmed around the whole ride back, abandoning Zaragoza to distribute lunch while I escaped to the intake bay to call her.

'Hey,' she said.

'Is everything all right?' I said.

'Uh, fine,' she said. 'Are *you* all right?'

Unlike me, she sounded calm, if a trifle perplexed. Nobody tapping on her window. Nobody crouched in the bushes. Only my unexplained urgency to trouble her.

'No no. I'm . . .' I let the adrenaline seep away. 'Busy day. What's up?'

'I wanted to let you know, I'm going to be heading out of town for a bit. In case you need to reach me about something.'

The best of news. Safer for her, at least in the short term. Mixed with my relief, though, was a stab of regret. 'Thanks for the heads-up,' I said. 'What's the plan?'

'Tahoe. My dad has a house there. Had. I need to start dealing with it.'

'Are you leaving soon?'

'Tomorrow morning,' she said. 'I found someone to cover my classes for the next few weeks. Figured I might as well get it over with.'

'Right,' I said. 'Would you be up for something before you go?'

'Up for . . .'

Smooth, Clay.

'Dinner,' I said.

A beat. 'You mean tonight?'

'That sounds like our only option. Unless you'll do breakfast at three a.m.'

'I don't know,' she said. 'I was planning on getting an early start.'

'Sure.'

'I mean,' she said. 'It depends.'

'On?'

144

'You said you needed to figure things out.'

'I know I did.'

'And. Have you?'

I said, 'I'd like to see you.'

Longer pause.

She said, 'Sorry, tonight's not going to work. I'm wiped.'

Steeerike!

'But,' she said, 'I could leave Monday instead.'

Before going home I tried Samuel Afton one final time. In my voicemail I informed him that the county was moving to cremate his stepfather as an indigent. I gave Cucinelli the green light, packed up, and headed down to the lockers. Zaragoza was already there, lethargically stowing his gear.

'Yo,' I said, 'I have to bail on Sunday night. Something came up.'

He took my flakery in stride, shrugging and starting to compose a text.

'Tell Priscilla thanks and I'm sorry,' I said.

He clucked his tongue. 'I'm telling Iris she doesn't need to come after all.'

18

Tatiana stepped from her apartment in jeans and a sleeveless top that fell straight and sheer, emphasizing her leanness. Black hair fanned over her shoulders. She'd put on a touch of makeup. Hoop earrings. She said, 'How do you feel about Mexican?'

'Some of my best friends are Mexican,' I said.

We set off walking.

'You look beautiful,' I said.

'Thank you.'

'Too strong?'

'No such thing,' she said.

She'd picked out not a restaurant, but a food truck, one of a dozen circled in the parking lot outside the North Berkeley BART station. A couple hundred people milled around under string lights, eating off paper plates. Unattended kids ran in giddy loops to the backing of a zydeco band. A banner behind the stage read OFF THE GRID.

'You are free to partake wherever and whatever you want,' she said. 'But I strongly recommend the *tacos al pastor* from Red Rooster.'

'Done.'

We got food and beer and found a pair of unclaimed plastic chairs.

'I think they do one of these around Lake Merritt,' she said.

'Saturdays,' I said. 'I'm working.'

'Poor you.' She held out her *lengua* for me to try. When I declined, she reached over, forking a piece of pork off my plate. 'I only offered so you'd give me some of yours.'

'You could've gotten your own.'

'Then we couldn't share.'

'We aren't actually sharing,' I said. 'You're just stealing politely.'

'Right, but this way I feel justified.'

'For some reason I had this idea you'd be a vegetarian.'

'Vegan,' she said. 'Thirteen years.'

'What happened?'

'*Tacos al pastor,*' she said.

I asked what she planned to do in Tahoe, other than dispose of furniture.

'Ski. Do yoga. Realistically it's my last chance to use the house before we sell it.' She paused. 'Barb – his first wife – she was the skier. My dad never cared for the cold. I don't know why he's held on to it all these years.'

'From what I've seen,' I said, 'he wasn't one for purging.'

'Yeah. Although you'd think, a house . . . He kept talking about renting it out, but he never got around to it. Most of the year it was unoccupied. He went up every few months to check on it. I can't remember the last time I was there.'

'You didn't go with him.'

'He never invited me. I'm sure he would've let me tag along, but I could tell he needed to get away, so I tried to respect that.'

'Away from what?'

'Me,' she said.

'Kind of harsh on yourself.'

She shrugged. 'I pestered him. I knew I was doing it. I wanted him to be healthy.'

I said, 'Your brothers are Barb's sons.'

Tatiana nodded. 'She's a nice lady. She flew in for the funeral. I was touched, but my mom threw a hissy fit.'

'About what?'

'What's it ever about? She seems to believe she still has an ownership stake in Dad. Their relationship was totally ridiculous. They'd be in divorce mediation during the day then go home and sleep together at night.'

'That's . . . different.'

'You think? I know because my mother told me. I was like, "I don't need to hear this, please." She told me I had a bourgeois sense of morality.'

'Meaning "a sense of morality."'

'It's the revenge of our generation.'

'What about your brothers?'

'Oh, they're way more uptight than I am. Charlie's a lawyer. Human rights. Stephen was in finance, but he quit to open a rock climbing gym.'

'That doesn't sound uptight.'

'He runs it like an investment bank,' she said. 'We don't fight, but we're not close. You?'

'I grew up in San Leandro. My folks are still there.'

'Siblings?'

'None to speak of.' I reached for her empty cup. 'Another?'

'Please.'

As I stood in line, listening to an accordion-driven version of 'Every Breath You Take', I glanced at the street sign.

We were on the 1400 block of Delaware.

Four blocks east of Julian Triplett's mother's house.

I looked over my shoulder at Tatiana.

She raised a hand.

I did the same.

I brought back a Corona and a margarita, giving her the choice.

'We'll share,' she said, taking the margarita.

'I know how that works with you.'

The band played 'Super Freak'.

Tatiana said, 'I want to tell you something but I'm not sure I should. Should I?'

'How about this,' I said. 'Why don't you tell me what it is first, and then I can decide if you should tell me or not.'

She laughed. 'Okay, I'm going to tell you. I was married.'

'Yes,' I said, 'you can tell me that.'

'It doesn't freak you out?'

'Why would it freak me out?'

'It freaks some guys out.'

'Not me.'

She tilted her head. 'Do you want to know why I got divorced?'

'If you want to tell me.'

'I met him in New York. We were married six months, then he came out.'

'That must've been a surprise.'

'*I* was surprised,' she said. 'Later I found out everybody knew except me.'

'I was married, too,' I said.

She raised her eyebrows.

I pointed to a gaunt woman in pigtails near the gelato truck. 'That's her.'

Tatiana balled up the napkin and threw it at me. I ducked and it landed on the asphalt behind me. A girl about seven years old ran over and snatched it up.

'Litterbug!' she yelled. Her T-shirt read LOCALLY GROWN.

She hopped around, waving the dirty napkin, chanting, 'Litterbug! Litterbug!'

'Sorry,' Tatiana said. 'It was an accident. I meant to hit him.'

'Litterbug!'

The girl's mother came over to apologize. 'Her class just finished a unit on recycling.'

The kid stuck out her tongue at us as she was yanked away. The band began to play 'Take On Me'.

Tatiana tossed back the dregs of her margarita. 'Smug little twat.'

I said, 'Let's get out of here.'

We walked east, through Ohlone Park.

'I vant to be Ohlone,' she said.

'Do you?'

'No.'

'Good,' I said. 'Up for a little walk?'

'Sure.'

Aside from the occasional booze wobble, she was graceful and purposeful, fluid in her movements, shivering against me.

'Here,' I said, giving her my coat.

'Thank you, gallant sir. Nobody's done that for me since eleventh grade. Where are you taking me?'

Ten minutes later, we arrived at University Avenue.

'You're taking me to campus,' she said.

'Ah, yes, but: *where* on campus.'

'Please tell me this isn't some hopeless attempt to relive our college days.'

'Who said anything about hopeless.'

We tottered happily through the eucalyptus grove, thumping over the bridge spanning Strawberry Creek, encountering bicycle racks and flapping banners but few faces. Mist hung in the trees, diffusing the greenish glow of pathway lighting. I imagined Donna Zhao, trudging home in the dark, bent-backed beneath the weight of her textbooks and notebooks and fatigue. In a strange way, she had brought me here now, to this moment and this place, to the feeling of Tatiana's arm, lost inside the sleeve of my coat, but gripping me fiercely as she laughed and swayed.

Up ahead loomed Haas Pavilion and the adjoining rec center.

'Where are you taking me,' she said. 'For real.'

'I want to show you something.'

We came to a side door. I fished my keycard out of my wallet, swiped it near the sensor. The lock retracted with a clack.

'An old teammate is an assistant coach,' I said. 'He got me the hookup.'

'Fancy.'

'That's how I roll.'

We went down a cinder-block corridor painted in blue and yellow and stenciled with motivational slogans. CHAMPIONS KEEP PLAYING UNTIL THEY GET IT RIGHT. BE STRONG IN BODY, CLEAN IN MIND, LOFTY IN IDEALS. The air burned with industrial cleaner. In the weight room, a few football physiques were grinding out reps with their earbuds in. They paid us no mind.

The practice court itself was at the end of the hall. I swiped in and hit the switches, and the floods flickered on, casting a sickly pall over the waxed floor.

'They take a couple minutes to warm up,' I said.

I unlocked a ball cart and dragged it to the top of the three-point line. Paused, squinting at the rim.

I have a low tolerance for alcohol. I never built one, never developed a taste; during college, when most people learn to drink, I had a strict diet and training regimen. Tonight, I'd consumed half a beer, walked it off for half an hour. Yet I still felt warm, my focus honed somewhat by the pressure of what I was about to do.

I took a basketball, spun it in my hand, breathed in, breathed out.

Pulled up.

Let fly.

It clanged off the back of the rim. Not the splashy opening I'd had in mind.

'I didn't see that,' Tatiana said.

'See what,' I said, reaching for another ball.

I pulled up.

This time I felt it as it left my hand; I saw myself from the outside, angles in agreement, head and neck, elbow and shoulder, wrist and fingers, collaborating. I felt the weightless instant, when gravity releases its stranglehold, and you float, and the ball becomes vapor, pebbled breath rolling back against the tips of your fingers. I felt it part from me with an understanding of its mission, an extension of me that continued to rise after I had softly retouched the earth; rising and rising, the seams spinning backward in a blur of symmetry and physics; peaking and then descending in a gentle arc, a faithful delivery.

The net snapped, was still.

I exhaled and took another ball.

Snap.

Another.

Snap. Snap. Snap.

I stopped when I reached into the cart and discovered that it was empty. Loose balls lay scattered like the aftermath of a cannon battle, the echo of the last bounce fading. I'd made twenty-three of twenty-nine shots.

Tatiana shifted.

I looked over at her. I'd forgotten she was there.

She said, 'That was beautiful.'

'Thanks.'

'Really, Clay. I – it was really wonderful.'

'Thank you.'

'Thank you for showing me,' she said.

I nodded.

She said, 'You do miss it.'

'Of course.'

'What most of all?'

The heat of the arena. Students with their faces painted and their throats stringy as they screamed. Truth be told, it never was my job to shoot. The three-pointer show makes for a good party trick, but no way could I hit half as many with a hand in my face.

I was a point guard. A setup man. Frame a situation, hand off to those more comfortable in the spotlight.

It's who I am, even today.

Sophomore year, somebody realized I was on pace to break Jason Kidd's single-season school record for assists. A group started showing up to the games. They called themselves the Claymakers. They sat in a line, a few rows in front of the band. Every time I got an assist, the next person in line would turn over a poster board with a picture of a light bulb and the words BRIGHT IDEA! Because: Edison. Get it? A very Cal kind of joke.

I ended up falling a few shy of the record. I didn't care. I had two seasons left, two more chances to beat it. The team had qualified for the NCAA tournament for the first time in three years. That was all that mattered.

Favored in our first game, we won by twenty. We cleared the round of thirty-two. That hadn't happened in a decade. We beat the three-seed, Maryland, to advance to the Elite Eight. You had to go back to 1960 to find the last time that had happened. I had seventeen assists in that game, one short of the tournament record. I scored twelve points, too. I was on *SportsCenter*. We were Cinderella. Things got nuts for a while.

When Tatiana said she'd recognized me, she was recalling the me from those few months, the italicized portion of my life. Agents turning up at our motel. One of them came to my dad's work. It was a time for imagining. Maybe I wouldn't go back for two more seasons, after all. Maybe I'd go pro. Get rich. Get richer. Get famous. Get *more* famous. It seemed so obviously desirable that I never stopped to wonder if, in fact, I wanted it.

I did want it. I know that, now.

We beat Miami in triple overtime and crashed into the Final Four against Kansas.

I had a lousy opening half. They had a great team that year, including three future NBA players, and I went into sloppy hyperdrive, turning the ball over a bunch. My coach sent me to the bench to cool off, keeping me there until five minutes remained in the half and we were down by eleven. Finally he sent me to the scorers' table to check in.

Rather than run the set play he'd drawn up, I gave in to frustration, coming off a screen and barreling down the lane. I remember, distinctly, the look on their center's face as I went straight at him: a mix of awe, pity, annoyance. He had eight inches and a hundred pounds on me. For me to dare — it wasn't in his mental playbook, and I'd wrong-footed him.

He reacted as best he could, sliding to cut me off, throwing his hands straight up and knocking me sideways in midair. I came down at an angle, landing on the inside of my right foot, the knee caving inward, the full weight and force of my heroism skewing laterally through my anterior cruciate ligament, medial collateral ligament, and medial meniscus.

I've heard other people talk about a catastrophic injury. They say things like *It's funny, there wasn't any pain*. I can't agree. It wasn't funny, and I felt more pain than I'd ever experienced. But pain, however bad, isn't what sticks in the long term. We can place it on a spectrum and assimilate it.

It's the unfamiliar sensations, the ones without a point of reference, that become the stuff of nightmares.

Take a wet bunch of celery.

Grip it with both hands.

Twist, as hard as you can.

That's what my knee felt like.

And the crowd, shrill and unforgiving.

And the floor, slick and unforgiving.

And the face of the trainer, scraped pale. He couldn't help himself. Consolation would follow; encouragement, planning, structure. But he'd shown me the truth in an instant, and to this day I can't help but feel a certain hatred for him.

I looked at Tatiana. 'Mostly, I miss my teammates.'

She slipped off my coat and her shoes and padded over. I tossed her a ball. She caught it awkwardly and dribbled a few times, slapping at it. She seemed to be seeking approval, and I started to step forward to give her a pointer.

She tore past me with a screech, chucking a wild shot that hit the top corner of the backboard and went flying.

'Fuck,' she yelled as we both ran after the rebound.

I got there first, corralling it and dribbling out to half-court. Tatiana faced me, cat-backed, grinning, rubbing her hands together, beckoning.

'Ones and twos,' I said.

'I don't know what that means,' she said.

'Normal shots are worth one. A three-pointer is worth two.'

'That makes zero sense.'

I ran toward her, stopped short, pulled up, and let fly. Snap.

'Two,' I said. I reached down and plucked a ball from the floor. 'Loser's out.'

'Oh fuck you "loser".'

We played with no regard for boundaries, running and heaving and traveling when convenient. When I blocked her path, she simply turned and sprinted downcourt toward the other basket; when I poked the ball from her hands, she snatched the nearest one off the floor. If I got within arm's reach of her she started hacking at me mercilessly, her shrieks caroming from the walls and the stands, lighting up the hush. Nobody came to see what the racket was all about or to tell us to keep it down. We were living in a one-room universe.

Flushed, her hair sticking to her forehead, her shirt glued to her ribs, she put up a particularly heinous airball from the free-throw line.

I backpedaled, leapt, snatched it from midair, rolled it in.

'We'll call that one for you,' I said.

'What's the score? I've lost count.'

'Me too.'

'I am so completely terrible at this.'

I took a ball and stood behind her, leaning down to wrap my arms around her, positioning her hands. 'The right provides the power. The left acts as a guide. Think of it as a one-handed push.'

I stepped back.

She bricked it, short.

'Closer,' I said, grabbing another ball. 'Put some height on it. The more you exaggerate the arc, the bigger your target gets.'

She dribbled once, twice. Shot.

Got the bounce.

I applauded. She turned and curtsied. Held out her hands.

'Come here right now,' she said. 'Please.'

We sank down together, tugging and prying at each other, fingers catching on fasteners and fabric, rolling around half naked on the hardwood. It seemed like a fun idea but she soon said, 'Know what, this is really uncomfortable,' and we both started laughing.

I said, 'We're not kids anymore,' and she said, 'Thank God for that.'

I got up and helped her up and then, before I could dwell on the risks to my knee, I swept my arms around her back and behind her legs and carried her to a stack of gym mats shoved into the corner. They smelled plasticky and sharp. Bodies had fought here.

I spread out my coat and she uncoiled, a creature released from captivity, running to trap and devour the first living thing it saw, which was me. She caged me with her arms, her fingers taloned my neck, light drilled down on us in high contrast, her perfect contours raised up above the surface of the world.

'Someone might come in,' she said.

'Does that bother you?'

She smiled. 'I like it.'

I should have figured: she was a performer.

19

IN THE morning I woke alone, blinking up at the blushing ceiling of her bedroom. My clothes lay folded on the floor. A dent in the sheets beside me. I flopped over the edge of the bed, scrabbling for my phone, dragging it toward me by my fingernails. Ten after eight.

I called Tatiana's name. No response.

Pulling on my pants, I went into the bathroom to wash my face.

I heard the front door open and came out to find her balancing a cardboard tray with coffee, a bulging waxed-paper bag in her other hand. A thoughtful gesture, but it sent a chill through me. The same items had been spilled across her father's foyer.

'I had to guess if you take milk,' she said, handing me the tray.

'I do.'

'That's what I thought,' she said. *'He's a big boy, he probably drank a lot of milk as a kid.'* She smiled and rose up on her tiptoes to kiss me. 'Good morning.'

'Morning. Thanks for this.'

'You're welcome.'

We sat cross-legged on the carpet and ate, surrounded by the stacks of banker's boxes.

'What are you going to do with all of it?' I asked.

'I rented a storage locker. I'm supposed to hang on to every-thing for a full year. There's even more stuff waiting for me in Tahoe. Just thinking about it stresses me out.'

'Then we won't think about it.'

'Too late.' She wiped her mouth. 'Did you sleep okay?'

'Great. You?'

She shrugged. 'You have long legs. Long, active legs.'

'Sorry.'

'It's all right. I need to be up anyway.' She tore at a croissant. 'Tell me the truth. You do that for all the girls?'

'What. The basketball thing?' I shook my head. 'Just you.'

'Uh-huh. Does it work?'

'Like forty percent of the time.'

She smiled.

I liked that about her. Quick to smile but hard to make laugh. It kept you honest.

We finished our breakfast and I carried her bags down to her car. My knee felt shockingly healthy.

'I'll call you when I'm back,' she said.

'Any sense of when that'll be?'

'Two weeks,' she said. 'Three.'

'Which one is it? Two or three?'

She kissed me, got into the Prius, and drove off toward the freeway.

It's true: I did want to see her again. But that wasn't my rea-son for asking.

However long she remained away — two weeks or three — that was how long I had to locate Julian Triplett.

It wasn't yet nine a.m. The day was clear. I moved my car to avoid a ticket and set out on foot for Delaware Street.

West of San Pablo, the neighborhood took a turn. Not for the worse, exactly; more for the tired. Weeds marching forth in their ranks. Indoor furniture living outdoors. Some creative soul had erected a two-foot-high 'fence' out of chicken wire, staked to tomato cages, everything held together with supermarket twist-ties. All manner of crap had been put on the sidewalk and left to the mercy of the elements: mattresses, crates of mushy paperbacks. Some folks had bothered to add a sign — FREE or PLEASE TAKE — as though words alone could transform junk into treasure.

Litterbug!

Julian Triplett's mother, Edwina, still lived at the same address as a decade ago, in the rearmost unit of a small stucco complex called Manor Le Grande. The name was goofy enough as is, without the cartoon-bubble lettering bolted to the brick façade. Something about it momentarily sapped my zeal. Most people would be at work at quarter to ten on a Monday morning, and even if Edwina Triplett was home, I couldn't make her talk to me. Nor could I see why she would do so willingly.

I had little to lose, though. Even if she refused to tell me where her son was, she might warn him that the cops had come around, and that might be enough to scare him off.

Concrete pavers led to a cracked trapezoidal courtyard. The curtains to #5 hung ajar.

I looked through the window. The living room beyond the glass was too sparse to qualify as messy; what I could see showed evidence of hard use. Tube TV squaring off with a soiled, defeated sofa. A tray on legs stood at the ready, but unhappily, like some dried-up butler. Dark puddles splotched the popcorn ceiling.

I rapped the screen door's frame.

No answer.

I got out my card and wrote on the back: *Please call when you have a chance*. I started to stick it in the mail slot but paused, worried about needlessly frightening her.

A note from the Coroner's Bureau, asking for a call, with no context?

Impetuously, I tacked on a smiley face.

Please call when you have a chance. :)

Well. That just looked ridiculous.

While I went through my wallet for a fresh card, the front door whined. An obese black woman of about fifty peered out through the screen. She wore a formidable floral-print house-dress and leaned on a shiny purple cane.

I raised a hand. 'Good morning, ma'am.'

'Good morning.'

I flashed my badge quickly, identifying myself as a deputy sheriff. 'I'm looking for Julian Triplett.'

She listed a little to the right, examining me. 'Is he in trouble?'

'No ma'am. I'm just trying to find him, and yours is the last address I have.'

'What you want him for?'

'Just checking in.'

She sniffed skeptically. 'He ain't around.' She reached for the door.

'It's important that I find him.'

'I said he ain't around.'

'When's the last time you saw him? Ma'am.'

She shut the door.

I crossed out the smiley face and pushed the card through the mail slot. If that made her anxious, so be it. Maybe it'd motivate her to cooperate.

I started back toward the street, jumping as the screen door banged open behind me.

Edwina Triplett came humping out, her gait jerky and pained. She was sweating, clutching the card fiercely, bending it into a U.

'You got no right.' She spoke quietly, her features glittering with rage. *No right.*

'All I want is to ask him a couple of questions.'

She whooped laughter. 'Coroner? You must think I'm some kind of stupid.' Squinting at the card: 'Edison? That's you?'

'Yes ma'am.'

'He's dead?'

'No ma'am.'

'Then why you harassing me, Mr Edison?'

'Ma'am —'

'What you think about this?' She tore the card in half, stacked the halves, tore them again. 'Huh, Mr Edison? Tell me what you think about that.'

She halved the card twice more. Getting through thirty-two layers proved a challenge – she strained with effort, the flesh of her arms and under her neck rippling like disturbed water – and she began shredding individual pieces, sprinkling them on the cement.

She said, panting, 'What you think about *that*.'

I said, 'I think I've upset you, and I apologize. For what it's worth, I'm not concerned with whatever happened before. This is something happening now.'

'I guess you didn't hear me the first five times,' she said. 'He. Ain't. *Around*.'

'I heard you.'

'Then why you still –' She broke off with a grunt, wincing and pressing a fist to her chest. The cane began to vibrate, her spine to bow.

I took a step forward.

'Don't touch me,' she wheezed. She sank down, slumping against the doorframe, her mouth gaping, grabbing at the air.

I asked if she could breathe.

She didn't reply. I took out my phone to call an ambulance.

'Nnn.' She tossed a hand over her shoulder. 'Pills.'

'Where are they?'

'. . . bathroom.'

I stepped around her carefully.

The air inside the apartment felt close, tens of thousands of cigarettes soaked into the walls. I went straight back, encountering a mess of amber bottles on the bathroom counter. Among numerous diabetes scrips I found nitroglycerin tabs. I shook a couple out, filled a water glass, and hustled back outside.

She stuck a pill under her tongue, ignoring the water. Within a few minutes her breathing had begun to ease. She closed her eyes, massaging her chest.

'Another?' I asked.

She shook her head.

'Who should we call? You have a primary doctor?'

'You can go,' she said.

'I can't until I know you're okay.'

At length she tried to stand. She couldn't manage it. I saw her grimace, weighing need against pride. She said, 'Help me up.'

I set the glass on the pavement and crouched, sliding an arm around her. Her skin was moist and warm and yeasty. I said a prayer for my knee, took a deep breath, and said, 'One two three *hup*.'

We rose together.

She directed me to the sofa, groaning as I got her settled, letting the cane fall to the carpet with a soft thud. I fetched the water glass. She gulped it down, droplets rolling over her jaw and down her throat, shading the lace at her neckline.

'More?'

'No.' Then: 'Thank you.'

I took the glass to the kitchen and rinsed it out. There was no dish drainer, so I upended it on a grungy towel. From beneath the sink came a fetid whiff. Overflowing five-gallon can, no bag.

I carried it through the living room, doing my best not to spill. Edwina Triplett still had her eyes closed.

Outside I found a row of gray city bins. I emptied the can, washing it out several times from a hose bibb and shaking the excess onto spiky, sere bushes.

When I returned, her eyes were open. She regarded me suspiciously.

'You have trash bags hidden somewhere?' I asked.

She didn't answer. I went into the kitchen and started opening drawers. The best I could come up with was a wrinkled paper sack from CVS.

I know how it reads: I was trying to worm into her good graces. No doubt that's what she thought. But at that moment, I was thinking of all the homes I walk into on a weekly basis, except that in those instances I'm there to remove a body. Few people get a chance to stage-manage their own exit. They die before they've had a chance to take out the trash. They die before they've finished wiping themselves. The last impression we leave is almost always inadvertent.

Seeing Edwina, the raft of drugs she depended on, I had a rare opportunity. For once I was here before – not after. It felt worth five minutes of my time to chip away, however slightly, at future indignity.

Also, I hate a mess.

I lined the can with the CVS bag and put it beneath the sink.

'I meant what I said,' she called. 'I don't know where he's at. That's honest. Not like you.'

I rejoined her in the living room. 'Even if you did know, I wouldn't blame you for not wanting to tell me.'

'You just tryin to sugar me up.'

'I'm gonna suggest one last time that we call a doctor.'

'I don't have a primary.'

'Someone else, then, to keep an eye on you,' I said. 'A neighbor.'

That got a snort.

'What about your daughter?'

She started. I'd done my research.

Then, as if giving up, she pursed her lips and faced away.

'We could call her together,' I said. 'Maybe she knows where Julian's at.'

'Ask her yourself.' Her voice was a hard matte shell, hinting at the terrible loneliness inside. 'I ain't even tryin to know.'

'Believe it or not, I'd like to help your son.'

She smirked.

'You've heard that before,' I said.

'Oh yes I have.'

'From the police.'

'Police,' she said. 'Lawyers. Social services. Everybody's so helpful. The folks from the experiment, they wanted to help, too, and you see what that got him.'

'I understand.'

'Oh you do, do you?'

'Maybe I don't,' I said. 'Help me out, then. Tell me about him.'

She looked at me. 'Tell you what?'

'About Julian.'

She fell silent for a moment. 'I don't know what you expect me to say.'

'You know him. I don't.'

'Yeah, and?'

'And maybe you share with me a little about who he is, what he's like, I can do what I can to keep him safe.'

'He's in danger.'

'He's out there,' I said.

'You think he did something.'

'I don't know that. Don't know him.'

'I don't know him, either,' she said. 'Not anymore. Maybe I never did.'

'Does he have friends? A girlfriend?'

'*Girl*friend? Be real, now.' She shook her head. 'You ask me as many times you want. The answer's still the same: I don't know where he's at. I ain't seen him in forever.'

'What's forever?'

'Ten years,' she said. 'More.'

I said, 'Back when he was living with you.'

'He got out and had no place to go.'

'You took him in.'

She stared at me. 'He's still my child.'

'All I meant was, you did right by him.'

'You definitely sugaring.' But she didn't seem to mind.

'How was it, having him home?' I asked.

She shrugged.

'Did he have a hard time adjusting to life on the outside?'

'Julian had a hard time ad*just*ing to everything,' she said.

Her anger wilted as quickly as it had come; she unballed her fists and began fiddling with her cuticles. 'I know God has His reasons, and He gives us each our gifts. And I know I ain't the greatest mother in the world, but I tried, I was trying. You need to realize, I wasn't like you see me now. I didn't sit here like this, I could get around. I had him young. Two kids and two jobs. I was tired all the time. I don't know what I did, to make him act like that.'

'You have a recent photo of him?'

She rolled her eyes. 'No.'

'All right,' I said. 'When he left, ten or so years ago, did something happen to make him take off? You two have a fight?'

'Wasn't like that. When he first came out he wouldn't do nothing. Just sat and watched TV. Reverend Willamette, bless him, he started coming round. He took Julian under his wing. He got him a job, helping part-time over at the church. You know – touch up the paint, whatever. He was doing all right. Then one day I wake up, and he's gone.'

She bit off a hangnail. 'I ain't seen him since. And that's the truth.'

She held the water glass out to me.

I took it to the kitchen, refilled it, calling, 'The reverend's a good man.'

'Yes he is.'

'Where's he preach at?'

'Dwight Baptist.'

'That's your church?' I said, coming back to the living room.

'I go when I can,' she said.

I handed her the glass. 'Lemme ask you about something else: those people from the experiment.'

Her face pinched. 'What about them.'

'You said they wanted to help.'

'That's what they *said*. They came to the high school, passing out flyers. Julian was all excited, begging me, "Can I please, Mama." I said, "What these people going to do to you?" I didn't want them giving him electric shocks or nothing.'

'What did they do?'

'He told me he got to play video games,' she said. 'He says he goes and does this experiment and also they gonna help him with his homework. You know, tutoring. He needed the help. The school already made him repeat the year. So, okay, I said.'

'He played video games, and they gave him help with school? Anything else?'

'That's what they *said* they were gonna do. But I didn't see none of that. Later I heard that the man, he said there was two groups, one got the tutoring and the other didn't get nothing. I say that's some bullshit.' She paused. 'They fed him, though.'

'Fed him.'

'He said the man got him a burger. He liked that.'

Rennert passing out McDonald's bags: life at Tolman Hall had improved since the days of free Oreos. 'Nice of him.'

She stared at me incredulously. 'You think a *hamburger* makes up for what they did?'

I was quick to agree that it did not.

'It was them made him crazy,' she said. 'He was normal before that.'

She seemed to believe it, too. A game had driven her son to violence. Because that was easier than the alternative, that a terrible crime had spilled forth from some poisonous well within his being.

Either way, she wasn't denying he'd done it.

I said, 'After he got out, did he ever talk about the people from the study?'

'Like what?'

'Was he mad at them? Talk about wanting to get revenge?'

'Julian didn't get mad,' she said. 'He got scared.'

'Scared of what.'

'Himself,' she said. 'People look, they see that big body of his and think the wrong things. I never seen a boy so scared his own shadow. I get scared, too, thinking about him out there, on his own. I just pray God keeps him safe. Nothing more I can do.'

'Is that where you think he is? On the street?'

She shook her head, dejectedly. 'I don't know.'

She yawned twice. 'I'm tired, Mr Edison. You made me tired.'

I stood. 'I'm leaving you another card. Maybe you'll like it better than the first.'

The barest smile. Another yawn.

'Ms Triplett, if you remember anything, think of something else that might make it easier for me to find Julian and help him, please give me a call.'

'Coroner,' she said. 'You sure he ain't dead?'

'Definitely not,' I said. 'We do other things, too.'

She said, 'Hmm.' Reached for the remote control.

20

DWIGHT BAPTIST Church was on my route home, a brick cube dressed up by a small steeple and an iron cross.

I rang the doorbell and spoke to an elderly lady in a smart navy suit who bid me please wait outside. The Reverend D. Geoffrey Willamette's name presided atop the letterboard. Tacked below the schedule of services was a poster for an upcoming event called Get Woke, Stay Woke: Empowering Our Youth! There would be free food, a DJ, a dance contest, a winter coat drive, a poetry slam.

There'd be a moment of silence to honor two young men, victims of gun violence. I recognized their names.

The woman returned to show me to the pastor's office.

Rail-thin, bald, in his sixties, Willamette greeted me with an open face, an open hand, a broad pleasant baritone that offered me a seat and a cup of water.

I accepted both and watched for a shift in demeanor as I explained who I was and why I was there. Employing the soft fib I'd told Edwina Triplett: main gig with dead people, but additional duties.

'How is Sister Edwina?' he asked. 'I haven't seen her here in too long.'

'She said she comes when she can.'

Willamette chuckled. 'I suppose she does. Which makes it my responsibility to seek after her.'

'She could stand a checkup at the doctor.'

'That's good to know. I'll arrange for it. I try to keep tabs on people, but things escape me. I used to be better at storing it all up here.' Tapping his temple. 'Nowadays, unless it's in front of my eyes . . . It pains me to think how much suffering might've been avoided, if I were a more diligent man.'

'I wouldn't blame yourself, Reverend.'

He smiled. 'Got to blame somebody. Might as well be me. As far as Julian is concerned, I haven't laid eyes on him for a long, long time. *That* pains me. The boy needs a certain degree of support to function.'

'What kind of support?'

'The kind that only a community can provide.'

'His mom said you got him a job here.'

He nodded. 'I'm not ashamed to admit that my motives were strictly charitable.'

'Why would you be ashamed to admit that?'

'Because in the end, charity is patronizing,' he said. 'I gave him that job to keep him out of trouble. I never suspected he would be any good at it.'

'But he was.'

'More than good,' Willamette said. 'He had a talent.'

'For?'

'Fixing things.'

The first kind words anyone had had to say about Julian Triplett.

Willamette tented his fingers. 'Let's agree, Deputy, at the outset, that he did a grievous wrong. Nevertheless he lives, he is a man, and he is free to make choices. So the question becomes: What will make a better world for him and everyone else? Tormenting him? Turning him into an outcast? These are the very forces that pushed him toward darkness. Whom do we serve, by serving the past? It's my belief that every man retains within him the light of God, just as each one of us who professes virtue bears the taint of sin. Julian revealed to me his godly spirit. For me that's reason enough to say: Praise be.'

'Did he ever express remorse for what he'd done?'

'He didn't often voice his thoughts.'

'So that's a no.'

'He has a unique mind. Whether he repented in his heart, I can't say. But he never gave us any problems.'

'Did you encourage him to repent?'

'I encouraged him to concentrate on building a worthy future.'

'By fixing things,' I said.

Willamette rubbed the top of his desk. 'Before I was called here, I had a prison ministry. Seven years. I looked into the faces of hundreds of men, some of whom had committed unspeakable acts. Comparable to Julian's. Worse, if you can imagine.'

'I can.'

'We must not be afraid to call evil deeds by their true name.

By the same token, we must not be so vested in our own right-eousness, so afraid of appearing weak to ourselves, that we deny goodness when it rises from the ashes. Many of those men were little more than frightened boys themselves.'

'That's what Edwina said about Julian.'

'It doesn't excuse him, of course. What I hoped for was to get him on the right path, so that he could exceed the sum total of his history.'

I said, 'What sort of things did he fix?'

'Whatever we needed. Drywall. Gutters. He installed those bookshelves.' He chinned at me. 'He made that chair you're sitting on.'

I tensed, feeling the imaginary pressure of Triplett's hands on my back, my legs. Willamette didn't seem to notice, and I forced myself to relax.

'I don't want to give you the impression that I took him on as my personal carpenter,' Willamette said. 'He was always paid fairly for his work. But the good it did went beyond that. It nourished him to create.'

I glanced at the bookshelves: straight and true, with tidy corners, the wood polished to a satin luster. 'Where'd he learn to make furniture?'

'He picked up the basics while he was incarcerated. When I saw that he had a gift, I arranged for him to take private lessons with a gentleman I know, a friend of mine who's a superior craftsman. Are you familiar with the Urban Foundry?'

I was: an industrial arts school in Oakland's warehouse district, not far from the old Coroner's building.

'My friend gave Julian permission to use their woodshop in

the off hours, so he could go in and work on projects of his own.'

While I admired the reverend's capacity to see decency in everyone, I did question the logic of granting a convicted murderer – who'd stabbed a woman to death – unsupervised access to a room full of sharp tools.

'May I please ask your friend's name?'

Willamette looked me in the eye. 'I'm sharing this information with you on the understanding that your goal is to help Julian.'

'You said it yourself, Reverend. It's better if he's not out there in the wind.'

A beat.

'Ellis Fletcher,' he said. 'He's retired now but I believe he comes in every now and again to teach.'

'Thank you.'

Before leaving I stepped back to have a look at the chair. Mahogany, delicate spindles at the back, sinuous legs, carved claw feet. Far more sophisticated than the shelves.

'Amazing, isn't it,' Willamette said.

I nodded. The finish on the seat had rubbed off over the years, leaving a blond center surrounded by a dark, reddish corona that reminded me of dried blood.

'Julian had big hands,' Willamette said, touching one of the spindles. 'Huge. Like those foam fingers they wave at sporting events. You'd never think a man with hands like that could produce such delicacy. It speaks to an underlying gentleness.'

I said, 'Thanks for your time, Reverend.'

* * *

176

That evening I took a walk down Grand Avenue, got myself a bento box and a kombucha to go. I sat on my couch and started to put my feet up on the coffee table.

My phone rang with an unfamiliar number.

I set my food aside, wiped my hands on my pants. 'Hello?'

A deep voice said, 'This is Ken Bascombe. I heard you were looking for me.'

'Oh. Yeah. Hi. Thanks for getting back to me. Did Nate Schickman fill you in?'

'He said something to do with the Zhao murder. You're with the Coroner?'

'That's right. Clay Edison.'

'Tell you upfront, Clay, I'm glad that shit's over and done with.'

'Bad one,' I said.

'The worst,' he said.

I told him about Linstad's death; about Rennert's.

'Rennert has a daughter who's local,' I said.

'Okay,' he said. 'And?'

'Triplett's out there, walking around. I can imagine he's carrying some ill will.'

'You think he's coming for her?'

'Just covering my bases,' I said.

'Uh-huh. Well, I mean, the guy's a fucking psycho, so . . . You're saying Rennert had a heart attack, though.'

'No question.'

'First I heard about Linstad kicking it, either. He fell down the stairs?'

'It was ruled an accident.'

'Accident's an accident,' he said. 'Unless you guys changed your policy since I left. When're we talking about, anyway?'

'Linstad was in oh-five.'

'I was gone by then.'

I asked how long he'd been with Berkeley PD.

'Eighty-one to ninety-seven.'

'You know when Triplett got out?'

'He was scheduled for release in oh-two. Everyone was pissed. We wanted him tried as an adult. I mean, shit. We're talking premeditation, lying in wait, some serious fucking animal brutality. Adult doesn't apply in that situation, when does it? You know how it goes around here. Get some idiot judge, find the soft spot, press on it, boom, Triplett's a victim.'

'Of what?'

'Society. The Man. The fast-food conspiracy. Listen, I'm not gonna sit here, tell you the kid wasn't holding a shitty hand. He's got an IQ of about eighty. He can barely read. I have to walk him through the Miranda sheet one word at a time. Lousy deal, no question. Dad's AWOL, mom's fucked up outta her head on dope twenty-four seven.'

'She seemed okay to me.'

A slight pause. 'You talked to her?'

'I went over to see if she'd clue me where he's hiding out.'

'Ah-huh. Lemme guess, she didn't know.'

'No. She looked clean, though.'

'Good for her. Maybe she did a twelve-step.' His laugh was harsh.

'What did she use?'

'Crack. The PD uses that to sob-story. Has people coming in

and saying Triplett's a nice kid, wouldn't hurt a fly. I get, it's the job, but enough is enough. He's hearing voices telling him to hurt people. He needs to be off the street.'

I said, 'Voices.'

'Oh yeah.'

'His mom didn't mention anything about that. Neither did his old pastor.'

'*Pastor*,' he said. 'You all over this motherfucker . . . Yeah, voices. Talk to him for two minutes – you don't have to be a fuckin psychologist to understand he ain't right. What do those guys do anyway, complicate simplicity. When we wanted to adult Triplett, the court ordered an eval. The shrink says he can't hack it at juvie, needs to be hospitalized. Okay, off he goes to the hospital. They put him on meds. Bingo! All better. Now he's not crazy anymore. Now he's a nice boy. Back to juvie. In juvie, he doesn't get his meds. So now he's crazy again. Back to the hospital. It was like that for eight, ten months. You get the picture.'

'I read your interviews,' I said. 'Thorough. Sometimes it's hard to tell if he's acting strange cause he's nervous, or a kid, or whatever.'

'Nervous? He was crazy,' Bascombe said. 'Half the stuff he said's not in there, it gets impossible to follow the thread of the conversation. He'd go on about all sorts of shit.'

'Like what?'

'Specifically? Christ, I don't . . . Okay. This I remember. He said the girl disappeared. Like, he stabs her, and – *poof*.'

'Yeah, I read that.'

'I mean, come on. Listen – what is it, Ed?'

'Edison.'

'Edison. You ever work homicide?'

'No.'

'Patrol?'

'Some. Before the Coroner I was mostly at the jail.'

'Jail, huh,' he said drily. 'Well, trust me. Whatever Triplett said, it was nothing special. We're talking about Berkeley, okay? I spent half my career talking to people who believe aliens ate their dog. It's noise. You learn to cut through it. But the eval made an impression on His Honor. Then you get the so-called expert witness banging on the table about this fucking experiment, he's vulnerable, he's triggered, blah blah.'

'Video games.'

'Right. Some shoot-em-up dealie they showed the kids. I think my son had it on Nintendo. I guess I should count myself lucky *he* didn't kill nobody.' He laughed. 'There you go. You know what you need to know. Remind me your name again.'

I said, 'Edison.'

'Edison. Okay. Well, Edison, don't work too hard,' he said. 'Trust me on that.'

21

BACK AT the office, I worked as hard as I could, but my head was elsewhere. Moffett and I took a callout for the 42nd Street overpass in Fruitvale – John Doe, indeterminate age, indeterminate race, in a state of advanced decomposition. Autopsy would have the final word, but a cursory inspection showed no signs of violence.

He had simply died, rotting in place because there was no one around to witness it, let alone help.

As Moffett and I crab-walked around the body, hacking, waving our hands to bat away the rising chimney of stink, I could not escape the thought that this could be Julian Triplett. Or someone who knew him. Or the person he could, would, become. Eventually. Inevitably.

If you'd asked me several months ago how I felt about such a case, I would've answered: *Sad but not surprised*. Now I listened to the traffic thundering along 880, thousands upon thousands of people pushing on overhead, oblivious to what lay below them. Moffett tried to adjust the corpse's arm, and a patch of skin sloughed free like the peel off a boiled peach. Behind his mask his features contorted in disgust, and I found myself filled with despair, and frustration, and anger.

We'd take this remnant of humanity, weigh him, stick him in the freezer. Tell someone he had passed, if someone could be found who cared.

So what?

In six-plus years on the job, I'd never questioned my purpose. I took the bad with the good because what I did was, foremost, *necessary*. That perfect fit, that sense of sealing airtight a crack in society, gave me deep satisfaction.

A setup man.

Now I felt pushed up against the limits of my mandate, and I had a sudden and awful premonition. Saw myself slide toward a darker state, where the work wasn't necessary, let alone fulfilling; just a temporary relief from uncertainty.

The question marks awaiting all of us.

'Earth to dude.'

I snapped to. 'Sorry.'

Moffett shook his head. 'One, two, three, *up*.'

We rose.

On my next day off, I drove over to Cal.

What I'd told Tatiana was true: I did come by every so often, to use the gym. But it had been years since I'd stepped foot in the psych building.

Sneakers chirping on linoleum.

Bulletin board soliciting human subjects.

One elevator out of service. Did it ever get fixed?

That things hadn't changed one bit was less charming than

terrifying: long before I'd arrived on campus, the structure had been condemned as seismically unstable.

I made my way up to the fourth floor. The halls were hushed and ill lit. I found the door and knocked.

A boyish voice said, 'Come in.'

Spellman-Rohatyn Professor of Psychology and Social Issues Paul J. Sandek taught in the department's social-personality track. He hadn't changed much, either. A few extra veins of white in his beard, a modest pouching around the eyes.

I'd never seen him in anything other than argyle sweaters, or maybe a sweater vest in late spring. The fluttering array of *Far Side* cartoons still blanketed the wall above his computer. At one point I'd known them all by heart. Cover up a caption and I could recite it.

'Clay.' He hugged me warmly. 'It's good to see you.'

'You too.'

He beamed up at me, inspecting me at arm's length. In his day, you could be five-ten and play Division I point guard. Granted, in the Ivy League. But still.

He clapped my shoulders. 'So good. Sit. You want some coffee?'

'Please.'

He pivoted to a side table set with a pod espresso machine and a stack of demitasses.

'That's new,' I said.

'Birthday present from Amy.' He pressed a button, and the machine gurgled to life. 'I use it way too much. Bad for the heart but I can't stop.'

'How is Amy?'

183

'Wonderful, thanks. Finishing up her PhD.'

I remembered Sandek's daughter as a pale, gangly high schooler, sneaking looks at me over the dinner table while her mother heaped me more mashed potatoes. 'Send her my congratulations.'

'Will do. Now comes the hard part: finding a job.'

'I'm sure she'll be fine.'

'Oh, she will. That's just me being parental. She's done some outstanding research, and to my amazement, having Yale on your diploma continues to mean something. It's a jungle out there, though.' He smiled and handed me my cup. 'Like I need to tell you that.'

Prior to getting hurt, I'd never paid attention to academics. No one on the team did. We got 'help' with our papers, prep for tests. To say nothing of those who preferred not to take their own tests. It happens everywhere. I had no reason to care. I was going pro.

Even after surgery, I entertained fantasies of a comeback. My first question upon waking in the recovery room was when I could start rehab. Junior year was a slog of stretching, ice, heat, water therapy, resistance bands, balance drills, speed drills, weights. By summertime, I'd been cleared to play. But I was different. I knew. Coach knew.

My first scrimmage back I was sluggish, wooden, ineffective. And – this was the dagger – timid where I once would have been bold. We had a sophomore, a transfer from San Diego State; he ran circles around me. Afterward Coach asked if I didn't think he showed real promise.

He offered me a spot on the roster, regardless, more as a

reward for previous performance than for anything I could contribute going forward.

I turned him down. Soon enough, the same people who had chanted my name were labeling me vain or selfish. Was I too good to come off the bench? Mentor my own replacement? I had obligations, they said, to set an example of leadership, of self-sacrifice and team spirit and loyalty.

Maybe they were right. I only know that my desire to play was gone, utterly, and that any physical pain was dwarfed by the agony of perceiving the chasm between *before* and *after*. It was the pain of a phantom limb. Reviewing myself on tape was unbearable, like watching a bird shot down, midflight.

That fall, I almost quit school. My transcript was in shambles. I had no declared major. I might as well have chosen classes by tossing darts at the course catalog. If not for Sandek – a fanatical team booster, but more important a profoundly kind and empathic human being – I doubt I would've graduated.

Now, waiting for the machine to finish sputtering his own cup of espresso, he wheeled his chair around from behind the desk. 'Theresa sends her love, too.'

'Same to her,' I said before breaking into laughter.

'What,' he said.

I pointed to his kneeling chair. 'I forgot you have one of those.'

He laughed. 'It's since been replaced by a newer model.'

'How's the back?' I asked.

'For shit. How's the knee?'

'Holding up.'

He took his coffee and knelt. 'I look like a supplicant, right? *Salùd.*'

We drank.

'So,' he said, wiping froth from his mustache. 'Pretty mysterious email you sent.'

'I wanted to speak to you in person,' I said. 'You were around in ninety-three, right? What can you tell me about Walter Rennert?'

He paused, the cup near his mouth. 'There's a name I haven't heard in a while.'

'Were you aware he passed away?'

'I wasn't, no. Shame.'

'How well did you know him?'

'Not very well at all. He was in the developmental track, I think, and I'd only come on board a year or two before. And then of course he got caught up in that sorry situation, so he wasn't doing a whole lot of fraternizing. I'd call us acquaintances.'

'It's his study that I'm trying to learn about, actually,' I said.

'Whatever for?'

'It may bear on a case of mine.'

'A current case.'

'Do you recall anything about the research? Or know who would?'

'Not offhand. I'd be surprised if you could get anyone to talk about it. The entire episode remains somewhat of a bugaboo around these parts. Same for Walter. I'm sure that's why nobody's mentioned his death. What happened to him?'

'Heart trouble.'

'Ah. Nothing sinister, then.'

'Not really.'

186

'I take it you're not going to tell me what's going on.'

I smiled. 'Do you remember anything about the victim, Donna Zhao?'

'Never met her. She was an undergrad, yes? There was also a grad student involved, I think. Walter's TA?'

'Nicholas Linstad.'

'That's the one. Big blond fellow.'

'Him you remember.'

'Only because I didn't much care for him. It's strange, given how little interaction we had. But there you have it.'

'What about him didn't you like?'

Sandek scratched his beard. 'I suppose I found him . . . superficial? He sounded like what an Ikea chair would sound like if it could talk. He ended up leaving the program.'

'When was that?'

'Right around the time Walter did. Not a happy parting for either of them. Extremely messy.'

'How so?'

Sandek finished his coffee. 'The department did what it always does when something goes wrong – and this was way beyond wrong. They established a review committee. If memory serves, the report put the blame partly on Linstad.'

'What for?'

He shook his head. 'I never read it. It wasn't made public. Everything I'm telling you is just scuttlebutt. Whatever the case may be, the buck stopped with Walter. It was his lab, so he ended up taking the brunt. I have no idea what became of Linstad after he left.'

'He's dead, too,' I said.

'Holy Toledo. That is one cursed study.'

'I'd like to know more about it,' I said.

'Honestly, Clay, I'm not sure there's anything to know. I don't think they'd finished collecting data before everything fell apart.'

'The design had to be submitted to IRB for approval.'

'Yes.'

'So that might be on file somewhere.'

A slow nod. 'It might.'

'The review committee's report, too,' I said. 'I'd like to get a copy of that.'

Sandek put his cup down. 'You know, my boy, I'm not some crime-solving whiz like you. I'm not sure what you think I can do.'

'Try to get the reports?'

He slapped his thighs. 'For you, I will.'

'Thanks.'

'Don't thank me yet,' he said, swiveling to the coffee machine. As he racked in a fresh pod, he said, 'You get a chance to play much these days?'

'Here and there.'

'I'm good for HORSE,' he said. 'Just don't ask me to run.'

'Is there money involved?'

'If you like.'

'I don't,' I said.

'Scared, are we?'

'Compassionate. You're on a teacher's salary.'

He laughed. 'Out of my office.'

The rain had let up, and I stood beyond the breezeway, filling my lungs with the scent of damp mulch. Tolman Hall was shaped like a squat H, two blocky legs and a low-slung bridge connecting them. Windows scaled its exterior, a move intended to soften the design's brutalism. Over time, the frames had rusted from the inside out, leaking streaky brown pennants down the raw concrete, so that the building appeared to be weeping, or bleeding, from a thousand eyes.

It struck me that the entire Greek tragedy – all its significant locales, spread out over twenty-plus years – fell within a five-mile radius. The poles were Edwina Triplett's apartment and Walter Rennert's house, lying at opposite corners of the city, a distance befitting the class disparity. The other places that mattered were bunched closer together. From where I stood, Donna Zhao's apartment was a fifteen-minute walk south. The spot where Nicholas Linstad had died was even closer – virtually across the street, up the hill on Le Conte.

Considering the circumstances of his departure from the university, I found it peculiar that he'd chosen to set up shop so close by.

I headed there to have a look.

Most of the block consisted of multi-unit dwellings catering to students. Halloween had recently come and gone, and the insides of some windows were still lined with paper jack-o'-lanterns and nylon cobwebs.

Twenty-four Halloweens since Donna Zhao died. The party never ended.

Nicholas Linstad's former residence, a skinny brown duplex, was set back from the sidewalk, cowed by a larger building of more recent provenance.

I knocked first at the downstairs unit, where he had worked. Receiving no answer, I went down the driveway to the exterior staircase, climbed up slowly. Sure enough, I spotted a series of waist-high grooves in the shingling, scrubbed down by a decade of weather but visible nonetheless. I remembered the pathologist's note that one of Linstad's nails had torn partway off in the fall. He really didn't want to die.

I reached the landing. The wobbly banister in Ming's report had since been repaired, a large nailhead driven into the base of the post.

My knock again met silence. I stuffed my hands in my jacket pockets and turned, scanning for sight lines. Steep, wavy terrain put the surrounding homes at relatively different heights. None had a perfectly unobstructed view of the landing. I saw, mostly, power lines and trees. Nearest was a majestic redwood, wide and woolly, rooted in the rear yard of the adjacent multi-unit, on the other side of a rough picket fence.

'Can I help you?'

Below, a woman in a flowing turquoise dress and matching chunky necklace was walking a ten-speed up the driveway. Long white hair cascaded from beneath her helmet.

'Admiring the tree,' I said, clomping down the stairs. 'Are you the upstairs tenant?'

'May I ask why you're interested?'

I showed her my badge. 'I'd like to take a look around inside, if you don't mind.'

'I'm afraid I do,' she said. 'I object to all manifestations of the fascist state.'

'It's for an old case,' I said.

She smiled pleasantly and flipped me off. 'Go fuck yourself.'

22

22

Julian Triplett's sister now went by the name of Kara Drummond. I phoned her at her place of employment, the Macdonald Avenue branch of Wells Fargo in Richmond, where she was an assistant manager. She agreed to speak to me during her lunch break.

With time to kill, I hung around in the parking lot, seeing ghosts. It was a neighborhood with a high body count. The year before I'd worked a shooting outside Target, two people dead, spillover of an argument that began with a dinged car door. More recently, I'd read that the city had begun paying high-risk kids a stipend for not getting arrested, a policy that kicked up controversy, folks arguing over whether it represented a new standard for creativity or a new low for desperation.

Noon thirty, a woman I knew from her DMV photo emerged, blinking against the cold bright sun. We headed into Starbucks. She declined my offer of a drink and we took a booth.

Kara Drummond was eight years younger than her brother, pretty, with good skin and quick, wide eyes. Heavy bone structure lurked beneath her surface; she'd put work into staying trim. She wore gray slacks, a white crepe blouse, black heels. No ring, leading me to wonder if she'd changed her surname in order to escape its notoriety. Could be divorced; a different father. She spoke with a polish that belied her age and origins. A pair of earrings, tiny dangling sunflowers, swung as she shook her head at me.

She said, 'I don't have contact with either of them. Edwina's toxic. God knows where he is.'

I asked when she'd seen Julian last.

'A long time ago. After he got out,' she said. 'I went over there to get him away from her. I didn't want him picking up her habits. I told him he could move in with me but he wouldn't budge.' She made a disgusted face. 'I was about ready to slap him. All that time he was inside, she never went once to see him. She wouldn't even pay for my bus tickets. You believe that? How cheap can you get?'

'Where'd they keep him?'

'Atascadero,' she said. Unconsciously she reached across the table and picked up my napkin, began twisting it. 'It took me all day to get down there. They never wanted to let me in, cause I didn't have ID. I was too young. I had to argue my way in.'

Her devotion impressed me. The youth camp was in San Luis Obispo, over two hundred miles to the south. 'You went by yourself?'

'Who else's going to take me?'

'Reverend Willamette?'

'I don't do church,' she said. 'Only thing I believe in is me.'

I decided I'd misread her reasons for changing her name.

She said, 'Have you ever seen a juvenile facility?'

I nodded. I had. Far more often than I'd ever wanted to.

'Those kids,' she said. 'They're not kids. They *look* like kids, but that's not what they are. They ate my brother alive. First time I show up, I haven't seen him in two years. He's got cuts all over his face. I'm twelve and he's crying to me like I'm the big sister instead of the other way around. "You gotta help me, I can't take it no more." I told him, "Julian, you fight back. They come for you, you hit them first. Hit them as hard you can." He couldn't do it. The next time I come he's got his arm in a cast.' The napkin was by now reduced to pieces. 'They broke his arm with a fencepost.'

She paused to compose herself. 'Once he got out, the last thing he needs is to end up back inside on account of Edwina doing something stupid. She's not the kind of person who can handle her own business, let alone someone else's. Let *alone* someone like him.'

Despite her efforts to the contrary, she was starting to get worked up again. 'I'm the one petitioning to seal his records,' she said. 'I'm the one filling out job applications. I'm not trying to sound selfish, but it's not like I don't have my own life.'

'It's not selfish,' I said.

'How'm I supposed to manage it when she's whispering in his ear the whole time?'

I shook my head. 'I don't know. I couldn't.'

She sat back, drained but restless, her hands active, searching for something new to destroy.

'Did Julian use?' I asked.

'I never saw him do it. But I don't know what he learned inside.'

'I'm asking cause I understand he suffers from mental health issues, and it's common to have substance abuse problems on top of that.'

'As long as he gets his meds, he's fine. That's another reason I couldn't have him living with her. She'd forget to give him his pills and next thing I know he's calling me up, talking crazy. I have to drop what I'm doing and run over there.'

'She seems to think it was the experiment that kicked off his problems.'

'That's because she was too high to notice,' Kara said. 'He's always been like that. Not dangerous. Just . . .' She bit her lip. 'Himself.'

'Does he have – did he have, at some point, before or after his release – someone monitoring him? Social worker? Anyone like that?'

That earned me an eye-roll. For an instant she looked just like her mother.

I asked where Julian had gotten his meds.

'Clinic, I think.'

Staff might have a bead on him. But I doubted they'd speak to me: confidentiality.

'What about old friends?' I said. 'Can you give me some names?'

She shook her head despondently. She said, 'All the other kids did was tease him.'

Her voice had fallen.

'They called him Grimace. Like the McDonald's character. The purple one? Big, dumb Julian. Ma – Edwina, she wanted him to play football. She saw a meal ticket. When he got into high school, she made him go out for the team. But he couldn't follow instructions, he'd wander around in circles. He didn't like to get hit, or to hit anybody else. He never could hurt another person, no matter what they did to him. Never.'

She was sticking up for him, and I felt for her, more deeply than she could imagine.

Kara stirred the remains of the napkin with a long, lacquered fingernail. 'So what do you think he's done this time?'

'Nothing. As I told your mother, I need to talk to him to make sure he's okay.'

'So you can arrest him.'

'I have no cause to do that.'

'That didn't stop you all before.'

We'd been circling this point, and as much as I dreaded it, it was almost a relief to have arrived. 'With respect, I read the file. There's no shortage of evidence.'

'With respect to you,' she said, 'that's wrong, because I know he didn't do it.'

I said, 'I'm listening.'

'I was with him,' she said. 'At home. That whole night.'

'The night of the murder.'

She nodded.

'You and Julian were together.'

'It was a Sunday. We were both in the house all day, watching TV.'

'He might've left the house after you were asleep.'

'He wasn't supposed to do that,' she said.

That didn't mean he hadn't. But she'd never concede. I said, 'You're sure it was that same night?'

A withering smile. 'I'm sure, Deputy.'

'How old were you?'

'Seven.'

'Okay, well, I'm thirty-four,' I said, 'and most of the time I couldn't tell you the date off the top of my head. I'd have to check my phone.'

'I'm sure,' she said. 'It was Halloween. People kept knocking on the door. I had to send them away because we didn't have any candy.'

'Where was your mother during this?'

Kara shrugged. 'Wherever she would go. Out.'

'Can I ask why you didn't tell this to the police?'

She chuffed. 'You don't think I tried? I went to the station myself. Nobody believed me.'

By now I'd read the complete file, some parts multiple times. There was no mention of Kara's statement, anywhere.

I said, 'You are aware that they had Julian's fingerprint on the knife.'

'I am.'

'Can you explain that?'

'I can't. But I know what I know.' She sat up straight and tall. 'My brother was sick. He needed help. But he wasn't evil, and he wasn't violent. He never killed that girl.'

There were lots of reasons to discount what Kara had told me, almost none to believe her, and as I relayed our conversation to Ken Bascombe, I tried to convey my own skepticism. All the same, I could sense his impatience growing, until finally he cut me off:

'What are we talking about. She was five?'

'Seven.'

'How many seven-year-olds can tell time?'

'That's what I told her.'

'You said you needed to find the guy for some other thing. Why're you messing with my case?'

'No messing,' I said. 'She's his sister, I thought she'd know where he is.'

'Yeah. And? What's that got to do with any of this other shit?'

'Nothing. It came up. I wanted to run it by you.'

'Uh-huh,' he said. 'It came up, or she brought it up?'

'She did.'

'Uh-huh.'

'That's why I checked the file. To verify her credibility.'

'And you didn't find it because she has none. I never spoke to her. Ever. Okay?'

'Is it possible somebody else did, though?'

'Is it *possible*? Sure. But they never told me. Listen, Thomas Edison, I don't have the file in front of me. I don't have it memorized. If you say it's not in there, there's a reason why not. And – and, let's pretend for a second I did speak to her, or someone did. It doesn't change a thing. Okay? I'm not about to rearrange reality to fit to some unsubstantiated thing, coming from a child, who by the way also happens to be an interested party. You said it yourself. She's his sister. Whatever bullshit she's spinning out does nothing to change the fact that we have physical evidence, an eyewitness, and a confession.'

'Her brother's been out for years,' I said. 'Why lie to me about it now?'

Bascombe laughed. 'I think even you can figure that out.'

'To rehabilitate his reputation.'

'Or to get you off his trail. Or just to yank your chain. You think she gives a shit?'

'Makes sense,' I said.

'Cause it's sensible,' he said. Another of his barking laughs. A seal after swallowing a sardine. 'Look. What you do, it's gotta be a drag. I know it must feel exciting, the detective thing. Take it from me. It dead-ends. Like everything.'

23

By Friday I knew that Freeway John Doe had died of liver failure. I still hadn't made much progress on identifying him. His height and weight didn't match any missing persons at our local PDs. The skin on his hands had degraded, making prints a nonstarter.

The best lead was a partial tattoo on his chest, the letters IVOR and numbers that could be a date. I worked the databases for surrounding counties, seeking persons named Ivor or Ivory or any variant thereof; executing public record searches for births and deaths.

From across the squad room came a mild commotion.

Sully said, 'Look what the cat dragged in.'

I followed her gaze toward the far door. An Asian man in jeans and a camouflage-patterned windbreaker had entered and was moving along an impromptu receiving line, fielding greetings, fist bumps, and hugs.

Shupfer scooted her chair back and went over to join the welcoming committee.

Marlborough Ming was a wiry five-eight, with a close-cropped goatee and thinning crew cut, TOUGH MUDDER printed along his jacket sleeves. Pushing sixty, he looked fit enough to outrun any one of us.

'Wassup people,' he said, adjusting rimless glasses after Moffett released him from a bear hug. Reaching into his backpack, he began distributing little cellophane bundles cinched with ribbon, each containing a couple dozen coin-sized cookies in various colors and flavors.

'Ooohhh,' Botero said.

'White chocolate matcha,' Ming said, 'sea salt caramel, dark chocolate raspberry, lemon crème.'

Ming's wife ran a bakery.

'Everybody loves tiny cookies,' he declared. 'They pay twice as much.'

I hadn't yet opened mine before I saw Moffett shaking crumbs into his mouth. 'Dude, these are the nuclear bomb.'

'You want more?'

'Hell yes.'

'Too bad, fat pig,' Ming said.

Vitti came down the hall. 'What's – hey now,' he said, as a package of cookies hit him in the chest.

Work ground to a halt so Ming could show off photos of his daughters sporting floppy chef's hats and flour-dusted faces. That in turn reminded him of the time some fool almost blew up the old building by drowning maggots in gasoline.

'Whose idea was it, Ming?'

'Shut up,' he said. 'Okay, maybe me, shut up.'

He mimed pouring from a canister. ' "Goodbye, little maggots," ' he sang.

The problem had come when some other fool decided to stuff

said dead maggots down the garbage disposal, then run the disposal, creating a spark that ignited the gas fumes and caused the entire building to jump like it had been bitch-slapped by God.

'It's true,' Shupfer said. 'I felt it on the fourth floor.'

'The old morgue didn't have no sprinklers,' Ming said. 'It had the chemical powder. *Whooooosh*. Everywhere, everybody, blinking, totally yellow except for the eyes.' He cackled, putting his hands in front of his own eyes and 'blinking' with his fingers. 'Like Wile E. Coyote!'

After several rounds of nostalgia, he and Shupfer drifted into quiet conversation, the rest of us resuming our respective tasks. It grew dark outside, wind anguishing the branches of the willows cantilevered along the building's northern slope.

I heard Shupfer say, 'Hey, Ming, did Edison ever end up calling you?'

I craned around my screen.

She was smiling genially.

I couldn't tell if she was doing me a favor or giving me the finger. The line's not so clear with her.

I said to Ming, 'I had a chance to review a case of yours.'

'Oh yeah.' Complete indifference.

'Accidental fall. Name of Linstad.'

'You had some questions for him, didn't you,' Shupfer said.

'Not really,' I said. 'Just that it was interesting.'

'Yeah,' Ming said. 'Very interesting.'

He rose and hefted his backpack, turned to Shupfer. 'See you.'

'Later, honey.'

He addressed the room: 'Goodbye, people.' He pointed to Moffett. 'Don't be like this fat pig.'

A round of farewells.

He left.

I said to Shupfer, 'What was that about?'

She was busy on her phone.

'Shoops.'

She handed me the phone, showing me a text.

Tell him come outside

In the parking lot Ming leaned against his Sentra, pushing open a blister pack of nicotine gum. He popped a piece in his mouth and began to chew, listening without interruption as I explained my interest in the death of Nicholas Linstad.

He said, 'Don't waste your time.'

'Is that what I'm doing?'

'Yeah.'

'Why?'

'He fell down. Hit his head. He's dead. It's closed.'

'I don't believe you believe that.'

'Why you care?'

'Same reason you did.'

'That's where you wrong,' he said, cackling. 'I don't give a shit. I got cookies.'

A gust of wind punched down. Ming ejected his spent gum into the broken blister, looked to me with stoic hope. 'You got a smoke?'

I shook my head.

He sighed and popped in another piece of gum. 'Last case before I retired.'

'I didn't realize.'

'Bad luck.'

'Not just for you,' I said. 'I spoke to the detective from the first murder. He left Berkeley PD soon after.'

He laughed, rubbed his eyes. 'You big brave stupid man.'

I waited. He shrugged, ticking off on his fingers: 'Two dents in the pillows. Two voices. Two wineglasses.'

'Someone else was with Linstad that night.'

He nodded.

I said, 'You don't know who it might've been.'

'Nope.'

'You don't know if they were present when he died.'

'Nope.'

'Theories?'

'Not my job.'

'But you do have one,' I said.

No reply.

I said, 'Julian Triplett.'

To my surprise Ming shook his head. 'I never heard about him.'

'You think someone else could've pushed Linstad?'

Ming said, 'I called his father. In Sweden. He told me the ex-wife was rich. Paying Linstad alimony.'

'*She* was paying *him*.'

'Like, twenty, thirty thousand a month. Good deal, huh?'

I whistled.

'Motive,' Ming said.

'Did you speak to the ex?'

'Not my job,' he said again. 'Not yours, either.'

'What'd the cops think?'

'They said no evidence,' he said. 'They were right.'

'There were two wineglasses.'

'So what?' Ming said. 'He had a friend. They got drunk. The friend went home. He fell down the stairs. So what?'

'Did they take prints off the glasses?'

'No evidence,' he said again.

'What about the guy who heard the gunshot?'

'Inconclusive,' he said. 'No casing. No bullet. No holes in the decedent. No holes in the wall.'

I understood. The case for a homicide was borderline at best, requiring that you squint and tilt your head. But Ming couldn't justify that – either to himself or to the cops – and so he'd done what he could.

'You must've had questions,' I said. 'You mannered it undetermined.'

'Okay, but I changed it.'

'Why?'

In the distance, the freeway had begun to clog with angry taillights.

He said, 'Pressure.'

'From who?'

'It came down through the lieutenant.'

'What was the source, though?'

He shook his head. Either *I don't know* or *I can't tell you*.

I said, 'How rich an ex-wife are we talking about?'

He tapped his chin thoughtfully. 'She could buy a lotta tiny cookies.'

'So what are you thinking? She knocked him off?'

'Skinny lady,' he said. 'Skinny rich lady.'

'She hired someone,' I said.

He chomped his gum.

'Maybe she hired Triplett,' I said.

He looked at me. 'Not your job.'

He spat out his gum. 'You should smoke,' he complained. He opened the driver's-side door. 'Good luck, stupid.'

'Thanks, Ming,' I said.

'Thank Shoops.'

'Yeah. Although I gotta say, I don't get why she's up my ass about it.'

He grinned, climbed into his car. 'Cause she loves you so much.'

While Google couldn't tell me how skinny Linstad's ex-wife was, it had lots to say about her financial status.

Her maiden name was Olivia Sowards, making her the daughter of John Sowards, CEO of CalCor, one of the Bay Area's largest commercial real estate developers. Her current married name was Olivia Harcourt, making her the wife of Richard Harcourt, cofounder of Snershy, which did something innovative involving cellphones, or had, until Verizon gobbled the company up for five hundred seventy-five million dollars.

Before departing for the day, I put in a call to her, leaving a message with an assistant.

On my way home I tried Tatiana from the car. As it rang, I wondered if I was using Snershy's proprietary technology.

She didn't pick up.

Not until nine p.m., as I was climbing into bed, did she call me back.

Since her departure, we'd spoken at least once or twice daily.

She wasn't loving Tahoe. Had locked horns with two realtors. One insisted on underpricing the house in order to spark a bidding war. The other insisted she repaint, top to bottom. She read me the ski report. Why didn't I come up to visit? They had eight inches of fresh powder. There was a good restaurant she wanted to try.

Banter; a transfusion, keeping the channels between us open.

I didn't know what we were working toward. Maybe nothing. I hoped it was something.

Expecting more of the same, I was totally unprepared for the panic in her voice.

'Thank God you're there,' she said.

'What's wrong?' I said. 'Are you okay?'

'The alarm company just called me,' she said. 'Someone broke into my father's house.'

24

My response was to tell her to hang up and call 911. But she meant the Berkeley house, not the one in Tahoe.

For the moment, at least, she was safe.

I threw on my uniform and sped over. Berkeley PD was already there. Pulling up the driveway, I parked behind a pair of squad cars, announcing myself in a loud voice.

A uniformed officer named Sherman stood guard out front. I showed him my badge and explained that I had come at the behest of the owner, a friend. For good measure, I name-dropped Nate Schickman.

Sherman didn't care one way or another. He wasn't about to let me inside the house, but he did show me the service door on the east side.

'It was open when we got here,' he said.

'No sign of forced entry.'

He shook his head. 'They're doing a walk-through.'

I didn't ask to join in. No sense putting him in the position of having to refuse me. He knew as well as I did that I had no business being there.

'All right if I take a look around the perimeter?' I asked.

'Knock yourself out.'

'Do me a favor and let them know I'm out there, okay? So they don't draw on me.'

He nodded.

I switched on my flashlight and began a circuit, passing the trash bins, the electrical box, a derelict potting shed. Turning the corner, I waded through knee-high ivy, playing my beam through the tree trunks. To my left, the earth sloped away severely; redwoods and thickets of fern screened off the street, far below. Wind came shrieking through in short blasts. I peered into the darkened living room.

Up on the second floor, lights blinked on as the cops cleared the bedrooms.

I reached the driveway, scrambled down an embankment, dropped over the retaining wall, stood on the gravel.

All quiet.

I jogged down to the cul-de-sac. Quiet.

I descended the footpath to the lower cul-de-sac where I'd chased Hoodie the Giant.

I wasn't expecting to find anything and I didn't.

As I hiked back up, I dialed Tatiana.

'They're checking the house as we speak.'

'How are they supposed to know what's missing?'

'They'll notice if anything's disturbed. Burglars aren't very subtle.'

'I don't fucking believe this.'

'Anything in particular you want me to have them look at? Paintings, jewelry?'

'You can't go inside?'

'It's not my jurisdiction,' I said.

She sighed. 'I'm sorry. I shouldn't've called you. I didn't know what else to do.'

'It's okay,' I said. 'It's going to be fine.'

I stayed on the phone with her for another twenty minutes, until the three uniformed officers finished their search. Their verdict: everything in order. Beds made, drawers un-tossed, clothes in the closets gathering lint.

Either the intruder had fled at the sound of the alarm or – and I could tell they were leaning this way – it was a false alarm.

Happened all the time, these old houses.

Rattly frames. Windy night.

Nothing more they could do.

Tatiana drove back to Berkeley the next day. I'd tried to persuade her to stay in Tahoe. She was adamant, of course; who wouldn't be? It was her house, now. Her stuff. Family heirlooms. She had to see for herself.

I still hadn't told her about Triplett. I hadn't yet decided what I was going to say when I met her at the house that evening.

She got out of her car and hurried toward me, casting nervous glances at the dark ranks of trees. Her smile was tremulous; the skin beneath the green eyes was smudged. I doubted she'd slept.

Not that I was at my best. Coming straight from work, I still smelled like death. If she noticed, she didn't let on as we hugged.

I pulled on gloves. Held out a pair for her.

'What're these for?'

'To do our own search. How was the drive?'

'Long.'

We started in the kitchen, going room by room, checking the contents against her memory and the catalog prepared by the appraiser. In the service porch, three wrinkled, smelly cardboard boxes sat shoved up against the wall: the same three boxes she'd left behind, the last time we were here. She grimaced.

'Why couldn't they steal those?' she said.

We swept the first floor, ascended to the bedrooms. Nothing looked out of place to her. All that remained was the attic. Tatiana seemed hesitant, as if afraid to enter a space where the traces of life might be in evidence, the tang of death still sharp.

I offered to go alone and report back.

She shook her head. 'I'm a big girl.'

We mounted the narrow stairs.

The smell in the attic was the same, only stronger: paper, bindings, dust, now underlined by months of neglect. Tatiana sneezed three times in quick succession.

'That's why I never come up here,' she said. 'Allergy hell.'

I switched on my flashlight and we began stepping over clutter, turning on lamps as we went, revealing the next few feet in a bright, bleaching spot.

'Anything look wrong?'

'I have no clue,' she said.

Neither did I. The place was such a disaster.

We came to the sleeping area. Tatiana switched on the reading lamp.

Rocker. Lounger. Blanket. Neck pillow.

'Look,' I said.

Several of the desk drawers were cracked, including the door to the liquor cabinet.

I crouched down. The bottles of scotch were intact, the levels about where they had been, so far as I could tell. The rack of tumblers, untouched. Three, not counting the one that I had tried and failed to return to Tatiana, presently sealed in an evidence bag and stashed, along with the leftover pill bottles, in the cabinet above my fridge.

I could understand why the cops had failed to note the open desk drawers. The attic was three hundred sixty degrees of distraction, including other cabinets not perfectly shut. Anyone glancing at the desk would have no reason to believe it had been messed with.

I turned my attention to the drawers on the right.

Pens, pencils, checkbooks, bills, bank statements, invoices, Post-its, confetti, crap.

Middle right, more of the same.

Bottom right.

Walter Rennert's revolver was missing.

We sat at the dining-room table, Tatiana's bloodless fingers woven around a juice glass filled high with Chardonnay.

I said, 'Who else has access to the house?'

'Nobody except me.'

'The real estate agent?'

'We haven't signed a contract yet.'

'A neighbor with a key?'

'No.'

'Cleaning service?'

'I canceled them.'

'Did they have a key when they worked here?'

'I don't know. Maybe.' She dropped her face in her hands. 'I can't remember. I think they were supposed to mail it back.'

'Are you sure you locked the side door, the last time you were here?'

'I think so.'

'Let me ask that a different way: Do you ever leave it unlocked? Like if you go to take the trash out.'

'I don't know.'

'Did your father keep a key hidden outside? Under a rock or something?'

'I don't *know*, Clay.'

'Okay,' I said. 'I'm sorry.'

She drank half the glass at one go.

'What about your brothers?' I asked.

She shot me a look: *Don't be ridiculous.*

'I'm just eliminating the obvious,' I said.

'They're hundreds of miles away,' she said. 'I gave them the appraiser's list. "Claim whatever you want." They don't need to break in. Anyway they wouldn't want it. We're not *gun* people. I'd forgotten he even had it.'

'Do you know when he bought it?'

She shook her head.

'Why'd he want one in the first place?'

'To protect himself from that maniac, I assume.'

I said, 'So, no one else who could get into the house.'

'What,' she said. Her lips were trembling. 'You're scaring me.'

I hadn't meant to. More than anything, I wanted to come up with a benign explanation. For her sake.

She pushed her glass away. 'What aren't you telling me?'

'That's his name?' she said. 'Julian Triplett?'

I nodded.

She bit her lip. 'I'm trying to figure out how to express this calmly. Because, right now, I'm *really* angry at you.'

She brushed hair off her face, took a deep breath, let it out. 'Okay. I'm telling myself it's considerate of you to want to protect me. Sweet, even. But dumb, Clay, stupid dumb. If I don't know I need to be careful, then I can't be careful.'

'I wasn't sure that you needed to be careful.'

'That's my decision to make.'

'You're right,' I said. 'I'm sorry.'

'Julian Triplett,' she said, enunciating slowly. 'He's about our age, isn't he?'

'A little older.'

'I wonder if my friends who went to Berkeley High knew him.'

'He was arrested freshman year.'

'Probably not, then.' She shivered, took a drink of wine. 'What should we do?'

'Report it to the cops. We can't have a loose weapon floating around. At least now we can give them a reason to keep an eye out for Triplett. For your safety –'

'I know what you're going to say. I'm not going back to Tahoe.'

'We're talking short-term.'

'No. Forget it.'

'Tatiana –'

214

'I will not let him intimidate me.'

'You could come back to my place.'

She looked at me, wide-eyed. 'You think he knows where *I* live?'

'No reason to assume that.'

'Then?'

'Humor me,' I said. 'At least for tonight.'

Her smile took effort. 'If you're tryinttg to sleep with me, there are easier ways.'

'I'll take the couch,' I said.

She didn't answer. She finished her wine, poured more. 'Are you convinced yet?'

'Of what?'

'That Dad was pushed.'

'It's late,' I said. 'We can talk about it tomorrow.'

A beat.

She shoved her chair back and dumped her refill in the sink.

'The couch,' she said, 'sounds like a good idea.'

215

25

THE NEXT day, I was a zombie at work, jittery and fatigued and doing a poor job of hiding it. On my lunch break I dashed out to the intake lot to call Nate Schickman. He hadn't heard about the incident at Rennert's house. As expected: a false alarm wasn't sufficiently noteworthy to make the rounds. And while he sounded duly concerned to learn about the gun, his responses were guarded. I'd worn out the welcome mat.

I said, 'I've been trying to track this Triplett guy down for a couple of weeks now. My best guess is he's on the street.'

'You have a recent photo?'

'Just the mugshot from his file.'

'From twenty years ago?'

'I know,' I said. 'It's not ideal.'

'No shit.'

'You'll keep it on your radar, though?'

'Yeah,' he said. 'No problem.'

I came home that evening to a quiet apartment, a note from Tatiana stuck to the TV. She needed to get out a bit, clear her head, had gone to dinner with a friend.

Don't wait up.

I ate a bowl of cereal, using my free hand to chicken-peck at my laptop. Got the data I needed, made a quick confirmation call, took a shower, and changed into street clothes.

The Urban Foundry occupied half a square block on 7th Street, about a mile west of downtown Oakland but light-years removed from any spirit of renewal. I parked up the block and stepped out into a puddle of safety glass; walking along, I passed several more, as if to suggest that the price of a spot was having your window smashed.

Even so, optimistic developers had begun to nose around, erecting a run of townhouses in full view of the freeway. On the other side of a weedy lot, a BART train shuffled toward the city, never looking back.

The Foundry itself was a hump of corrugated sheet metal, part hangar, part bunker. The first sensation that registered as I entered – before I could take in the concrete vastness; before I smelled the slag or heard the grinding of machinery – was heat. Immense, pressing heat; heat with mass and force.

The floor plan was sectioned by craft, with signs rendered in the appropriate medium. SMITHY in black iron. BIKE SHOP in gears and chains. Multicolor NEON. Closest to the door was GLASS, three bellowing furnaces that were the source of the roasting air.

The folks working the various stations wore goggles and steel-toes and old-timey facial hair stylings. I had the feeling most of them had been to Burning Man and found it too corporate. They reminded me of kids I knew in high school who built the sets for plays, sneering and striding around purposefully, fistlike masses of keys clashing on carabiner belt clips.

The woman at the front desk had a tattoo on the inside of her wrist: a unicorn, vomiting up a rainbow. I asked for Ellis Fletcher and she pointed me toward the woodshop.

Class was winding down, nine men and three women doing last-minute sanding or returning tools to wall racks. A dozen incomplete Shaker tables sat out, degrees of wonkiness attesting to the broad range of native ability. Anyone could, and did, enroll.

It was easy to spot Fletcher; he was the one eyeballing the surface of a tabletop, checking it for evenness while its maker looked on anxiously. Age was also a clue: mid-sixties, the only person there over thirty.

He wore a broadcloth button-down shirt tucked into Levi's. Both belt and suspenders had been enlisted in the battle between pants and gut. I liked the gut's chances. It had gravity on its side.

I waited till the last student had finished sweeping up to make myself known.

'Reverend Willamette said you might be by,' Fletcher said. His hand felt like one single callus.

'I saw you were scheduled to teach tonight,' I said.

'Wish you'd called first,' he said, settling on a work stool. 'I could've saved you the trouble of coming down here.'

'You're going to tell me you don't know where Julian is.'

'I do not. Haven't seen him in ages.'

For form's sake, I asked how long, expecting the same answer I'd gotten from everyone I'd spoken to so far: more than ten years. But Ellis Fletcher said, 'Hell,' and removed his cap, blue with VIETNAM VETERAN stitched in gold. He rubbed at his forehead with the heel of his hand. 'Must be two or three years now.'

'No kidding,' I said. 'That recently?'

He gave me a strange smile. 'You call that recent?'

'No one else's seen him since two thousand five,' I said.

Fletcher looked puzzled. 'I – okay, I guess.'

'The pastor told me you let him come in to use the shop in off hours.'

'That was way back in the beginning,' Fletcher said. 'Geoff said he had this boy, special case, would I show him the ropes. All right, why not, send him on over. For a little while Julian was here all the time. Then he sorta dropped out of sight.'

'When was that?'

He paused. 'Come to think, right around when you said.'

'Oh-five.'

'That sounds about right.'

'But you did see him after that,' I said.

He slapped the cap against his knee, knocking loose a cloud of sawdust. 'Not frequently. Once a year at most. He didn't give me any warning, he'd just turn up. Like you.'

I smiled. 'What did he come to see you about?'

'Nothing special. Showing his face, I think.'

'You're the one he chose to show it to.'

The suggestion seemed to unsettle him. 'If you say so.'

'His mother. His sister. Reverend Willamette,' I said. 'They haven't seen him. You must've meant a lot to him.'

'I really don't know what to tell you,' he said.

Aware of his growing discomfort, I backed off a hair. 'What'd you two discuss?'

'We didn't "discuss" anything,' he said. 'That wasn't the nature of the relationship. I'd ask him what he'd been building, so forth. You know, chitchat.'

He tugged the cap back on. 'The man's not one for talk.'

'So I've heard.'

'Good with his hands, though.'

'Heard that, too,' I said. 'Did he mention where he was living, or who with?'

'I always assumed he was with her. His mother.' Concern came into his face. 'You're here because he's done something.'

'Not necessarily.'

'You're here,' Fletcher repeated.

'I'm trying to be careful, Mr Fletcher. Stay ahead of things. For Julian's sake, as much as anyone's. When he came by did he talk about having a job?'

'No.'

'Do you know how he got by?'

He shook his head.

'All right,' I said. 'More generally, could you get a sense of where his head was at?'

Fletcher stared out the shop window, at the main floor. The presses and saws and lathes made a gruff but steady chant, oddly soothing. 'I get these students,' he said, shifting on the stool, 'kids. They buy everything on the internet. They don't need to touch it first. You bet they never stopped to think how it got that way. Where it started from. It's click click click click, until one morning they wake up starving and they don't know why. They can't put a name on it. It doesn't have a name. So away they go on the internet again, click click click, until they end up in my class, asking me questions. They want to lock everything down in rules. "How do I know when to change the grit?" ' He paused. 'I do what I can. But I can't make them feel.'

'And Julian?'

'Nothing was for show. He didn't crave praise, or attention. He did what he did.'

'You taught him well.'

Fletcher shook his head. 'Can't teach talent. Intuition for the wood – you're born with it or you're not. I gave him pointers now and again. Showed him pictures or plans from my books and magazines. Most the time I just kept an eye out so he wouldn't steal my tools.'

'You thought he might?'

'In the beginning, sure. All I knew about him is, here's this kid just came out of prison. After a while I got to see him for who he was.'

'You know what he went to prison for.'

'I do,' he said and left it at that.

'Did he ever speak to you about the murder?'

'Never.'

'Did the name Walter Rennert ever come up?'

'I don't know who that is.'

'Nicholas Linstad?'

'Him neither.'

'Did he ever talk about wanting to hurt anyone? Get revenge?'

'No,' Fletcher said. 'You're worrying me, Deputy.'

'Please don't.' Yet. 'Like I said, this is me being extra-careful.'

'Ounce of prevention,' he said.

I nodded.

He gave me a long look, let his features go slack. 'Hell, you're just doing your job.'

I wasn't. But I appreciated his attitude.

Fletcher said, 'Ask me, it's hard to see him hurting anyone. Ever. Not by the time I met him.'

He raised his arm. 'That was his table, in the back. He'd shove himself in there and put his earmuffs on, working by himself, not talking, not asking questions. Maybe I go over there to see how he is, and he shows me. But otherwise he does his thing in peace.' A crooked smile. 'Big as he was, I sometimes forgot he was there.'

A chop saw howled, devoured, was satisfied.

'This way a second,' Fletcher said.

Exiting the shop, he led me past an emergency eyewash station and through a door marked STAFF ONLY BEYOND THIS POINT THANK YOU. He stopped at a stainless-steel trough sink to rinse his hands before heading down a row of school lockers. A pale young woman with black ear gauges and a purple Mohawk sat on the bolted bench, blotting her armpits with a hand towel. She waved to Fletcher, who acknowledged her with a salute.

His was the second-to-last locker on the left. He dialed in the combination. 'I keep this around for when folks get in their heads they want me to make them something.'

The locker didn't hold much: a crusty bottle of Gold Bond, a brown paper lunch sack, a spare shirt on the hook. From the shelf, he took down a photo album – not the twenty-first-century ready-made version, but crack-spined, with pocket pages housing three-by-five snapshots.

It was a portfolio of sorts, although it focused more on process than on results, documenting the creation of several pieces, step by step, from raw material to finished product. Fletcher himself hovered at the margins, like some almighty set of hands. He did beautiful work.

He flipped a page, put his finger down. 'That's him.'

I had yet to see a picture of Triplett as an adult. The Zhao murder file contained his mugshot, one of six in a photo array provided to Nicholas Linstad, who had circled him and written in the margin *this is the person I saw outside Donna Zhao's apartment building on 31-10-1993.*

The photo in the album was a candid, taken while Triplett leaned over a plane.

He sure hadn't grown up any smaller.

Wearing a gray hoodie. Same as the guy I'd chased. Same as the person Linstad spotted lurking near Donna Zhao's building. The same gray hoodie found blood-soaked and wrapped around the murder weapon.

I said, 'That his usual getup?'

Fletcher laughed softly. 'I guess you'd call it his uniform. I told him he could keep it on as long as he left the hood down. So as not to obscure his peripheral vision, you know? Can't have people bumping into each other, especially not someone his size. But he'd forget.'

'Is this the only photo you have of him?'

He paged forward, finding a second candid. Useless, because Triplett had spotted the camera and was averting his face, blurring his features.

I said, 'He didn't like having his picture taken.'

'You got that right,' Fletcher said. 'Shy boy. Afraid of his own shadow, except when he got into the work.'

I pointed to the adjacent photo. 'What's that?'

Fletcher squinted. 'The rocker? Julian made it. Based on a Hans Wegner design. I'd gotten him away from my stuff, away from Chippendale, the usual. I wanted him to have a broader notion of what was possible. Yeah, I forgot about that. He worked on it a long time. The original has a woven seat, but we didn't want to start messing with caning, and the grain was nice, so we kept it plain mahogany. Real pretty. And that's before we put the stain on. Finish it in cherry, you get some good depth of color.'

I said, 'May I?'

He waved consent, and I slipped the print out of the sleeve. I turned it over to read the date printed on the back: *Mar*-19-03.

'Chairs were his thing,' Fletcher said. 'He loved making them. Regular sitting chairs. The rocker was a one-off.'

I'd sat in one of Julian Triplett's chairs, in the reverend's office.

I'd seen the rocker, too, before. Or its twin.

'What'd he do with it?' I asked. 'Did he sell it to someone?'

'I told him he should go around to the local stores, he could get some good money. He didn't care, gave all his work away. Mostly we auctioned the pieces off. We do an auction every June, to raise money for this place.'

'This particular piece, though, the rocker,' I said. 'Any idea who has it?'

'Shoot, I couldn't begin to tell you.'

I nodded. 'Mind if I borrow this? The ones of Julian, too. I'll get them back to you, promise.'

He hesitated, then removed the prints from their plastic, taking a last look before handing them over to me. 'You've seen it, now. He did some fine, fine work.'

26

HUSTLING TO my parked car, I called Tatiana. She didn't pick up.

'Call me,' I said, getting in. 'It's important.'

I drove to my office.

It was eleven thirty, the building sleepy. In the squad room a single DC sat at his desk, a rookie named Jurow. He did a double take as I entered.

'Can't stay away, huh?'

'Working for God and Country.'

'And overtime.'

I gave him a thumbs-up and went to my computer. I propped the print of the rocking-chair-in-progress against the monitor and opened the Rennert file, scrolling through the flicks Zaragoza had taken at the scene.

Exterior; body; downstairs; second floor.

Attic.

The rocker only appeared in a couple of shots, and when it did, it was off to the side, or out of focus in the background, caught in the frame as Zaragoza captured something of greater evidentiary value.

I called Jurow over.

'Take a look at these and tell me if you think it's the same chair.'

He set down his coffee mug, studied the screen, the print. 'Could be.'

'Not definitely.'

'This one' – the print – 'looks lighter to me.'

'It's unfinished,' I said.

'Hold the phone. This guy has seven thingies. And this one has eight. Right?'

I saw what he meant: spindles. The one on the screen appeared to have fewer, which would blow my theory out of the water.

'It might be the angle,' I said. 'Or this one here has a broken spindle.'

He shrugged. 'You asked. I'm telling you what I see.'

'Yes or no?'

'Gun to my head?' he said. 'Sixty–forty, no.'

'Thanks, man. Have a good night.'

'You too,' he said, mystified.

En route to my apartment, I tried Tatiana. Voicemail yet again.

'Hey,' I said. 'I really need to talk to you. I'll be home in ten minutes. If you get this before, call me. I need to get into your father's house. Call me, please. Thanks.'

Back at my apartment I put all three photos on my coffee table and began pacing around the living room. I kept stopping to stare at the print of the unfinished rocker, straining to match it to the image in my mind of the one in Rennert's attic.

Why was it so hard? I'd just seen the goddamn thing, twenty-four hours ago. Ellis Fletcher had better recall for detail than I did, and it had been more than a decade for him. But he was a professional. His brain trafficked in shapes and colors.

Really, though, I knew I was correct. Had to be. Because the photo solved a problem that had been gnawing at me ever since I'd opened the drawer to find the gun gone.

Why would anyone — either a random burglar or Triplett himself — proceed straight upstairs to the attic? Ignoring the art, the porcelain, furniture, televisions.

He went there with a goal in mind.

He knew what he wanted and where to find it.

He'd seen it before.

He'd *been* there before.

Although Tatiana hadn't said so, I had to believe the same problem had occurred to her. Possibly not. The violation of the break-in left her distraught. Learning Triplett's name had staggered her all over again. She wasn't thinking clearly.

Footsteps thumped up the stairs, uneven gait on the uneven carpet.

I glanced at the clock on my DVR.

Two thirty-nine a.m.

The lock turned and Tatiana entered in a burgundy cashmere sweater, skinny jeans, and heels. She saw me and bristled. 'I said don't wait up.'

'Where've you been? I've been trying to reach you.'

She stooped to remove her shoes. 'I didn't realize I had a curfew.'

'Can I borrow the key to your dad's house?'

She straightened. 'Why?'

'I need to check something.'

'What?'

'Maybe nothing. Can I have it, please?'

She stared at me like I was crazy. I'm sure I looked it.

'What's going on, Clay?'

Hands on hips, eyes blazing.

No way to avoid the truth. I showed her the print. 'That, I believe, is your father's rocking chair.'

'So?' She brought her face closer to the picture. Only then did I realize that she reeked of pot. Green irises, red sclera. Like Christmas come early.

'In the attic,' I said. 'You don't recognize it?'

'I never noticed every piece of furniture he has. It's chaos up there. Does that make me . . . what, unobservant? Why's it matter?'

'It might not,' I said. 'That's why I need to go over there. To find out.'

'You're weird,' she said. 'Who gives a shit?' Giggling. 'You're the *chair*-man.'

I tapped the photo. 'This was made by Julian Triplett. I spoke to a man tonight who knew him personally. He made furniture after he got out of prison.'

A beat. Then her gaze snapped back toward the coffee table. I'd carelessly left the candids of Triplett in plain view.

She said, 'Is that *him*?'

She snatched up one of the prints, gripping it with two hands.

'Careful, please. It's not mine.'

'That's him,' she said. 'God. He's huge. He's a . . . a monster.'

'Tatiana.' I gently pried open her fingers, extracted the print

229

before she could damage it. 'Sit down. Let me get you some water.'

'I don't want any water,' she said, grabbing at my arm. 'I want to look at him.'

I removed the prints to the safety of the kitchen and filled a glass from the tap.

'I *said* I don't want water.'

'You'll feel better.'

'What's that supposed to mean?'

I gave a noncommittal shrug.

'Don't you fucking judge me,' she said.

'I'm not.'

'I am dealing with a lot of shit in my life,' she said.

'I know.'

I don't judge people who get high. Nor do I want to have to reason with them.

I said, 'Please give me the house key.'

She said, 'I'm coming with you.'

On the ride over, she said, 'Just so you know, I was fully intending to wake you up and fuck you.'

'Huh,' I said. 'Rain check?'

She declined to respond.

We pulled up to the house.

'I feel like we were just here,' she said.

'We were.'

I let Tatiana go ahead of me on the stairs, so I could catch her if she fell. Her ass pumped furiously.

In the attic, we switched on lamps, climbed over junk to reach the rocker.

It had one broken spindle in back.

I hadn't noticed before. It was at the extreme left end and it had been sanded flush with the top and bottom rails.

Tatiana gestured for the print of the rocker-in-progress. I handed it to her, watching her eyes flick back and forth, her lips purse and retract in concentration. I'd seen her like this before, on the morning we met.

She said, 'I'm sure there are a billion others out there that look exactly like it.'

A concession, of sorts. She hadn't said *no*.

'Humor me for a second,' I said. 'Say it's the same chair. How'd it get here?'

'The chair fairy brought it.'

'The man I spoke to said Triplett auctioned off some of his pieces for the school benefit. He wasn't sure of this one. Maybe your dad reached out to them.'

'How would he know about it in the first place?'

'He got word Triplett was out of prison and decided to make amends.'

'Amends for what?' She shoved the print at me. 'He did nothing wrong.'

'I'm not saying he did. But maybe he *felt* he did. Several people told me he was broken up. You yourself said he didn't like to talk about it.'

'Yeah, cause it destroyed his life.'

'That's my point. He needed to find a way to deal with it.'

'He did deal with it,' she said. 'He bought a gun. You don't do that if you're feeling guilty, you do it if you're scared.'

'I'm sure he was scared, at one point. But what if he got to know Triplett –'

'Whoa. Whoa. They're not *friends*.'

'Is that impossible?'

'Yes. It is.'

'Why?'

'Because it *is*.'

'Your father was a psychologist,' I said. 'Maybe he saw Triplett as a patient.'

'He didn't have patients. He was a researcher.'

'That doesn't mean he didn't think clinically.'

'*Clinically?* You're a shrink, now? Well, sorry, you need to go to school for that. Who gives a shit? *Chairs?* I don't understand what you're *doing*.'

'Keeping an open mind,' I said. 'Like you asked me to.'

'You made it sound like there was nothing left to think about,' she said. 'First you're telling me he wasn't pushed –'

'He wasn't.'

'Then I don't get what you're trying to achieve. Okay. Fine. They knew each other. They played checkers. Why's it *matter*?'

'That doesn't strike you as significant?'

'What strikes me as significant, Clay, is that a homicidal maniac broke into my father's house and took a *gun*. I mean for God's sake, yesterday you're like, he's on the loose and my life is in danger, now you're putting him and my dad in a fucking buddy comedy –'

'I didn't say any of that.'

She backed away from me. Held out her hands. 'Stop. Please. Stop.'

Her eyes were wet.

I said, 'I didn't –'

'You *implied* it,' she said. 'All right? *Okay?* Is that accurate enough, Mr Officer? I thought you wanted to *help* me.'

'I'm trying to.'

'Then why are we wasting time with stupid shit? You should be looking for him. Whatever.' She pushed on her closed eyes with forefinger and thumb. 'I can't deal with this right now. My head is fucking splitting.'

She brushed past me and went downstairs.

As I reached the freeway on-ramp, she said, 'Take me home, please.'

'To your place?'

She nodded.

'If that's what you want,' I said.

'I do.'

We didn't speak for the rest of the ride.

I pulled up outside her duplex. Tatiana unbuckled herself and opened the door, pausing to glance at me resentfully. 'Are you coming or not?'

I felt briefly lost for words. 'You want me to?'

'I said I want to go home,' she said. 'I didn't say I want to be by myself.'

I sighed and got out of the car.

27

IT WAS my second consecutive late night, and the next day I woke up late. Like the last time I'd stayed over, Tatiana was nowhere to be seen. Somehow I didn't think she'd be bringing breakfast.

Nevertheless, I decided to stick around a bit, in case she did return. I texted to let her know I was up, made myself a cup of tea, and sat on her living room futon. The banker's boxes had been shoved up into one corner like refugees. I laid the ukulele in my lap, plucking at it as I charted the possibilities that had been brewing overnight.

Scenario one: the chairs were not the same.

End of story.

A no-frills explanation, and Tatiana's obvious preference. For years she had conceived of Julian Triplett as a malicious force, nameless and faceless, responsible for everything that had gone wrong in her father's life. Having to redraw the boundaries galled and disoriented her.

Scenario two: the chairs were the same, but Rennert had come into possession of it indirectly – buying it at the school auction, say.

His little secret. Write a check, take the thing home, lug it upstairs, give it a place of honor. An object, hard, undeniable, taking up space where he lived, giving him something tangible to focus on when he meditated on his sins.

No relationship between him and Triplett, other than the fantasies in Walter Rennert's head.

End of story.

Scenario three: the connection between the two men was not slight, but personal and ongoing. I gravitated toward this explanation for the same reasons Tatiana hated it.

How else would Triplett know where Rennert lived?

How had Triplett, a man of limited intelligence and resources, gotten into the house?

Simple, once you assumed a direct link: he knew where the spare key was hidden.

Or – too terrifying for Tatiana to consider – he had a key of his own.

If Triplett and Rennert did have a relationship, what kind?

How far back did it go?

The ugliest question of them all: why did Triplett need a gun?

Why now?

Hearing voices again? Frantic to purge them, by any means necessary?

Another target in mind?

Maybe Rennert, once upon a time, had promised him something. Money. A token of reconciliation, offered rashly. Offered to put him in the will, even.

Triplett's disappointment when his prize didn't materialize.

Hatred toward the true heirs.

Tatiana's face was plastered all over the house.

The gun drawer wasn't the only part of the desk that had been messed with.

The liquor cabinet had been opened.

Abandoned bottles, racked tumblers.

But that wasn't true a few months ago.

A few months ago, there'd also been pills. One of which was an antipsychotic. Prescribed by a urologist who got squirrelly when questioned.

Pills Walter Rennert had no medical reason to take. Pills you took if you were schizophrenic, if you suffered from hallucinations and delusions.

Rennert was a psychologist, not a psychiatrist. He could talk to Triplett for hours, months, years, but he couldn't prescribe medication.

He'd have to get someone to do that for him.

The time had come to pay Louis Vannen, MD, another visit.

Back at my apartment, I texted Nate Schickman the candid of Triplett. Still ten years out of date. But better than twenty.

The rest of the day went to small tasks: stripping sheets off my couch, restocking the fridge, jogging. Waiting for Tatiana to call or write back. By sundown I had yet to hear from her. I pushed it out of my mind and sat down with my laptop.

I'd tried going to Vannen's office and gotten the brush-off. A little more aggression was in order.

If I'd been at work, doing actual work-related stuff, I could've used Accurint. Inside of ten seconds I'd know everything about him. Current address, previous addresses, relatives, associates. But I was at home, on my own time, and he was unlisted, forcing me to get creative.

Using an archived article in a community newsletter ('Local Sisters Turn Old Sweaters into Warm Hugs for Foster Kids'), I was able to connect him to his daughters, both at Stanford, both with hyphenated last names. That led me to Vannen's wife, Suzanne Barnes. Plugging her into a people finder yielded a residential address in Orinda.

The daughters, I hoped, were away at school.

No need to embarrass the old man unduly.

I went to his house.

The same silver BMW sat in the driveway, beside a Lexus SUV. I trotted up the front walk a few minutes after eight p.m.: late enough for them to have finished eating but before they got too far into whatever show they liked to watch together.

He would groan, hit PAUSE.

She would start to get up off the couch.

He'd stop her.

Better he go, that hour.

I stood at the door, listening to faint, lilting voices.

I rang the bell.

The sound cut off.

Inside: *Let me.*

Footsteps. Porch light coming on. Interval, as an eye flitted behind the peephole.

I already had my badge up.

The door swung wide. 'Yes?'

'Dr Vannen?'

'Yes.'

'You don't remember me,' I said, so that he would.

And he did. He drew back half a foot, seeking the safety of his domain. 'I told you before, I can't help you.'

'Actually, that isn't what you said. I asked you about Walter Rennert and you said you didn't know him, which isn't the same thing as saying you can't help me. Either way, it's not true. You did know him and you can help me.'

His wife called, 'Lou? Who's there?'

'Nobody,' he called. To me: 'I don't know who the hell you think you are —'

'Are you okay, honey?'

'One second,' he yelled, his voice cracking.

'Your name was in Rennert's phone,' I said. 'Two numbers, home and cell. So you tell me you didn't know him, I call bullshit on you.'

'This is outrageous,' he said, starting to shut the door.

'When he asked you for the Risperdal,' I said, stopping it, 'who'd he say it was for? I have to think he gave a name, or else you were going to have a problem playing along. You and I both know it wasn't for him. So what did he tell you? "It's for a friend"?'

'Lou.' A woman with a pleasant, round face appeared, tightening her bathrobe. 'What's going on.'

'Evening, ma'am.' I lifted my badge again. 'How are you tonight?'

'Is everything okay?' she said.

'It's fine, honey,' Vannen said. 'Go back. I'll be there in a minute.'

'I'm here about Walter Rennert,' I said to her.

'What about him?' Suzanne Barnes asked. 'Is he okay?'

Vannen's mouth compressed into a line.

'You didn't tell her?' I said to him.

'Tell me what.'

'Dr Rennert passed away,' I said.

She gasped. 'Oh no. How horrible. Poor Walter,' she said. 'Recently?'

'Few months ago. September.'

'God, I had no idea.' Turning to her husband. 'You didn't say anything.'

Vannen said, 'I –'

'I'm sure he was too upset to talk about it,' I said. 'I know they were close.'

'Why didn't you say anything?' Suzanne said to him.

'I apologize for disturbing you,' I said. 'I have a few quick questions for your husband, if it's all right.'

She smiled at me. 'Of course it's all right. Would you like to come in?'

I smiled back. 'I'd love to, thanks.'

Passing the den, I glanced at the paused TV.

'Foyle's War,' I said.

'Are you a fan?' Suzanne asked.

'Great show.'

They saw me into the home office. I asked Suzanne if we might have privacy.

Vannen waited for her footsteps to fade, then glared at me. 'You're a real asshole.'

'I'm an officer of the law,' I said, 'and you're writing bogus scrips and lying to me about it. So let's not start with name-calling.'

A beat.

'They weren't bogus,' he said. 'He told me it was for a nephew of his.'

'And you took him at his word.'

'I decided that if Walter was willing to go out on a limb, then he had a good reason. Of all the drugs people have asked me for over the years – and they ask, believe me, all the time – that's not one I'm going to worry about. He wasn't begging for opioids.'

'Why didn't he go to a psychiatrist?'

'It was a private matter. The kid's out of a job, no health insurance, estranged from his family. What's Walter supposed to do, drop him off at the county clinic?'

Vannen lolled back, laced his fingers behind his head. 'He's a psychologist, not just some layman. I saw I could help and I did. I'd do it again.'

On the wall hung his medical degree as well as various professional certifications. The desk and shelves displayed a variety of pharmaceutical company swag, including a plastic cutaway model of male genitalia. Half of one bookcase belonged to trophies – tiny, cheerless, golden men swinging rackets.

He saw me staring and said, 'We play once a month. Played.'

'You and Rennert? That's how you met?'

He nodded. 'We moved up here in ninety-nine, I joined the club about a year after that, so I knew him – what. Seventeen years, give or take.'

'Did you socialize outside of tennis?'

'We might have a drink together after the game, but not much else. I think he liked that I didn't belong to his usual circle.'

'How long had you two known each other before he asked you for the drugs?'

'I couldn't tell you off the top of my head. A few years.' He smiled to himself. 'It became sort of a running joke between us. 'Gee, Lou, I hate to bother you."'

'You ever meet other members of Rennert's family? His daughter? Wife?'

'No. I think he was divorced by the time we met. Or pretty soon after.'

'And you never met the nephew in question.'

'I never even learned his name. All I can tell you is that Walter cared about him.'

'He said so.'

'He didn't need to. It was obvious. You don't make that kind of request lightly. He knew he was making himself vulnerable by asking me. And, look, we didn't have long discussions, about the nephew or anything else. We met strictly to play. It's an escape for me and for him, too. Only thing Walter would say was, I was being a big help. Some folks respond better than others to antipsychotics. The kid was one of those.'

'He's not getting them now,' I said.

Vannen nodded. 'I realize that.'

'What do you think's happening to him?'

He poked his tongue around in his mouth. 'I prefer not to think about it.'

'Think about it,' I said.

Vannen stared down at his desktop.

'That's why I'm here. I need to find him,' I said. 'So whatever you can remember, any hint of his whereabouts – I need to know.'

I let him take his time. Lot of history to review.

He said, 'There's one thing. I'm not sure it'll help.'

'Go on.'

'Walter called, once, to cancel our game. This was years ago. Very out of character for him; he was a fanatical player. I'm sure I canceled on him a dozen times or more, but he never did. He sounded pretty bothered, so I asked if everything was all right. He said no, his nephew was in trouble and he had to go out of town.'

'What kind of trouble?'

'He didn't say. I said, "Anything I can do . . ." He told me he had it under control. He canceled the next game, as well.'

'Out of town where?'

'I don't know.'

'When was this?' Seeing Vannen hesitate, I said: 'Around two thousand five?'

'Could be.'

'Dr Vannen, are you aware of what happened in Walter Rennert's life before you met him? How he lost his position?'

'Something about his research,' he said. 'I make it my business not to make other people's business my business. If a person comes to me first, all right. But I don't like to pry. I wish I had more to tell you.'

I glanced at the trophies. 'You must be one heck of a tennis player.'

He flexed his hands. 'We all do what we can to stave off death.'

'I spoke to Rennert's primary doctor,' I said. 'He said he played like a maniac.'

'That's one word for it.'

'What word would you use?'

A long silence.

'Punitive,' he said. 'Like he wanted to punish himself.'

28

IN THE days leading up to Thanksgiving, we got slammed at work. I spent the holiday on duty, hours taken up by a hit-and-run that left a sixteen-year-old dead and a fifteen-year-old who shouldn't have been driving on a ventilator. We were short-staffed again, though it wasn't Shupfer causing the crunch, it was Zaragoza. His wife had prevailed upon him to take time off. He was due – overdue – and nobody could stop him, though Vitti chewed him out about the timing.

The sergeant prowled around the squad room in a sour mood. His fantasy team sat in dead last, and his admiration for my coaching had curdled into disdain. He made sure to drop by my desk at least once every couple of hours to harass me, swipe my food, tell me to quit spending so much energy on football and get back to doing real work.

If he only knew.

Tatiana wasn't returning my calls or texts. Nor had I heard back from Paul Sandek, Nate Schickman, or Nicholas Linstad's ex-wife. I was starting to feel unloved.

I missed Tatiana. The challenge of her personality. The landscape of her body.

I could understand her reluctance to probe. In the aftermath of death, you flail around, hoarding mementos. You think you want that: *Any scrap.* But in truth we advance through grief via an act of willful ignorance.

Take your idea of the deceased. Frame and seal it.

New information requires you to update the image. It forces you to smash the glass and unfreeze time. It reminds you that, no matter how much you loved someone, there are things about him you will never know. That uncrossable space between two people, painful in life, widens unbearably.

I'd broken open a disturbing perspective on Tatiana's father – yet continued to dismiss her beliefs about his manner of death.

For her, dredging up the past was a no-win.

But I'd begun. I'd put myself in debt. Not merely to Tatiana. To her father. To Nicholas Linstad. To Donna Zhao. And I knew, better than most, that the dead never forget. On quiet nights, nights of reckoning, they come to collect.

'Coroner's Bureau, Deputy Edison.'

'Yeesss, hello, I need to speak to you, sir, because I have received some very disturbing information, and we need to have a conversation about this, like right away now.'

'Mr Afton? Is that you?'

'Yes and I am sorry to tell you but this is not acceptable.'

'What isn't?'

'I cannot accept this situation and I am very unhappy, *very* unhappy.'

'One second,' I said. 'Can you hold on a second, please?'

'Well okay but we need to talk.'

'We will, I promise, I'm just – gimme a second.'

I hit MUTE, called up the file on Jose Manuel Provencio, skimmed through it. I unmuted the phone. 'Mr Afton.'

'Yes sir.'

'Okay, let's talk about what's bothering you.'

'Yes sir, I am bothered because I just went down to the place where they had him and I was informed that he's not there because they already cremated him already.'

'You went to Cucinelli Brothers.'

'Yes sir, and I'll tell you, I was very surprised because I thought you and me, we had an understanding.'

'Right, but we also agreed that if I hadn't heard from you by a certain –'

'And so that, that is, what. He's in a *jar*? I'm sorry, but that is unacceptable, I cannot accept that.'

'Hang on, please, Mr Afton. Let's review this together, okay?' I moved the phone to my other ear. 'Last time you and I spoke, you were getting together funds to cover the cost of burial. You sounded like you were ready to move. I don't know what happened in the interim, but I get a call from Mr Cucinelli and he tells me you never followed up.'

'I was, I was doing that.'

'I attempted to reach you, more than once. I tried the number I had for you, I left messages. My hands are tied. I authorized them to proceed with a county indigent –'

'Excuse me, sir.'

'I'm sorry if you're unhappy with that outcome, but –'

'Excuse me. Sir. Excuse me, please.'

'Go ahead.'

He said, 'I was in the process of assembling the funds.'

'Okay.'

'And I got, okay, *delayed*. Okay? So, but I was handling it.'

'I get that, but if you tell me it's all set, and then it turns out there's going to be a holdup, I need to know that. I'm working in the dark here.'

'I asked you to wait.'

'I did wait,' I said. 'I waited six months. What happened?'

'I had a situation and I was unavailable,' he said.

'Why didn't you call me?'

'Well, okay, listen, I was not in a position to do that.'

'Uh-huh,' I said. 'Hang on a second, please.'

I muted him again and clicked over to the main Sheriff's Department server.

On October seventh – days after our last conversation, in which he assured me he was on top of things – Samuel Afton pleaded no contest to a charge of possession of a controlled substance and was booked into Santa Rita Jail to begin a forty-five-day sentence.

I came back on the line. 'Hi, Mr Afton. I completely understand why you're upset. Unfortunately, this is what we're looking at. I'm sorry, but I can't undo it. We do have his remains, and I'm happy to arrange for you to –'

'What do I want that for?'

'Well,' I said, 'this way you could bury them when the time is right for you.'

'Did I ask for your advice? I didn't ask for it. No, you don't say nothing.'

I did not reply.

'Hello?'

I shut my eyes. 'I'm here.'

He paused. 'You did the wrong thing.'

'Mr Afton,' I said, but I was talking to a dead line.

I set the receiver down. Immediately it rang again.

I jabbed the speakerphone. 'Coroner's Bureau,' I barked.

'Eh. May I please speak to Clay Edison?'

It was Paul Sandek.

I picked up. 'Hi. Sorry. I'm here.'

'Clay? You sounded like somebody else.'

'It's been a long week.'

'Oh. Well, hopefully I can make it better for you.'

'You got the files.'

'Only some of them,' he said. 'I'm sorry about the delay. It got a bit weird, actually. I'll tell you about it when I see you. Dinner tomorrow? Theresa's making stew.'

I glanced at Vitti, stalking the floor like a big disgruntled toddler. 'I might be on the late side.'

I didn't make it to the Sandeks' till a quarter to nine.

'It's perfectly fine,' he said, dismissing my apology and leading me into the kitchen. 'We saved you some.'

I sat down and right away felt at ease – like putting on an old bathrobe. So many hours spent in this room: studying at the breakfast nook when my apartment got to be too loud and the library felt too lonely. Talking to Paul or his wife or the both of them about the meaning of life. Two smart adults I respected, hearing me out and taking my fears seriously.

Now I saw the same cream-colored wall tiles, every third

embossed with a different farm animal. An espresso machine, identical to the one in Sandek's office, had joined other counter appliances lucky enough to have received tenure.

Theresa Sandek pecked me on the cheek and took a cling-wrapped bowl from the fridge. 'Let me heat it up first.'

Same maternal instinct. Theresa had a doctorate of her own; she taught at the business school. Around me, though, it was always food and comfort.

'Don't bother,' I said. 'I'm starving.'

'It's better hot.'

'She's right,' Sandek said.

'I'm always right.'

'She's always right,' he said, taking the bowl and opening the microwave.

A voice from the living room said, 'Clay?'

I poked my head out. A young woman was coming down the stairs. She wore square-toed canvas slip-ons and jeans, a bright-blue flannel shirt that offset a swarm of glossy blond curls – bobbed, not pulled back carelessly like I remembered.

She had changed in a lot of respects.

'Amy,' I said.

She gave me a hug. 'It's so good to see you.'

'You too.'

'I can't believe how long it's been,' she said. 'How are you?'

'Busy,' I said. 'In a good way. You?'

'Same.'

'Your dad said you're almost done with your doctorate.'

'You know what ABD stands for.'

' "All But Dissertation." '

' "A Big Disappointment." '

From the kitchen, Sandek called, 'Not true.'

'You cut your hair,' I said.

'I did?' she said. 'I guess I did. It was a while ago. I wanted "professorial". Instead I got 'preemptive lurch toward middle age".'

'It's nice,' I said.

'Thanks.' Curls tossed. Teeth flashed. 'I'm sorry I can't stay and catch up. I'm meeting a friend for a drink. Nobody told me you were coming.'

'I didn't want to spoil the surprise,' Sandek called.

I made jazz hands. 'Surprise.'

Amy smiled. 'I'd love to hear more about what you're doing, though. What's your email address?'

I gave it to her. 'Are you around next week?'

'Sunday-night red-eye,' she said. 'I have to TA on Monday morning.'

'She's back for Christmas,' Sandek called.

Amy mimed strangling him, then smiled again and squeezed my arm. 'Nice seeing you.'

'Safe travels.'

She grabbed her jacket off the sofa and went.

Sandek called, 'Stew's on.'

I lingered briefly, examining the negative space created by Amy's departure.

'Awesome,' I called, heading into the kitchen.

I found it telling that neither Paul nor Theresa attempted to stop me from taking my bowl to the sink and washing it. I belonged. 'Delicious,' I said. 'Thanks so much.'

'Pleasure,' Theresa said. 'Can I get you anything else? We have leftover meatloaf.'

'I was going to eat that for lunch,' Sandek said.

'Paul. He's our guest.'

'I was going to make a sandwich.'

'I'm good, thanks,' I said. I ran a dish towel over the bowl, placed it in the cupboard.

Sandek and I adjourned to the living room sectional. From his work bag he produced a rubber-banded photocopy of the review committee's report.

'Strings were pulled,' he said.

'I appreciate it.' I riffled the document; it ran to three hundred fifteen heavily footnoted pages. 'You read it?'

'Not to the end. I wanted to get it to you ASAP. The parts I did see were interesting.'

'How so?'

'I won't bias you,' he said. 'I'll let you draw your own conclusions.'

Theresa walked through en route to bed. 'I left you something on the counter.'

'Thanks again,' I said. 'Have a good night.'

'I'll be there soon,' Sandek said.

She went upstairs.

'You also asked for the file on Rennert's experiment,' Sandek said. 'I didn't know this, because now we do everything online, but they keep all the old paper. IRBs, raw data, reimbursement forms, and so on, boxed up at an offsite facility.' He fished in his bag, handed me a single sheet of paper. 'That's the reference number. I put in the request and got an email back saying the file was unavailable.'

'What's that mean, unavailable?'

'That's what I wondered. I spoke to the social sciences librarian, who spoke to offsite, who told her there's a gap on the shelf where the box ought to be.'

'Who was the last person to check it out?'

'She wouldn't tell me,' Sandek said. 'Borrowing histories are confidential.'

'Damn. Think it was Rennert?'

'Your guess is as good as mine,' he said. 'I'm sure he wasn't the only person interested in it. There was a lawsuit, remember. They might be more responsive to a request from law enforcement.'

'They might be less responsive, too.'

'Always a possibility,' he said.

'I don't mean to sound ungrateful.' I held up the report. 'This is fantastic.'

He grinned. 'When do I get my badge and gun?'

The 'something' Theresa had left on the counter was a meatloaf sandwich, wrapped in foil. On it she had written in blue Sharpie: FOR CLAY!!!!

'Treachery,' Sandek said, 'thy name is Theresa.'

I reached for the sandwich but he snatched it away. 'We'll play for it.'

Out in the driveway, I eyed the hoop hanging askew over the garage door. No external lighting, just starlight to shoot by.

'You're not worried about waking your neighbors?' I said.

Sandek strode across the street, jouncing a basketball.

'We'll keep it quick,' he said. 'PIG instead of HORSE.'

He stepped onto the opposite curb, spun on his heel, and drilled it. Forty-footer.

I set my backpack down and went to collect the ball. 'You've been practicing.'

'Goddamn right I have.' He pointed to the curb. 'Your shot.'

I crossed the street. He stepped aside, yielding the spot to me.

I hesitated. 'Do I have to start with my back to the basket?'

'In the spirit of hospitality, I'll say no.'

All the same, I missed by a country mile.

'This is not fair,' I said, jogging after the rebound.

'Don't talk to me about fair,' he said. 'That's my fucking sandwich. *P.*'

29

THE FIRST thing I did when I got home was order Sandek a plastic sheriff's badge and pistol. To qualify for free shipping, I also bought him a child's ten-gallon hat and a cookbook with a hundred and one recipes for meatloaf.

It was too late to start reading the Psych Department's internal report. Sunday I got called out on another homeless man, dead in an alley behind a machine shop on 12th Street in Oakland. This one was ID'd as 'Big John' by his fellow street people. Five-three and ninety-nine malnourished pounds. By day's end, I'd failed to make any headway on next of kin, and I left the office feeling thrashed but eager.

I sat on my couch, opened the report; turned the last page at one a.m.

My conclusion: Tatiana was right, perhaps more so than she realized. Her father had done nothing wrong.

Sandek had heard that the review committee placed partial blame on Nicholas Linstad. Truth turned out to be more interesting than rumor. More or less *all* the blame went on him. The experiment had been conducted in Rennert's lab, under his auspices, but Linstad had been the doer, his advisor a remote presence.

They'd worked together on one previous paper. A lot of profs in that situation would take first authorship, but Rennert had done the ethical thing, giving Linstad credit.

For their second collaboration, Linstad took over wholesale. He devised the idea for the study and drafted the initial proposal.

The subjects, thirty-seven males between the ages of fourteen and eighteen, began by taking a memory test. For the next two months, they came into the lab on a weekly basis. Half of them played twenty minutes of a violent video game, half a nonviolent game. Following that, each group was further divided into two subgroups, one performing a neutral task, the other receiving thirty minutes of unspecified 'memory training'.

Here was Edwina Triplett's 'tutoring' – useless beyond the confines of the Cal Psych Department.

At the end of eight weeks, the kids were retested. Linstad's hypothesis was that exposure to the violent game would diminish the kids' memories and mute the effects of the tutoring. In order: nonviolent-plus-training would do best; violent-no-training would do worst; the other two groups, somewhere in the middle.

The design sounded convoluted to me, and the committee agreed, labeling it 'riddled with confounding variables'. Departmental ass-covering; no one had objected the first time around, when the proposal passed the human subjects panel.

By week five, scholarly concerns were rendered irrelevant:

Julian Triplett slaughtered Donna Zhao and the experiment came to a crashing halt.

The report referred to the murder euphemistically as 'the events of October 31, 1993'.

Every kid who applied for the study was required first to complete a psychological screen called the Meeks School Checklist. The committee devoted twenty pages to dissecting its strengths and weaknesses. While the test did a fair job of detecting learning disorders, it was not sensitive to other types of mental illness, certainly not early signs of psychosis.

Bearing in mind the goal of the experiment, it seemed unreasonable to fault Linstad for choosing to use the Meeks. Why would he think to be on the lookout for latent schizophrenia? But that wasn't the real problem.

The real problem was that Linstad had personally screened Julian Triplett and rejected him, only to change his mind and allow the boy in.

The committee comprised five members. Two were psychology professors; I had taken classes with both of them, found one okay, the other an insufferable ass. In addition, there was Michael Filson, dean of the College of Letters and Science, a former cognitive psych prof. A UC regent named S. Davis Auerbach. Finally, outside legal counsel, Sussana Khoury, of Stanwick and Green, LLC.

Reviewing Triplett's results on the Meeks, the committee noted that Linstad had only scored eleven of the twenty items.

His explanation, verbatim: *Based on this individual's responses and his behavior during the interview, I felt that he was unfit to participate in the study. I therefore discontinued the interview early.*

They continued to press: What did he see that made Julian Triplett appear unfit?

Linstad gave several evasive replies before admitting that Triplett had muttered to himself throughout the interview 'in an incoherent manner'.

Then how, they demanded to know, had Triplett ended up in the study anyway?

I believed he could benefit from what we were offering, education-ally. It was always my intention to throw out his data.

A nice guy, wanting to help an underprivileged kid.

The committee asked Linstad to address the allegation that he had taken an inappropriate interest in Triplett; the two of them had been seen walking into the Free Speech Movement Café together.

Linstad flatly denied any such contact had ever occurred.

The man got him a burger.

Edwina had said that to me, and I'd taken her to mean Rennert. Now I wondered. Though I didn't remember burgers on the menu at the FSM Café.

In any event, the committee abruptly dropped the line of inquiry, as though steering itself out of dangerous waters.

There was, I noted, a troubling lack of information about or concern for the victim. The committee spent more page space on video games than on Donna Zhao.

Flipping back to the title page, I read the date.

August 3, 1997. Right after the Zhaos settled their law-suit against the university, and Walter Rennert handed in his notice.

Another CYA move, perhaps: delaying release of the report,

minimizing mention of Donna, lest the Zhaos' attorneys find something to exploit in front of a jury.

Like most committees, they were amoral.

By the report's end, their recommendations felt inevitable.

Nicholas Linstad was suspended indefinitely from the PhD program.

A lighter touch for Professor Rennert: a scolding, for not being more aware of the actions of his staff; a suggested leave of absence, temporary and voluntary.

He'd never been asked to resign. Yet he had.

That meshed with my sense of Rennert as a man crushed by guilt.

Could lead to savior fantasies.

Extending a hand to a psychotic killer. Buying a chair. Soliciting iffy prescriptions.

A relationship founded on pity and shame.

I lay in bed, my mind afire, sifting through connections, motivations, actions.

One thing was clear: this research, aimed at curbing violence, had resulted in a hell of a lot of violence.

Too amped up to sleep, I clawed my laptop toward me.

The game Linstad selected for his media stimulus was called *Bloodbrick: 3D*.

Some shoot-em-up dealie.

I think my son had it on Nintendo.

I guess I should count myself lucky he didn't kill nobody.

In thirty seconds I'd found it freely available on a Korean website dedicated to preserving 'classic vintage arcade nostalgic and video games'. You didn't need a Nintendo console. You didn't have to download anything. Some helpful, under-employed dude sitting in an internet café in Seoul had taken the time to convert the old code into Java. Now anyone could experience the two-hundred-fifty-six-color glory of *Bloodbrick: 3D* anywhere in the world, right from the comfort of his or her own keyboard.

I decided to see what all the fuss was about.

The game took a familiar format: first-person shooter, the player as a disembodied hand, clutching a weapon, hovering at the bottom of the screen. Dropped into an urban maze popu-lated by a variety of baddies, you had to blast your way to safety, receiving points for every direct hit. Targeting an innocent lost you points, as I discovered when I inadvertently mowed down a woman pushing a baby carriage.

By today's standard, the blocky graphics and crinkly sound sucked. Nevertheless I recoiled in disgust, watching mother and child shred into pixelated strips, screeching in tinny agony for a few seconds before dissolving to nothingness.

All the same, I found it hard to believe that twenty minutes, once a week, could inspire anyone to pick up a knife and kill. Kids in 1993 saw far worse stuff, far more often.

Nonpsychotic kids.

But most mentally ill people – the vast, statistical majority – weren't violent.

I closed the laptop, stretched toward my nightstand to shut off the lamp.

I had a text from Tatiana, five minutes old.

R u up

I slid to reply. Yes

Did I wake u she wrote.

No I was up. Whats going on where are you

Her answer, slow in coming, had me scratching my head.

Protons

?

*portland she wrote fucking autocorrect

The tone, so nonchalant, taking for granted that her being in Portland was any easier for me to accept than her being inside an atom smasher.

Whats in portland I wrote.

Friends

I didn't know you had friends there

Of course I didn't. I didn't know anything about her, not really.

Yup she wrote.

I'd given her an opening to explain; she'd passed. I chose not to force the issue. Ok when are you back

Don't know

I need to tell you some things

About

I read the psych dept report I wrote. Also spoke to Vannen

Please can u just leave it alone

I started to type a reply; reconsidered and dialed her instead. She picked up after half a ring.

'Hey,' I said.

Amid the rustle of sheets, she whispered, 'Hang on.'

'First off, I wanted to say that if you're feeling like I –'

'Hang on.'

Her voice, breathy, then the sound of a door closing. When she spoke again there was a ceramic echo; she'd gone into a bathroom or kitchen. 'It can't wait until the morning?'

'You texted me,' I said.

'I know, I – look, I recognize that it's my fault you're doing this.'

'Doing what?'

'Digging. I provoked you, but I was being –'

'You didn't provoke me.'

'I did. But I'm over it. I don't want to hear it,' she said. 'I *can't* hear it, right now.'

I heard a man's voice, muffled and sleep-addled: 'Baby?'

A knock; a lull; a blossoming hollow-point of silence.

'Just a second,' she called.

'Who're you talking to?' the man said.

'Nobody,' she called.

'Come back to bed.'

'In a *second*.'

'You know what,' I said, 'we can talk later.'

'Clay –'

'Enjoy Portland.'

I hung up and shut off my phone.

I slept poorly, waking at dawn and stumbling out to my living room. Gray sun smeared the soiled carpet. I needed to call my landlord, have it steam-cleaned.

Clinging to the corner of my TV was Tatiana's note.

She needed to get out. Clear her head. I shouldn't wait up.

She's what you'd call a runner.

I removed the note and crumpled it.

In the kitchen I opened the cabinet above the fridge. At the back of the highest shelf sat the plastic evidence bag containing her father's whisky tumbler. I fetched it down, stood turning it in my hands.

You made it sound like there was nothing left to think about.

Yes, I had.

I don't get what you're trying to achieve.

I started to carry the tumbler to the trash.

I thought you wanted to help me.

Everything I'd told myself, about owing a debt to the dead — it was true, too.

But there was something else at play.

Me.

No longer relegated to setting up shots.

Finding myself wide open, behind the three-point line.

I tore the bag open, took the tumbler out, went back to my living room.

I put the tumbler on the mantel, in full view of the front door.

I'd see it whenever I walked in, and I'd remember.

Not for her.

Not for them.

For me.

30

NICHOLAS LINSTAD's ex-wife, Olivia Harcourt, lived in Piedmont, an island of privilege surrounded by the socioeconomic typhoon that is Oakland. We don't take many coroner's calls there. I'd been inside one home, two years ago, an eye-popping Dutch Colonial where a ninety-year-old society doyenne had drowned in her pool.

Olivia Harcourt's place made that one look like a cottage. Soaring walls of dove gray peeked through old-growth redwoods as I leaned out to ring the call box. A large curlicued *S* emblazoned the gate panels. I hadn't yet figured out what it stood for when they swung back.

I inched up the drive, around the bend, took in a clearer view.

Olivia Harcourt lived in a castle.

By 'castle' I don't mean that it was really big or that it had a weak medieval flavor. I mean stone, mortar, towers, heraldic flags, a gatehouse, a drawbridge. The turrets – I could see three – had those skinny little windows cut in the masonry, for archers to shoot through.

I couldn't see any archers, but that didn't mean they weren't there.

A cobbled parking circle, a gushing fountain. The lady of the manor stood in the shade of a marble pergola. In her late forties, she was attractive in a print ad sort of way, blond-haired and blade-faced, wearing a sleeveless blouse that showed off taut, tan arms. Her face had been reengineered and chemically relaxed, but subtly, and to good effect. Wide-cut slacks gave her a sunken appearance from behind, calling to mind an old remark of Moffett's. *Legs for days but ass for the next five minutes.*

She met me with a winning smile. She was prepared. It had taken me weeks to get past her snotty assistant.

'Thanks for agreeing to see me,' I said.

She said, 'How could I say no?' As if consent had been immediate. 'It's not every day I get a call from the police.'

Walking beneath the raised portcullis, we entered a stone corridor adorned with period weaponry. Broadswords, a lance, a crossbow, a pair of battle-axes, and a bunch more I couldn't name. Tied to each was a gigantic Christmas candy cane. Grievous bodily harm, followed by tetanus, and tooth decay.

Olivia Harcourt saw me ogling. A well-worn smile. She was used to explaining.

'The structure is based on a thirteenth-century monastery in Toulouse. My parents summered there one year and liked it so much they decided to copy it.'

The *S* on the gates: Sowards.

'It's not a hundred percent accurate,' she said.

'No monks.'

'Indoor plumbing.'

The hall opened into a cloister lined with gothic arches. I saw tinsel. Birds flitted across the gleaming, hazy courtyard.

I said, 'Is that a well?'

She crooked a finger and we detoured. I peered down at cloudy water, specks of vegetal matter floating on the surface. Dragonflies mated in midair.

'It's drinkable,' she said. 'We've had it tested. But I wouldn't recommend it.'

Inside the great room, we sat in high-backed chairs. A unicorn tapestry topped the fireplace; there was a fire going. Too close to a fifteen-foot fir awaiting ornaments. A uniformed maid emerged from behind a suit of armor to serve tea on a silver tray.

From the photos scattered about, I deduced that Olivia Harcourt had had her fill of lanky Scandinavians: her current husband was squat and swarthy and thick-necked, traits he'd passed to their children, son and daughter alike.

Aside from the maid, who vanished as silently as she had appeared, joining us was a silver-haired man dressed in a fitted blue suit, white shirt, and gray tie one shade lighter than the castle's stone.

He introduced himself as Robert Dutton Stanwick, Mrs Harcourt's attorney.

'Of Stanwick and Green, LLC,' I said.

He puffed up a bit. 'That's right.'

'I hope you don't mind,' Olivia Harcourt said.

I smiled. 'Don't imagine there's a choice.'

'None at all,' the lawyer said.

Olivia crossed her legs, a maneuver that took a long time and ought to have involved the FAA.

'Before we begin,' Stanwick said, 'I'd like to clarify the purpose of this meeting.'

'Information gathering,' I said.

'To what end?'

Expecting I'd be called upon to explain myself, I'd assembled a curated version of the facts.

'You think some person or persons unknown may have been responsible for Mrs Harcourt's ex-husband's death,' Stanwick said.

'I'm exploring alternative explanations for his death.'

I watched Olivia for a reaction: nothing.

Stanwick said, 'What's it got to do with my client?'

'You knew him,' I said to Olivia.

'Once upon a time,' she said.

'Was there anyone you can think of who might have wanted to harm him?'

'Besides me, you mean.'

Stanwick said, 'Nothing my client says should be construed as an admission of any kind.'

'Relax, please, Bob, I'm joking . . . I honestly wouldn't know, Officer. Nicholas and I didn't have much contact after the divorce.'

'Did it end on bad terms?' I asked.

'It was a divorce,' Stanwick said. 'It's on bad terms by definition.'

'Not true,' Olivia said. 'I have a girlfriend who engineered a very meaningful uncoupling. It actually brought them closer together than they'd ever been. Isn't that remarkable?'

'Is that what occurred between you and Nicholas?'

'No comment,' Stanwick said.

'I can answer for myself, thank you,' Olivia said. 'We tried our hardest to be graceful, but it wasn't perfect. There were tears.'

'What was your reaction when you heard that he'd died?'

'Don't answer that,' Stanwick said.

She recrossed her legs. 'You'll have to excuse him, Officer. Bob's always been a strong advocate for my interests.'

Warm smile at the lawyer, who grunted bashfully.

'Well, let's see,' Olivia Harcourt said. 'I have to put myself back in that frame of mind. It feels like another life . . . My reaction? I suppose I thought: *Too bad for him.*'

'You weren't still angry at him.'

'Don't answer that.'

'No, I wasn't angry,' she said. 'Not anymore. I'd moved on. I found love again. I had my children. My life was – is – very full. I was barely twenty when I married Nicholas. Swept up. We all do things we regret when we're young.'

The lawyer ground a fist in a palm.

'If it wasn't an accident,' Olivia said, 'what do you think happened?'

'I'm exploring several possibilities.'

'A little unfair of you, don't you think? Come in and ask me questions and yet you won't answer mine.'

'My assumption is that if someone did harm him, they had a reason to do so.'

'I'm going to insist we put an end to this,' Stanwick said. 'You're just trying to scare her, and I won't accept that.'

'I'm not, sir,' I said. 'As I said, I'm interested in Mrs Harcourt's perspective, and I appreciate her letting me into her home.'

'Then start showing some respect,' Stanwick said.

'More tea?' Olivia said.

'Yes, please,' I said.

She plucked a golden bell from the end table and jangled it. The maid reappeared.

'Officer . . .' She looked to me.

'Edison,' I said. 'Deputy, actually.'

'Sandra, Deputy Edison would like more tea.'

'Yes, Mrs.'

'And you know what, I'll have a glass of rosé. From the bottle in the fridge. Thank you, Sandra.'

I heard Ming's voice: *Two wineglasses.*

'Unless you'd like some, too,' Olivia said to me.

'Good with tea, thanks.'

'Bob?' Olivia said.

The lawyer shook his head and fooled with his tie. The maid went off.

I said, 'Am I correct that you were paying alimony to your ex-husband?'

'Well, he wasn't in a position to pay me,' Olivia said.

Stanwick unsnapped his briefcase and produced a binder-clipped document. 'We were more than generous with him,' he said, handing it to me.

It was the Linstads' mediated marriage settlement, dated January 4, 1997.

He'd come prepared, too.

'Let me save you some time,' Stanwick said. 'Mrs Harcourt and Mr Linstad agree to the dissolution of their marriage according to the following terms as established by their prenuptial agreement' – out came another document, dated July 17,

268

1992. 'One, in the event that the marriage is terminated within thirty-six months of its taking effect, Mr Linstad waives any claim to spousal support. Should the marriage be terminated subsequent to that point, Mr Linstad is granted spousal support of seventy-five hundred dollars a month for a term of twenty-four months, which term may not be extended, and after which he waives any further claim to spousal support.'

So Ming had it wrong. Or Linstad's father had gotten it wrong and misinformed Ming. The millstone around Olivia Harcourt's neck was far smaller than they'd believed, had long dropped off by the time Linstad died.

More to the point, seeing her in her natural habitat, I realized that the millstone was no millstone. She probably spent that much every month on scented candles.

'Two,' Stanwick said, 'and bear in mind that this was *not* part of the prenuptial, but an adjunct thereto, offered voluntarily by Mrs Harcourt as a gesture of good faith – Mr Linstad is granted full title to the property located at twenty-three thirty-six Le Conte Avenue.'

'The duplex,' I said.

'Mm,' Olivia said.

'You paid for it originally.'

'I paid for everything,' she said.

'And then you gave it to him?'

She shrugged. 'For all practical purposes, he was already living there.'

'While you were separated.'

'Well before that,' she said. 'We purchased it in – I don't know. Bob?'

Stanwick said, 'September ninety-two.'

'Thank you, Bob.' To me: 'The idea was that Nicholas would have someplace close by campus to sleep when he worked late. Little did I know.'

'He was using it for other activities,' I said.

She beamed. 'Bravo, Deputy Edison.'

The maid brought the tea and a generous balloon glass of wine and retreated.

'I'm sorry to be dense,' I said, 'but why give him the property, at that point? It's not like he deserved it.'

'I wanted him to have a permanent reminder,' Olivia said.

'Of his cheating.'

She sipped, dabbed at her mouth with a linen napkin. 'More that he'd never earned anything on his own.'

'Like he gave a shit one way or the other,' Stanwick said. 'Free real estate.'

'I know,' Olivia said. 'You were right.' To me: 'Bob didn't want me to do it.'

'I told you at the time it was a waste.'

'C'est la vie,' she said, raising her glass. 'I gave Nicholas a gift in order to punish him. Never in a million years did I imagine it would actually work.'

A gleeful note had appeared in her voice.

Money didn't have to be the motive.

There was always spite.

She took a deep gulp of wine.

I asked how she'd found out about Linstad's affair.

'A friend of mine spotted them at a bar in San Francisco, groping each other in a booth. She didn't tell me for months.

She didn't want to upset me. But she got drunk at a party and let it slip. She felt awful, apologizing right and left. "I don't judge, I don't know what kind of arrangement you two have." Believe that? "Arrangement." '

Her laughter disintegrated, and her posture caved, leaving her gazing at the fire in wonderment. 'Looking back, I can hardly believe my*self*. I mean, it seems so obvious now. He wasn't especially sneaky. But I loved him. I really did. I was hypnotized.'

I couldn't envision her successfully pushing a man Linstad's size down a flight of stairs. Then again, if you rewound ten years – pumped them full of Cabernet – charged her up with righteous indignation –

'It's not your fault,' Stanwick said.

She yawned. 'It is and it isn't. I was young and vain. I thought I was immune. He'd never risk losing me. But now I think that was at the heart of it. No danger, no pleasure.'

'He was a fool,' Stanwick said. 'A woman like her? What kind of idiot goes and screws that up?'

'Thank you, Bob.'

'It's true,' he said.

'Of course, Nicholas denied everything when I confronted him. He said it wasn't him, my friend must've confused him with someone else. I wanted to believe him. Then I started to wonder about the late nights.'

'We hired a private detective,' Stanwick said.

'He was taking his mistress to the duplex,' I said.

'Among other places,' Olivia said.

'At the risk of offending you,' I said, 'can you tell me her name?'

'I never wanted to know. I saw the pictures and that was enough.'

She paused, chewing at her bottom lip. 'Nicholas . . . He had such funny taste, you know? You imagine – if you ever do think about your husband cheating on you, and I suppose most women do, whether they admit it or not. But. You imagine it's going to be with somebody prettier, or – I don't know. At least then there would be a . . . not a *reason*, but at least it would make sense, on some level. And – I don't mean to sound small about it. But she was . . . I'm not sure how best to put it.'

'Dumpy,' Stanwick said.

'Yes,' she said. She tossed back the rest of her wine, scrunched her face, reached for the bell. 'A dumpy little girl.'

The maid appeared. 'Another, Mrs?'

'Yes, please, thank you, Sandra.'

I said, 'Do you think I could talk to the PI?'

'I can't see why that's necessary,' Stanwick said.

'I'm looking for anyone who knew Nicholas,' I said. 'Anyone who might've had a reason to harm him.'

Olivia said, 'Bob will give you the phone number.'

'I'll need your written permission.'

She looked at Stanwick. He said, 'Fine. Are we done here?'

'Almost,' I said. 'Ms Harcourt, could you please tell me about Nicholas's relationship with Walter Rennert.'

'What about it?' Olivia said.

'Were they close?'

'Walter was very fond of him.'

'It wasn't mutual?'

'I always got the impression he considered Nicholas sort of a

272

surrogate son. Nicholas told me Walter didn't always get along with his own kids. As if he was explaining his own feelings.'

There you go: new data.

I said, 'There was a university committee that looked into the circumstances surrounding the murder. Maybe you've seen their report.'

Stanwick stiffened.

'I have,' she said. 'After the divorce –'

'Totally on the up and up,' the lawyer said. Meaning: skids had been greased. 'If there's nothing more –'

I said, 'It seemed to throw a lot of the blame on your ex-husband's shoulders. I'm wondering if Walter tried to intervene on his behalf.'

Stanwick clapped his hands. 'That's it. We're finished.'

I sat there.

'You've had your time, Deputy.' He meant it, now. 'Move along.'

I stood up as the maid reentered with a refill containing the second half of the bottle. Olivia Harcourt had changed her mind: she shook her head and waved the glass away. She stared at the floor.

'If you do speak to the girl,' she said, 'tell her I said hello.'

31

THE PI Bob Stanwick had hired was named Faith Raine. She worked out of a room above a ramen shop in downtown Oakland, spitting distance from the county courthouse. Thick tendrils of steam laced with MSG wafted up through the floor vents.

Olivia Harcourt had given me the impression that her ex-husband had screwed up but the once. Either she was still in denial or she was downplaying her humiliation. Or else Stanwick had hidden the truth from her. Nicholas Linstad was a repeat offender. In five months of surveillance, Raine had photographed him meeting with four different women.

As she laid out the evidence – names and addresses, grainy zoom-lens snaps – I felt the hair on the back of my neck stand up.

I asked Raine if she knew about any affairs prior to 1997.

She shook her head. 'I'd assume there were plenty, though. Guys like him, it's an instinct. They're collectors.'

He had such funny taste.

I don't mean to sound small about it.

A dumpy little girl.

Olivia couldn't say what she meant out loud, of course. That would be racist.

274

Put a pint of rosé in her, though – she couldn't stop herself from saying *something*.

All the women Nicholas Linstad had collected were in their early twenties, with straight black hair and a medium build. They all stood in the neighborhood of five foot three.

All four were Asian or Asian American.

A perfect description of Donna Zhao.

Li Hsieh, Donna's former roommate, worked as a supply chain manager for a supermarket conglomerate headquartered in Hong Kong. I pulled her email address from the UC Berkeley alumni database. In the murder file, Ken Bascombe had noted that she spoke minimal English, so I kept my questions to her simple and direct.

As it turned out, her English was just fine – vastly improved since her days at Cal, a point she herself made in her initial reply.

I didn't speak with the police, I was embarrassed they wouldn't understand me she wrote. *Wendy was American, I thought it would be better for her to talk to them.*

Unsatisfied by her own excuse, she went on to offer another.

Donna's family was very traditional. Every night her mother called to make sure she was at home studying. They got angry when she switched her major from business to psychology. They wanted to bring her back to Beijing but she convinced them to let her stay. They didn't know she had a boyfriend, they would not approve, it's a big distraction. I don't think she discussed it with Wendy either, they were not close. She spoke to me a few times. She was unhappy because he did not respect her. I told her it's better to find a man who shows you respect, but she said she loved him. I never met him.

She would not tell me his name, she was afraid her parents would find out.

There was another, more powerful reason for Li Hsieh not to raise the subject of Donna Zhao's boyfriend, with the police or anyone else: he was a married man.

This is a very shameful thing. I did not want to cause any more pain to Donna's family. If they found out they would be very embarrassed and angry, it would be to them like she died another time. The police caught the person who was responsible, I decided to forget about it.

Ken Bascombe had retired to Crockett, a waterfront enclave north of Richmond. For not much money, you could get a neat little condo with bay views – not San Francisco Bay, granted, and you had to overlook the refinery. But to a lot of ex-cops, some water is better than no water. I know guys who have dumped their life savings into a boat or a beach cottage, when really what they need is ten years of therapy.

Still, as far as coping mechanisms go, almost anything beats liquor.

Bascombe answered the door with highball in hand. Meaty, with a seamed, sunburnt face and a good head of hair, some gray but mostly brown. His arms were thick; bowling pin legs stuck out from cargo shorts. 'Yeah?'

'I'm Clay Edison,' I said.

He squeezed the doorframe. A gold bracelet swung on his left wrist, links rattling.

'You said I could swing by today,' I said.

He hadn't meant it. Or hadn't expected me to show.

He wobbled, turned, and went inside, leaving the door open.

The theme was tourist-trap nautical: rope and lanterns, a bar cart fashioned from two ship's wheels. He pointed me toward the sofa and fell into a La-Z-Boy.

His expression never changed as I spoke. When I gave him a printout of the email from Li Hsieh, he scanned it impassively, reaching the end far too quickly to have read it.

I said, 'I can't prove she's talking about Linstad. But overall, it's a good fit. He worked with Donna. She assisted him on the study. She matches his preferred physical type.'

Hard to say which of us was more uncomfortable. I'd figured it would be an easier conversation in person, but that meant having to look him in the eye. Ask him to consider the possibility that he'd stumbled during the most significant case of his career.

He wasn't looking me in the eye.

He was looking anywhere but at me.

He folded the page in half and waggled it between two loose fingers. 'I'm waiting for the part where you tell me why any of this matters a shit.'

'I got in touch with one of the women Linstad messed around with,' I said, retrieving it and returning to my place on the sofa. 'Tammy Wong. She said Linstad once went at her, physically. Held her against a wall and got up in her face. I haven't heard back from the other two, but it wouldn't surprise me if they said something similar.'

Bascombe said nothing.

'If so, it feels like a pattern.'

'Big if.'

'Right, but ... Let's just, for a minute, take it as a framework.'

'Framework,' he said.

'Say Linstad is sleeping with Donna Zhao.'

Bascombe yawned, didn't bother to cover his mouth. 'You wanna say that, say that.'

'Something happens between them. He dumps her, she gets mad, starts making noise, threatening to tell his wife.'

Bascombe waved a finger like a conductor's baton. The music goes on. Yawn.

I said, 'Nineteen ninety-three, Linstad and Olivia have been married less than two years. Their prenup says he doesn't get anything till year three.'

'So.'

'That's motive for him to want to shut Donna up.'

Bascombe raked the chair arm upholstery, as if trying to quash an unpleasant urge. 'You are one creative guy, Tommy Ed.'

'I know it's not a lot to go on that's concrete –'

'It's nothing concrete,' he said. 'Don't let me stop you, though, I'm finding it really entertaining.'

'Linstad puts himself at the scene,' I said.

'As a witness.'

'Okay, but what's he doing there to begin with? His office is across campus. He lives in Piedmont. He's spending nights at the duplex, which is in the opposite direction. There's no reason for him to be on foot anywhere near her apartment. Why's he there?'

'Ask him.'

'I can't,' I said. 'He's dead.'

'Yup,' Bascombe said. 'You said it.'

'Did you consider him as anything other than a witness? At any point?'

'Sure I did,' he said. 'You think I'm a fuckin idiot? It don't mean shit, because we have a print and a confession. So unless you can explain that I got nothing to say to you.'

He finished his drink, heaved himself up out of the chair, went over to the bar cart, and uncorked a bottle of Wild Turkey. He poured, plodded back to the recliner. His drink sloshed as he sat down. He licked the spillage off his thumb.

'Triplett was vulnerable,' I said, drawing a smirk from Bascombe. 'He's young. He's suggestible and unstable. Linstad had to be aware of that; he screened Triplett for the study. There's a report — I emailed you copies of a few pages.'

'I saw.'

'Then you know: the two of them had this weird relationship. Triplett flunks the screening procedure, Linstad goes, "No thanks, see you later." Then all of a sudden he changes his mind and enrolls him.'

''Cause he felt bad for him.'

'Maybe. Or maybe he realizes, *Wait a second, this kid could be useful.* He starts buying him food, taking him out. He's grooming him.'

'Brainwashing. Just like on TV. I love it.'

'Maybe Triplett acted alone,' I said. 'Maybe he and Linstad did it together.'

'Hmm,' Bascombe said. 'Did you check out Lee Harvey Oswald?'

'Maybe Triplett was home that night, like his sister says, and he was nowhere near the scene and Linstad acted alone.'

'You love that word *maybe*.'

'You don't think Triplett's confession comes across as confused?'

'Of course it does. He's fucking crazy.'

'You ask him, after he stabbed her, what happened? He says: "She like disappeared." You tell him come on, be serious, what are you talking about, she disappeared? You know what he says?'

'Please, tell me.'

' "Like in the air." ' I looked at him. 'In the air.'

He stared at me: *Who the fuck cares*.

'The study had the kids playing a video game,' I said. 'I checked it out. The way it works is, you kill people, they break into pieces and dissolve into the air. It's possible, right, that Triplett's imagining that? What's that mean, "in the air"?'

'It means,' Bascombe said, his voice dangerously soft, 'jack shit.'

Silence.

I said, 'I know this case is important to you.'

'Shut up,' he said. 'All right? You had your turn. Now shut the fuck up and listen.'

He leaned over to set his glass on the carpet, coming back up red in the face, busted capillaries etching the flesh of his nose.

He said, 'This is finished. It's dead. Understand?'

'I'm thinking about the family,' I said.

'You arrogant goddamn muppet, I told you to *shut up*.' He sputtered a laugh. 'You're thinking about the family? All right. Let's "think about the family". When *I* think about the family, it's that they've had twenty-four years to come to terms with what happened to their daughter, their only child, which – if you had a shred of real-world experience whatsoever, which you don't, you sad fucking wannabe – then you'd know that it's not nearly enough. The fuck you know? You don't deal with alive people. You're a vulture. You go through pockets. But I can promise you one thing: dragging them back into it will do nothing, *nothing*, to "help" them. You want to help them? Shut up. Everything you're saying, all this garbage you're spewing, even if it was true, accomplishes nothing. There's nothing *to* accomplish. One guy is out of prison, the other guy is dead. Not to mention everything you're saying is a hypothetical load of shit.'

He smiled. 'I've tried to be patient with you. I let you call me on the phone, come to my house, where I live, waste my time, tell me this that the other, make up stories about people you don't know and never met, and then I'm supposed to give you a pat on the back?'

He leaned over, feeling around for the glass. 'We're gonna be good boys and do our jobs. I already did mine. I put that fuckin animal in jail. Now I get to have fun. You seem a little unclear about yours, so I'll review it for you again: shut up. Go back to being a maid. Unless you're as terrible at that as you are at police work, in which case, my recommendation is, go out and find a job more suited to your skill set. Try clowning.'

He found the glass, pushed himself to his feet, headed to the bar cart.

I said, 'Linstad's ex-father-in-law is John Sowards.'

He froze, thick shoulders bunched. 'Jesus fucking Christ, you're still talking.'

'He's worth about half a billion dollars. There's one business partner he's done several deals with. Dave Auerbach. He used to be a UC regent. Dave is short for S. Davis. That's him, on the committee that throws Linstad under the bus. The lawyer, Khoury? She's from the Sowards family firm.'

Bascombe kept his back to me as he poured more Wild Turkey.

I stood up. 'The report comes out right around when Olivia and Nicholas's marriage hit the rocks. You'd think Sowards would have no reason to protect Linstad. Quite the contrary. Let the bastard burn. But the big rich think differently, right? Reputation is everything. Their daughter marries a murderer, they get tainted by association.'

Bascombe recorked the bottle.

'I spoke to the coroner who handled Linstad's death. He told me his boss was leaning on him to close the case quickly and quietly. I'm figuring Sowards got spooked. He may've even suspected his daughter had something to do with it. So he circled the wagons.'

Bascombe faced me. Red gone to purple.

He extruded words, like a machine making sausage links. 'Never. In my. Career. Did I. Let *anyone*. Influence. Me.'

'I'm not saying you did,' I said.

The room was small, and, drunk as he was, he covered the distance with impressive speed. Barely enough time for me to see him cock a fist back, the bracelet jangling, the big hairy right forearm swinging in a shallow, sideways arc.

What's true for a free throw is true for a punch: the flatter the trajectory, the more accurate it has to be. Try to club me over the head but miss, you still might break my collarbone. Aim straight for my nose and your margin of error shrinks. It's not a perfect analogy, but it was what I was thinking as I juked to the left and Bascombe's momentum carried him past me and into a bookcase.

Kitschy piece, shaped like a canoe with the bottom third chopped off so it stood upright. A few books, mostly knick-knacks: brass compass, ship-in-a-bottle, autographed baseball on a plastic stand. All of which came raining down as the book-case slammed back and then pitched forward, leaving a moon-shaped cleft in the drywall.

Bascombe tangled with a floor lamp, which went down, the bulb blowing out with a pop. He came to rest in a deep one-legged squat against the wall, arms flung out, fingers spread and palms flattened, as though he'd been shot from a cannon. A Tom Clancy paperback lay at his feet.

His wrist was bleeding. I put out a hand to help him up.

He slapped it away, struggled up, and lurched toward the back of the house, swallowed up by the unlit hallway.

A door slammed.

I put the canoe-case back where it belonged. The baseball had a Giants logo; the signature was Willie McCovey's. The ship-in-a-bottle was toast. The glass hadn't broken, but the insides had collapsed into a slurry of matchsticks and fabric. I set it on an end table and saw myself out.

32

'I DON'T blame him,' Shupfer said.

She swung the van around and began backing up toward the intake bay. 'You got into his personal space and accused him of being on the take.'

'I was careful not to say that.'

'I'm sure he totally appreciated the distinction.'

'Somebody took a statement from Triplett's sister,' I said. 'What happened to it?'

'I'm gonna go with "garden-variety incompetence",' she said.

She jammed the gearshift into park and noted the mileage, and we got out to unload the latest decedent. Seventy-nine-year-old Hispanic woman found in the bath by her caretaker. We hadn't noted any obvious signs of elder abuse, but the location of the body warranted bringing her in.

'Forget Bascombe getting paid off,' I said, unlocking the gurney wheels. 'It doesn't have to be that overt. It could be much subtler – like what Ming felt. Linstad cooks up his story. He tells his wife he's going to the police, give a statement. She freaks out, calls her father. He freaks out, calls his lawyer, and so on and so forth, up the chain, until the message trickles back down to Bascombe: 'Handle with care.' Now, in his mind, he's no longer talking to a potential suspect. He's talking to a helpful witness with important friends. Anyone would start to see the situation through that lens.'

'What about you?' she said. 'What lens are you seeing it through?'

We wheeled the body over to the scale. I switched it on and saw Shupfer raise her eyebrows. The dead woman weighed just eighty-one pounds.

'You ask the caretaker about her nutrition?' Shupfer asked.

'She said she ate okay. I saw a box of Ensure in the pantry. Couple cans missing.'

'Mm. Could still be FS.'

Frailty Syndrome. Old bodies deteriorating, the damage hastened by neglect and sometimes worse. A memo had directed us, last year, to look for it.

We rolled the gurney into the intake bay. While Shupfer scribbled on the clipboard, I began unwrapping the body. The old woman was already naked – her skin waxy and shrunken – saving us the trouble of having to undress her and catalog her clothing.

I picked up the camera, began taking flicks. 'You're right, though.'

'Am I now.'

'Bascombe. I shouldn't have gone there,' I said. 'No reason to think he'd cooperate.'

'Yup.'

'Anyway I don't have enough.'

'Nope.'

'But he just – he pissed me off, Shoops. Super-smug.'

She stopped writing. 'Just be glad he didn't hurt you, princess.'

She spoke too soon.

Entering the squad room, wringing out wet hands, I proceeded down the corridor past the sergeants' offices. Vitti's door was propped, the man himself slumped over his desk like he'd been sucker-punched. He saw me and sat up, curled a finger, telling me to shut the door and close the blinds.

'If this is about trading for Odell Beckham, Junior,' I said, sitting down, 'forget it.'

He ran a hand back and forth over his scalp. 'I just got off the phone with Chief Ames at Berkeley PD.'

'Okay.'

'Any guesses why he's calling me?'

'No sir.'

'None at all?'

'Sir?'

Vitti said, 'Have you been harassing one of their guys?'

I said, 'Sir?'

'Have you?'

'No, sir. I haven't.'

'Did you go over to some guy's house?'

'With permission,' I said. 'I didn't show up out of the blue.'

'But you did go to see him.'

'I spoke to him, yeah.'

Vitti's eyes went to slits. 'God's sake, what were you thinking?'

'I was thinking he and I could have a civilized conversation.'

'The guy's retired. With health issues, I might add.'

'That's what he said? I'm harassing him?'

'It's a little worse than that, actually. He said you took a swing at him.'

'*I* –? Sorry, sir. That's bullshit. He came at me. All I did was avoid him.'

Vitti sighed and began fiddling with his Word-A-Day desk calendar – part of his relentless, half-assed pursuit of self-improvement. 'What the hell are you into?'

'One of my cases,' I said, 'led me to one of his cases. I did due diligence and noticed parts of Bascombe's report don't add up. So I went over there to get clarification.'

'How's that lead to him hitting you?'

'He didn't hit me,' I said. 'He missed, cause he was drunk off his ass.'

'Christ, Clay, don't pick nits. How does Bascombe's case impact yours?'

'It doesn't, directly. But –'

'Jesus.'

I said, 'We're still cops, sir.'

'There are cops whose job it is to deal with things like that and we're not them.'

'I don't see anyone else volunteering.'

'Did you bother to ask?'

'No one seems interested, sir. And I know when someone's screwed up.'

'Ames doesn't see it that way,' he said. 'He told me the guy's a decorated veteran.'

'Veterans make mistakes.'

'I don't care,' Vitti said. 'All right? I do *not* care. What I — what *we* — have to worry about is relationships. We gotta work with these people. Not just today. Every single day. People, agencies, they rely on us. They need to know that when we show up we're there to handle our business, and nothing else. I can't have you running around stirring up shit.'

He paused. 'Is everything good with you?'

'Sir?'

'Is there something in your life going on I need to know about?'

Was he really going to do this? Play Papa Bear? 'No sir.'

'You can tell me,' he said. 'We look after each other, that's how we do around here. You are an important member of this team.'

What supermarket checkout aisle management handbook had he picked up? 'I appreciate that, sir.'

'I checked your logs. You worked Thanksgiving.'

'Yes, sir.'

'You're signed up to work Christmas.'

'Yes, sir, I am.'

'You worked Christmas last year,' he said. 'Year before that, too. I checked.'

He waited for an explanation.

I said, 'I don't believe in Santa Claus.'

'Don't be a wiseass.'

'Sorry, sir.'

Vitti looked at me pleadingly. His instincts were to ream me out, but he wanted so badly to be a Good Guy. 'I think you need a break.'

'I'm good.'

'You haven't taken time in two years,' he said.

He'd never complained about it before. 'Trying to do my bit, sir.'

'That's fine, Clay, but it's not good for the soul.' He plucked a tissue, blew his nose. 'Look, I know how shit gets, okay? I been there. I wasn't even going to mention it to you, but now, in light of this Bascombe thing, I feel like I gotta say something. This is the second call I've had about you in the last week.'

I said, 'Pardon me?'

'A guy phoned up hollering about you cremated his father against his wishes.'

Samuel Afton.

I said, 'That is a hundred percent not what happened.'

'Be that as it may, he's going on about he wants to make a formal complaint.'

'You're kidding.'

'Wish I was.'

'What did you tell him?'

'I talked him out of it. I went to bat for you, same way I did with Ames. You're welcome. But now sitting here listening to you argue with me I'm starting to feel like a prick. Don't make me into a prick, Clay. If you're starting to get overwhelmed –'

'Honestly, sir, I'm not.'

'– you need to be clear with me about your state of mind. Things pile up, understandable. But you need to be self-aware. Okay? You need to come to me: *Sarge, I'm starting to feel it*. Nobody's going to judge you for that.'

His eyes said otherwise.

'Sir –'

'Overall,' he said, 'I appreciate your contributions. But if this

289

isn't working for you, you can be at a new duty station in twenty-four hours.'

'I don't want that.'

Interminable silence. 'I'll assume for the moment that's true.'

I nodded. 'Thank you, sir.'

'The case led you to Bascombe,' he said. 'What's the decedent's name?'

'Walter Rennert.'

He swiveled to his computer, moused, clicked. 'You've had this open since September.'

'Yes, sir.'

His lips moved as he ran over the narrative. 'What am I missing here? Cause to me this reads like a straightforward natural.'

'I agree, sir.'

'What are you waiting on?'

I said nothing.

Vitti squinted at me, as though I'd receded into the distance. 'Okay, here's what we're going to do. First thing, you need to call this Bascombe guy up and apologize.'

'Sarge –'

'Just do it, all right? Be the bigger person. Call the guy up and make it right.'

He slid his desk phone toward me.

I stared at him. 'Now?'

'No time like the present.'

I brought up the number on my cell and keyed it into the desk phone.

It rang and rang.

'He's not answering,' I said, hanging up.

'Then leave a message.' He leaned over and turned on the speakerphone.

I gritted my teeth, redialed.

This is Ken, I'm gone fishin.

Beep.

Vitti prompted me with a hand flourish.

'Mr Bascombe, Deputy Coroner Edison calling' – tasting bile, swallowing it – 'calling to say I'm sorry if I offended you. I'm sorry if it came across that way. All best.'

I punched off.

'Good,' Vitti said. 'Thank you. Now I want you to be done with the Rennert case. Get it out of your system. And – hey. While you're at it, take some time off.'

'You're suspending me?'

'Clay. Will you listen to yourself? Stop being paranoid. I'm saying go home. Visit your family. Whatever you need to do. See a fuckin movie. Get your head right and then let's get back on track. Okay? I don't want to hear no more about this. Go home.'

'Can I get my coffee mug first?'

He said, 'Mind your tone, Deputy. You're dismissed.'

33

If I owed anyone an apology, it was Nate Schickman. I could guess he'd paid for helping me out. I called him the next day.

'No worries,' he said, unconvincingly. 'Ames is annoyed, but nothing I can't survive.'

'Annoyed at you or at me?'

'Both. Bascombe, too.'

'Oh yeah?'

'He seemed more put out than angry. Like – pissed about having to go through the motions. I get the impression the two of them aren't friends.'

I filed that tidbit away. 'I owe you one.'

'I'd say we're up to three or four by now.'

'True. Speaking of, any sign of Triplett?'

'None. I have an eye out.'

'Thanks.'

'Yeah,' Schickman said. 'I gotta ask, though. You seriously hit him?'

Trucking in gossip. Good trait for a detective.

'Bascombe? Hell no. He tried to hit me.'

'Damn,' Schickman said. 'What'd you say to get him so mad?'

292

I hesitated.

'Hey,' Schickman said. 'All that owing deserves no bullshit.'

'I might've implied that he arrested the wrong guy.'

He laughed for a good long time. 'No shit. Really?'

'Really.'

'Balls,' he said.

'Thanks.'

'I pulled down the Donna Zhao file again,' he said. 'After you left? I took another peek at it. It seemed solid to me.'

'First glance, it does.'

'What does second glance do?'

I said, 'You really want to hear this?'

'I asked, didn't I?'

Get it out of your system.

Whatever you need to do.

Ask me, that sounded like permission.

An order, even.

Vitti hadn't meant it that way.

Next time, Sarge, choose your words more carefully.

'Tell you what,' I said to Schickman. 'Let me buy you a drink. You be the judge.'

We met at a bar of his choosing, on San Pablo near the Albany-Berkeley line. The place had a Day of the Dead theme, the menu boasting a hundred thirty-one different tequilas and mezcals. Schickman asked for a Dos Equis. I asked for water. The waitress smiled in desperation and beat a retreat.

I laid out the case for him, just as I had for Bascombe.

'I started off thinking Linstad roped Triplett into doing his

293

dirty work,' I said. 'More I go over it, more I feel like that's wrong. Linstad isn't going to rely on a kid who he knows is not all there. And Triplett's sister gives him a solid alibi.'

'Seven years old,' said Schickman.

'She's a smart adult, seems totally together,' I said. 'Which, given her upbringing, is impressive.'

'You think Linstad framed him.'

'If you're going to pick someone to frame, Triplett's pretty much your ideal candidate. Young, black, physically imposing. Borderline intelligence, a loose sense of reality.'

Schickman shifted around in his chair.

'I mean, it's very interesting,' he said.

I laughed. 'Please,' I said. 'Don't hold back.'

He sipped beer, tapped the table, collected his thoughts.

'Start off by saying what I like,' he said. 'The affairs, the roommate's statement – that's useful information. I'm the lead, I'm starting from scratch, all that shit is hugely significant to the fact pattern.'

'I know,' I said. 'Circumstantial.'

He nodded. 'Which isn't the end of the world. Lots of guys in San Quentin got there on circumstantial evidence. You're *not* starting from scratch, though. There's a confession. Maybe not perfect, but not a whole lot worse than most. It's on paper now, part of the record. You have Triplett's fingerprint on the murder weapon.'

'Linstad could've gotten him to handle it,' I said. 'I showed you the report. They were hanging out together, outside the lab.'

'Allegedly.'

'Nobody ran DNA,' I said. 'Not on the knife, on the

sweatshirt, on the blood at the scene, anything. It was nineteen ninety-three.'

'You're lucky enough to get viable material, you still need a known sample for comparison.'

'I have a name and address for Linstad's father in Sweden.'

Schickman smiled. 'I'm trying to imagine how that phone call goes.'

'Yeah, no shit.'

'A fine morning to you, sir. Your son, who's dead, we'd like to destroy his memory by pinning him for a vicious murder. You mind please spitting into this tube for me? We'll cover postage.'

'It's all in the delivery,' I said.

'Look at it from my perspective. I bring this to my boss, what's he gonna say?'

'You need more.'

'To start resurrecting old shit, spend time and money? Lot more.'

'Gimme the evidence box,' I said. 'I'll take it to the lab myself. They're one floor up from me. Nobody has to know.'

Schickman laughed. 'Aaaand he's gone rogue.'

He raised his empty to the waitress. 'I'm not saying I won't help you out, if I can.'

In essence, he was answering me just as Bascombe had, and Shupfer had, and Vitti had – only a little more nicely, and he'd left the door open a crack.

'One thing that does get to me,' he said, 'is both Rennert and Linstad, going down the stairs. But you say Rennert was natural.'

'Doesn't exclude Linstad being a homicide. The night he

died, he was drinking with someone. Ming said they leaned on him to close it as accidental. He suggested I look at Linstad's ex, all that family money. But I met her and I don't see it. Too risky. She'd hire somebody.'

'From what you've told me about Linstad,' he said, 'any number of women would've done it for free.'

The waitress brought Schickman a fresh beer. He drank, using his lower lip to pull foam from the upper. 'Find Triplett. Without him, none of this matters.'

I nodded, debating whether to voice my thoughts. We seemed to get along, Schickman and I, but I didn't know him well enough to be sure he wouldn't regard me as naïve or overzealous.

I said, 'He didn't do it. Triplett.'

Schickman watched me closely.

'I'm not asking you or anyone else to accept that on faith,' I said. 'I'm just stating what I know to be true. What's left for me now is to prove it.'

His slow nod could have been wariness or agreement.

'Do us both a favor,' he said. 'Don't step on any more toes.'

He tipped his beer to me.

Vitti's order made me think about Christmas.

The sergeant was right: I'd worked every one since joining the Sheriff's. It never felt like much of a sacrifice. When I was growing up, our family didn't do religion, and the secularized version of the holiday we'd once celebrated had fallen by the wayside, along with every other ritual that called for full participation.

Gathering as three underlined the missing fourth.

This year, I didn't have any excuse.

Saturday morning, I caught a matinee of the latest installment of *Fast and Furious*, calling my mother as I left the theater to give her twenty-four hours' notice that I was free for Christmas Eve dinner.

'We don't have anything planned,' she said, managing to sound both apologetic and accusing.

'If it's too much trouble –'

'No no,' she said. 'I don't want you to be disappointed, is all.'

These conversations always went the same way: I reached out, stirred by duty and guilt and love. As soon as she answered, I started mapping my escape route.

I forced myself to stay on the line, knowing I'd only feel worse if I hung up. 'I can pick up food.'

'Would you? Thanks. I'm sorry, I'm just so tired.'

'No problem.'

'I was down to see Luke last week,' she said. 'It takes a lot out of me.'

I said, 'Chinese okay?'

Dragon Deluxe Palace was packed, whizzing trays and parties of eight, a comforting din. We weren't the only family too jaded or lazy to put a turkey in the oven.

Waiting at the hostess stand, hunched in the rippling light of a murky fish tank, I scrolled through my inbox, deleting spam, pausing as I came to one headed IN TOWN.

The sender was Amy Sandek.

I opened it.

. . . as promised.
Love,
A

I composed my reply, hitting SEND as the hostess gave me a warm plastic bag and wishes for a merry Christmas.

Sliding down East 14th through patchy traffic, I saw crowds in the windows of the pho counters and the curry houses. Back in the sixties and seventies, San Leandro was the whitest city in the Bay Area. That began to change as the courts struck down neighborhood covenants. By the time I was born, the process had been well under way for years, and my own group of friends resembled a mini–United Nations, a broad coalition formed on the basketball courts, united by our love of the game and our disregard for posted playing hours.

We roamed in packs, seeking out anyplace with a hoop and a little space, climbing fences, taking on all challengers. Washington Elementary; high school blacktop; curving driveways and buckling courtyards. In those open-air chambers, I began my career in diplomacy.

I learned how to talk to people as individuals. How to align common interests. How to derive pleasure from the success of others.

My brother Luke was half an inch taller than I was and nearly as fast. At eleven he could dunk a tennis ball; at thirteen, the real thing. His nickname was White Boy Can Jump. He worked on his shot incessantly, developing a beautiful stroke, like calligraphy. For raw talent, you'd take him over me, every time.

Yet he spent many of our playground hours squatting on the sidelines, impatiently waiting on next, flapping his arms and pounding on his bony, scabby knees. His teams never seemed to be able to grab onto winning streaks like mine did.

Standard rules called for game till eleven by ones. Luke would start off hot, knocking down five, six in a row. Then the opposition would gang up on him, smothering him in double and triple teams. He'd continue to hold the ball, passing only to clap his hands and demand it back, jacking up hero shots as he fell out of bounds. Every so often one went gliding in, causing everyone in the vicinity to erupt, clutch their heads, fall over in exaggerated faints, *ohhhhhdaaayyuuummm*. Their reactions provided enough reinforcement to keep him chucking away.

More often, the ball skipped off the top of the backboard.

For him, it was glory or death, all or nothing.

He easily made our high school team but clashed with the coach and ended up quitting after a year, leaving a legacy – ball hog, arrogant, uncoachable – that tarred me. I had to work twice as hard to earn my spot, and I made sure to pass more than I shot, sometimes at a ridiculous ratio. I was once benched for forgoing an open layup.

I can't say for certain when Luke began using drugs. I wasn't around the first time someone offered him a joint. I don't know where I was. Probably at practice.

I can, however, guess about where he acquired the habit: the very same courts where we'd once lived in innocence.

His first arrest came during junior year. They picked him up, along with two other guys from our childhood circle, for misdemeanor possession. The judge saw a decent kid, no priors, intact family, parents gainfully employed. Luke pleaded no contest and received a suspended sentence plus community service.

For a while he managed to stay clear of the law. He'd learned his lesson, and it was: don't get caught. At home, though, things got ugly. He fought bitterly with my parents. It takes a lot to rile my father up, and one of the more unreal and cartoonish moments of my teenage life was watching him and Luke come to blows, after my brother announced he was dropping out of college. Trying to get between them earned me a black eye.

My mother's response was to detach and deny. Casting about for a place to put her attention, she landed on me. Luke had flushed his future away. I, on the other hand, had no ceiling. She never missed a game of mine. She heaped praise on me.

Me, I couldn't decide what to feel about my brother. Pity. Contempt. Guilt, for the canyon widening between us, our fortunes diverging in lockstep. I entered Cal, and he moved in with a friend in Fruitvale, taking part-time work as a clerk at a sporting goods store. I shouldered the rising hopes of a team and a school, and Luke bounced in and out of jail on minor drug offenses or petty theft. Sixty days here, ninety there, each stint setting him up for the next screwup.

We had no idea how badly he would screw up.

I doubt he did, either.

Nobody wanted to deal with him. I was the one worth rooting for, even after my injury. More so: everybody loves an underdog.

One night – high on crack, reeling under a blood alcohol level of .15 – Luke stole a car. He later claimed that his intention was merely to joyride. Careering north on International Boulevard, doing seventy in a thirty-five zone, he blew through a red at 29th, T-boning a Kia.

The driver, a twenty-eight-year-old woman named Rosa Arias, was killed instantly.

The passenger, Arias's nineteen-year-old niece, died the next day of her injuries.

Luke suffered a broken femur, broken ribs, a punctured lung, a lacerated spleen. He spent four days in a coma. The first person he saw when he came to was a nurse. The second person he saw was the arresting officer.

Pleading guilty to two counts of gross vehicular manslaughter enabled him to avoid prosecution with the intoxication enhancement, shaving a couple of years off his sentence.

Even with Mom's gift for denial, this was overload. She reevaluated the past, all those miles driven to and from arenas in San Jose, Sacramento, Las Vegas. The mornings she'd woken up hoarse from screaming nonstop through the fourth quarter.

With me hobbling through rehab, and Luke headed off to prison, her division of resources must have seemed to her beyond neglectful. Criminal.

When I enrolled in the police academy, she became fixated on the idea that I could use my newfound knowledge and position to help Luke. She was wrong, of course. His fate was out of my hands. But what truly got to her was realizing that, even if I'd had leverage, I wouldn't have used it. Not for him.

I was embarking on a career as an officer of the law. My duty was to the community – to protect decent folks from outliers like my brother.

Those were the days when Christmas stumbled and fell, and Thanksgiving, too, and birthdays devolved from dinner to a phone call.

Once I was at the Coroner's, I softened to her a bit, chastened by death and what it does to people. But there was still nothing I could do to pry Luke free any faster. And I don't think I'm alone in struggling to be as generous with my family as I am with strangers.

The biggest sticking point remains my spotty visiting record. Like most state prisons, Pleasant Valley is open to the public on weekends. Usually I'm working, a built-in excuse. I manage to think up others for those rare instances when I am free.

If nothing else, there's the drive, which is abysmal: three hours, more with traffic.

My mom goes twice a month, and every so often she'll call and invite me to join her. Already knowing the answer, she plays up her disbelief when I say no. But her hurt, her regret, her continuing sense of failure – those are genuine.

Now, sitting in my car outside my parents' house, I gazed down the block at a ladder of windows brimming with milky cheer. LED icicles strung from the gutters dripped into the void. On the passenger seat, the takeout bag crinkled, its contents breathing sweetly.

The majority of the surrounding houses had been redone, ranch homes leveled, replaced by McMini-Mansions pushing at the margins of their lots. The house where I'd grown up remained the same: fifteen hundred square feet of lumpy tan stucco, a sun-melted caramel fronted by succulents and weird red gravel, like a transplanted piece of Mars. Thirty-year mortgage, manageable on the combined salary of a public school teacher and an office manager. With the housing market back up, it might be worth it for them to sell, downsize, take early retirement. I'd raised the point before and met breezy dismissal.

Why in the world would they leave?

If it was worth X now, it would be worth more in five years.

Luke could have his old room, once he got out.

I stepped from the car, carrying the bag of takeout on two fingers and humming 'The Little Drummer Boy'.

The evening went better than expected. Mom was in a decent mood. Following her cues, my father relaxed, rubbing at his sunken stomach as he discussed his current crop of sixth graders with a mix of fondness and despair. Each new incoming class demanded an increasing degree of vigilance on his part. The world had succumbed to phones. You couldn't confiscate the damn things fast enough. The dumb kids disseminated pictures of their genitals. The smart kids fact-checked him in real time, correcting him with a smirk. It was enough to break a lesser man.

He laughed, his legs scribbling restlessly beneath the table. There was a patch worn in the carpet by his heels, dragging over the same spot. He coped with stress by breaking it down into more manageable forms: anxiety about his pension, his bad back, the electricity bill. Over the years I'd watched him turn into an old man.

A baseball player in his youth, he was by his own admission never very good. It was from my mother – a collegiate long jumper – and her northern European forebears that Luke and I got our height and wiry strength.

We ate moo shu pork and chicken with broccoli and fried rice. We cracked our fortune cookies and read them aloud.

' "Today's questions yield tomorrow's answers," ' I said.

'What questions do you have today?' my father asked.

I smiled. 'How much time do you have?'

He chuckled and went into the kitchen with the plates.

My mother said, 'I'm glad you decided to join us.'

'Sorry to spring it on you.'

'You're here now,' she said. Then: 'I meant to call you last week.'

Seeing where this was going, I said, 'I had work. I wouldn't've been able to come.'

She shook her head, dry blond and gray, a shivering haystack. 'I'm not going to ask when was the last time you went.'

'Okay.'

'Do you know when was it?'

'You just said you're not going to ask.'

'More than two years,' she said.

'There you go,' I said. 'You answered your own question.'

'I thought maybe you didn't realize how long it's been.'

Keeping my voice even required a supreme effort. 'How's he doing?'

'The same.'

'Did he ask you for commissary money?'

'They feed them like slaves, Clay. He lives on ramen. It's the only way for him not to starve to death.'

'Ramen is currency, there. You know that, right? He trades it for drugs.'

'Stop.'

'Did he look well nourished to you?'

She spread tight, pale hands. 'I don't want to hear it, please.'

In the kitchen, the dishwasher gurgled to life.

'He has a girlfriend,' my mother said.

It took me a second to process. 'Luke?'

'She started writing to him. Her name is Andrea. He showed me her picture. She lives in Salinas.'

'Pen pal, huh.'

'She's been to see him,' my mother said. 'Twice.'

I resented the implicit comparison. 'And we're sure this isn't some sort of scam?'

'I don't see what she could possibly expect to get out of him,' she said.

'I'm trying to figure out why a woman would write to him out of nowhere.'

'People are lonely,' she said. '*He's* lonely. It makes him happy.'

'Good for him.'

She tilted her head. 'Why are you so angry at him?'

I said, 'Why aren't *you*?'

She clasped her hands, as if in prayer. 'He's going to get out, you know.'

'I'm aware.'

'And? What's going to happen then? Because soon – let me

finish, please. Sooner than you realize, he'll get out, and you won't have been to visit him. You'll both know it. That's going to be hanging between the two of you.'

I brushed at crumbs on the tablecloth.

'He's still your brother,' she said. 'That's never going away.'

That was the problem.

Family. It's an incurable disease.

34

LYDIA DELAVIGNE — Rennert's ex-wife; Tatiana's mother — lived on the thirty-first floor of a newly built high-rise in San Francisco, a torqued platinum phallus blocks from the Embarcadero.

I left my car with the valet, made myself known to the concierge. While he called up to her 'suite' I answered another email from Amy, confirming our plans for that evening.

The concierge said, 'You can go up.'

I headed for the elevator bank.

A high-speed car shot into the sky, spat me out into a silent corridor carpeted in near-black blue and painted barely-above-white gray.

A woman was waiting in the doorway to 3109. She was thin, her spine arrow-straight, making the most of her small stature. Black hair tied in a tight bun; ivory skin, with smoky nuances, same as Tatiana. She wore black leggings, navy shoes with kitten heels, a billowing gray silk tunic patterned with deep-blue butterflies.

Color-coordinated with the hallway.

'Behold,' she said, 'the man fucking my daughter.'

What can you say to that other than nothing?

She didn't seem bothered. It was more like she was assigning me a classification.

She went inside, leaving me to follow.

She kicked off her shoes in the entry hall and padded ahead. 'Make yourself comfortable,' she said.

Her apartment evoked The Future, circa 1975: a single room, open, vaulted, and finished in white from top to bottom – surfaces, fixtures, and furnishings. It made for disorienting effect, washing away depth and compressing space. Steps led down to a sunken sitting area with two white sofas, a lustrous white coffee table, piles of white pillows on a stitched cowhide rug.

In its immensity, its blankness, the place felt like a photographic and philosophical negative to Walter Rennert's attic. Their marriage must've been interesting.

'Tea?' she said, moving toward the kitchen area, a speed kettle already piping.

'Yes, please.' I faced the eastern wall, a solid sheet of glass overlooking the Financial District, skyscrapers reduced to ash by a scouring midwinter sun. 'Nice view.'

'On a clear day you can see forever.'

'How many clear days do you get a year?'

'Not a one,' she said gaily. 'But who wants to see forever? That sounds hideous.'

She brought a tray down to the sitting area and placed it on the table, curling up against the sofa arm, her legs folded beneath her. She had tiny hands; tiny, delicate fingers. They barely reached around her mug. The veins in her neck and wrists were Delft blue. The resemblance to Tatiana was so striking that her comment about sex began to bother me.

She sidled closer, allowing the tunic to ride up. My chest got tight.

She said, 'Beauty is editing.'

I took a gulp, scalding the roof of my mouth. 'Tatiana said the same thing.'

Lydia halted her advance. 'Did she.'

'She said she's a minimalist at heart.'

'I'm sure she would never admit that to me.'

'She doesn't seem to have a problem admitting things to you.'

'Who else should she tell, if not her mother?'

'Is she required to tell anyone?'

'Oh but yes,' she said. 'Otherwise it might never have happened. We talk, we share our experiences, so that we exist.'

She lolled back, inspecting me. 'You know, she said you were a big boy, but hearing and seeing are not the same. Don't worry, she didn't go into excessive detail. Look, you're blushing, how perfectly charming.'

'How's it going for her in Portland?'

'If you're fishing to find out whether she returned, she did. A few days ago.'

I set the mug aside. 'Does she know I'm here?'

'Not yet. Should we make it our little secret?'

'No need,' I said. 'If you speak to her, send my best.'

'If I speak to her before you do, I will,' Lydia said. She mirrored me, putting down her own mug. 'I birthed a free spirit, I honored that as I raised her, allowing her to be who she wanted to be. Watching her evolve was lovely. She's always been so much like me. Though by her age, I'd accomplished what I'd set out to accomplish.'

Her arms had begun to twine toward the ceiling. I couldn't tell if it was deliberate or simply a reflex – the world her stage.

'Yet despite that' – she wilted – 'a critical piece of my psyche remained unfinished: I wasn't free. It had of course to do with my own mother. She was such a terrible scold. Art to her was a competition. I wasn't going to make that mistake with my child.'

She smiled. 'I know you must miss Tatiana, how could you not? But it's for the best. You're an authority figure by nature. You can boss her around but it will never work.'

'I wouldn't dream of trying.'

'Oh, don't say that, don't ever say that. What else have we, but our dreams?'

Said the woman in the eight-million-dollar apartment.

'So,' she said, 'young, strapping Mr Edison, what can I do for you? I know you didn't come here to talk about *her*. Or did you?' She leaned in. 'I do hope you aren't going to ask me to carry a message to her.'

'I'm not.'

'Good, because I'm enjoined against that. By the rules of rational parenting: we all must make our own choices. Although if you give up that easily, then you don't deserve her.'

'You're probably right,' I said.

Having won her point, she smiled again, though I detected a certain disappointment that I hadn't fought back. 'Tell me, then, what are we going to talk about?'

'Dr Rennert,' I said.

'Ah,' she said.

'I understand you two kept in touch after the divorce.'

'Naturally. We're connected on a cellular level. Our living

styles became incompatible but that doesn't mean he ceased to adore me and I, him. The same applies to everyone I've loved. The web of intimacy, sticky and ever-expanding.'

She pursed her lips, kissed air, looking as satisfied as though she'd made contact with flesh. 'I don't believe we're meant as a species to be monogamous.'

'Right.'

'Nobody is perfect,' she said. 'And thank goodness, perfect is boring. *Walter* wasn't perfect, though he would've liked people to think he was. Do you believe – do you expect *me* to believe – that he didn't take his fair share of comfort in the arms of others? I don't begrudge anyone the pursuit of happiness.'

'It's his connection to Julian Triplett that interests me.'

Another disappointed nod. 'If we must.'

'You've been expecting this conversation,' I said.

'At some point, perhaps. I didn't expect to be having it with you.'

'Who, then?'

'Tatiana, if she took the time to find out. Has she?'

'Not in detail.'

'You've tried to discuss it with her,' she said. 'She got angry. Yes?'

I stared.

Lydia Delavigne said, 'A mother knows. She idolized Walter. And idealized him. And he encouraged it.'

'Aside from you, did he tell anyone else about his relationship with Triplett?'

'Oh no. He was afraid of more scandal. For himself and for the boy.' She smiled. 'I'm extraordinarily discreet. It's one of my best qualities.'

'Clearly.'

'That's very sweet of you to say,' she said. 'May I ask what led you to investigate?'

'The rocking chair.'

She shuddered. 'That thing. It put a nobler face on what was essentially charity. You know, teach a man to fish, versus give him a hunk of halibut. Walter tried to convince me to buy one, as well. I said let's not get carried away.'

I said, 'How did it start between them?'

She sighed. 'I don't suppose there's much harm in telling you, now that he's gone . . . He wrote the boy a letter.'

'While Triplett was in prison?'

'I warned him not to. I thought it was unhealthy. But he got into one of his righteous funks.'

'When did this happen?'

'Oh, don't quiz me, it's boring. Three or four years after the fact? We were still married. I remember Walter's excitement when he got the reply. What do you know, but it was quite articulate, too, once you got past the atrocious spelling and grammar. They corresponded for a while. Eventually Walter went to visit him, where they kept him.'

'How many times?'

'More than once. I wasn't keeping count. The boy had no one.'

'He had a sister.'

'Well, all I know is that Walter felt he had a moral obligation.'

'To do what.'

Her answer surprised me. 'I suppose you could say he viewed it as a personal research project,' she said. 'An attempt to grapple with the same question he always grappled with. How does it happen that a person can come to commit such a horrible act?'

I said, 'Triplett was a case study?'

'You make it sound so *sterile* . . . No. It was never Walter's intention to exploit. And he never could have published it, that would have been impossible.'

'Then what was he trying to accomplish?'

'He was curious,' she said. 'One of *his* best qualities.'

She took a sip of tea. 'Walter was very badly beaten as a child. Did you know that?'

I shook my head.

'His own father was a wicked man. Creative, but horrible. That's not accidental. True cruelty is its own form of genius. He owned property all over San Francisco.'

'That's where the money comes from.'

'You didn't think Walter got rich in a lab, did you? The house he grew up in – it's still there, in Pacific Heights. Landmarked. Some twenty-five-year-old computer person lives there now . . . Walter showed me pictures once. There's a grand marble foyer, and a pair of staircases, shaped like this.'

She traced a female form.

'When Randolph – that was his father – when he wanted to punish Walter, he would make him run up one side and down the other, for hours on end. If he slowed down, or tripped, Randolph would whip him.'

I said, 'Does Tatiana know about this?'

'Certainly not. And you're not to tell her. I'm only telling you so that you'll understand why Walter was so drawn to darkness. It mesmerized him. It wasn't simple voyeurism. He genuinely wanted to understand. That's how it started, at any rate. With time, I think he came to view the boy as a kind of ward.'

'When did Walter start supplying him meds?'

'After his release. Practically from day one. It was the right thing to do. They just punted him out and locked the gate behind. Shameful, but predictable.'

'Did he give him anything else? Money?'

'It's certainly possible. By then I had moved out. I didn't keep close tabs.'

'I'm trying to figure out how Walter felt comfortable hanging out with a convicted murderer. Having him over to the house.'

'I suppose he was confident in his own ability to manage the situation.'

'Ms Delavigne, did your ex-husband ever express the belief that Julian Triplett was innocent?'

'Not in so many words.'

'But?'

'Well, actions speak louder, don't they.'

'Which actions do you mean?'

For the first time her bravado seemed to falter. She pursed her lips. 'More tea?'

We'd hardly touched the mugs, but before I could answer she had snatched them up and carried them to the kitchen, dumping them out in the sink. She poured refills. To her own mug she added a slug of caramel-colored liquid from a bottle kept in a drawer. She did not offer to do the same for me.

I waited for her to return to the couch. 'I spoke to Nicholas Linstad's ex-wife, Olivia,' I said. 'She told me Walter regarded Linstad as a surrogate son.'

Lydia said, 'Well, he would have. You've never met his sons from his first marriage.'

I shook my head.

'They have more in common with their mother than with Walter.'

'How's that.'

'Materialistic.'

I bit my tongue.

'Not to mention that they moved away,' she said. 'Far, far away, making it clear that they had no intention to return. Walter took their life choices as personal insults.'

'And Nicholas?'

'He didn't need to be grasping,' she said. 'He'd married up. With Walter he could afford to play the intellectual.'

'Meaning, he wasn't, really.'

'I don't know if Nicholas was *really* anything, at his core,' Lydia said. 'He was magnetic. Let's give him that. Handsome, intelligent, capable of making conversation with anyone – for a short while. He had the most intense gaze. It made you feel as if you were the only person in the world that mattered. That Scandinavian sangfroid. You could interpret it as interest, if you wanted to see it as such. Personally, I was impervious. But Walter was rather swept off his feet.'

'When did they fall out?'

'I couldn't give you a date and time,' she said. 'As I said, I was no longer around.'

'It seems like Walter tried to stand up for him during the internal hearing,' I said. 'Deflect some of the blame.'

'Yes.'

'So at that point, at least, they were still close.'

'Yes, noble Walter, falling on his sword. You see, my dear, what you fail to grasp is how much it pleased him to martyr himself.'

The notion of Rennert as masochist rang true. And it pointed to a line of succession for Walter Rennert's self-destructive affection: from his sons to Linstad. From Linstad to Triplett.

Not much room left for Tatiana. With her, the pattern was reversed: she was the one sacrificing herself for him.

I said, 'What caused the rift between him and Linstad?'

'Everyone disappoints in the end.'

A logical conclusion for a woman married five times. 'How did Walter react to the news of Nicholas's death?'

No answer.

'He talked to you about everything else,' I said. 'He didn't talk to you about that?'

For a moment she sat motionless.

She said, 'Let's get one thing perfectly clear: I don't know where the boy is now.'

She looked at me. 'All right? You can put me in the rack, it won't do any good.'

I nodded.

She cleared her throat, took a sip of her tea. 'The night Nicholas died, Walter phoned me up.' She paused, corrected: 'Not that night, the next day, early. He said he needed to see me, right away. He was adamant. He said, "I can't drive, you have to come here." I refused, of course, and next thing I know he's pounding at my door. I was living in the Sunset then. He showed up looking like a wet dog, with his hair stuck down to the top of his scalp. He was drunk, which I suppose is why he didn't want to drive. I almost slammed the door in his face but he looked so pitiful. He said, "There's been an accident."'

'What kind of accident?'

'He wouldn't elaborate,' she said. 'He had the boy with him in the car. He asked, would I put him up for a few days while he thought things through. The place I was in had a little garage. I said he could sleep there temporarily.' Wistful smile. 'That tells you what you need to know about the depth of our love. For all I knew, I was sheltering a killer. But Walter assured me I'd be safe, and I trusted him.'

'How long did Triplett stay with you?'

'Walter picked him up the next day.'

'Where did they go?'

She shook her head. 'I told you. I don't know.'

I assumed she was lying. But I could detect her patience thinning, and I didn't think that going at her any harder would yield the truth.

'You never reported any of this,' I said.

'Report what? I had no idea Nicholas had died until weeks later. Then I drew my own conclusions.'

'That?'

'The boy had killed Nicholas, Walter was protecting him.'

'Is that what you still believe?'

She said, 'I believe people get what they deserve.'

35

At Amy's insistence, I chose the restaurant. She'd lived away for nearly a decade, and her ideas about where to go and what to do were 'fossilized in adolescence'.

She left her car at my place, and we drove together to Temescal, parking on a grim, unlit side street. In her gray peacoat and scarf, she looked like an authentic New Englander, moving comfortably in the cold, our sleeves brushing as we reached the bright, sharp scene sprung up along Telegraph Avenue.

All around us was the same head-on collision – between poverty and frivolity, bleeding need and fussy want – resonating throughout Oakland.

Art gallery. Bike co-op. Flannel and stiff denim.

Drugstore. Bus stop. Abandoned lottery tickets and blackened gum.

'We never used to call it Temescal,' Amy said.

'What did you call it?'

'The ghetto.'

Outside the Burmese restaurant there was, as always, a crowd.

'They don't take reservations,' I said. 'We can go somewhere else if you're hungry.'

I pointed north. 'Organic pizza.'
I pointed south. 'Jack in the Box.'
Amy smiled. 'I'm fine waiting.'

Over bowls of samusa soup, we caught each other up. She was in the clinical track at Yale, writing her dissertation on PTSD in female veterans, working at the West Haven VA. Proximity to damaged souls had converted her into a zealous advocate for small pleasures.

'I cannot believe you've never watched *Naked and Afraid*,' she said. 'It's the best example of my absolute favorite TV genre.'

'Which is.'

' "Idiots in the woods".'

She shared an apartment with one of her old volleyball teammates who was at the divinity school. She didn't get to play her game much, either, these days.

She hadn't told her parents yet – she didn't want to get their hopes up – but she was toying with moving back to the Bay Area. She'd poked around the job market.

'Lot of demand,' she said, wiping her mouth, 'lot of supply.'

I kidded her about her father's ham-fisted attempts at matchmaking; our laughter chased by a secondary laugh, as we both acknowledged, inwardly, that he'd succeeded.

Reaching to dish her more garlic noodles, I noticed that I was sitting up taller, my body big and open. I'd been carrying around so much tension for so long that it had become my resting state, imperceptible until I was free of it.

No conflicts of interest hissing in the background. No power dynamics to negotiate.

319

It tells you a lot about my state of mind just then that our ease with each other made me suspicious. There we were, behaving as though we had a history – detailed, rich, important – when in reality, we'd seldom gone beyond *hi how are you fine thanks*. What else could we have said? Back then she was the Professor's Daughter: sixteen, lovestruck, dumbstruck. I was twenty-one, riding the hardest downward slope of my life, myopic and full of self-pity. But they call those years formative for a reason. Memories retain their pungency. Faces and personalities imprint, assuming an importance out of proportion. The context had shifted; we had shed those selves. And yet they remained molds, priming us for this present, a reincarnation in more compatible shapes.

Now she was a sly, funny, beautiful, perceptive woman.

Now we were equals.

She asked about my family.

'They're okay,' I said. 'I saw my folks on Sunday.' I felt the same blockage rising in my throat as when Tatiana asked me if I had siblings.

Amy already knew, though. I didn't need to hide anything from her.

I said, 'I've been thinking about something my mom said.'

She put down her utensils and paid attention.

'She asked why I'm so angry at Luke. She wants to know why I don't visit him.'

'What did you say?'

'I didn't. I turned it around on her. I couldn't help myself, she put me on the spot.'

Amy nodded. 'All right,' she said. 'Do-over. What would you say to her now?'

I thought about it. 'I'm not angry at him. I mean, I am, on some level. But that's not the reason I don't go.'

I paused. 'Have you ever seen him?'

She shook her head.

'He looks like me,' I said. 'We could switch clothes and trade seats and nobody would notice. He could walk out of there and I'd be stuck behind bars.'

'Too close for comfort,' she said.

'I worshiped him,' I said. 'What are we going to say to each other now? I can't go. I used to. Every time I'd feel like shit for days afterward. I can't do it.'

We let the babble of the restaurant briefly insulate us.

I said, 'I've been thinking about him a lot lately. It has to do with this case. They're not the same, not remotely. I can't stop, though.'

Amy reached across the table and took my hand.

'Thanks,' I said. Forced a smile. 'I'm actually a lot more fun than this.'

She smiled.

I said, 'I'll be right back.'

She held on to me a moment, squeezed, let go.

I locked myself in a bathroom stall, feeling foolish for having bolted the table.

I fished out my phone to check the time.

Tatiana had texted me, twice.

U went to see my mom

Wtf

The more recent message had come in twelve minutes prior. I fussed with my reply, aware that my date was waiting for me. Before I could finish, the phone dinged in my hand.

U need to call me she wrote. And then: Right now please

Busy I typed. Tomorrow

I silenced the phone and put it away.

Back at the table, Amy was helping herself to more tea leaf salad. 'I heard my dad kicked your ass at HORSE.'

'PIG,' I said, sitting down. 'And I let him.'

'Did you, now.'

'Can't beat up on an old man.'

'I'm going to tell him you said that.'

'Please don't.'

'What's it worth to you?'

'I'll pay for dinner.'

'Didn't you know?' One corner of her mouth went up. 'You already are.'

Bellies full, we walked to my car, stopping to kiss on the cracked sidewalk beneath a gaudy streetlight halo.

It was easier than kissing Tatiana, because Amy was five foot ten and because I didn't have to worry about her reporting me to my superiors. I could feel her long torso through the dense wool of her coat. She pressed into me and the lapels parted, and I tugged my jacket open, allowing the warmth of her body to find mine. She was trembling slightly.

She pulled away. 'Is this weird for you?'

'A little. You?'

'Definitely,' she said, moving in again.

We didn't talk much on the drive back to Lake Merritt, letting the air between us build up a charge.

Turning onto Euclid, I slowed beside her car to let her out. It seemed like the gentlemanly thing to do: don't make assumptions.

Amy said, 'You can keep going.'

I kept going. I found a spot and parked, and we got out, walking in sync, fingers linked, bag of leftovers swinging in my right hand. We rounded the corner onto my block.

Whoever designed my building cared enough to mind the details. Fine exterior molding, for instance. Or the shallow alcove, framed in elegant green tile, enabling you to duck out of the rain while searching for your keys.

Amy's grip tightened as a small dark buzzing shape stepped out to block our path.

'You went to see my *mother*?'

My heart was a fist. 'What are you doing here.'

'You didn't want to run that by me first?'

'We can talk about this later,' I said.

'I'd like to talk about it now,' Tatiana said. She rocked on her heels, speaking to me as though Amy wasn't there.

'Tatiana –'

'You really upset her. And me.'

'I –'

'Are you *even aware*,' she shouted.

Her voice slammed off the asphalt and brick.

I said, 'I'm sorry if I did.'

'Oh well that's a superb apology,' she said.

I started to move forward, but Amy tugged me back. She

323

didn't know what Tatiana was capable of. Frankly, I didn't, either. She was stinking drunk.

'Not to mention,' Tatiana said, 'it's pretty insulting you would believe she has *any* control over what I do.'

I said, 'I don't think that.'

'You must think *something* if you're begging her to speak to me on your behalf.'

'That's . . . No. If that's what she told you, she lied.'

Tatiana pivoted toward Amy, acknowledging her at last, making a big show of looking her up and down, clocking her height, whistling. 'Wow. *Look* at *you*.'

Amy said, 'I'm Amy.'

'Tatiana.'

'Nice to meet you, Tatiana.'

'You, too, Amy. Some advice, Amy? Keep him away from your mom.'

'You know what,' Amy said, 'I think I'm gonna head home.'

'You don't need to do that,' I said, smiling hard at her. But the moment was dead, and her own smile was bruised.

'Walk me to my car?' she said.

Tatiana plopped down on the middle step. 'I'll wait right here.'

I tried to go slowly, buy myself a little time. But Amy had her own ideas and was taking giant, athletic strides, forcing me to keep pace.

'I'm so sorry about this,' I said.

'It's fine.'

'We're not together,' I said. 'Tatiana and I.'

324

'Okay.'

'Just so you know. We – not anymore, though.'

'Roger that.'

'She's in a bad place right now,' I said.

'So I gathered.'

'I really don't know what's gotten into her.'

'I'd estimate about nine beers.'

I almost said *Her father just died* but stopped myself. Not only would that be a violation of Tatiana's privacy, it would make me look like an uncaring dickhead. 'I'm sorry.'

'I said it's fine, Clay.'

'How much longer are you in town?' I asked.

'I leave Thursday.'

'I'm free tomorrow,' I said. 'We could have lunch.'

'Why don't you sort things out with her first?'

'Nothing to sort. I swear.'

She did not reply.

We reached her car. Last chance. 'You really don't have to go. I can . . .'

Amy tilted her head. 'Can what?'

Choke Tatiana out? Cuff her to a lamppost?

I said, 'I'll go talk to her.'

'I think that's a good idea.' She kissed me on the cheek. 'It was good to see you, Clay. Don't be a stranger.'

I watched her drive away.

Tatiana moved aside to allow me access to the entrance.

'Amy seems lovely,' she said.

I ignored her and went inside.

Tatiana clomped after me, up the stairs. 'She's the right size, anyway.'

'Please go home,' I said, not looking back.

She kept on coming. We reached the third floor. I let myself into my apartment and she pitched forward to block the closing door.

I was too tired to argue. Maybe my lizard brain was still holding out hope that I'd get laid before night's end. I don't know.

I started toward the kitchen to put the leftovers in the fridge.

'Is that what I think it is?'

I paused and turned. Tatiana was pointing at the tumbler on the mantel — the first thing you saw, as soon as you walked into the apartment.

'That's my father's,' she said.

'It used to be,' I said. I hurried to grab hold of the tumbler before she hurled it out the window or did something equally melodramatic. 'Then it was yours. Now it's mine.'

I took it into the kitchen.

'Clay.'

I stashed the glass up on a high shelf.

'I'm talking to you,' she said.

I put the leftovers away, opened a carton of milk and sniffed.

'Can you *look* at me? *Please?*'

I put the milk back, poked around for another prop to demonstrate my indifference. Mine is a bachelor's refrigerator, heavy on condiments. I pretended to examine pickles.

'Please listen to me,' she said softly.

I closed the fridge, faced her.

She was crying.

She said, 'I'm sorry.'

'What for? Ruining my night? The part where you don't answer me for a *month*?'

'I needed to work through some things,' she said.

'It didn't occur to you that I might be *worried* about you?'

'I – no,' she said, blinking. 'It didn't.'

I threw up my hands.

'Thank you,' she said. 'That means a lot.'

'Whatever,' I said. 'We didn't set any rules. You're entitled to do what you want.'

'I'm sorry you had to find out the way you did.'

'Not sorry you did it, though.'

She sat down at the kitchen table, waited for me to join her.

I continued to stand.

'If it's any consolation,' she said, 'he kicked me out.'

'He' being Portland Guy. I pictured a stringy neck-bearded dude sporting a woolen beanie and toting an artisanal ax on his shoulder.

'I'm not interested,' I said. 'And no, it's no consolation.'

'He said he couldn't let me stay because I'm not making good decisions at the moment and he didn't feel right taking advantage of me.'

'Did you hear me?' I updated Mr Sensitive's image: subtract ax, add sweater vest and corncob pipe. His analysis, though – that I couldn't argue with. She *wasn't* making good decisions. 'I don't care.'

She looked stung. I hadn't meant I didn't care about her, just that I had no intention of validating her odyssey of self-discovery.

Even so, I felt bad for her, almost against my will. Having to defend her behavior to Amy had shifted me into a sympathetic frame of mind.

I said, 'Look, it happened. Okay? No hard feelings.'

'But time to move on,' she said, and she twirled a finger in the air, just as she had on a warmer night some months ago.

'Yes,' I said.

Silence.

She said, 'Do you know why I went up to Tahoe?'

'To sell the house.'

'I could have done that from here,' she said. 'I went to grieve,' she said. 'I couldn't while I was here. I tried. I couldn't do it.'

'There isn't a wrong way –'

She held up a hand. 'Please? This is hard for me.'

My knee had begun to ache. Cursing myself, I pulled out a chair and sat opposite her.

She gave me a sad, grateful smile. 'The estate, my mom, my brothers – it was just too much. I went thinking I'm going to get there, all of that is going to fall away, I'll be able to focus and look reality in the face.' A bewildered laugh. 'It worked. For about an hour, until I realized that the reality I'm facing is, actually, fucking horrendous. It's my father. And he's dead.'

She'd begun tugging at a piece of dry skin on her lip. She caught herself doing it and shoved her hands under her thighs. 'Then I get back, and you're telling me all these crazy things about him . . . I wasn't ready.'

She looked at me. 'I'm ready, now.'

'Are we talking about your father, or are we talking about us?'

'Either. Both.'

I rubbed my knee. 'What did your mother tell you?'

'That you went to see her and asked about me.'

'I went to talk to her about your father and Julian Triplett,' I said. 'That was the subject of conversation. The *only* subject of conversation.'

She looked down at her lap.

I said, 'Still want to help?'

After a beat, she nodded.

'Fine,' I said. 'I ask, you answer. That's the deal.'

Silence.

'All right,' she said.

She sounded so meek that I started feeling bad for her all over again.

I squelched it.

'The locker where you put your father's documents,' I said. 'Where is it?'

'Eastshore Highway. The big place. I don't remember the name.'

'Text me the address,' I said. 'Meet me there tomorrow morning. Nine a.m.'

She nodded again. Then she said, 'We could go together.'

She raised her face to me.

'Tomorrow,' she said. 'We could go over there together.'

She meant: *I could stay the night*.

Lizard brain perked up.

I said, 'I'll meet you there at nine a.m.'

For a moment I thought she'd rescind the offer. But she conceded with a half smile.

'Nine a.m.,' she said.

*   *   *

I ordered her a car. She started to argue, but this time I wasn't having it: I threatened to arrest her if she attempted to drive away. We sat in the kitchen, waiting in silence. Every second offered another tough choice for lizard brain. She was willing and present and no less attractive than she had been a month ago. Finally my phone chimed, saving me from myself.

At the door, she said, 'I'm sorry I ruined your evening.'

'I'll figure it out.'

'I can call her and explain.'

'I'm going to veto that.'

'For the record, Amy really does seem nice.'

'She is. Although I'm not sure how you could tell. You met her for ten seconds.'

Tatiana said, 'I'm a good judge of character.'

Like mother, like daughter.

I bid her good night and went to restore the tumbler to its place.

36

EN ROUTE to East Bay Premium Storage the next morning, I left Amy a voicemail, fumbling through an apology that ended with me saying, 'Look, do-over? Please? Just, call me. Okay. Thanks. Bye. Call me.'

Smooth.

I arrived a few minutes early, waited in the parking lot till ten after.

I texted Tatiana. I'm here where are you

Still no sign of her by nine twenty. I was on the verge of leaving when she replied.

Locker 216

Combo 4-54-17

Good luck

My first impulse was to get annoyed. But what was the point? I had what I needed.

Thanks I wrote.

I headed over to the front office to sign in.

The 'premium' part of 'Premium Storage' was a free cup of lukewarm coffee. I stepped from the freight elevator into a concrete corridor lined with rolling steel doors, numbers stenciled on the wall in red paint.

The unit Tatiana had rented measured ten by fifteen – enough to house the contents of a one-room apartment, and far more space than she needed. Running my flashlight over the piles, I counted about forty boxes. Stacked up, unlabeled, in no particular order, they gave off that diluted campfire odor characteristic of old paper.

I moved quickly through the first few stacks. Utility bills and auto insurance policies. What I wanted were credit card statements, bank statements, copies of canceled checks, correspondence – anything that might prove Rennert had been sending Triplett money or that divulged Triplett's whereabouts.

The likelihood of finding a clear trail was low. Easier for Rennert to fork over a packet of cash. Even so, I might be able to detect a pattern of withdrawals, find an ATM, narrow it down to a neighborhood.

I was fishing. It was going to take time.

Working cross-legged on the unswept concrete, I fell into a sort of trance state. Distant sounds reverberated: humming elevator, dollies clattering. The financial paper I came across revealed nothing about Julian Triplett but drove home how rich Rennert had been. All those commas and zeros gave me a new understanding of how drastically Tatiana's life had changed in recent months.

Even with a three-way split she'd never have to work again. A blessing, I guess, but maybe a source of shame?

I stopped myself. No need to sink back into caring for her.

I stood up, knee cracking, and went downstairs for a second free cup of coffee.

Checked my phone. No reply from Amy.

I started composing a text to her.

Thought better of it and deleted.

Ninety minutes in, I came across a box slightly larger than the others, UC library system bar-code stickers on the body, lid taped shut.

Pulse racing, I slit the tape, beheld the remains of Nicholas Linstad's experiment.

I found the Meeks score sheets, anonymized. I found the master document that decoded participant numbers into names and noted other demographic data.

Nowhere did Julian Triplett's name appear.

A whole mess of waivers, dual signatures, participant and parent/guardian.

No Julian Triplett. No Edwina.

Linstad, avoiding putting Triplett's name on record?

I held up a red three-and-a-half-inch floppy disk labeled BB. *Bloodbrick: 3D.* The game that had started it all.

Or hadn't, depending on who you asked.

A blue floppy disk, labeled T. Linstad had used *Tetris* as a control.

Next: a thin, wrinkled manila envelope containing reimbursement forms – three of them, filled out in the same, slashing hand and signed *N. Linstad*. The first form was for five hundred dollars, the licensing fee for using the Meeks.

The second was for several hundred dollars' worth of cash incentives, doled out to subjects as an inducement to show up, week after week.

The third reimbursement form asked for twenty dollars for 'miscellaneous expenses'. Like the other two forms, it bore Linstad's signature. An attached receipt gave the breakdown.

SAMMIE'S STEAK SAMMICH
'home of the original'
1898 Shattuck Ave, Berkeley 94709
Ticket #10012116   User: Max Z.
10/31/93   01:39:28 PM PST

ITEM	QTY	PRICE	TOTAL
Double Steak Sam Plate	1	9.95	9.95
Curly Fries			
Honey Slaw			
Lg Fountain Beverage	1	2.95	2.95
Whoopie Pie	2	2.50	5.00
Subtotal			17.90
Tax			1.35
Total			19.25
Visa XXXXXXXXXXXX8549			19.25
Auth: 015672			
Tip			0.75
Total			20.00

Thank You For Your Business Please Come Again

I knew Sammie's – a greasy spoon off the northwest corner of campus, known for its cheap, gargantuan portions and don't-give-a-fuck-bout-chu waitstaff; a lowbrow bastion in a culinary

334

landscape that got increasingly precious with every passing year. My teammates liked to go there after practice. They'd egg one another on, see who could eat the most without throwing up. Athletes will turn anything into a competition. I'd go along, not for the food, but for the sake of team unity.

Neither the reimbursement form nor the receipt indicated who the meal was for.

But I had a theory.

He said the man got him a burger.

Steak sandwich. Burger.

A reasonable enough mistake.

I slid the form into the envelope, put the envelope in the box, took the whole thing with me down to my car.

Sammie's Steak Sammich had not changed in ten years, twenty years – the entirety of its sixty-seven-year existence, to judge from the black-and-white photos on the wall.

The décor consisted of rickety wooden tables and chairs, upholstered in torn yellow vinyl; a chipped Formica counter with torn blue stools; UFO-shaped ceiling pendants. The fare consisted of overlarge cuts of chewy, oily meat – pounded into submission, fried gray, and set adrift on a kaiser roll, only to be drowned in barbecue sauce.

A bell jangled as I entered, prompting the line cooks to shout, 'Yo, siddown.'

At quarter to eleven in the morning, I was the sole customer. I slid onto a stool and scanned the menu board above the kitchen window, plastic letters pressed into grimy felt. Prices had risen since ninety-three. The Double Steak Sandwich Plate now ran you $11.95. At the bottom of the dessert list, below soft serve and the ubiquitous whoopie pie, block capitals declared WE CHEAT DODGERS FANS!

'Yo,' the counterman said.

'Yo,' I said. 'Whoopie pie, please.'

He raised a glass cake dome. Each cookie was half a foot across. He took one off the top of the pile with his bare hand and put it on a plate. 'Yo, here you go.'

'Can I get a knife, please?' I asked.

'What for.'

'This thing is huge.'

He frowned, craned to address the kitchen. 'Yo,' he yelled.

'Yo,' the line cooks yelled.

'Yo, sir here wants to eat his whoopie pie with a knife.'

The line cooks booed.

The counterman turned to me. 'You don't eat no whoopie pie with no knife.'

'All right, give me an original.'

'Fries or onion rings for a dollar extra.'

'Neither.'

'*Fries* or *rings*.'

'Rings.'

'Beans or slaw.'

'Slaw,' I said. 'And a knife, please.'

He scowled and put the order in. Within seconds I heard the sizzle of meat hitting the flattop. Within minutes I had before me a glorious plate of slop. The counterman set out a squeeze bottle, colored an unappetizing brown – more barbecue sauce.

'In case I get thirsty,' I said.

His face was stone.

I looked at him expectantly. He grunted and reached down and brought out a knife from behind the counter, slapping it down in front of me.

It was a big honking thing, heavy-duty black plastic handle and a thick-spined, serrated blade about four inches long. The teeth were worn down with use but the tip still looked menacingly sharp. You needed such a weapon to vanquish a Sammie's Steak Sandwich. They put up a fight.

I said to the counterman, 'You always use these same knives?'

'What?'

'The knives. Are they the same brand you were using, say, twenty years ago?'

'Yo, I look like I worked here twenty years?'

'Ask them,' I said, pointing to the cooks in the kitchen.

'Man, they don't know.'

'Is there a manager around?'

'Me.'

I'd recheck the murder file, but to my eye the knife was an exact match for the one recovered from a garbage can on the corner of Dwight and Telegraph, wrapped in a bloody gray sweatshirt and stuffed in a plastic bag.

I raised my phone to take a picture of it.

'Yo,' the counterman said. 'No pictures.'

He pointed to a sign on the wall that read NO PICTURES.

I asked for a to-go box.

'Yo, you didn't eat nothing.'

'I need to go.'

'Then why didn't you say *to go*.'

I'd had enough of this. I put my badge on the counter. 'Yo. Box, please.'

He fetched it quick, transferred the food from my plate.

I held up my unused knife. 'And I need to borrow this for a little.'

'Yo,' he said, breaking off uncertainly.

When in doubt, be tall. I stood up, spread my hands on the Formica, loomed. 'Yes?'

'Yeah, boss,' he said, 'no problem at all.'

The Berkeley PD station was six blocks away. On the walk over I bit into my sandwich. It tasted like buffalo hide. I got through a quarter of it before dumping it in the trash.

37

I DIDN'T go in the building. I didn't know what the situation was with Schickman – how much static I'd caused him, how lightly he had to tread. From half a block away, on Allston, I texted him. Fifteen minutes later he jogged up.

'Need to be quick,' he said. 'What's going on?'

I showed him the reimbursement form, the receipt, the knife.

'We were wondering how Linstad got Triplett's fingerprint on the murder weapon,' I said. 'That's how.'

'Could mean the opposite: Triplett took the knife on his own.'

'You don't think it's interesting?'

He grinned. 'Like I said. Interesting.'

'Check out the date on the receipt,' I said.

He stared. 'October thirty-first.'

I nodded. 'Day of the murder. Less than twelve hours prior. Wrap the handle in something,' I said, 'keep the print nice and fresh. For all we know, the knife you have in evidence isn't the real murder weapon. If Linstad was smart, he ditched it some-place far away and planted the one with the print.'

Schickman continued to study the receipt. 'Why would he put in for reimbursement?'

'Because he's a cheap bastard who couldn't help himself,' I said. 'He wanted his twenty bucks back.'

'He tipped seventy-five cents on a nineteen-dollar bill.'

'Add it to a growing list of character flaws,' I said.

Schickman laughed.

'So?' I said. 'This change your mind any?'

'You are one persistent son of a bitch,' he said.

He took the knife from me. 'Let me compare it with the one in evidence.'

'That's all I ask,' I said.

'Whatever I decide to do – and I'm not deciding anything yet – we need to keep it on the DL, all right? Least till we have more.'

'Understood. I'm back at the Coroner's starting tomorrow.'

He held the knife up. 'I need to return this when I'm done?'

I shrugged. 'If the spirit moves you.'

My co-workers greeted me normally, asking how I'd spent my vacation days. I responded in kind, although in truth I felt on edge, my forehead a marquee, my secrets blaring brightly for all to read. Did they know why I'd taken time off in the first place?

I took my seat across from Shupfer, working diligently, aloof as always.

She said, 'Welcome home, princess.'

Las Vegas PD had responded to my request for information regarding Freeway John Doe. They might know my guy. It sounded promising.

The next order of business was to review my queue, updating

cases to reflect the autopsies that had been completed in my absence.

The old lady who'd died in her bathtub: stroke. Nothing sinister.

I clicked SUBMIT.

Overdose. Car accident.

SUBMIT. SUBMIT.

Way down at the bottom, last name on the list: RENNERT, WALTER J.

Get it out of your system.

My failure to close the case out wasn't intentional. Subconscious, maybe. I'd left last week in a hurry, pissed off and eager to get out of there before I shot my mouth off.

Down the hall, Vitti's door was propped, open to anyone who needed him, as per his policy. We were all friends here. He was my superior, sure, but he preferred that we think of him like a father. Or uncle, but not the creepy kind.

He knew I was back today. Probably he was waiting for me to get off my ass and go in there and pay homage, thank him for the R&R, confirm the wisdom of an enforced break.

No, thanks.

Midafternoon he sauntered in to remind everyone to finalize rosters in time for kickoff. It was the final weekend of the regular season. I realized I hadn't lifted a finger to manage my team in over a month.

Opening the website, I saw that I'd slipped to fifth place. Moffett was out front, followed by Sully. Vitti's team sat in third.

'How the mighty have fallen.'

A hand on my shoulder. I fought not to squirm.

'Always next year, Coach,' Vitti said. He was leaning down on me pretty hard, bent over to look at my screen. I could smell the aftershave he applied to his scalp.

I said, 'I'm still in it.'

'You say so, Chief.'

'I mean I don't think I'm eliminated, mathematically.'

I waited for him to make a comment about the Rennert case still sitting in my queue. Instead he just chuckled and walked off. 'Hope springs eternal.'

Outside in the intake lot, I slotted myself behind a concrete pillar, the closest a man my size can get to hiding. I hadn't escaped with any other purpose in mind other than to get some air, but I found myself dialing Amy's number.

Right after pressing SEND, I remembered she was headed back to the East Coast today. I'd left her two voicemails yesterday. A third would push me past 'determined' and on into 'pathetic'. I started to hang up.

But I heard her voice, far away: 'Clay?'

'Hey,' I said. 'Where are you? Are you at the airport?'

'I'm in New Haven,' she said. 'I left this morning and got in an hour ago.'

'Right. Okay. Well. Glad you're back in one piece.'

'That's not morbid at all,' she said, laughing.

I laughed, too.

We spoke at the same time: 'Listen –' 'I meant to –'

'Me first,' she said.

'Okay.'

'I want to apologize for the way I reacted,' she said.

'You don't need to apologize.'

'I do. I was caught off guard.'

'That makes two of us.'

'I had no idea what was going on.'

'Can I please explain?'

'I'm sure I'll want an explanation at some point. Not right now, though.'

'Okay,' I said. 'I had a good time with you, regardless.'

'Me too.'

'. . . but?'

'But nothing,' she said. 'Just. I don't know. I think maybe I packed too much expectation into one night.'

'Uh-huh,' I said.

'I don't mean I didn't enjoy myself, or that I don't want to do it again, when we can.' She paused. 'Seeing you brought back all these memories of how I used to feel.'

I wanted to be able to tell her I felt the same way – that I'd always felt that way about her. But I'd be lying, and she'd know.

I asked when she was next in the Bay Area.

'Not till the semester's over. The plan is to lock myself in my room and write.'

'Spring break?'

She said, 'Let's see how my work goes. Okay?'

'If that's the best I can get,' I said, 'I'll take it.'

'Be well, Clay.'

'Thanks. Happy New Year.'

'You too.'

The day was dying. I should've gone back upstairs, finished

up, done my job. I didn't move. I thought about the dozen or so boxes at the storage unit that I hadn't gotten to yet. I'd planned on heading over there after work. Now I didn't know if I had the energy.

I thought about Amy, and Tatiana, and I remembered a conversation with an old girlfriend. We were fighting, or I should say that she was fighting with me, getting more and more upset at my failure to match her rising ire.

Care she yelled.

About what I asked.

Anything.

We didn't last long after that. It was a familiar pattern. I went along agreeably until all that remained was agreeability.

I called Amy back.

'Hi?' she said.

'I want to see you,' I said.

'Uh. Well –'

'Hang on,' I said. 'Let me speak. You said let's see how it goes, and I said I'll take what I can get. But that's polite, and it's bullshit. I'm not okay with that. I want to see you, soon, and I don't want anything less than that. I know it's new. I know we're at the beginning. I'm putting on record that I want it to *be* a beginning. If you don't want the same thing, that's up to you. But I won't apologize for thinking you're fantastic, or wanting to be with you more, a lot more, as soon as possible.'

Silence.

She said, 'I want to see you, too.'

'Good. Then let's find a way to make that happen. I'll come to you. Or you come here. One or the other. Maybe we have to wait a week or two months, or maybe you really can't get away until the end of the semester, which would suck. But be aware: I'm not letting this go.'

A beat. She laughed softly.

'What,' I said, smiling.

'You,' she said.

'What.'

'You're different than I remember.'

I said, 'I hope so.'

345

38

On Sunday morning, I got a call from Ivory Richards, daughter of Freeway John Doe, his identity now confirmed through dental records as that of Henry Richards, age fifty-eight, formerly of Las Vegas and missing since April.

'I wanted to thank you for what you did,' she said, 'taking the time to find me.'

'You're very welcome.'

'He's still gone. Least now I don't have to wonder.'

'I hope it gives you some comfort.'

She said, 'He used to talk about going to California. He was going to retire, live on the beach. Too hot here. As soon as he could get some money he was going to go. But he lost his house when the bubble burst. I said he could move in with me. I told him: "Just till you get back on your feet again." He didn't want to, it hurt his pride.'

'Yes,' I said, so she'd know I was still listening.

'When he took off, I thought he was living out there. That's what I told myself. I didn't know he was in trouble. I didn't know how bad it had gotten, he hid it. I asked the police to see pictures. They told me better I don't. I can't stop thinking about it. In my mind . . .' Her voice wrenched. 'In my mind, I see such horrible things.'

She was weeping. 'Please tell me it wasn't as bad as I think.'

The scream of the freeway overhead; a body unable to hold its own skin.

I said, 'Not that bad.'

'You're telling stories,' she said. 'It's okay. I appreciate that. I asked you to.'

The last dozen boxes at the storage unit contained nothing that pointed me toward Julian Triplett. I locked up and drove home.

Unsure if I'd need to make this call, I'd waited. Now I didn't think I had a choice.

'Hey,' Tatiana said.

'Hey.' Silence. 'Got a second?'

'Sure.'

'I've been through the boxes.'

'Anything?'

'Sort of,' I said. 'Can I ask you: those last few, that you left at your father's house?'

'You want to look at them,' she said.

'If possible,' I said.

'I was going to get to them eventually,' she said defensively. 'Every time I come near them my eyes water.'

'Right,' I said. 'What do you say?'

'I'm not around to let you in,' she said.

'Later this week, then.'

'No. I mean I'm not *around* around.'

347

A shroud of formality covered her tone.

'Okay,' I said.

Relenting a little, she said, 'I can send you the key, if you'd like.'

'If you don't mind.'

If this. *If* that. So tactful, we were.

'You'll need the alarm code, too,' she said.

'Please.'

She gave it to me: 7-9-7-8. I thought back to when I was having trouble unlocking Rennert's iPhone. I couldn't remember if that was one of the combinations she'd suggested. Probably would've been worth trying. I asked her what it meant.

'I don't know, actually,' she said. She sounded miffed to admit it.

'Thanks,' I said. 'I'll try not to disturb you again.'

'Clay?' she said. 'Let me know what you find?'

'I will if you want me to,' I said. 'Are you sure you do?'

A long silence.

She said, 'My father obviously believed he was doing the right thing. I don't know his reasons, but I have to trust he had them. He was a good man.'

She expected an answer.

'From what I've seen,' I said, 'yes, he was.'

'People don't appreciate that. They never did. They know one thing about him and they think they know everything. But it's not that simple.'

'Nobody is,' I said.

An urge welled up inside me: to ask when she'd be back.

'I'll put the key in the mail tomorrow,' she said.

'Thank you,' I said.

'Take care, Clay,' she said.

The key arrived four days later, postmarked Portland, OR.

I was still laughing as I got into my car and drove over to Berkeley.

Three boxes, mildewed and spongy, tucked in the corner of the basement, caged in by a shelving unit.

We'd had to work to get them out, which meant that Rennert had had to work to put them in. A precaution.

Months drying out in the service porch had helped: they no longer stank so bad. The black stains in the cardboard had faded to a dull greenish gray, shedding a powdery residue that came off on my hands as I lifted the lid off box number one.

It was a quarter full, the contents not sitting high enough to escape the annual flooding. They appeared to be some sort of manuscript. The top few pages were legible, but only just: water damage had caused them to curl and shrivel, the printer ink bleeding, leaving teasing fragments.

never met J before
process of rehabilitation
coinciding with my own interests as a psychologist
arrogance, which prevented me
an alternative explanation presented itself

Beyond page five, the paper had disintegrated, fusing into a single moldering brick, like crude papier-mâché. Trying to separate them only worsened the damage.

The second box was in slightly better shape. The pages had been folded and unfolded, giving them some loft, and they weren't packed down, leaving the uppermost portion unscathed, sixty or seventy pages in total.

Letters, written in a tight, uniform hand.

dear doctor rennert thank you for comming to see me

Lydia Delavigne had commented disparagingly on Triplett's poor spelling and grammar. Considering his learning difficulties and the fact that he'd never finished ninth grade, I thought he got by pretty well.

The neatness of the script struck me as particularly apt.

Big hands doing delicate work.

None of the letters bore a date, and most were brief, one or two lines on a short list of concrete topics: the weather, the food, a stomach ailment that appeared to drag on.

If Triplett ever expressed emotion, it was gratitude for Rennert's visits – simple gratitude, ritualistic, the kind a young child offers when prompted.

The crime, the victim, Nicholas Linstad: none of that came up.

It would be easy to read into the tone a lack of empathy. A low-functioning psychopath, unable to grasp or care about the consequences of his behavior.

I took away a different message. I heard a disoriented mind, brimming with anxiety and loneliness, clinging hungrily to anything consistent.

Two pieces of toast for 'brekfist' one day; three the next.

His way of marking time, like scratch marks on a cell wall.

The sheer volume of the correspondence suggested the depth

of the connection between Walter Rennert and the boy he'd helped put away. Writing must've presented a serious challenge to Triplett.

Yet he'd persisted, seeking to communicate, taking comfort in repetition.

He told Dr Rennert. Who else could he tell?

I moved on to the third box.

Atop the pile sat a loose sheaf of yellowed newspaper clippings, speckled with mold. The murder; the trial. I skimmed them. Nothing I didn't already know.

Lastly, a pair of plastic shopping bags that rattled when I picked them up. I unknotted the handles and saw a jumble of microcassette tapes, cases dated in blue or black ink.

I gathered up the bags, along with the surviving letters.

Stopping in the foyer to reset the alarm, I glanced at the spot on the tiles where Walter Rennert's body had lain. Another small patch of my world marked by death, a shadow invisible to nearly everyone except me.

The clerk at Radio Shack tried to discourage me from buying a microcassette player.

'We don't even make those anymore,' he said.

'The website says you have one in stock.'

He trudged off, returning after a while with a scratched clamshell case.

He scanned it. 'Two eighty-four sixty-nine.'

'That can't be right.'

''Swhat I mean. Shit's discontinued. Get a digital recorder, they're like forty bucks.'

I couldn't be sure that the tapes were good: the water might have ruined them. But the plastic bags gave me hope.

'What's your return policy?' I asked.

'Thirty days.'

I handed him my debit card. 'Receipt, please.'

At home I brewed a pot of coffee and set myself up at the kitchen table with notepad, pen, and my new, expensive, semi-vintage microcassette player.

I sifted the tapes, arranging them in chronological order. The oldest went back to March 2006 – shortly after Julian Triplett disappeared. Fifty-seven in all, roughly one a month. But not evenly spaced out: the first few bunched together weekly. Then monthly, bimonthly.

Seven months separated the second-to-last tape from the final one, in January 2011.

I put in the first tape and rewound to the beginning.

Expecting something along the lines of an audio letter – garbled updates from Triplett, sent to reassure Rennert – I sat up at the first voice I heard.

A woman, crystal clear.

All right, Julian. Before we begin I wanted to make sure that you're settling in okay.

The response came slowly.

Uh-huh.

I'd never heard Triplett speak before. His voice was deep, so muted that you could mistake it for a distortion in the recording. As though he were hiding beneath the covers.

How are you liking the new place? the woman asked.

Pretty good.

Okay. Okay, good. Well. I spoke to Dr Rennert about your medication. You remember I told you that I can't do that for you, write prescriptions? He and I agreed that he'll continue to handle it, like you've done so far. I'll check in with him periodically. But if you ever run out, or you're having a problem, and it doesn't feel right, you should come talk to me and I'll do what I can to help. That's what I'm here for. Okay?

Okay.

Okay she said. *Great.*

Silence; hiss.

She said *How've you been feeling recently?*

Okay.

I know you've had a lot of changes. No response. *Do you want to talk about that?*

All right.

The silence went on so long I started to think the tape had ended.

How about your symptoms? Are you hearing voices?

No.

The conversation lasted another twenty-five minutes, much of it empty air. The therapist probing gently, Triplett mumbling *yes* or *no* or *I guess.*

I'm so glad we're talking, Julian. I really look forward to getting to know you better.

No answer.

The hiss cut off.

I reached for the next cassette.

* * *

As in his letters to Rennert, in his speech Triplett gave an unsettling initial impression. He sat silent for uncomfortably long stretches, ignoring – or seeming to ignore – questions that would have sparked an emotional response in most people. I could imagine him sitting there, taking up a vast amount of space, like some dormant volcano. I could guess how he had come across in court.

The therapist never lost patience, slowly building up a rapport over many sessions. While Triplett was never chatty, his replies got a hair more expansive, his mood less skittish. On tape eight he referred to a job. He'd been hired as some sort of shop hand.

During the following session, she asked how work was going.

I don't like it Triplett said.

What don't you like?

He thinks I'm stupid.

Has he said that?

No.

So why do you think he thinks that about you?

He don't let me touch nothing.

Touch what? The tools?

I wanted to use the band saw. He said I don't know how.

But you do know.

Yeah I know.

You could try telling him that she said. Pause. *Why are you shaking your head?*

He won't listen.

Well, you don't know that unless you try.

As their relationship deepened, I began to feel guilty, eavesdropping. But not enough to stop.

From tape eleven:

Happy birthday, Julian. It's tomorrow, isn't it?

Yeah.

Doing anything special to celebrate?

I don't know.

What about the friend you mentioned? From work?

You mean Wayne he said.

That's the one she said. *You could invite him to do something.*

I don't know.

It seems like you two get along fairly well. What's something you both like to do?

He wants to see the X-Men.

Would you like that?

Silence.

He's got a girlfriend Triplett said.

Well, fine, but if he wants to go to the movies with you, I bet she'll be okay with that.

I don't know.

Well. Whatever you decide to do she said *I hope it's a good day for you.*

I picked up the cassette case. July 8, 2006.

Triplett's birthday was the next day, the ninth. He had a few years on me. Born in '78.

7-9-78.

Rennert's alarm code.

* * *

Come midnight, I'd been listening off and on for over six hours and had yet to learn the therapist's name. Triplett never addressed her, and the recordings picked up in the middle of their talks, as though she waited until they'd said their hellos to start taping.

Then, toward the middle of tape thirteen:

Dr Weatherfeld?

Yes, Julian?

When

I rewound to make sure I'd heard right.

Dr Weatherfeld?

I stopped the tape, opened my laptop.

No mental health professional by that name showed up in the Bay Area.

But I did find a Karen Weatherfeld, farther afield.

About Me

I am a Licensed Clinical Social Worker, offering individual and group therapy for adults facing a wide variety of challenges, including depression, bipolar disorder, and schizophrenia.

She had an office in Truckee. About a twenty-minute drive north of Lake Tahoe.

I kept my email to her casual and quick, asking for a callback, identifying myself as a sheriff but mentioning nothing about Rennert or Triplett.

Within seconds I received an automated reply.

Thank you for your inquiry. I will be away from the office until January 13th. During that time I will be checking email infrequently. If you are experiencing a mental health emergency, please contact the Nevada County Crisis Center at —

Over the ensuing week I called carpenters and cabinetmakers in the Truckee-Tahoe area. There were a lot of them; construction appeared to be one of the main local trades. Vacation homes needed building, refurbishing.

No one I spoke to knew Julian, let alone admitted having employed him.

The day of Karen Weatherfeld's return, I sent a follow-up email. No response. I sent another; same result. Called her. Called her again.

On Saturday we took a homicide in Oakland, guys beefing over a debt, the vic mouthing off about the shooter's girl. While Shupfer finished up with the cops, I perched on the van bumper, dragging my finger down my screen to refresh the inbox, again and again.

Nothing.

I gave Karen Weatherfeld the rest of the weekend. By Sunday night my patience was gone. I had forty-eight hours of my own time and I intended to use them. I checked the weather report and road conditions, threw some clothes in a bag, and set an alarm for four a.m.

39

I<small>T WAS</small> still dark out when I reached Sacramento and stopped at Walmart to buy chains for my tires. The streets of the capital were wet, and after another hour on 80 North, snow appeared at the margins, wispy strands that thickened with the climbing elevation.

I hadn't spent any time in the western Sierras; for obvious reasons, I don't ski. Operating on a gallon of coffee, I gazed out over a surreal landscape – unimaginably beautiful from a distance, terrifyingly harsh up close – and felt an unpleasant tickle in my heart.

A crumpled moonscape, massive blades of granite. Blackened, limbless remnants of forest fires; stark pine mobs. Coppery light oozed down the mountainsides, like the blood of some giant beast caught and thrashing on a jagged peak.

Names on road signs were strange and unsettling. Rawhide. Secret Town. Red Dog. You Bet. At the turnoff for Emigrant Gap, the California Highway Patrol had set up a tire chain checkpoint. Enterprising young guys in parkas hunkered on the shoulder, offering to help with installation for twenty bucks. I hired one and we got down together on the salt-slimed asphalt, pebbles biting through the knees of my jeans.

I rumbled onward, toward Donner Lake, Donner Pass, Donner Memorial State Park. While I could summon a pang over the plight of folks forced to eat their dead, the decision to name every local landmark after them seemed macabre.

There was even a Donner Golf Course. Think of the club-house lunch menu.

The town of Truckee lay hushed under a night's snow. Along the main drag, people shoveled off the sidewalks, clearing the doorways of cafés and gift shops, ski outfitters and rustic chic boutiques. Businesses catering to the tourist trade, spillover from the resorts scattered to the south and west.

Traces of an older, grittier past persisted. At one such establishment – rotten shingles, guttering neon – I stopped to fuel up. A certificate declared the fare BEST BREAKFAST IN TRUC-KEE 1994. In celebration of this achievement, the bathroom hadn't been cleaned since.

Karen Weatherfeld's practice was located out past the muni-cipal airport, where alpine greenery yielded to a flat, featureless scrub. I pulled around back of a bland commercial complex that hosted several other mental health practitioners, along with a cosmetic dentist, a snack shop, a paint emporium, and a fitness boot camp. Only the last of these was up and running, elec-tronic bass juddering through the parking lot. How anyone could conduct therapy amid that racket, I had no idea. For her sake I hoped she'd signed either a great lease or a short one.

Her office hours began at ten. At a quarter to, a forest-green Jeep Cherokee pulled into the lot. The driver was a tall, hand-some redhead in her mid-fifties, dressed in a shiny, quilted winter coat, emerald scarf, and jeans tucked into cowboy boots. I recognized her from the headshot on her website.

Keys in hand, she headed for the exterior stairs.

I made myself known from ten yards off, so as not to startle her. 'Ms Weatherfeld?'

She faced me. 'Yes?'

'Deputy Clay Edison,' I came forward, badge up. 'I've been trying to reach you.'

A series of quick blinks. 'May I?' she said, reaching for my ID. I gave it to her. 'I don't know if you got my emails.'

She examined my picture longer than seemed necessary. 'What can I do for you?'

'Can we go inside? Talk a moment?'

'I have a client scheduled at ten.'

'I can come back later.'

She returned the badge. 'May I ask what this is about?'

'It's better if I have a chance to explain in detail. In the meantime, though, please don't worry. It's a routine matter.'

'Your saying that makes me extremely worried,' she said.

'How does noon work for you?'

A beat.

She said, 'I take lunch at twelve thirty. Meet me here.'

She started up the stairs, glancing over her shoulder. 'For the sake of my client's privacy, I'd appreciate it if you left now.'

Walter Rennert's vacation home sat on the northwest shore of the lake. Easing down the private road, I could see why Tatiana came here to retreat from the world. It was secluded and still;

the trees were majestic and the frost on the water glistened and the earth smelled everywhere of freshness and rebirth.

The house itself was smaller than I'd envisioned, a real cozy cottage, log walls and a black stovepipe jutting from the roof. I strolled around the property in ankle-deep snow, imagining Tatiana and her brothers running through the woods, cramming wet handfuls down one another's shirts.

Most of the shutters had been left open, and I played my flashlight through the windows. I'm not sure what I expected to discover – Triplett himself, perhaps, peering out timidly from beneath a rug? I found it blackly funny to imagine him, the giant lump of him, living hidden beneath Tatiana's feet for weeks on end.

I saw only a mild disorder. Following the break-in, she'd left in a hurry, running back to Berkeley before she had a chance to clean up or prepare for winter. The firewood rack on the back porch hadn't been stocked. She hadn't managed to sell off all the furniture. The living room had been denuded, but in the kitchen I spotted an overflowing ashtray left out on the breakfast table. The table was nothing special. But the chairs that surrounded it made a set. There were four of them, exquisitely carved.

Stepping into Karen Weatherfeld's waiting room, I added my coat next to hers on the rack and pushed the button to notify her of my arrival.

The inner door swung wide, and she beckoned me into a warm office with a neutral color scheme, a jute rug, bookcases.

With the door shut, the throb of the gym subsided to a gentle pulse, reminiscent of a heartbeat.

Diplomas on the wall: BA in sociology from Arizona State University; master's in social work from the University of California, Berkeley.

'Please,' she said, inviting me to the couch. Running horses patterned her navy blouse. She sat at the desk, opened a canvas lunch sack, began setting out neat little glass containers of vegetables and grains. 'You don't mind if I eat.'

'Of course not.'

'I did get your emails,' she said. She shook up a mason jar of dressing, tipped a thimble's worth onto sliced cucumbers. 'I couldn't tell if they were legit.'

Credible excuse. I'd written to her from my personal account instead of from work; I'd referred to myself as a sheriff but had not identified the county. I couldn't afford to have her calling my office to confirm.

I offered her my bona fides again.

'I believe you,' she said, stirring her salad. 'Long way to come for a routine matter.'

'It's a nice drive.'

She chuffed. 'In this weather?'

I said, 'I need to get a message to Julian Triplett.'

A hitch in her expression. She set down the fork and reached for her water bottle. 'You realize, Deputy, that we can't have this conversation. Any answer I give you constitutes an ethical violation.'

'I'm not asking you to reveal anything. I'm asking you to deliver a message.'

She shook her head.

'Is that a no?' I asked.

'It's not a yes or a no. It's not anything. I told you, there's nothing I can say to you.'

'Are you aware that Walter Rennert passed away?'

She paled, and her mouth opened involuntarily.

'When?' she said.

'September.'

'How?'

'His heart,' I said.

She shut her eyes. 'God.'

She sounded shell-shocked.

'I'm sorry to have to tell you,' I said.

She shook her head. 'I'd rather know.'

'How often were you two in contact?' I asked.

'Once or twice a year.' Her eyes remained closed. 'Usually it was over the phone.'

'When he came up here, you didn't see him?'

She shook her head. 'No, we . . . No.'

I said, 'You knew Walter at Cal.'

'Yes.'

'Did you work together?'

She cleared her throat, came to attention. 'We were friends.'

Lydia Delavigne's words came into my mind.

Walter wasn't perfect.

Do you expect me to believe that he didn't take his fair share of comfort in the arms of others?

'I found the audiotapes you made for him,' I said. 'The sessions you did with Julian. I listened to some of them. Not all. I stopped once I figured out who you were.'

Karen Weatherfeld said nothing. She appeared to have lost interest in her lunch.

'Walter calls you up,' I said. 'He says, I have this kid, he's in some trouble and I need to get him out of town. He asks you to keep an eye on him. How am I doing, so far?'

She stared at her lap.

'You must have been surprised when he showed up with Triplett. Unless you already knew about the relationship between the two of them.'

No answer.

'The tapes stop about six years ago. Have you kept up with Julian since?'

No answer.

'You're juggling several competing priorities, I get that,' I said. 'But let's remember what the purpose of this arrangement was originally: to help Julian.'

She seized her fork and scooped quinoa into her mouth.

'I'm not here to create problems for him,' I said. 'The opposite. I know he didn't kill Donna Zhao. Tell him that, please.'

She chewed, chewed.

I said, 'His sister Kara is concerned about him. So's his mom. His pastor; Ellis Fletcher. People haven't forgotten about him. They want to hear from him.'

I took out my card, scratched out the office number, wrote my cell on the back.

'I'm not in town long,' I said. 'I have to go back tomorrow afternoon. I was hoping to speak to him before then.'

I pushed the card across the desk.

She didn't touch it.

Reaching in my pocket again, I took out an amber pill bottle. Held it up.

'This is a thirty-day supply of Risperdal,' I said. 'Julian came looking for it a couple months back. I don't know how he's fixed now. But at the time he was desperate enough to break into Walter's house. He's lucky he wasn't arrested.'

I placed the bottle on the desk, atop my card.

'If nothing else, I want him to know that somebody believes him.' I stood up. '*I* believe him. Please tell him that.'

I headed south out of the parking lot, driving a hundred yards before making a U-turn and pulling over. I had an unobstructed view of anyone entering or exiting the parking lot. Which meant they would have the same view of me.

I reclined the seatback as far as I could without losing my sight line.

I listened to the radio.

I ate beef jerky and a gas station muffin.

Intermittent snow fell.

I guessed she'd stay through the end of the workday.

Close.

At four fifteen, the Jeep made a rolling stop at the lot entrance and headed north, away from me.

I started my car.

40

THE ROADS were icy, and practically every vehicle on them was an SUV, which added to the challenge of keeping an eyeball on the Jeep. At that hour the winter sun drooped on the horizon, the glare giving me a slight advantage when she got on the freeway heading east.

Moving within one car length, I opened the map on my phone, tracking our location, trying to get a sense of where she was headed.

Not home; I knew that much. I'd looked up her address, south of the lake.

Traffic had begun to congeal well before we reached the Nevada state line. I fiddled with the map, pressing my head up against the window to check on the Jeep. Its green paint job stood out at first, but the oncoming dusk reduced every not-white color to a generic muddy hue, pierced by hundreds of stuttering brake lights.

The land curved and swelled, loosely mimicking the river. Billboards began to poke their heads up, rodent-like. Tawdry, bright, and basic; promising jackpots of every kind. Cheap food. Cheap sex. Easy money. Salvation in the Lord's embrace.

I crested the hill and the lights of Reno exploded into view.

The procession squeezed through the pass, groping toward the city. Two lanes became four. I struggled to keep sight of the Jeep, repeatedly losing it in a shifting maze of panel trucks. Gunning ahead, only to discover it behind me. It was rush hour. I was driving like an asshole.

My phone vibrated in the cup holder.

I muttered and reached down to silence it.

The caller ID read NATE SCHICKMAN.

I hit SPEAKER.

'Yo,' I said. 'Can I call you back? I'm right in the middle of something.'

'You can,' he said, 'but I think you want to hear this.'

The Jeep had moved into the rightmost lane, toward the 395 interchange. I signaled and began forcing my way into line. 'Go ahead.'

'I looked in the evidence box,' he said. 'The knife's a match: brand and model.'

'Excellent,' I said.

'Hang on, not done,' he said. 'Seeing that, I thought I'd take a poke through the rest of it.'

I throttled the steering wheel eagerly. 'And?'

'In the hood of the sweatshirt,' he said. 'I found hairs. Nice, long blond ones.'

'Please tell me you're not kidding.'

'Three of them. Root and all.'

'Holy shit,' I said. 'That's him. That's Linstad.'

'Well, I'm pretty sure they don't belong to your boy Triplett.'

367

'Fuck *me*.'

He was laughing. 'Don't get too excited.'

'Fuck *that*. I'm *excited*. How soon can we run them?'

'I still need to clear it with my lieutenant. I think he'll bite, though. While I'm at it I want to run the knife, too. If it is the murder weapon – no guarantee there, but if it is – we might be able to pick up offender blood. That'd be even better.'

'You think Linstad cut himself while stabbing her?'

'Happens all the time. Especially if the victim puts up a fight.'

I remembered the crime scene photos. 'She sure did.'

The Jeep juked toward Susanville. I went after it, cutting off a van. The driver leaned on his horn.

'Where are you, anyway?' Schickman said.

'Let you know when I get there. Hey, but, that's fucking fantastic, man. Thanks.'

'No worries,' he said. 'Thank *you*.'

The bulk of the traffic split off southbound: downtown Reno, airport, Carson City.

Karen Weatherfeld went north, toward the hilly fringes of civilization.

Finding myself directly behind her, I eased off on the accelerator. I still had my chains on, and whenever I broke forty miles an hour, a guttural protest rose up from the undercarriage. The Jeep had no such trouble. It had snow tires. The gap between us began to grow, until all I could see was two dancing red spots.

We'd been traveling for over an hour and a half. It was fully night now. In my rearview mirror, the lurid glow of downtown receded. Homes and businesses began to thin, blank patches appearing on the phone map.

Without warning, the Jeep veered from the middle lane toward the exit.

I cursed and gave chase.

The off-ramp bent violently, forcing me to jam on the brake. Once I'd straightened out, I spotted her taillights far ahead. The highway had dwindled to a single, unlit lane. I sped up, ignoring the noise, the steering wheel battling me. Drawing closer, I made out the Jeep's square profile as it turned left, toward Panther Valley.

The road doubled back under the freeway, and for the next half mile the modern world flared up in the form of freight yards, an RV park, off-brand gasoline. Soon, though, darkness pressed down its thumb, and the asphalt broke up into gravel, warped spurs running off into oblivion. Fists of cloud silenced the stars, smothered the moon.

It was just the two of us out there. No streetlamps. If she was even the slightest bit aware of her surroundings, she would've realized I was following her.

Quickly I consulted the map. The neighborhood we had entered was stubby and self-contained, petering out in dead ends. There was only one way out, the same way we'd come in. Unless she intended to go off-road, she couldn't get very far.

I took a measured risk: I pulled over and cut my engine, letting her drive on.

The Jeep bobbed, swayed, vanished.

I sat out five long minutes, restarted the car, and crept forward.

According to the map I was on Moab Lane. Snow clumped in the desert scrub. Shoved back from the road, every hundred yards or so, were small clapboard houses, half a step above trailers, dropped down at nonsensical angles. Weak moonlight touched mangy grass, woodpiles, lengths of collapsing chain-link, propane canisters, lots of vehicles in varying states of decay. The odd mailbox, sitting atop a four-by-four post, hammered into the dirt.

Near the end of the road I came to a compound of sorts, though nothing to inspire envy in the likes of, say, Olivia Harcourt. To the right of the main house stood a pair of padlocked wooden sheds. Junk lay out like rejected offerings: hubcaps, a smashed-up bicycle. A hammock drooped. I could make out the shape of a fourth structure toward the back of the property, most of it hidden behind an orange pickup a quarter of a century old. A black Camaro, no more recent, sat up on blocks.

Parked a few yards away – as if to distance itself – was Karen Weatherfeld's green Jeep Cherokee.

Dark.

My phone was getting one bar, but the data network refused to budge. I mulled it over, then took another measured risk.

I called my office.

'Coroner's Bureau, Deputy Bagoyo.'

My lucky night. Lindsey Bagoyo was good people.

'Hey there,' I said. 'It's Clay Edison, from B shift.'

'Oh hey, Clay,' she said, her voice cutting in and out. 'What's up.'

'Not much. Listen, I'm checking something out here, and I can't get reception for shit. Can you do me a favor and look up an address for me?'

'Yeah, no problem.'

I gave it to her. Added, 'It's in Reno.'

'As in Nevada?'

'The very one.'

'What's up there?'

'Long story,' I said. 'Remind me to tell you sometime.'

I heard her typing.

She said, 'I'm getting a couple names associated with that address. Arnold Edgar Crahan. Michael Wayne Crahan.'

What about the friend you mentioned from work?

You mean Wayne.

'Can you see if either of them have a record? I need to know who I'm dealing with.'

More typing; a beat.

'Nothing on our end,' she said.

'Okay. Great. Thank you.'

'Clay? Everything all right?'

'Fine,' I said. 'I'll fill you in later. Have a good night.'

'You too.'

I put down the phone and strapped up, vest and gun.

Dry frigid air constricted around me, tightening the skin on my throat as I approached the gate and lifted the latch.

It squeaked.

A thousand dogs began howling.

I stopped dead, my hand hovering at my pistol.

I could hear the dogs, but I couldn't see them. The ruckus echoed across the frozen earth, fracturing crazily: claws on wood, steel chains tested, meaty bodies slapping together. All from the sheds to my right.

The main house porch light snapped on.

The screen door banged open.

A man in a flannel shirt leaned out. He swept a flashlight over the yard, landing on me. I raised an arm against the glare. 'Mr Crahan.'

'Who's that.'

'Sheriff. I'm gonna put up my badge. Okay?'

'Stay put.'

He ducked inside, reemerged dragging a baseball bat, his moccasins crunching snow and gravel. In his late forties, he was Anglo and sinewy, with thin brown hair and a wire of scar tissue connecting his left ear to the left corner of his mouth, where a lit cigarette dangled.

He stopped within swinging range. 'Lemme see it.'

I held out my badge. He snatched it and scurried back.

The dogs bayed and scratched and wailed.

'Are you Wayne or Arnold?' I asked.

'Arnold's my uncle,' he said.

He tossed me the badge. 'What do you want?'

'I'd like to speak to Julian, please,' I said.

No reply.

'Is he in the house?' I asked.

'I don't know what you're talking about.'

'Wayne. Come on. That's Karen Weatherfeld's Jeep.'

'Jeep's mine.'

'With California plates.'

'I used to live in California,' he said.

I squinted past the pickup truck. 'Is he out back?'

Wayne Crahan took a drag. 'What's the problem?'

'No problem. Just want to say hello to him.'

He chuckled, smoke billowing. The dogs were still going crazy.

I said, 'You have my word.'

'See, friend, I don't know what your word's worth.'

He flicked ash toward the sheds. 'Hush,' he said.

The barking ceased.

'Well trained,' I said.

'Nobody wants a pit bull don't listen to instructions,' he said.

He sucked the cigarette down to the filter, dropped the butt, and toed it out.

'Do I have your permission to look around?' I said.

Before he could reply, footsteps came up the side of the house. Karen Weatherfeld emerged from the shadows, saw me, and stopped short.

I raised my eyebrows at Crahan, who shrugged.

'You followed me?' she said.

I said, 'How's he doing?'

She seemed torn over whether to yell at me or thank me. At last she sighed, rubbed her forehead, came over to join us. 'Not great.'

'Can I talk to him?'

'Not tonight. He needs to rest and let the medication take effect.'

'Tomorrow, then.'

'Let's see how he is,' she said. 'I was planning on coming by to check on him.'

'Did you give him my message?' I asked.

'I think it's a bit much for him to handle right now.' She turned to Crahan. 'You'll keep an eye on him overnight.'

'Yup,' he said.

'Thank you,' she said. Adding: 'I wish you'd called me sooner.'

Crahan sniffed. 'We're fine.'

'I'm sure you are,' she said. 'But that's what I'm here for.'

'I said we're fine.'

They regarded each other tautly.

'Here's what I don't understand,' I said. 'It's been probably two, three months since he ran out of meds. How's he been managing this whole time?'

'I split him some of mine,' Crahan said.

We both looked at him.

'What,' he said.

We all arranged to touch base in the morning. Before leaving, Karen Weatherfeld went back to check on Julian once more. I stood in the yard, chapping my hands against the cold. Crahan fired up another cigarette and offered me the pack.

'I'm good, thanks.'

He blew out smoke. 'Sorry I had to lie to you there.'

'I get it,' I said. 'He's your friend.'

He nodded.

'You two lived together long?' I said.

'Couple years. My uncle don't charge no rent cept he takes half what we make from the dogs. Good dog get you three, four hunnerd.'

'You and Julian used to work together,' I said.

'Not since I hurt my back. He still likes to mess around. Him and tools, they get along.'

'I know, I've seen his stuff.'

'Oh yeah? Cool. I was the one helped him get the site set up.'

'Site . . . Website?'

'Yup.'

I said, 'Julian has a website.'

'Etsy, man,' Crahan said. 'People go crazy for that shit.'

'What's he make? Chairs?'

'Nah, not no more. We don't got the room for a workshop, pretty much just the lathe. Cutting boards, bowls. Little sells quicker and anyhow it's easier to ship. He helps out with the dogs, too. The dogs like him.' He coughed. 'Straight up: what trouble's he in, huh?'

'None. I gave you my word.'

He nodded skeptically. 'Then what's your message for him?'

'That it's okay for him to come home.'

Crahan sniffed, sucked in smoke.

'Whatever, man,' he said. 'He's home.'

41

I CHECKED into a hotel-casino in downtown Reno, fifty dollars for a nonsmoking room that smelled like a bonfire of used jock-straps. The window opened a maximum of six inches. I left it cracked and cranked up the thermostat. Let the elements slug it out.

For the next couple of hours I wandered neon streets, breathing steam, enjoying my anonymity. Dinner was a cheeseburger and fries. From my booth I watched through fogged glass as the lucky and the unlucky stumbled by.

Wayne Crahan's words kept coming back to me.

He's home.

Crahan had given me the address of Triplett's Etsy page. The shop was called Two Dogs Woodworking; it made no mention of either man by name, which was why it had escaped my previous searches. Licking grease from my fingers, I thumbed through the catalog on my phone, browsing pet food bowls, salad bowls, birdhouses, coasters, bracelets. By and large, their feedback was positive. *Beautiful item. Well made. Good deal.* A few people had complaints about the seller's slow response time or his grouchy attitude, which I had to laugh at. Michael Wayne Crahan, friendly face of customer service.

Back at the hotel, the heater and the window had fought to a comfortable stalemate. I showered off a day's worth of driving, then called Nate Schickman to tell him the news.

He congratulated me, asking if I could collect a DNA sample from Triplett.

'Let me see first how's his state of mind,' I said. 'I'm not sure trying to swab him is the best way to establish trust.'

'Gotcha,' he said. 'Listen, I've been thinking on what we do next. Say we get everyone on the same page, it pans out, we wind up with enough to show it wasn't Triplett. That only takes us so far. Overturning a conviction?'

'Bigger deal.'

'Exactly. So I was thinking. There's this group over at the law school works on these sorts of cases. We could throw it to them.'

'Your bosses okay with that?'

'Ordinarily, hell no. Right now? You know how shit is.'

I did. Trust was at a low ebb. Even a cop like me, largely removed from the grind of the streets, felt it. I thought about the woman in Berkeley who'd cussed me out, flipped me off, called me a fascist. Both sides felt misused, hamstrung, frustrated, spooked.

'This prof, Berkowitz, runs the place,' he said. 'It's not like we're her favorite people in the world. Or vice versa, frankly. Now imagine we bring her this on a platter.'

'Building bridges,' I said.

'Ames is a politician at heart. That's as good a reason as any for him to sign off.'

'Plus he gets to put Bascombe on a spike,' I said.

Schickman laughed. 'Yeah, that too. So what do you say?'

'Fine by me.' Then, thinking of Vitti, I said, 'You'll have to keep my name out of it.'

'No way, dude. I'm not taking credit for your work.'

'Still plenty left to do,' I said. 'I'll call you tomorrow, after I've met with Triplett.'

'Enjoy Reno,' he said. 'Stay classy.'

The price of my room included the breakfast buffet. Eight a.m., Karen Weatherfeld met me in the restaurant, nursing tap water while I feasted on tough eggs and pale toast.

'I wish Wayne had come to me sooner,' she said. She looked exhausted and sounded anguished. 'I had no idea things had deteriorated to this point.'

'I'm sure he would've called if it became an emergency.'

She waved, denying herself forgiveness. Then, reconsidering, she said: 'The fact of the matter is, Julian has done very well. As well as you can expect for someone with schizophrenia. If that's really what he has.'

'You don't think so?'

'I wish it was so clear-cut,' she said.

I thought about Alex Delaware's reply when I asked what was wrong with Triplett.

It would be convenient if everyone fit into a diagnosis. Or if a diagnosis was all you needed.

'You have two kinds of symptoms,' she said. 'Positive, like

hearing voices or paranoia, and negative, like social withdrawal or diminished affect. Julian has always shown more of the latter. Certainly he's shy.'

'That's what comes across on the tapes.'

She nodded. 'It could simply be that he's an extreme case of social anxiety, or that he doesn't understand social cues the same way most people do. To me it feels more appropriate to put him on the autism spectrum. Even that's not a perfect fit.'

'He hears voices,' I said.

'Does he, though?'

I looked at her with surprise.

'He never complained about it to me,' she said. 'Personally? I witnessed what you'd regard as irrefutable proof. Mumbling to yourself when you're experiencing stress isn't quite the same as being plagued by an internal monologue that you can't turn off. I'm not a psychiatrist, granted. But, again, it feels like we have a hammer and we're seeing nails everywhere.'

He's always been like that. Not dangerous. Just . . . himself.

Kara Drummond had said that.

I said, 'His mother described him as afraid of his own shadow.'

'That's definitely true,' Weatherfeld said. 'He was – is – extremely anxious. You could label it paranoia. It's a fine line. If it were me, I'd probably be paranoid, too, at least by now. Think about what he's been through.'

Enough to induce a false confession.

Enough to hide and stay hidden.

I said, 'Why keep him on antipsychotics, then?'

'Because they make him feel better,' she said. 'Risperdal

helps with other things, too, like mood. Understanding the mechanism isn't as important as knowing that it works for him.'

'Does he see a psychiatrist?'

She shook her head. 'In the beginning we wanted to keep a low profile. If I'd noticed anything worrying I would have insisted. In fact, later on I tried to refer him for a checkup. Meds aren't a silver bullet. There are side effects, and it pays to recalibrate every once in a while. But he refused. He has a hard time trusting people. It was hard enough for him to learn to trust me.'

'I can't blame him for that.'

'Me neither.' She clutched her water. 'It was supposed to be temporary.'

'Him being up here.'

'Just till things calmed down. Walter and I never explicitly discussed the terms, or how long it would last. If I had any idea it'd turn into a permanent arrangement, I never would've agreed. You have to realize: after Nicholas died, Walter was in a frenzy. He was absolutely convinced the police would come swooping down on him, or Julian, or both of them. Talk about paranoia . . . He had me convinced, too. All I had to go on was what he told me.'

'Which was what?'

'There was an accident,' she said. 'It looked bad for Julian.'

'He didn't say Julian was involved.'

'No. Walter was adamant about that.'

'Did you and Julian ever discuss him going back?'

'It never came up. In the beginning I was more concerned with short-term goals, managing his stress level. Once he did get settled, a certain amount of inertia set in, I guess.' She paused. 'He never raised the subject, either. For the first time, he was living on his own terms.'

Point taken. What did Triplett have to return to in the East Bay?

People did love him, but love didn't guarantee safety.

I said, 'What was the deal with the tapes?'

'Walter's idea. He wanted to hear Julian's voice, to know he was okay.'

But she had broken eye contact. I said, 'Any other reason?'

She said, 'I'm not going to say he had ulterior motives. He really did care about Julian. Immensely.' She pinched the bridge of her nose, sighed. 'He wanted to write a book.'

'Walter did?'

'Explain it all. The murder, the trial. Put the record straight. He thought he could fix everything.'

The manuscript.

an alternative explanation presented itself

She faced me. 'He meant well.'

I said, 'What was it that changed his mind?'

'I'm not sure there was one specific moment,' she said. 'He got to know Julian. That's a process that takes a long time. It requires serious dedication.'

'Let me put it another way,' I said. 'Did he learn something from Julian that would have caused him to shift his attention to Nicholas Linstad? Confront him?'

'I don't know,' she said. 'Again, I doubt it was so cut-and-dried. Few things in life are. And, believe me, Walter could be . . . fickle. With his affections.'

Everyone disappoints in the end.

She cleared her throat softly, drank water, moved her lips against each other. 'As far as the book's concerned, I think he ran out of steam once I stopped recording. By then I was seeing Julian far less often. He didn't need me as much. He had a routine. Unconventional, but stable. In my experience, Deputy, much of mental illness is about losing autonomy. When someone starts to regain that, you want to encourage them.'

I nodded.

'I don't know,' she said. 'Maybe I'm letting myself off the hook too easy.'

'Julian and Wayne seem to get along.'

She smiled faintly. 'Yes. And thanks for changing the subject.'

She checked the time on her phone. 'Should we get going?'

In daylight, the neighborhood looked less menacing – worn out but bright. Crahan sat on his porch steps, smoking, while a pair of dogs chased each other in circles. One brindle, one white with half a black head. Compact tubs of gristle and teeth, well short of purebred, they ceased their game to watch Weatherfeld and me. We waited at the gate for Crahan to stub out his cigarette and amble over.

A third dog, crazily pied, older and larger, trotted out from behind the Camaro and joined the other two.

Mom and puppies.

'Safe,' Crahan announced in a loud voice.

He lifted the squeaky latch.

I tensed.

The dogs stood locked in place, vigilant, calm, nothing like the hellhounds that had produced last night's earsplitting racket.

Crahan held the gate for us. 'He's up,' he said. 'I heard him moving around.'

We walked toward the back of the property. The roofline I'd discerned in the dark belonged to a trailer that had seen better days. Exterior paint crackled, and the whole structure listed toward the ass-end. Orange extension cords originating in the main house snaked through open windows, where gingham curtains hung slack in the frozen, windless morning. The dimensions looked utterly inadequate for a man of Triplett's size. I pictured him wedged in there like a fetus.

Crahan thumped the door gently. 'Yo, JT. Company.'

A wooden croak.

The trailer tilted forward.

No matter how often you tell yourself not to make assumptions, you can't help it. I believed – knew – that Julian Triplett was innocent. Yet as the door opened and his torso filled up the frame, the reality of him startled me nonetheless.

I felt a click in my throat. I'd taken a step back, reflexively.

He was bending over to peer out, clad in a 5XL blue T-shirt and camo mesh basketball shorts. Barefoot, or so I thought initially. Then I saw flip-flops, black plastic straps stretched to their limit and cutting into his insteps, foam soles squashed flat, toes the size of plum tomatoes overhanging in front.

My work has taught me to know at a glance what lies beneath a person's clothes. Calves say a lot. They describe the burdens a body imposes on itself. Julian Triplett's were hewn cliffs of muscle, suggesting that the load above was balanced despite its outrageous proportions.

He appeared to have just woken up. His skin bore an oily sheen. Cloudy eyes went from Crahan to Karen Weatherfeld. To me.

His face pinched, as though he was bracing for a punch.

'Good morning, Julian,' Weatherfeld said. 'Feeling any better today?'

A cautious nod.

'I'm glad to hear it. Did you sleep okay?'

Triplett kept looking at me.

He recognized me. I could tell. I worried he might run.

'Julian,' Weatherfeld said. 'I want to introduce you to someone. This is –'

Crahan strode over and slapped me on the back, interrupting her: 'You gonna let us inside or what? I'm freezing my nuts off out here.'

After a moment, Triplett withdrew.

The trailer tilted backward again.

'Come on,' Crahan said, waving us along.

Stepping inside solved at least one mystery: while the sink and cabinetry were intact, the far end of the trailer, where you'd expect to find a dining table and banquette, had been gutted. A pair of mattresses crammed in on the floor formed an oversized sleeping area. I saw a stack of four pillows, crushed into V's by the nightly weight of Triplett's head. The sheets were old, but they were clean enough, and there was a distinct lack of smell, much less than I'd expect from so much human in so cramped a space. The open windows helped.

The floor felt gritty underfoot, and the air tasted of sawdust. A fine layer of it covered the surfaces; swirling paisley clouds diffused the sunlight that insisted through cracks in the curtains. Again, if not for the open windows, it would have been intolerable. As it was, the atmosphere was hazy and unreal.

On the counter, a tabletop lathe. Beside it, a cardboard box, labeled REAL CALIFORNIA AVOCADOS and piled halfway up with scraps of wood.

Crahan's line about wanting to get out of the cold was just that, a line. The temperature inside the trailer was the same as out. I suppose Triplett's bulk provided him enough insulation to walk around in T-shirt and shorts.

He plopped down on the mattresses, scooted back against the wall, and hugged his knees to his chest.

Crahan crawled over to join him. They sat side by side, shoulders touching.

'Julian,' Karen Weatherfeld said, kneeling, 'this is Deputy Edison.'

'Hi,' I said. I got down and pulled myself cross-legged. It was awkward but I didn't want to loom. 'You can call me Clay.'

Triplett had hooded eyes, dark nearly to the edges, narrow-set and too small for his face. The effects of years on antipsychotics showed in his wrists, which flexed and extended; in fingers that snatched at the air. A pink nub of tongue skated over his lips periodically.

For all that, he exuded an otherworldly silence, a monumental Buddha, hardly breathing. He kept staring at me, finally saying, 'I seen him.'

Weatherfeld gave me an uncertain look.

385

'At Dr Rennert's house,' I said.

Triplett nodded.

'I'm sorry I scared you,' I said. 'I didn't realize it was you.'

He clenched his hands to stop their fidgeting.

'It's cool, JT,' Crahan said. 'We're all good here.'

He looked at me. 'Right?'

'Absolutely,' I said.

Karen Weatherfeld said, 'Julian, Clay has some questions for you. You don't have to answer them if you don't want. I'll stay here with you the whole time.'

'Me too,' Crahan said. 'Okay?'

Triplett said, 'Yeah, okay.'

'Thank you, Julian,' I said. 'First off, I want to tell you that you're not in any trouble. I came here because I think people blamed you for things you didn't do.'

Silence.

I said, 'I know you went through a lot. I can't change what's already happened. But I *am* sorry that it happened, and I want to try to prove that you didn't deserve it.'

'Lookie there,' Crahan said. 'The man's apologizing.'

Triplett shrugged.

'Is it all right if I ask you about Dr Rennert?' I said.

Triplett nodded.

'You know he passed away?'

'Yes, sir.'

'How'd you find out?'

'I can tell you that,' Crahan said. 'We didn't get meds like usual. I tried calling but it said the phone was off. So I put his name in the computer and we saw the notice.'

'It must be hard for you,' I said to Triplett. 'You two were close.'

Triplett nodded. 'Yes, sir. He's a nice man.'

'Is that why you went down to Berkeley?' I said. 'To look for your meds?'

Crahan said, 'He didn't say nothing to me, he just took off.'

'How'd you get down there?' I asked.

'Bus,' Triplett said.

Crahan nudged him with his elbow. 'I was mad.'

Triplett shrugged, a small smile playing at his mouth before vanishing. It occurred to me that the relationship between him and Wayne might go beyond friendship.

'You have a key to Dr Rennert's house?' I asked Triplett.

'No, sir. He keeps it in the shed.'

'The potting shed.'

'Yes, sir. In the jar.'

'How come you didn't shut the alarm off?'

Triplett shrugged. 'I didn't know it.'

'The alarm code.'

'No, sir. He never turned it on before.'

I said, 'It was your birthday. The code.'

A tangle of emotions passed over the massive face, slow and inexorable as a caravan pressing across the desert.

He said, 'I didn't know that.'

'You did know where he kept the pills, though, in his desk.'

'Yes, sir. I didn't find nothing.'

'You could have come to me, Julian,' Weatherfeld said. 'I would've helped you.'

Triplett averted his eyes.

'You used to do that,' I said. 'Take the bus down, visit people. You stopped.'

He shrugged. 'I don't like it.'

'What don't you like?'

'The bus,' he said.

'How come.'

'They look at me.'

'Uh-huh,' I said. 'I get that. People stare at me, too, sometimes.'

He regarded me quizzically.

'I mean,' I said. 'I'm pretty tall.'

For the first time, Triplett broke into a full grin. 'Yeah, you ain't nothing.'

That had us all laughing, and the tension released a notch.

'I spoke to some folks who're worried about you,' I said. 'They haven't heard from you in so long. Ellis Fletcher?'

Triplett appeared briefly surprised, then shook his head. 'I don't think so.'

'It's true,' I said. 'Your sister Kara, she misses you, too.'

He swallowed hard.

'She'd like to hear from you,' I said.

Rather than answer, he looked to Crahan, who said, 'You tell him what you think, JT.'

Triplett said, 'I like it fine here.'

I nodded. 'Well, sure. Peace and quiet like you got, I'd like it, too.'

He gave another small smile. 'Yeah.'

'All right,' I said. 'You two discuss it and decide what you want.'

388

Triplett nodded.

I said, 'I want to ask you about the night you and Dr Rennert left to come up here.'

Silence.

'It was raining,' he said.

'That's right. Good memory. Did he say why you had to leave?'

'The man got hurt.'

'Nicholas Linstad.'

'Yes, sir. Doctor went to talk to him about me, that I ain't done nothing wrong.'

'Was Dr Rennert planning to go to the police?'

Mere mention of the police caused Triplett to seize up with apprehension.

'It's okay,' I said. 'Never mind that. What about you? Where were you, that night?'

'Home.'

'At your mom's.'

He nodded.

'Was anyone with you? Your mom? Was she there?'

He scratched his chin. 'I can't remember.'

'That's okay,' I said. 'You're doing great. So you're home. Dr Rennert shows up.'

'Yes, sir. He said to get in the car.'

'He took you someplace in the city, in San Francisco. Is that right?'

'Yes, sir. I was there the one night and then doctor said we got to go. The man got hurt, he didn't want nobody thinking I did it to him.'

'Did he explain what had happened?'

He hesitated.

'Did the two of them have an argument?' I asked.

Again, Triplett looked to Crahan.

'Up to you,' Crahan said.

Triplett said, 'He shot him.'

I said, 'Renn – Dr Rennert told you that?'

'No, sir. I heard him tell the lady when we was at the house.'

'Lydia,' I said. When Triplett regarded me blankly: 'That was the name of the woman whose house you stayed at, Lydia. You overheard Dr Rennert tell her he'd shot Linstad?'

'Yes, sir.'

'Shot him, or shot *at* him.'

Triplett made a helpless face.

'It's all right, Julian,' Weatherfeld said. 'It was a long time ago.'

She gave me a warning look, and I relented. 'We can leave it there for now.'

Triplett's hands had resumed their fitful dance.

He said, 'He was a nice man, too.'

'Dr Rennert cared a lot about you,' I said. 'And I know you cared about him.'

But Triplett was shaking his head. 'The other one.'

I grasped his intention. 'Linstad?'

'Yes, sir,' Triplett said. 'He was always nice to me.'

He showed no trace of bitterness. Had Rennert given him the whole truth? Maybe, maybe not. Perhaps, over time, Walter Rennert arrived at the same conclusion that I had, after years of dealing with death: truth, like any vital substance, can be fatal in large doses.

If Julian Triplett could suffer his ordeal while retaining his humanity – his quiet, somber grace – by what right did Rennert or I or anyone else interfere?

Crahan said, 'You said you can prove he's innocent.'

I said, 'I can try.'

'How?'

'First thing I need is for Julian to take a DNA test,' I said. To Triplett: 'It's your choice. Nothing's going to happen if you decide not to do it.'

Crahan said, 'We got a lot to think about. Right, JT?'

Karen Weatherfeld said, 'Maybe we should let Julian rest.'

She got to her feet, waited for me to follow suit.

'One last thing, before I go,' I said. 'I'm going to need you to give me back the other item you took from Dr Rennert's house.'

Triplett stared at his twitching hands.

'Nobody's mad,' I said. 'But it belongs to someone who wants it back.'

Triplett said nothing.

'JT?' Crahan said.

'Yeah,' Triplett said. 'Okay.'

He got up – I felt the floor dip beneath me – and pointed to a kitchen drawer.

'Excuse me,' he said.

Weatherfeld and I backed out of his way.

The drawer housed a variety of woodworking tools: X-Acto knives, chisels, files. Buried in the mix was Walter Rennert's .38.

Triplett picked it up by the butt. Pinched in his fingers, it looked like a toy.

Weatherfeld sucked in a sharp breath. 'Oh, Julian,' she said softly.

Crahan was on his feet now, too, scowling. 'The hell you got that for?'

Triplett shrugged.

'It's okay,' I said. 'You got scared and you grabbed it.'

Triplett nodded.

'We both know you wouldn't use it.'

'No, sir.'

'You don't need it anymore, though. Right? You're safe. So can I have it, please?'

Triplett offered me the gun, barrel-first.

'Thanks,' I said, taking it carefully. 'I want you to know this, okay? You don't have to be scared anymore.'

He thought it over awhile, then nodded. 'Okay.'

I smiled. 'Good.'

We started to go, but Triplett stopped us: 'Hold on.'

He rooted in the avocado box, coming up with a piece of wood he liked. Selecting a knife from the tool drawer, he began rapidly to whittle.

He worked inches from me, like a close-up magician. I couldn't tell what he was making; it was lost in his huge hands. He paused but briefly to inspect the piece from a new angle before resuming with swift, short strokes, shavings spiraling to the floor. The tremors had left him, and he was steady and confident. I could hear the whisper of the blade. His big chest moved up and down like the tide.

Crahan looked on fondly. Karen Weatherfeld watched, rapt.

The strokes slowed. Ceased.

Julian set the knife in the drawer, exchanging it for a crumpled square of sandpaper. He gave the piece several quick wipes, blew dust into the sink, regarded his handiwork with a satisfied smile.

A sunflower.

Start to finish, it had taken him perhaps three minutes.

'Twenty bucks,' Crahan said, 'and it's all yours.'

Triplett pressed the carving into my palm. For an instant his flesh touched mine, and what I felt was smooth and warm, strong and heavy and present, impossible to ignore.

'Kara,' he said.

I said, 'I'll make sure she gets it.'

42

Nine weeks later, on a balmy Tuesday afternoon, I met Nate Schickman in the lobby of Boalt Hall, the main law school building.

He was in uniform. I was not, though I'd put on a decent shirt. No jacket: spring had arrived on campus, overnight. When I was a student, my friends and I had a term for it – that moment when you looked up and noticed that the mud had unfolded into grass, and girls went out in tank tops and shorts. We called it The Day.

The Institute for Wrongful Convictions operated out of room 373, also the office of Yount Professor of Law and Criminal Justice Michelle George Berkowitz.

The door was ajar. Schickman rapped the frame.

'Come in.'

I saw Michelle Berkowitz and thought: assumptions.

She was a petite black woman with regal cheekbones and sculpted eyebrows. Tight braids lined her scalp, blossoming into an auburn cloud at the base of her neck. Stacks of photocopies, forms, folders, textbooks, journals – the stuff of appeals-in-progress – cluttered the floor and bookcases. The desk itself was clean, save a laptop whose wallpaper showed her with a white man and a grinning braces-faced girl of about eleven, the trio mugging in leis.

She told us to sit.

'Thanks for agreeing to meet,' I said.

'How could I not?' She spoke with a Caribbean lilt. 'The curiosity was overpowering. You must realize how rare it is to be approached by the police. In fact, it's never happened in the eleven years I've run this clinic.'

'First time for everything,' Schickman said.

'Mm.' An inscrutable smile. 'Let's begin with the same question I would ask Mr Triplett himself: what's your goal?'

'To clear his name,' I said.

'Yes,' she said. 'But to what end?'

Schickman glanced at me. I won't say we'd been expecting a hero's welcome, but her leeriness caught us off guard.

'Legally, your options are limited,' she said. 'He's no longer incarcerated. We could pursue a pardon, but in this instance any potential practical benefits are, in my view, outweighed by the potential costs. So the question then becomes one of personal or psychological benefit. From what you've described to me, he's living quite contentedly.'

Schickman laced his fingers in his lap, as if to belt himself in the chair.

'Maybe you can help us understand the costs,' I said.

'Set aside, for the moment, the toll on Mr Triplett, which may be significant,' she said. 'There's also a significant cost to me, and by extension to the men and women who *are* wrongly incarcerated, at this very moment. While we sit here chatting, their lives are slipping away. If I agree to take on Mr Triplett's case, I'm depriving those people of our clinic's time, money, and resources. Does that seem fair to you?'

'He deserves to be able to hold his head up,' I said.

'Can't he do that already?'

I said, 'Could you?'

Berkowitz smiled again, a touch more appreciatively. 'You must forgive my skepticism. As I said, I've never been approached by law enforcement.'

'We're here now,' Schickman said. 'That counts for something.'

'It does. Although, at the risk of being cynical, I could point out that, if Mr Triplett were to be granted a pardon, the police officers who stand to be embarrassed are not presently employed by either of your departments. Whereas I have a roomful of pending cases that *do* create problems for active officers, some of whom *are* in your departments.'

'We're not running cover,' Schickman said.

'I believe that your intentions are sincere,' she said. 'But let's be honest with each other, shall we? I've known Chief Ames a long time. Don't tell me he isn't happy to score a few points.'

Schickman smiled neutrally. 'Our duty is to the public, ma'am.'

'Yes, yes, of course.'

'But, look,' he said, 'you don't want it, we respect that.'

'I didn't say I don't want it,' she said. 'Other aspects of the case make it attractive, vis-à-vis precedent. The juvenile angle. Mental health. There's value in revisiting it. It's more a question of timing. And I'd like to emphasize that I meant what I said, about the cost to Mr Triplett. It's not a quick process. It could take years. He'll be forced to revisit a traumatic experience.

Even with your superiors on board there will be pushback, I guarantee.'

I elected not to mention the fact that my superior wasn't on board. If he knew I was sitting here, he'd hit the roof.

'Pushback from the prosecutor,' Schickman said.

'Certainly,' Berkowitz said. 'The victim's family, too.'

'We're bringing them the real killer.'

She shook her head. 'They won't look at it that way. I've seen it happen, in cases far stronger than this. To them, we are ripping off a scab. Nor can I control how people react toward Mr Triplett once the information becomes public.'

She turned to me. 'When we first spoke on the phone, you described him as shy.'

'He is,' I said.

'Well, yes, I should say so. I spoke to his sister, as you suggested, but so far he hasn't returned my calls. So I'd ask you to consider carefully whether he's equipped, emotionally, to handle the backlash. People will rush to reconvict him. In the press. On social media. They won't show thoughtful restraint. He needs to be made aware of the risks.'

'I'll talk to him again,' I said.

'Please do. And have him call me.'

'Say we do move,' Schickman said. 'Can you ballpark our chance of success?'

She yawed her head. 'I try not to make predictions.'

'With respect, Professor,' I said, 'this is a two-way street. He *is* shy, and if he senses that you don't believe him, or that you're not invested, or that you expect to fail, how are we supposed to win him over?'

'Fair enough,' she said. 'I'm going to say "possible." '

'Better than impossible,' Schickman said.

She chuckled, took a pen and a pad from her desk drawer. 'These are the names of two individuals in the clinic who I feel would be best suited to handle the case. It might make more sense for them to speak with Mr Triplett, rather than me.'

She tore the page off and held it out it for Schickman.

'Thanks,' he said.

She nodded. Back to me: 'I remember you. From your playing days.'

Schickman raised his eyebrows. I guess he'd never bothered googling me.

'My husband is a basketball maniac,' she said. 'He was in the crowd the night you got hurt.'

'I'm sorry he had to see that,' I said.

'I'm sorry it happened,' she said.

'Don't be,' I said, rising. 'I'm not.'

43

When Marlborough Ming heard what I had to say about the death of Nicholas Linstad, he responded, 'Ah, screw you.'

I told him I'd take that as a compliment.

The following Tuesday we convened at 2338 Le Conte Avenue, the four-story multi-unit adjacent to Linstad's former duplex. Joining us was the superintendent, a lanky, easygoing Albanian. He led us to the base of the giant redwood that dominated the building's backyard. He'd gone to the trouble of hauling up from the basement a thirty-six-foot extension ladder – in turn saving me the trouble of renting one, along with a truck to transport it. He'd also brought his toolbox. Ming had brought his mouth and a bulging bag of pastries.

We propped the ladder against the tree and the manager racked it out to thirty feet. I paused, one sneaker on the lowest rung. The top looked ridiculously far away.

'Okay there, buddy?' the super asked.

'You should make him sign a waiver,' Ming said.

I started up before the super could see the wisdom in this advice.

The bark of a California redwood is thick, spongy, hairy, and furrowed, to the touch more like fur than plant matter. Entire ecosystems occupy its crevices; its mass creates a microclimate. Within a few short feet I had entered an unknown dimension, hidden in plain sight, just beyond the tip of my nose. Hectic insects. Spiky leaves tickling my face and neck.

About two-thirds of the way up, I twisted around. I was standing a bit below the duplex's second-story exterior landing.

I glanced down.

The super, securing the base of the ladder, gave me a thumbs-up.

'Don't fall, stupid,' Ming called.

My search zone was a band of bark six to eight feet high, that portion of the tree in line with the landing. Starting at the bottom, I moved from left to right, examining one square foot at a time, using my penlight to investigate the hollows, inserting the tip of a screwdriver, feeling for variations in the surface of the wood. When I got to the rightmost edge of the band, I shuttled back like a typewriter carriage, climbed a rung, and began again.

It was tedious, uncomfortable work. Gnats swarmed my eyes, ears, upper lip, forearms, neck. Although I did my best to avoid damaging the tree, inevitably bits and pieces flaked off, red threads that found their way into my sinuses. Pouring sweat, fighting vertigo, I rubbed my face against my shoulder. I really did not want to sneeze, mostly due to the potential for humiliation. I imagined Zaragoza and Shupfer struggling to keep a straight face as they explained to my parents how I'd come to lose balance and break my neck. I imagined Moffett typing up the intake report, unable to stop giggling. Where on the form did you check the box for 'dumbass'? Just thinking about it prompted a nervous burst of laughter.

The ladder rocked.

I clung to the rails, held still.

'I think he gonna piss himself,' Ming said.

After half an hour, the super went inside to handle some tasks. Seizing on the chance for a break, I descended. My back ached, my throat was parched, and my knee felt like tissue paper. I accepted a cranberry-orange scone from Ming and uncapped a bottle of water.

I said, offhandedly, 'What I really need is a metal detector.'

'What a coincidence,' Ming said. 'I got one in my butthole.'

I stared up at the canopy. 'How'd you know when it was time for you to get out?'

Ming shrugged. 'When you start spending days off climbing trees.'

I laughed.

'You ready to give up,' he said, 'I have a job for you at the bakery. Sweeping.'

I drained the water. 'Not yet.' Stepped on the bottom rung. 'Spot me.'

I'd been at it for fifteen minutes when, behind me, a woman's voice rang out.

'What do you think you're doing.'

I risked a glance over my shoulder. She was back: the crotchety neighbor I'd spoken to on my previous visit. She was standing on the landing – her landing – wearing a sleeveless floral dress, a floppy straw hat, and a necklace made of knuckles of pink stone. She had her hands on her hips and was gawking at me in furious disbelief.

I blinked at her across thirty feet of open air. We were almost exactly eye level. I doubt she recognized me. Months had elapsed since our last encounter, and I was in street clothes, my face speckled with dirt and redwood bark.

I tried to smile. 'Hi there.'

'What do you think you're *doing*?' she shouted. 'Get *down* from there.'

'I'll just be a sec,' I said.

I turned my back on her, climbed another rung, began a new sweep.

'*You can't do that.*'

I called down to Ming. 'Little help, please?'

'*You're hurting it.*'

To my dismay, Ming released his grip on the ladder and trotted over to the fence separating the two properties, standing on a rock to address her.

'Hey, lady,' he said. 'Chill out.'

Somebody give this man the Nobel Peace Prize.

'Do you *see* what he's *doing*? *Are you witnessing this?*'

'Yeah, I see.'

'He is *raping the tree*.'

'Hey, lady, please. You giving me a headache.'

'Silence is a form of consent. *I do not consent.*'

The super poked his head out, saw what was happening, sighed volubly.

Meanwhile Ming had fetched the bakery bag and thrust an arm over the fence, waving the pastries at her. 'Have a croissant.'

The super said, 'Ms Parker, these men come from the police.'

An ominous lull.

'*Rape.*' Her voice had risen steeply in pitch and volume. '*State, sponsored, rape.*'

'Lady,' Ming said, 'you need a dictionary.'

The next short while felt like an eternity, as I continued to search the bark and she continued to torch me as a prime example of the worst of white male privilege. Curtains began shifting in neighboring windows, sleepy faces peering out, concerned and confused. In retrospect I'm amazed we didn't attract more attention. Although I'm not sure what anyone could've done, other than call the cops (ha!) or kick the ladder out from under me.

At one point a young man with a backpack wandered up the duplex driveway. He looked at the shrieking lady, at me, at her, adjusted his glasses, and departed.

At last she spun on her heel and stormed inside her apartment. A moment of silence.

Ming said, 'Oh come on, lady.'

'It is ten fifty-eight in the morning on the twentieth of March . . .'

She was recording me with her phone.

'When I arrived on the scene,' she said, 'the assault was already in progress.'

I resumed my search.

Impressively, she never stopped talking, though she soon ran out of ways to describe my crimes and shifted to invoking theories of power and control, darting back inside her house to retrieve a copy of a Judith Butler reader.

Nearing the top of the search area, I slid the screwdriver between two ridges of bark and watched the shank sink several inches deep, the blade landing on a bumpy patch. By then I'd gotten accustomed to a certain texture, a responsiveness in the surface of the wood.

This was different.

I began prying at the bark with my fingers, stripping away chunks and tossing them aside. I'll admit it did feel a tad invasive.

Having tunneled down to bare wood, I beheld a partially healed fissure, at its center a sunken gray smudge. I worked the tip of the screwdriver into the crack.

'The male tool becomes an inflictor of forcible penetration,' the woman said.

I tried unsuccessfully to pry the object loose. The trouble was the length of my limbs: I had crappy leverage. I was swaying all over the place, my palms slick, my shoes failing to keep their grip.

Ming called, 'Fool, come down.'

I did. 'Definitely something,' I said, stepping off the ladder. 'I can't get it out.'

He took the screwdriver from me, clamped it between his teeth, and scampered up, heedless of the wobbling.

'And so violation multiplies,' the woman said, 'rape becoming gang rape.'

It took Ming all of ninety seconds to extract the object. He came down and lovingly displayed it in the palm of his hand.

He said, 'Check out this little motherfucker.'

'This little motherfucker' was the mutilated remnant of a bullet.

Caliber indeterminate. Full metal jacket.

I faced the duplex landing. The woman was still there, still ranting, though I'd begun to mentally edit her out.

I said, 'Rennert's disturbed by what he's learned from Julian Triplett over the years. He pieces together what really happened – maybe not with a hundred percent conviction, but enough to wonder. He feels betrayed. Linstad was like a son to him. He decides to confront him about it. He's concerned for his own safety, so he takes the gun along. Or maybe he meant to scare him. Rennert was prone to grandiose gestures, we've seen evidence of that. They get drunk, words are exchanged –'

'Bang bang,' Ming said.

'They're fighting,' I said. 'It goes off by accident.'

'Don't be stupid, stupid,' Ming said.

I looked at him.

'No sign of struggle,' he said. 'No holes in the walls. No holes in the windows.'

'So?'

'So,' he said, 'how's he hit the tree?'

I traced the imaginary path of the bullet. 'Through the open doorway.'

'Who opened it.'

I let the scene play in my mind.

A big body, crashing onto the landing.

Slamming into the banister, jarring it loose.

Slipping on the wet wood. Tumbling down the stairs.

'Linstad,' I said. 'He was trying to get away.'

I looked at Ming. 'Rennert shot at him as he ran.'

Ming smiled dreamily. 'In the back, I think.'

Midnight; rain; blood everywhere. I could understand why Rennert mistakenly thought his shot had been fatal.

'Never forget,' the woman yelled.

'You gonna tell his daughter?' Ming asked.

Let me know what you find.

I shook my head.

Ming cackled. He dropped the bullet fragment in his breast pocket. 'For a stupid guy, you pretty smart.'

44

IN JULY, our team threw a party to celebrate Moffett's promotion to sergeant. Sully baked a carrot cake. Carmen Woolsey brought five-layer Mexican dip. Even Shupfer got into the act, slopping down a Costco bag of caramel corn.

A strong showing, considering that, until quite recently, none of us – not me, not Zaragoza, not even Dani Botero – had any idea Moffett had taken the exam, let alone passed. Let alone gotten the highest score in four years.

'Ninety-*six*,' Vitti said. He juked and jived, proud as if it were his own son. He'd known, of course.

The man of the hour held court at his cubicle, bumping fists and toasting with ginger ale beside a glittery sign: CONGRAD BRAD! He was to oversee graveyard shift, and we'd scheduled the festivities for the five p.m. changeover, enabling members of both teams to attend. The outgoing sergeant was there, as was Lindsey Bagoyo. In two weeks' time, she would be joining us to fill the vacancy.

I wondered if she and I would ever get around to discussing my call from Reno.

Noticing me staring, she gave a friendly little wave.

I tipped my cup to her, went over to shake Moffett's hand.

He grinned. 'Thanks, hoss.'

'This whole goofy-dude vibe,' Zaragoza said. 'I get that that's an act. My question is: How deep does it go? Are we *supposed* to think you're an idiot? Or is the idea that first we think you're an idiot, then go, No, he can't be that dumb, he must actually be a secret genius. Or is it a triple-cross: No, he can't possibly be smart enough to act that dumb, he must *actually be* an idiot, and so we miss the fact that you *aren't*.' He paused. 'Which is it?'

Moffett said, 'I'm just good at standardized tests.'

Standing in the burnished evening, tapping our feet to the sound of pop music through portable speakers, we laughed readily, talked more quickly than normal. Hurry up and live, because at any moment a call could come in. The dead don't care.

Not long after, returning from a removal on Alameda Island, I peeled a folded Post-it from my computer screen.

my office

The handwriting was Vitti's.

I scanned the squad room. Nobody paying me any special attention. Either they didn't know I was in trouble or they were determined not to become collateral damage.

As usual, his door was open. I found him reading at his desk. 'What's up, Sarge?'

He told me to shut the door and have a seat.

I crossed my legs, aiming for casual. My body didn't cooperate. I was perspiring madly. It was a scorcher out, and in my haste I'd neglected to remove my vest. The ceiling vent thundered frigid air, patches at my lower back and chest going clammy.

Vitti let me stew a little before handing me the sheet of paper he'd been reading.

It was the intake form for a body that had come in several nights prior. The primary making the report was Rex Jurow. The decedent was a white male, age thirty-seven, found in an abandoned house near Oakland Airport, a needle jutting from his arm. Marital status as yet unknown. Manner of death accidental, pending autopsy. Identification was made from a California driver's license, found in a wallet in the vicinity, stripped of cash.

The decedent, Samuel Afton, stood five-five and weighed a hundred and twenty-one pounds. He had brown hair and blue eyes. He resided at an address in West Oakland.

'You knew him,' Vitti said.

'His father was one of mine.' I set the page down. 'Mind if I ask how it landed on your desk?'

Vitti said, 'Moffett saw him come up in queue and remembered you mentioning the name. He thought you might want to know. He asked would I pass it along.'

'Right,' I said. 'Thanks.'

'Don't thank me, thank him.'

'Will do,' I said. Silence. 'That all?'

Vitti scrunched his eyes, rubbed them. 'Why're you doing this to me, Clay?'

'Sir?'

'Did I do something to you, in this life or another, that you feel the need to put me in this position?'

'I'm not sure what you mean, sir.'

Vitti said, 'I see the name, I go, "Why's that sound so familiar?" I'm bananas, tryna figure it out. Then it hits me: this is the same guy who called to make a complaint about you.'

I said nothing.

'Which gets me thinking,' he said, 'about our conversation that we had last year. You know the one I'm talking about.'

'Yes, sir.'

He grimaced. 'So? You like to tell me why you're doing this to me?'

I didn't answer, and he made an exasperated sound, grabbing at his computer screen and swiveling it around to show me my own queue. He pointed to the bottom of the list.

RENNERT, WALTER J.

He said, 'I asked you – I *ordered* you – to close that case out. Did I not?'

'Yes, sir, you did.'

He drummed the desk with his fingers.

I said, 'It slipped my mind.'

'I'm giving you a chance to explain yourself, you're gonna sit here and *tell* me that?'

'I'll do it right now,' I said, starting to stand.

'Sit your ass down,' he said.

I obeyed.

He said, 'Something like this, I have to ask myself, What else is he doing? Huh? What else is he up to, that he's not supposed to be? Because clearly, whatever the deal is with you and this case, clearly it's affecting your judgment.'

'I'm very sorry, sir,' I said. 'It wasn't my –'

He waved me silent. 'I called Berkeley PD,' he said. 'Turns out Chief Ames has nothing but nice things to say about you. You and this homicide guy, all the good things you're doing. I have to play along like I know what the hell he's talking about. How's that make me look? How's it make me *feel*.'

'I don't know, sir.'

'Wrong answer, Deputy. Try again.'

'Like a prick,' I said.

'Ding ding ding ding ding. Like a grade-A prick.'

I said, 'I'm truly sorry, sir.'

He regarded me with a pained expression. 'That's not what we're about here.'

'I know.'

'We're a family. Family doesn't treat each other like this.'

I thought: Maybe not yours.

'What'm I supposed to do here?' he said. 'Huh? You know me. Am I the kind of guy who goes around, *Blah this, blah that, Big Me in charge*? Huh? I don't want to be like that. That's not me. I hate it. But *this*, here? What you're doing? You're basically forcing me.'

I said, 'I'm sorry, sir.'

He shook his head. 'That's really all you got to say?'

'I'll close the case out.'

'Of course you fucking will,' he said. 'You're gonna do that, first thing. Second thing, from this point forward, you have nothing to do with the appeal. Any further developments – a reporter comes to you – you don't speak to them. You don't know shit. You refer them to me. Three,' he said, 'you're suspended. One week without pay. Fight it if you like, but my advice to you – and I say this as a friend, who cares about you and your future – take your medicine. Dismissed.'

I left his office in a fog, stripping off my vest and hanging it on the edge of my cubicle. Phones rang. The copier coughed and spat. People minded their own business.

It all looked plasticky, deformed.

Punch line? I'd never meant to keep the case open. I really had forgotten. Tatiana and I hadn't spoken in nine-plus months. My focus had become Julian Triplett, and him alone.

I hunched over my desk, mousing.

RENNERT, WALTER J.

SUBMIT

Stare at something long enough, you cease to see it at all.

'You okay, princess?'

I raised my eyes. Shupfer had craned around her monitor.

I said, 'Knee's acting up.'

She held her gaze on me.

I said, 'Gonna give it a rest.'

Her smile was soft and sad and knowing.

'Feel better,' she said.

I nodded and she shrank behind her screen.

I clicked SUBMIT.

45

KARA DRUMMOND said, 'My treat.'

I put my money away.

We took our coffees to the same table, at the same Starbucks, in the same Richmond shopping center. She still worked next door at the bank, though she'd recently been promoted to manager. The added responsibility, on top of a bi-weekly drive to Reno, had begun to wear her down. Since February, she'd put an extra seven thousand miles on her car.

She gave me the latest from the lawyers handling her brother's application for pardon. 'The girlfriend whose name you gave them, they heard from her.'

She was referring to Francie Nguyen, one of Nicholas Linstad's former paramours. I'd tried repeatedly to get in touch with her, but she had failed to return my calls, and I'd passed along her contact information more as an afterthought.

Now she'd changed her mind, following the appearance of a news item about the appeal. As expected, Nicholas Linstad's father had declined to provide a DNA sample, and there was no legal means to compel him to do so. Nguyen had read the article on *Berkeleyside* and promptly called the Institute for Wrongful Convictions.

'She filed a paternity suit against him,' Kara said. 'The court made him take a test. She has the whole profile.'

'How long till they get the comparison with the hairs back?'

'End of the week,' she said, crossing her fingers.

'Congratulations,' I said.

'Thank you,' Kara said, beaming. She was thrilled, and I was thrilled for her. At the same time, a tiny part of me felt shaken. I wondered if Francie Nguyen realized how fortunate she was to still be alive.

The other big news was that, after endless cajoling, Julian had agreed to come down and meet with his legal team in person.

'About time,' I said. 'What's on the agenda?'

'Antonio and Sarah' – the lawyers. 'After that? Depends on how much time we have. We'll visit who we can. I told him he could stay over with me. I said I'd give him the bed, Wayne can take the sofa.' She laughed. 'I sleep in the bathtub.'

She paused. 'He didn't want to. He said he has to get back. It's hard for him, being here. He gets nervous.'

'Bad memories,' I said.

She nodded.

I said, 'Does your mom know he's coming?'

'I didn't tell her.' She toyed with the lid of her coffee cup. 'You're right, though. It's up to him if he wants to have a relationship with her. I need to start thinking of him that way. You know? A person who can make his own decisions.'

I asked when they got in.

'Thursday,' she said.

'Send them my best.'

'I will,' she said. Then: 'You have any time? In case Julian wants to see you.'

A beat.

I said, 'I'm working.'

Her face loosened, settling in a half smile. 'Sure.'

'I'll see if I can get away.'

'Don't worry if you can't,' she said. 'You've done enough. More than enough.'

Before returning to work, she needed to grab something from her car. I walked her across the softened asphalt and stood by in the broiling heat while she rummaged in the glove compartment. When she came up, holding a tube of hand cream, her necklace had fallen free of her blouse. The wooden sunflower.

She touched it. 'Last time I went up, I had him fix the chain on.'

'It looks nice,' I said.

'Thanks.'

'I'll let you know about Thursday.'

She tucked the necklace away; shut the car and locked it.

Hesitating, she stepped forward and embraced me.

It lasted a second or two. She pulled away with a short, embarrassed laugh, shaking her head, wiping her eyes. She started to speak, but thought better of it, leaving me alone in the punishing glare.

46

I PULLED to the curb, tapped the horn. The front door opened, and Paul Sandek came down the walkway. I lowered the passenger window to return his greeting.

'She said to tell you she'll be out in a sec,' he said.

'Thanks.'

'Realistically, though, it could be hours.' He leaned in through the open window. 'We probably have enough time for PIG.'

I pointed: behind him, Amy had stepped from the house.

'Dammit,' he said.

She was toting a paper grocery bag – 'Snacks,' she said – which she stashed in the footwell before sliding in next to me.

'Drive safely,' Sandek said.

'We will,' Amy said.

'As for you,' he said to me, 'consider yourself lucky.'

'I do,' I said.

I couldn't pretend to be familiar with the route, so I had Amy navigate. Google Maps predicted a drive time of two hours and fifty-eight minutes.

We spent the better part of that discussing her, which was

fine by me. I wasn't in a talkative mood, and anyway she had more news to share. A complete draft of her dissertation. A job lined up at the VA clinic in downtown San Francisco. Aside from seeing individual clients, she was to lead the weekly stress reduction group.

'I'm sure I'll be burnt out soon enough,' she said. 'But for right now I'm choosing to be excited.'

The question remained: hunt for an apartment in the city or remain in the East Bay? Convenience or affordability?

'I could probably swing a one-bedroom in the Tenderloin,' she said. 'Either that, or I'm going to have to split with five other people. I feel like I'm getting a little old to be labeling my cottage cheese.'

'You could always stay at your parents',' I said.

'That's super-helpful, thanks.'

'Laundry service,' I said. 'Free food.'

'Unwanted advice. Personal questions.'

'Learn to focus on the positives.'

'You think it's so great,' she said, 'I'm sure they'd be happy to have you.'

She pulled the snack bag onto her lap. 'I have egg salad and turkey with Swiss. Oh – but. My mom really wanted you to have this for some reason.'

She unwrapped the sandwich to its waist. Meatloaf.

I laughed and took it.

The route was a straight shot down I-5, offering precious little scenery: monotonous stretches of wrinkled highway, beige hills relieved by farmland. Billboards advertised berries, fudge,

417

antiques – always, it seemed, a bit farther on, a promise infinitely receding.

'In two miles,' the phone said, 'the exit is on the right.'

'How're you feeling?' Amy asked.

I shrugged. 'Fine,' I said. 'Little nervous.'

'Do you want to talk about it?'

'That would be the healthy thing to do, wouldn't it.'

'Only if you want to,' she said.

'I don't really.'

'Then don't.'

A green sign loomed.

Jayne Ave

1 mile

Pleasant Valley

State Prison

The phone said, 'In one mile –'

Amy muted it.

The last stretch before the exit consisted of citrus groves – row after row of round-topped trees, studded with underripe fruit. It was easy to pretend we were headed someplace fun. A day of U-pick, followed by lunch, a nap, a blanket in the shade.

Then we crossed over a dry riverbed and the terrain sank and withered, becoming a terrible blankness, baked and sterile, only the sandy margins of the road and drooping power lines separating us from oblivion.

It was a vision of hell.

I reached for Amy, and she took my hand.

The prison campus revealed itself in stages. Barbed wire, protecting nothing but empty acreage; bleached green trans- former boxes and orange traffic delineators and a duo of blinking amber lights that warned of the upcoming intersection. Low- slung cement structures: a sister facility: state hospital for mentally ill and sexually violent offenders.

The left turn lane stretched for hundreds of yards, as if to allow you time to change your mind.

I put on my signal.

The run-up to the guard booth was long, too, trimmed with agave and rocks.

Amy squeezed my hand. 'You do know how to woo a lady.'

I said, 'Wait'll you see what I got lined up for our third date.'

The guard checked my driver's license, raised the barrier arm. 'Ahead on your right.'

I lifted my foot off the brake.

The visitors' lot was already crowded, slack-faced folks trudging between the cars, like the breakup of some awful tail- gate. They knew enough to get here early.

I killed the engine. In an instant, suffocating heat slammed through the windshield.

I turned to Amy. 'Ready?'

Easier to ask her than myself.

We got out and she took my hand and we joined the back of a discontented line, shuffling toward the door, out of the sun and into a scratched, boomy concrete room. Clearing the metal detector required that she let go of me, but she was waiting for me, hand out, when I came through, and she held on to me as I approached the booth, the impassive face behind Plexiglas.

I felt her walking close beside me, and I felt her fingers tighten on mine as I formed the words:

Clay Edison, here to see my brother.

ACKNOWLEDGMENTS

Jesse Grant, Ariana Heller, Sam Ginsburg, Jeff Shannon, Lauri Weiner, Janice Thomas.

Alameda County Sheriff Gregory Ahern.

Capt. Melanie Ditzenberger, Lt. Riddic Bowers.

Dep. Rebecca Lorenzana, Sgt. Howard Baron, and all the members of the Alameda County Coroner's Bureau.

Special thanks to Dep. Erik Bordi.

Don't miss the next gripping
Alex Delaware thriller

THE NO. 1 INTERNATIONAL BESTSELLING AUTHOR
JONATHAN KELLERMAN

NIGHT MOVES

AN ALEX DELAWARE THRILLER

Available from Headline

HEADLINE

THRILLINGLY GOOD BOOKS FROM CRIMINALLY GOOD WRITERS

CRIME FILES BRINGS YOU THE LATEST RELEASES FROM TOP CRIME AND THRILLER AUTHORS.

SIGN UP ONLINE FOR OUR MONTHLY NEWSLETTER AND BE THE FIRST TO KNOW ABOUT OUR COMPETITIONS, NEW BOOKS AND MORE.